"If you're looking for a suspense thriller that will grab you, spin you around, then pin you to your chair until you finish, this is it. *Amber Dawn* is terrific entertainment by a writer working at the top of his game."

William Martin, *New York Times*-bestselling author of *The Lincoln Letter*

"*Amber Dawn* is for everyone who loves action-packed international thrillers that pit a talented but fallible protagonist and his team against a complex yet completely intriguing opponent for the highest possible stakes."

Rick Ludwig, author of *Pele's Fire*

"A great action-packed novel. It lets you in on the complexities of the United States intelligence community in our war on terrorism. The author obviously knows his way around the territory!"

Robert Miller, former Navy intelligence officer

"Intrigue, action, terrorist plots, political maneuvering. *Amber Dawn* has it all. Ken Andrus weaves an intricate, complicated web as this tale winds toward its exciting climax."

George Wallace, author of *Warshot*

AMBER DAWN

AMBER DAWN

KENNETH ANDRUS

BABYLON
BOOKS

This book is dedicated to the memory of HM2 Allan M. Cundanga Espiritu FMF/PJ, United States Navy, who lost his life in Ar Ramdi, Iraq 1 November 2005 while serving as a Corpsman with the 2ⁿᵈ Force Service Support Group.

"It is foolish and wrong to mourn the men who died. Rather, we should thank God such men lived." George S. Patton

You are what you have done; what you have done is in your memory; what you remember is what defines who you are.

Julian Barnes, *Nothing to be Afraid Of*

Chapter One

OZERSK
THE RUSSIAN FEDERATION
TUESDAY 7 OCTOBER

Bashir al-Khultyer's finger caressed the smooth, cold metal of the AK-47's trigger guard, the corners of his mouth twisting into a tight smile. The faint sounds of the Techna River flowing along the eastern flank of the Ural Mountains one hundred meters further down the slope returned him to another time. Time spent with family.

His finger froze on the trigger. His face hardened at the other memories that forced their way into his consciousness, erasing his smile. The mistakes he'd made. The mistakes for which he would soon atone.

He inhaled through his nostrils, taking deep, controlled breaths, embracing the pine-scented air of the forest slowing his heart rate. Four seconds in...hold...four seconds out. Calming. Suppressing his anger. Preparing for what he must do.

He shifted his weight on the slab of worn granite that dominated the hill of his vantage point and set the rifle aside to focus on the remote stretch of highway. The dense ground fog began to lift, the bend in the macadam road now visible through the swirling mist still clinging to the boughs of the low hanging branches of the fir and spruce trees. The Russian drivers would have to brake when they entered the curve.

Each Tuesday, their three-vehicle convoy traveled from the Mayak Reprocessing Plant to the industrial city of Karabakh. Their cargo: nuclear fuel rods. Bashir passed the convoy several times during the previous month while driving his truck to the farmer's market outside the city of Ozersk. His surveillance verified the route and timing of the Russian trucks that had been provided by his informant. Not that he had doubted the accuracy of her information.

He reached for his iPhone and touched his thumb to the home button. The light from the device's screen cast an eerie shadow across his face, weathered by harsh summers and winters spent in the rugged mountains of southern Afghanistan. He checked the time, then slipped the phone back into the pocket of his worn fatigue jacket.

He nodded at Azad. His comrade hefted a canvas carrier and pulled out a rocket-propelled grenade for his RPG-7. He slid the warhead assembly into the firing tube and settled the weapon to his shoulder.

Ushiska trotted across the road and crouched behind a slight berm. Salim squatted behind a large boulder on the opposite side of the road. He and Ushiska were now positioned to sweep the ambush site with an intersecting field of fire.

The sound of a laboring engine shattered the serenity of the forest. Bashir looked in the direction of the approaching vehicle. Not the one he waited for. He caught movement out of the corner of his eye. Ushiska stood, rifle sighted on the road.

He leapt to his feet and ran down the slope waving his

arms. "Don't fire. Don't fire! Get down. It's not them." His over-zealous comrade lowered his weapon.

No sooner had the old Lada Vesta sedan sped out of sight than Bashir picked up the rumble of the convoy's approach. He dropped to a crouch and pulled out the key fob. The lead vehicle rounded the bend faster than he expected. He braced for the concussive thump of the blast and pressed UNLOCK.

An enormous explosion ripped the air, hurling the truck upward in a dirty red-orange fireball. The twisted wreckage slammed back down, showered by a rain of smoking debris.

Azad steadied the grenade launcher on his shoulder, waiting. The troop carrier's driver jerked his wheel to the left at the sight of the carnage in front of him—just as expected.

Flame and exhaust gasses blew out the back of the weapon as the RPG roared toward the truck. The grenade's rocket motor ignited after traveling ten yards, its stabilizing fins deploying to steady the projectile on its course. The five-pound warhead impacted on the engine compartment sending the truck careening onto the berm. The objective of Bashir's ambush, the transport van, was now trapped between the burning hulks of the destroyed trucks.

Ushiska shouldered his AK-47 and directed its fire on the windshield of the lead vehicle. He emptied the entire magazine, hit the release button dropping the empty, and slammed home a fresh one. He yanked back on the charging handle to seat the first round, swung the barrel around, and found a new target—a Russian crawling away from the blazing wreckage. He fired a short burst that shredded the smoldering fabric covering the man's back.

Salim raced to the bend in the road and cut down four men who were tumbling out of the bed of the truck. One struggled to his feet, trying for the safety of the adjoining woods. Salim fired from the hip. There could be no survivors. The 7.62mm rounds sent the Russian sprawling face-first onto the gravel easement.

Bashir ran through the dirty-brown haze. Greasy, black smoke billowed from the fire in the engine compartment of the lead vehicle. Acrid fumes from the explosives and the stench of burning rubber filled his nostrils. He failed to see a Russian leap from behind the vehicle until the man leveled an automatic rifle at his chest. Bullets whipped the air. He threw himself on the ground and rolled under the van.

Salim fired a three-shot burst at the shooter. The Russian screamed, spinning around from the impact, and fell. He tried to regain his feet, but a single round from Salim's rifle dropped him to his knees. The man toppled over, wide-eyed, his blood spreading over the pavement.

Bashir pushed the corpse out of the way and crawled out from under the transport, swiveling his head checking for threats. There were none. He kept his back to the van, side-stepping to the rear of the vehicle. The twin rear doors were secured with a massive padlock. Undeterred, he molded a small block of PETN explosive around the lock and stuck in a detonator with a ten-second delay.

He ran to the front, seeking cover behind the mass of the engine block. Six seconds, three....

The sharp crack of the explosion punched through the sporadic sound of rifle fire coming from the rest of his team. He looked over the hood. *Clear.* He jogged to the rear of the truck.

The right door hung by its lower hinge, blocking his way. He jerked it open. Before him were dozens of twelve-foot long aluminum tubes neatly arranged on wooden racks. Each tube contained a single zirconium alloy-encased fuel rod containing hundreds of radioactive fuel pellets. These individual rods were to be bundled in clusters to become part of the core of a new reactor.

Secured to the forward bulkhead of the carrier was another container, one he hadn't expected. He recognized it immediately—the containment vessel for VIPAC fuel rods.

The barrel-shaped transporter would hold four-inch-high metallic tubes packed with a mixture of depleted plutonium-238 and uranium-235. If the containers were breeched by an explosive, the resulting radioactive particles would be dispersed in a deadly aerosol.

Unbelievable. They were ideal. But how to hide them? The VIPAC rods would be too wide to fit in the steel pipes welded under the chassis of his truck. And it wouldn't be safe to remove them from their containment vessel because of the radiation.

He sorted through the options. They'd have to conceal the three-foot-high transporter under the produce piled in the bed of his truck. Could the container be wrapped with staves from the sauerkraut barrel?

He grabbed the doorframe and pulled himself up. "Salim. Give me a hand. We've got to get these rods out."

The two of them released the metal bands securing the containment vessel and rocked it down the narrow aisle between the racks of fuel rods. Azad and Ushiska turned their attention to the team's truck, concealed in a copse of trees a short distance away. Azad jumped behind the wheel and eased the vehicle past the burning hulk of the first truck, braking at Salim's hand signal. Ushiska remained in the woods erasing their truck's tire tracks.

Bashir waited until his truck was positioned, then chose one of the rods. Salim and Azad pulled a zirconium tube out its aluminum container while Bashir scanned its length ensuring there were no cracks that would allow the helium gas pressurizing the container to escape.

"It's good."

Bashir nodded affirmation. The two men slid the control rod into its new carrier under their truck, capped the end, and smeared the stopper with a coating of grease and dirt.

Bashir moved to his next task, pulling a brown plastic-wrapped package and a detonator from the satchel slung over his shoulder. He set the detonator's timer for five minutes and placed the two-kilogram block of C4 explosives in the van. The Russians wouldn't be able to take an accurate inventory for weeks.

"I'll drive. Azad, you and Ushiska ride in the back and hide that container. Salim, up here with me."

Bashir pulled around the burning truck and headed north leaving the destroyed vehicles behind. The entire operation had taken less than fifteen minutes.

He drove several miles and pulled off the road adjacent to one of the many lakes dotting the area. The team hurled their weapons into the water. He then continued northeast skirting the East Ural Radioactive Trace, site of a devastating explosion of an underground storage tank that had released seventy tons of liquid radioactive waste into the area years before.

––––––

The police who patrolled the highway were familiar with Bashir and his team's identification papers and travel documents were in order. After the first month, the police didn't bother to check anymore. In their only inspection of the truck, they never noticed the two rust-encrusted iron pipes welded to the inside flange of the undercarriage frames—one of which now contained the fuel rod. If questioned, Bashir would have explained he added the pipes to provide additional support to the rickety1980's truck he bought to transport his farm goods. No one ever asked.

Salim interrupted his thoughts. "Uh, oh. Checkpoint."

Bashir tensed, then relaxed his grip on the steering wheel. He recognized the paramilitary policeman waving them to halt. He downshifted and the old truck rattled to a stop.

The guard unslung his rifle and approached the window. He pointed the weapon at Bashir's head. "Credentials."

"Da, da. Just a moment."

The man looked into the cab and lowered the barrel as he

accepted the papers. "Ah, my friend. Heading to the market? How are you?"

"Better now that you're not pointing that thing at me."

The guard gave a cursory glance at Bashir's documents and handed them back before heading around to the back to check the produce and Bashir's men. Ushiska gave a friendly wave and tossed him a couple cabbages. It was their customary bribe.

"*Spasibo.*"

"*Bis prabl'Em.*"

Bashir hollered from the cab, "What's going on? We saw the paramilitaries driving like madmen going the other way."

"No idea. Maybe an accident," the guard said.

Bashir shrugged. "As long as they've cleared it before we head home."

They had no sooner collected their papers and gotten back on the highway than three more police vans flew by them heading south. Bashir watched them in his rearview mirror and smiled.

———

Bashir directed his team to pack the truck just after noon. They headed south before turning east on the M5 highway toward their farm on the outskirts of Chelyabinsk. He considered bypassing the city and continuing to Kostanoy in bordering Kazakhstan but discarded the idea. He needed to trust his plan.

They hadn't gone more than twenty kilometers before they encountered another roadblock. Bashir joined the long line of vehicles inching their way forward toward the military police. He spotted a pair of them walking toward the truck. One peeled off and stepped up to the cab.

The guard's voice was clipped, nervous. "Road's closed. You can't go this way."

The other policeman fingered the trigger of his AK-47. He studied the other three with suspicion before climbing into the bed of the truck and pointing the barrel of his rifle at the cask. "What's that?"

"Sauerkraut," Azad replied.

"Open it."

Azad pried open the wooden lid while keeping his eyes on the military policeman. He pressed against the wooden side rails of the truck to let the man past. He watched in horror when the MP peered into the vat and began stirring the contents with his bayonet.

Bashir seethed in helpless fury. He shouted out the window to Azad. "Perhaps he wants some."

The policeman turned at the shouted question, then leaned over to sniff the contents of the cask. "Nyet. My wife makes better." He straightened and gestured with his gun to Azad and Ushiska. "Papers."

The guard snatched the documents out of their hands and climbed down. He flipped through them, looked up to scrutinize their faces, and then walked away, talking into his radio. In a few minutes he returned, a look of disapproval on his face. "Move on."

Bashir released the brake and eased back into traffic. Tomorrow he would set to work, the payout of nearly a year of meticulous planning. Based on his calculations, he had more than enough material to construct five dirty bombs. The VIPAC fuel was an unexpected bonus he'd use in his first device.

Chapter Two

NATIONAL COUNTERINTELLIGENCE CENTER
McLEAN, VIRGINIA
FRIDAY 10 OCTOBER

"The director wants to see you."

Nick Parkos jerked his chair back upright. *The director?*

"Mr. Strickland?" Nick stuttered to the reflection in his computer screen.

"No, the DNI."

"Mr. Gilmore wants to see me?"

"That's what I said."

"Right now?"

"Ten-thirty."

Nick looked at his watch—twenty-seven minutes. "Any idea what it's about?"

"No." The inflection in his supervisor's voice indicated that he wasn't in the best of moods.

Nick screwed up his forehead. He turned to ask another question, but his supervisor had disappeared. He slumped in his chair. This didn't make any sense. *Why does the director want to see me?*

Nick worked as an intelligence analyst focused on the Balkans and the former Soviet Republics. He'd backed into his Washington job with the Director of National Intelligence, signing up on a whim while wandering the job fair booths set up for graduating seniors at Ohio State. The recruiter had convinced him he would be able to use his degree in criminology. That piece proved to be problematic, but he did exhibit some competency in his analysis of the various terrorist and transnational crime organizations vying for power following the collapse of the Soviet Union. He found his work interesting, but not particularly inspiring.

His office, a windowless room in the National Counterterrorism Center building in McLean, mirrored his status within an obscure division of the DDII, the Deputy Director Intelligence Integration. The third-floor office door had no identification except for the room number. The anonymity seemed fitting.

He didn't present a particularly imposing figure at five-nine and one hundred forty-seven pounds. Attempts to tame his unruly long brown hair failed and he always harbored the feeling he looked like his driver's license photo. His clothes didn't help either. His wardrobe belonged in a men's episode of *What Not to Wear,* yet anything he tried on looked better on the hanger than it did on him. He'd learned early on to keep his mouth shut and use his brain.

His eyes drifted from the computer screen to a photograph of his child and ex-wife. The picture had been taken during vacation to Hawaii—another attempt to salvage their marriage. The trip was a failure with one notable exception. The time he'd spent with his daughter playing in the sands of Waikiki beach.

The transition from the carefree college life to the responsibilities of adulthood hadn't worked out so well for either of them, but he tried not to blame her. Marty moved to be near her parents in Miami, taking six-year-old Emma with her. She'd even taken the family pet, Taz, his little dog buddy. The stray cat he'd adopted wasn't quite the same.

He dropped the picture in a desk drawer. Recess was over.

From a stack of files he selected a report on the Novorossiysk Business Group. The Russian transnational crime group was pushing its way into the Balkans. He sorted through the scant information and read that the NBG had just acquired a controlling interest in Meycek Exports. He entered the company's name into his search engine. There wasn't much, but it was a start. He began to type, but stopped in mid-sentence.

He stared at the letters on his keyboard for a moment before logging off. The answer to why he'd been summoned wasn't going to come from the databases. He fingered his computer access card for a moment before pulling it from its slot on the keyboard. The screen went black.

"Well, here goes," he spoke to the empty room, fighting the urge to retreat within himself. The summons left him no choice. He slid the access card into the plastic holder dangling around his neck and made for the seventh-floor office of the Director of National Intelligence.

His footfalls echoed in the empty corridor as he crossed the breezeway that connected his building to the ODNI, wondering what he could have done wrong. The one person he encountered while waiting for the elevator kept his head down to avoid eye contact and moved out of the way. *Am I contaminated?*

Nick paused at the closed double doors of the Director's office and took a deep breath. He stepped over the threshold, only to be confronted by the DNI's secretary.

"May I help you?" She looked annoyed at the interruption.

"I have a ten-thirty appointment."

Nick noted the secretary's eyes running over him with obvious skepticism before they came to rest on his scarlet and gray striped tie.

"I'll let the director know you're here."

He watched the woman disappear into Gilmore's office. When she was out of sight, he lifted the end of his tie. It was a Christmas gift from Emma and his favorite. He let it fall from his hand and surveyed several large red-leather armchairs and a matching couch before deciding to remain standing.

The secretary reappeared followed by the DNI. Gilmore looked just like his pictures. Aside from the silver-gray hair, he could easily pass for someone years younger.

"Do you prefer Nikola or Nick?"

"Ah, I go by Nick, sir."

Gilmore gestured toward his door. "Well, Nick it is. Ever been in here?"

"No, sir."

"Come on, then. First time for everything."

Gilmore settled in behind his formidable desk and flipped open one of two documents. He waved to an empty chair. "Your family is from Czechoslovakia."

Nick reached out for the chair's arm to steady his descent. "Yes, sir. I'm second generation. My grandfather immigrated after the second world war."

Gilmore scanned Nick's file. "And fluent in Russian. That will be useful."

Nick plucked at the loose button on the cuff of his left shirtsleeve. *Useful for what?*

Gilmore made a note in Nick's personnel folder and closed the file. He picked up the second document. "We may have a situation. Take a moment to read this."

The folder contained only two items: a double-spaced page of analysis and a high resolution satellite image of three destroyed trucks. The fact the document was double-spaced spoke volumes. Not much was known about what happened. The typed analysis did provide a cargo manifest for one of the vehicles. *How did they know that?*

"Sir, this— "

"Best case," Gilmore interrupted, "it's a random terrorist attack. My gut's telling me there's more. For starters, I want to know who did this and why."

Nick concluded the question was rhetorical and waited for Gilmore to continue.

"I'm reassigning you to the NCPC."

Nick's eyebrows shot up. *The National Counterproliferation Center? A promotion?* "Wha…?"

Gilmore's eyes locked on him. He tapped Nick's personnel folder with his index finger. "Your supervisor gave me three names. I've reviewed your work. Bottom line—you have a unique ability to link seemingly unrelated events to a common element. I want you to figure out what just happened in Ozersk and what the risks are to our national security."

Nick placed the intelligence report on the desk.

"No, keep that. I want your analysis tomorrow afternoon. You'll use your current office until we find you a new place to hang your hat. Questions?"

"Sir, I'm working the Novorossiysk Business Group. Do you think there's a connection?"

"That's for you to figure out. Anything else?"

Nick tightened his lips. "No, sir."

"Because of the sensitivity of this incident, you'll report directly to Mr. Strickland. You need anything, ask him." Gilmore popped the top back on his fountain pen. "That should cover it."

Nick took 'that' to mean the meeting was over. "Thank you, sir." He got up and took several lightheaded, wobbly steps toward the door.

Gilmore addressed his back. "And Nick?"

"Yes, sir?"

"Don't disappoint me."

The receptionist waited in the outer office to escort him out. "We'll be in touch," she said. "Good luck."

Nick noted a bemused look on her face but barely heard her voice. He didn't answer.

The short walk back to his office gave him the opportunity to complete a quick self-assessment. He hadn't been fired. That was a positive. But now what? He dropped the intelligence report on his desk. *Where to begin?*

For starters, he knew very little about the NCPC. The betrayal of the National Security Agency operations in the Snowden Affair had changed everything. While the various shops still mined information, the exchange of that intelligence within the ODNI or between the ODNI and the CIA, NSA, FBI, and DoD was again highly compartmentalized. It ran counter to the rationale behind the restructuring of U.S. intelligence after 9/11, but no one person could be permitted to have enough access to threaten the country's security.

He would need to access and cross-reference data points from multiple agencies. For those he would need to send his queries through the DDII. He might even be assigned a supernumerary who would stand peering over his shoulder to verify and enter into a logbook those documents he accessed, what agency provided them, and when he viewed them. He shook his head at the prospect, "Well, there's not much to do, but start."

Let's start with what I do know. First thing: The cargo manifest. Nuclear fuel rods. These were not your typical terrorists. Nick typed in the subject lines for his spreadsheet: Leader, Cell Members, Financing, Support Networks, Intent, Motive, Personality Traits, and Device.

With those as a starting point, he opened the folder the DNI had given him and pulled out the photograph of the ambush site. The header read: 'National Geospatial-Intelligence Agency.' A National Reconnaissance Office satellite had taken the photo from its elliptical orbit over the Mayak Production Facility. Placed to keep an eye on the sprawling facilities responsible for producing and reprocessing the material for Russia's nuclear weapons, the satellite carried a sixty-inch focal camera that provided two-foot resolution of any object under its gaze.

Nick studied the imagery of the three trucks but couldn't glean any more information than was already in the report. He scrutinized the sides of the road. Nothing caught his eye, but a question did flash through his mind. Were there other images of the road that might reveal details of what the terrorists were doing leading up to and after the ambush? He made a note to find out.

He slipped the photograph back into its folder and pulled a clean sheet of paper from his desktop printer. On it, he inscribed a series of circles creating a Venn diagram. He likened the circles to throwing any number of rocks into a pond. The ensuing ripples from the strikes would spread outward, overlap, and eventually create a common center. At the center of his intersecting lines he wrote LEADER.

He wondered how many gigabytes of information the DNI's supercomputers would eventually consume to fill in the blanks of his spreadsheet. There had to be other images of the ambush site. Who else had been on that road?

He next reviewed the headings of the Analytic Sources Catalog to get a better idea of what databases he could tap. One header caught his eye: the Database on Nuclear Smuggling, Theft, and Orphan Radiation Sources. Perhaps the DSTO could provide the historical context to help guide his investigation?

This investigation was going to be tough and things wouldn't be any easier if everyone involved wasn't acting off the same page. There needed to be a Principles Committee. He opened a new document and drafted the letter. The

request would be under Strickland's signature and routed to
the DNI for approval. That was the easy part.

His finger froze on the letter "C." He considered the
implications of who should be on his list. The information-
sharing environment was not optimal. He had no idea if the
CIA would play ball.

Chapter Three

MOSCOW
THE RUSSIAN FEDERATION
WEDNESDAY 4 NOVEMBER

B ashir settled on the train's wooden bench and extended his left leg to relieve the ache in his thigh. The pain from the old wound was always there, an intruder into his thoughts from that fateful fifth day of February.

He slowed his breathing and studied the other passengers. They had boarded with him at the provincial city of Ryazan for the three-hour trip to the capital. Most of them fell asleep. The remainder stared out the windows at the passing countryside. None of them looked like FSB, the Russian Federal Security Service, whose presence on the trains had increased following the bombing of the Lubyanka Metro Station in September.

A half-smile crossed his face. To be blown up by a suicide bomber would indeed be ironic.

He lifted his satchel onto his lap and pulled out a copy of *Pravda*. A photograph of the American President shaking hands with Anatoly Srevnenko, President of the Russian

Federation, dominated the front page. Their eyes lied, their gesture hollow. The nuclear disarmament treaty they had just signed included a provision for the Russians to reprocess another seventy-five tons of weapons grade plutonium. The document meant nothing. The two most powerful men on earth stared at him from the page.

He studied the picture for a moment before dropping the newspaper on the floor. He drove his boot into their faces, grinding them both out of existence. In a few hours, their mighty armies would mean nothing.

Bashir hadn't chosen this day at random, but his selection couldn't have been more fortuitous. The prevailing winds during the first week of November would spread death across Red Square and the Kremlin. Better yet, the temperature was an unseasonably warm two degrees Celsius. Holiday crowds were descending on Moscow to celebrate Unity Day.

The rhythmic beat of the commuter train's wheels slowed, prompting him to look out his frost-etched window. Repetitious slabs of worker housing jammed together in a near treeless landscape rolled by. A light snow had fallen during the night, providing some visual relief to the monotonous gray suburbs of Moscow. He checked his iPhone to verify the arrival time and settled back into his seat for the remainder of the trip.

———

The train screeched to a stop at the Kazansky Station, one of the three rail stations bordering Kosomolskaya Square in northeast Moscow. Bashir grabbed his satchel and waited for the others to leave the car before stepping into utter mayhem. Hundreds of people pressed toward the exits.

His eyes passed over neoclassical crystal chandeliers, turn-of-the-century sculpted ironwork, fluted pylons, and bas-relief yellow-gold ceilings. When he first visited Moscow years before as a teenager, he thought the station beautiful. Now he looked at the cavernous space with disdain. The murals depicting the glory of the Revolution mocked him.

He blended in with the crush of humanity and exited the terminal through a pedestrian tunnel. He hesitated at an arched doorway leading to a narrow alleyway of shuttered kiosks.

The smell of vomit and stale urine assailed him. Danger. His right hand ran across the bulk of his coat that concealed the Markarov 9mm pistol. He understood this world—so different from the one he'd known as a student at the Moscow Institute of Physics and Technology.

He turned left and made his way through the clutter, circumventing uniformed security police intent on disposing the drunks littering the street. He wasn't concerned. He'd seen this act played out many times. The drunks were being dumped in the adjacent alleyways to keep them out of sight of the morning commuters. Wrapped in old newspapers and tattered blankets, they had passed out or been beaten unconscious by thugs of the Izmayovaskaya gang the night before.

The militiamen and private security guards were bent over, their backs to him while searching the derelicts for any money overlooked by those who preyed on the homeless. He hurried past, continuing on to meet the rest of his team at the kiosk they'd rented months before.

Bashir made his way down the dark alley, senses alert. The smell of freshly baked bread replaced the stench of human squalor. The aroma prompted him to pause. He crossed the corridor to the bakery, dropped a couple of rubles on the counter for a loaf of black rye bread, and exited the shop.

His destination was a few doors down. A flickering fluorescent light dangling from two rusted chains advertised its wares: Electronics.

He stopped and pretended to look through the smudged display window at the haphazard collection of cheap electronic devices, knockoffs of watches, and pirated CDs. The store had opened six months earlier and did little business.

He scanned the reverse image of the street behind him but saw nothing to rouse suspicion in the few people sharing the alleyway. None appeared the least interested in him or the store. He turned his head toward Ushiska who sat on a wrought iron bench guarding the kiosk.

"Nothing," Ushiska confirmed from behind the newspaper he pretended to read.

"The others?"

"Inside."

Bashir pushed open the door of the cramped shop. Discarded cell phones that had been cannibalized for their parts littered a small workbench. Salim sat behind the clutter. His strength, and thus his value to Bashir, was his expertise in fabricating remote detonator devices. Salim, oiling the action of an automatic pistol, didn't look up.

"You won't be needing that," Bashir said.

Salim took a long pull on his cheap Russian cigarette and exhaled a plume of acrid smoke. "It deters the scum who try to steal from me." He studied the tip of his cigarette and tapped the ash into a red salt-rock ashtray he'd picked up in Afghanistan. He replaced the cigarette in the corner of his mouth, opened a drawer in his workbench, removed two cell-phones, and handed them to Bashir.

Bashir chose one at random and turned it over in his hand before flipping open the cover. Inside the device, Salim had mated a car remote with the cell-phone circuitry to create a detonation circuit.

"Just turn it on and press CALL."

Bashir handed the phones back without comment. Azad sat in the corner wearing a clean white-cotton shirt, reading a worn copy of the Koran. He looked remarkably composed for a man about to die.

For his part, Bashir held no desire to seek martyrdom. He

had no interest in killing people for God. He was driven by more personal reasons.

Bashir pulled out the black bread from his satchel and handed it to Salim. Salim nodded, tore off a hunk, and tossed the rest across the room to Azad.

"Is the package ready?"

Azad ripped off a piece from the loaf and stuffed it in his mouth. "Over there, in the box."

Bashir walked to the corner of the shop. Inside the box were two bandoleers of explosives and a black leather Coach daypack. He removed one of the bandoleers. *Excellent.* The device could easily be concealed under a winter coat.

He hefted the daypack by its single sling, judging its weight. It was heavier than he would have wished. He set it on the floor and unzipped the top. Inside the twenty by fifty-centimeter compartment nestled a sealed box that once contained a leaded-glass decanter. The box now contained two clusters of the four-inch high VIPAC cylinders they'd taken from the ambush. Packed around the cylinders were one-hundred dark-gray pellets from the reactor fuel rod.

He had purchased the crystal decanter the week before. If someone were to check his bag, he could produce the receipt from the *Hrustal and Farfor* shop and explain he was returning the decanter.

Bashir slipped the backpack over his shoulder. "Time to go."

Chapter Four

Bashir walked up the stairs leading from the subway station to the northeast corner of Red Square. He paused at the exit and scanned the imposing walls of the Kremlin before continuing across the cobbled expanse toward his destination, the world-famous GUM department store.

He suppressed a slight limp, skirted the workers re-striping the square in preparation for the military parade later in the day, and strode across the barren expanse without a glance from the police patrolling the area. He scanned the main entrance. A small group of shoppers lined up behind a new checkpoint. The extra security didn't surprise him. He veered to the left and stopped before a large plate glass window displaying the latest Dior perfume, J'Adore.

"*Ah, oui, ma petite. J'adore en effet,*" he whispered. "*J'adore toujours.*"

He studied the guards while pretending to admire a shimmering red-silk dress draping a mannequin that shared the window of the Dior display. Far from a random check, the guards were selecting every tenth customer. Amateurs. He counted off seven shoppers, worked his way into the queue in the eighth position, and passed through the revolving glass doors of the main entrance into a previous life.

Like him, the GUM had transformed from when he and Nadia use to window-shop. He met her while an undergraduate at the Moscow Institute of Physics and Technology. They married a year later following his acceptance to the Master's program in Radiation and Radiobiology at the Joint Institute for Nuclear Research. During the frigid Moscow nights they would huddle together in their walk-up apartment, Nadia sharing her dreams of the day they would shop in the boutiques of Paris. She'd made him laugh. There hadn't been any laughter in his life for a long time.

Bashir slowed as he passed the ornate fountain dominating the center of the main concourse. The sound of cascading water blended with the undertone of shopper's voices and piped-in jazz saxophone music. Sunlight flowed through the iron scrollwork of the glass-domed ceiling three stories above, adding warmth to the gold and white walls of the mall. Strands of sparkling crystal pendants suspended from the ceilings enticed the shoppers below. The entire effect was magical —and calculated.

A group of noisy teenagers burst through the rotating doors of the entrance, interrupting his observations. He stepped to one side allowing them to pass. His eyes fell on a young blonde in an expensive fur coat standing on the opposite side of the fountain. She cast him a coy look and said a few rapid words into her cellphone.

At forty-two years of age, he could have made it past the thugs exercising face control at one of Moscow's exclusive clubs if he had so chosen. But he wasn't the least bit interested in these dens of the fornicators like the GQ Bar on Propaganda Street that only granted admission to the beautiful, privileged New Russians.

Bashir frowned and made his way to the Colour's Café on the second floor gallery. The Café's paired tables lined one side of a bridge that spanned two arcades of shops, providing the diners a vista of the fountain below. A large umbrella with panels of alternating primary colors topped each table. He selected an inside table, slid his daypack off his shoulder, and pushed it out of sight next to the wrought iron railing.

A menu appeared. "May I offer you a coffee?"

Bashir smiled at the waitress. "A cappuccino please. I won't need the menu."

She started to clear the other place setting, but he stopped her. "I have a friend joining me."

The waitress answered with a knowing smile. "Would she like a pastry?"

"*Nyet spaseeba*. I should be so lucky. It's a friend from work. Could you bring him a black coffee?"

The waitress disappeared with his order leaving Bashir lost in thought. He caught himself rubbing his ring finger and dropped his hand. The cappuccino arrived. Resting beside it on the saucer, a biscotti.

"It's on the house. Enjoy."

Bashir stirred a packet of sugar into his cappuccino and took several reflective sips before Azad arrived and pulled out his chair. The waitress delivered his coffee and sauntered off with a seductive swing of her hips.

"I didn't know you had such a way with women," Azad quipped.

"They no longer interest me."

Azad grunted in disbelief and reached under his coat to unclip his bandoleer. He slipped off his heavy coat and deposited both in a pile on the chair next to the railing.

Bashir didn't see anyone take note of Azad's actions. "Did you encounter any difficulties at the check point?"

"None. I used the side entrance off Nikol'Skayash Street. Ushiska was to wait until I was through in case there were problems. In fact, there he is."

Bashir searched the concourse.

"See him? Over there. Looks like he's heading for Gastronome. Probably hoping for free samples."

Bashir snorted and pushed the plate with the biscotti across the table. "Wouldn't surprise me. Here, you have this. You're looking hungry."

Azad hefted his coffee in salute. "*Spasibo*."

Neither man said anything more until Bashir noted a clutch of well-dressed women loaded down with shopping bags approaching the empty table next to them. "Wait until they start moving things around, then pretend one of them knocked your coat off the chair. Use that as cover to ready the package. I'll distract them."

Bashir selected his moment when one of the women pulled out a chair and deposited her bags on the floor. He pretended she bumped his elbow. The coffee cup toppled over with a conspicuous clatter, spilling the last of his cappuccino across the table. Azad pushed his coat off the chair in the resulting confusion and disappeared under the table.

"Oh, I am so sorry," the woman said. "May I buy you another?"

"No. No, thank you. Everything is fine," Bashir said, mopping up the mess with his napkin.

"And your friend's coat. Let me—"

Azad's head popped into sight. "No need. It's perfect where it is."

The woman looked puzzled. Her eyes clouded with suspicion as if something about the man disturbed her. She checked the safety of her belongings and turned her attention back to her friends.

"We set?" Bashir asked Azad.

"Yes. There is nothing to do but finish my coffee and the rest of your biscotti. You are off then?"

Bashir pushed away from the table and offered his hand. "We will meet again, brother."

"Perhaps things will be different."

"I am sure of it."

"*Inshallah,* if Allah wills," Azad whispered.

Bashir didn't look back as he made his way down to the first floor. He had a final errand to complete.

He turned right and entered the food court of Gastronome, his stomach emitting a grumble in response to the smell of fresh pastries and cheese. He ignored the impulse to buy a Pastila and made his way to a display of fresh flowers near the rear exit. He selected a simple bouquet of bright-yellow sunflowers and paid for them.

He clutched his bouquet, pushed through the rotating doors onto Vetoshny Lane, and walked past the display windows. He stopped in front of the Armani Emporium to admire their jeans. Nadia would have looked stunning in them.

———

The first explosion came as he rounded the far corner of the department store. The blast should have destroyed one of the restrooms killing anyone using the facilities. But the intention of the bomb was to create panic and drive the GUM shoppers to the main entrance where they would be caught in the blast of the second device. Ushiska had used the tactic many times in Afghanistan.

The second explosion dropped the Colour's bridge onto the mass of terrified shoppers herded together at the store's exit and blew apart the elegant glass dome above the fountain. The shattered fragments showered the concourse with a deadly rain of contaminated debris and crystal pendants. The screams of the wounded drowned out the sound of buoyant jazz still playing over the mall's speakers.

Bashir worked his way through the stampeding crowd of Muscovites gathered across the GUM for the parade and descended the stairs to the Metro Station. He boarded the Blue Line to the Kursk train station as the plume of aerosolized plutonium and uranium from his bomb drifted over Red Square toward the Kremlin.

Chapter Five

THE WHITE HOUSE
WASHINGTON, DC
THURSDAY 5 NOVEMBER

"Mr. President?"

Randal Stuart swiveled his black-leather chair to face the Chief White House Usher. The Usher stood at the door to the study, an apprehensive look clouding his face.

"I hate to intrude, sir, but Mr. Gilmore would like a moment of your time."

Stuart suppressed a frown, capped his pen, and deliberately set it on his desk. The staff understood he was not to be disturbed during his private time before the day started. "He's up here?"

"Yes, sir. I tried to dissuade him."

Stuart knew enough not to doubt the Chief Usher's word. He took a deep breath, pushed away from the desk, and followed him down the second floor hallway of the residence to the Treaty Room.

"Thank you for seeing me, sir," Gilmore said. "I need to speak with you before the morning brief."

Stuart braced himself. Gilmore's intrusion was highly irregular as was his use of 'sir'. "This have something to do with the Moscow incident?"

"The operation turned out badly."

Gilmore extracted a dozen 8x10 color photographs from his red leather-bound intelligence folder and handed them to Stuart. "We had an understanding with our source in the FSB that this operation would not target civilians ... assurances the attack would target a Spetsnaz GRU headquarters in Chechnya."

Stuart worked his way through the photos, only half-listening. He stopped at the seventh—a bloodied young blonde wearing a white fur coat sprawled across the wreckage of a fountain, crushed by a steel beam. Mercifully, a spray of hair covered most of her face. He turned to stare out the window overlooking the front lawn. "What are you doing to contain this?"

"We're taking measures to ensure the incident isn't traced back to us."

"Not good enough, Bryce. We've got blood on our hands."

"We're going to identify and take out the perpetrator."

Stuart glared at his Director of National Intelligence. "What the hell, Bryce? You're telling me, we don't even know who did this?"

"No, sir. We felt it better if—"

Stuart cut him off. "Cut through the bullshit and get this mess cleaned up."

"Yes, sir."

"We need to get downstairs."

Stuart didn't say another word as they descended the stairs leading to the West Wing and walked along the colonnade bordering the Rose Garden. The cold air did him good. He managed to calm himself before taking his seat behind the imposing bulk of the Resolute desk. Dan Lantis, his Chief of

Staff, joined them, entering from the small reception area just outside the Oval Office.

If Lantis was surprised to see Gilmore, he didn't let on. "Good morning, Mr. President."

Justin Brown, Stuart's National Security Advisor set his coffee cup down when the president entered the room. "Good morning, Mr. President. Morn'in, Bryce. How're things in your world?"

"Could be better," Gilmore replied.

"Let's get the day started, shall we?" Stuart cast a sideways glance at Gilmore, then opened the intelligence binder containing the photographs of the carnage at the GUM. "Bryce, let's get up to speed on the Moscow incident. What are the Russians saying?"

"Nothing's come through official channels," Gilmore replied. "The embassy is sorting through the releases coming from the Russian media. *Pravda* and *Interfax* are blaming Chechen terrorists, but there are enough inconsistencies in the reports to make me wonder if the Kremlin isn't trying to hide something."

Stuart couldn't erase the image of the bloodied young blonde from his mind. He looked at the picture of his wife and daughter on the right corner of his desk. *She can't be much older than my own Jennifer.* "Any word on casualties?"

"Nothing specific. But there's something odd going on. The first responders were pulled and Red Square's been sealed off."

"We're getting that from the media?"

"In part," Gilmore said. "One of our embassy staffers is the primary source. She happened to be in the square with some friends when the bombs went off. Several of the photos in your packet are from her iPhone."

"Does she have any idea why the EMT's were pulled?" Lantis asked. "The security makes sense, but the first responders?"

Stuart leaned forward, elbows on the desktop. "What's the worst case scenario?"

Brown gave the edge of his bowtie a thoughtful tug. "Worst case? I'd say we've just seen a dirty bomb."

Stuart looked at Gilmore to judge his reaction. Gilmore's face remained impassive. "Bryce?"

"It's possible. I have an unverified report that the decontamination unit from the Fifth Guards Independent Motorized Rifle Brigade is setting up outside the Kremlin. The unit tests the Red Army's latest equipment and procedures for nuclear, biologic, and chemical incident containment."

"What do you think's going on?" Brown asked.

Stuart nodded to Gilmore.

"Last month there was a terrorist attack on a Russian convoy transporting nuclear fuel rods from their reprocessing plant at the Mayak Production Facility."

"I never heard a word about it," Brown responded.

"We felt it better—"

Stuart intervened. In hindsight, he knew he should have brought Brown in on the attack and the CIA's source within the FSB. "Sorry, Justin. My call. I decided it best to work this through our back channels."

Brown turned to Gilmore. "The Russians never said a thing?"

"Let's say, they haven't exactly been forthcoming about the incident."

"How'd we know?"

"We've had the Mayak facility under constant surveillance since the beginning of the Cold War. Our satellite caught the incident. We haven't shared the photographs with the Russians."

"Why not?"

"It wasn't anything they couldn't have already known. From a national security standpoint, we wouldn't have given anything away to the Russians with the photos, but we weren't about to inadvertently disclose the identity of our source within the facility."

"That's how we know what was taken?"

"Yes."

"You think the incidents are linked?" Brown asked.

"We don't have any direct evidence to suggest they are, but there's a high probability. A couple weeks ago, I put a team together to determine our risk."

"Any leads?" Stuart asked.

"The team's first meeting is tomorrow."

"Who's on it?"

"Reps from Defense, CIA, FBI, Homeland Security, Treasury, and the National Counterterrorism Center. The lead is one of my people. Nick Parkos, from the Counterproliferation Center."

Stuart set his pen down after jotting down the names of the departments. "Interesting choice."

"I wanted someone with the cognitive skills to analyze a lot of disparate information and find the common points."

"So he's not one of your old-guard 'Blue Flamers?'" Brown asked.

"Far from it. He's a specialist in Transnational Crime Organizations."

Brown's eyebrows popped up. "Really? I'm intrigued. What makes you think a TCO's involved?"

"Just a hunch. If this is a one-time incident, we're done. But if the perpetrators are planning further attacks, those will require a sophisticated operation."

"You're looking at ISIS or Al Qaeda?"

"Justin, I must emphasize that making any assumptions at this point would be based on pure conjecture. We'd run the risk of missing something. You have to put the history in the proper context to make any sense of what's going on over there."

"So, what about the Chechens?" Brown asked.

"As I said," Gilmore replied. "We'll pursue all possibilities.'"

Brown raised an eyebrow at the edge in the DNI's voice. "How's this going to impact our relationship with Srevnenko? His record of dealing with the Balkans hasn't exactly been one of measured response."

"We'll have to see how this plays out over the next couple days," Stuart said.

"If this was a dirty bomb, it could be a game changer," Brown noted.

"I'd say, 'could' is the operative word." Gilmore appeared to collect himself. "If I were you, I wouldn't be holding my breath for Srevnenko's cooperation. His track record is pretty clear from all the pre-conditions he threw at us before agreeing to renew the Nunn-Lugar Cooperative Threat Reduction Treaty."

Brown tugged at his bow tie. "We all agreed in our preparatory meetings that we'd take the broad view during the negotiations, and that it was best to create separation with the treaty and his actions in Chechnya, Georgia, and the Ukraine."

Gilmore remained tight-lipped. Not everyone had agreed. He'd had any number of heated discussions with the Secretary of State, Richard Valardi, over the negotiating points. "We knew there'd be a price to pay, but this... If whoever carried out this attack feels we're somehow complicit, our risk increases exponentially."

"Bryce, I know you weren't happy, but don't you think that's a bit of a stretch?" Brown replied.

"My gut's telling me we haven't seen the last of this."

Stuart had heard enough. He was more than cognizant of the price that might have to be paid, but he needed to turn the conversation away from Srevnenko.

He released his grip on his pen and set it on his desk, flexing his fingers to restore their color. "Gentlemen, we're not going to solve this now. We need to move on. Bryce, I'd like you to include what you have on the French for my trip book. I need to get up to speed for my summit with President Lemaire."

Gilmore turned to Brown. "Can you send me a copy of the preliminary discussion points?"

"Richard and I went over them yesterday. Stop by my office on your way out. We've got some blanks to fill in regarding both their domestic and foreign counter-terrorism programs. Considering the event in Moscow, they're particularly germane."

"Justin," Stuart said.

"Sir?"

"You got me thinking. I'd like to bring someone from State's Bureau of Political-Military Affairs along to Paris. Touch base with Richard and make sure Captain Rohrbaugh gets on the manifest. I want him to work our joint counter-terrorism programs and firm up our basing agreement in Djibouti."

"Camp Lemonnier?" Gilmore asked.

"Yes. And, Bryce, I don't recall you mentioning that you had a rep from State on your team investigating the Mayak incident. Something to think about."

Chapter Six

Nick had never been in Committee Briefing Room A—COBRA in shorthand. The title of the fifth-floor room in the National Counterterrorism Center conveyed a sense of strength and lethality. He felt neither at the moment.

He took a deep breath, wiped his palms on his pants legs, then placed them flat on the conference room table to stop the trembling.

One of the eight chairs remained vacant and the aloof body language of the man seated at the far end of the table unnerved him. Nick sensed he was in a stare-down similar to those he had with his cat. He ended the visual standoff by flipping open his briefing book to the page with the seating chart.

The empty seat belonged to the Department of Defense's representative from the Central Security Service. The place cards didn't match. It read: Taylor Ferguson, CIA.

Nick cocked his head. *He must have changed places. That's odd.*

He filed the thought and scanned the remainder of the place cards matching them with his chart to make sure nobody else had moved. The internal politics of the ODNI were such that he didn't want to ruffle any feathers by screwing up the formal pecking order around the table. He sucked in his lower lip as he addressed his first official decision: *Was it important enough to press the point of the altered seating arrangement? No—at least not yet.*

He started with the only woman in the room. On the right side of the empty chair was the FBI's National Security Branch representative, Jessica Caudry. She wore red, in contrast to the standard Washington dark-blue suits for the men. She returned his look with a bemused one of her own before acknowledging him with a slight nod.

Nick wondered if she read his thoughts. He nodded back and moved on to the person immediately to his left, Mark Arita, from Treasury's Office of Terrorism and Finance Intelligence. They had worked together on other cases and Nick had made a special request to have him on the team. A wry smile crossed Arita's face accompanied by a subtle shake of his head.

Damn, am I that easy to read?

He turned his chair to observe the remaining seats. The immense bulk of the Assistant Deputy Director for the Office of National Counterintelligence Executive, John Elliot, filled the first. The middle seat belonged to the Special Collections Service. This outfit, whose existence wasn't even officially acknowledged outside of the intelligence community, fascinated him.

He tossed a look of recognition to Frank Garcia who held the last chair at the table. Frank worked for Homeland Security's Directorate of Intelligence Analysis and Infrastructure Protection. Nick looked forward to picking his brain.

An impressive assemblage, although Strickland cautioned

him they might have to adjust the membership to reflect whatever direction his investigation took.

A voice from his right interrupted his thoughts. "What do you say we get started?"

"DoD's rep isn't here." Nick pulled up his sleeve and glanced at his watch. "He has five minutes."

The Assistant DD had a reputation of starting meetings early and this one wasn't going to be an exception even though Nick sat in the place of authority at the head of the table. "He's probably hung up in traffic."

Nick couldn't see any point in wasting energy discussing the point, so he opened his iPad and tabbed to his notes. He steadied himself remembering a doctor friend's advice for dealing with medical emergencies; 'If you don't know what you're doing, at least look like you do.' He pressed the ON switch of his voice recorder.

"Good morning. Welcome to Liberty Crossing. These discussions will be classified Top-Secret, SCI code-name 'Amber Dawn.' Questions?"

Nick didn't expect any, but you never knew. He surveyed the faces around him. Ferguson raised his pen, signaling he was about to speak, then dropped it and wrote something on his notepad.

"Two days ago, I presented my preliminary assessment to the DNI. We'll start there. Mr. Gilmore has tasked us to explore the broader implications of the Moscow incident as they pertain to our national security. If we confirm a credible threat exists, we are to recommend the specific actions required to eliminate it."

Ferguson's pen went back up.

"Yes, Mr. Ferguson?"

"You said, *confirm*. Are we to presume, then, a credible threat exists?"

Nick swore to himself at his word choice and took a

different tact. "The Russian government has acknowledged a low-yield dirty bomb was detonated at the GUM department store. They have not been forthcoming with the particular details of the device. We can only surmise why they've chosen not to do so. To that end, I've been authorized to travel to Moscow and meet with a representative of the FSB to—"

"Has your trip been vetted through the appropriate entities?"

Nick saw Jessica Caudry shoot Ferguson a '*What the hell?*' look before he responded. "I believe Mr. Gilmore's approval will suffice."

Arita was first to respond. "Nick, what's your assessment based on?"

"I created a matrix consisting of eight major elements that I've begun to populate. The DNI felt there was enough information to pursue a threat analysis."

"And those are?"Feguson asked.

Nick's hesitance vanished as he found familiar footing. "Leader, Cell Members, Personality Traits, Motive, Intent, Device, Financing, and Support Networks. With those, I've drawn a Venn diagram to allow us to visualize the data we collect to populate these sets. How this data overlaps will identify the common elements and help focus our investigation."

"I presume we're going to review the data you've compiled?" Ferguson replied. "We shouldn't waste our time drawing circles and chasing phantoms."

Nick detected a trace of a smirk from the CIA rep. "I couldn't agree more, so let me answer your question this way. I've established five premises that we can use as our starting point."

"Shouldn't—"

"I'll open the meeting for discussion in a moment. Number one, the perpetrator has experience in handling radioactive materials.

"Two, he will likely avoid contact with known terrorist organizations.

"Three, he has a sophisticated support network.

"Four, his cell is small.

"Five, he has a secure financial base.

"Now, I'll take your questions."

"I'll presume our greatest risk is from a terrorist network we haven't identified," Caudry said. "Do we have any leads?"

"The known separatist and radical Islamic groups have remained silent," Garcia said.

"Then we'll need to think out of the box," Arita responded.

"Nick, I'd focus on motive," Caudry added. "Beyond the psychological impact, what is the ultimate intent of the malicious use of such a device?"

"Exactly my thoughts."

Garcia consulted his notes. "I'd suggest we frame our analysis by thinking in terms of the perpetrator's intent. We shouldn't confine ourselves by assuming this was an isolated event."

"Could this be the work of some internal network intent on destabilizing the government?"

Nick noticed Ferguson startle at Caudry's comment. "I wouldn't want to dismiss any motive at this point. Let's start with what we know and work from there. We can think in terms of the material used in the device, the amount released, distribution pattern, and the detonation device.

"Frank, could you review what you have from the Nuclear Security Administration?"

"We've completed our forensic studies of the material from Moscow and matched the results with samples from the National Uranium Materials Archives at Oak Ridge. The material used in the radiologic dispersal device was an alpha-emitter consistent with a fuel pellet composed of reprocessed weapons grade uranium: Plutonium-239. There were also traces of Uranium-235. These suggest two sources were used in the device."

"Nothing surprising," Caudry said.

"In short, no it isn't. We're not dealing with your average terrorist."

"The data does provide a pertinent negative," Garcia added. "The scientists at Oak Ridge were able to match the radioactive isotopes of the Red Square sample with known material submitted by the Mayak Production Facility several years ago as one of the conditions of the nuclear disarmament treaty. With that, we can exclude the use of material from the other known cases of smuggled or stolen material in our black market data base and narrow our search to those responsible."

"We're to presume that group conducted the attack in Moscow?"

"Yes," Nick replied.

"We also conducted a review of the International Atomic Energy Agency records looking for any evidence of trafficking of nuclear material during the past year," Frank said.

"Are you prepared to defend your position?" Ferguson asked.

"The nuclear forensics, the images of the ambush site, and those of a farm truck identified on the highway leaving the ambush site are the key. I'll leverage this information to identify those responsible."

Elliot stared down the table. "Mr. Ferguson, do you have something further you'd like to say?"

"No, I'm good."

Nick closed his iPad. "Let's wrap up. I'll draft a point paper of today's meeting and send it out for review along with any specific taskings. We'll meet in two weeks, Friday, same place and time."

The room cleared except for Caudry who approached Nick. "Did you pick up on the CIA rep?"

"Ferguson?"

"I'm the one who changed seats. I've worked with him before. He's a prick."

Nick kept his face expressionless. Not quite sure what to make of her comment, he inwardly agreed that something wasn't quite right with the guy. He slipped the voice recorder into his coat pocket. "See you in a couple weeks."

Chapter Seven

MOSCOW
RUSSIAN REPUBLIC
THURSDAY 13 NOVEMBER

Nick settled into the back seat of the black Mercedes sedan. He gazed out the side window, thankful it was only a short trip to the embassy. His United flight from Dulles to Moscow via Geneva had taken thirteen hours and with the time zones turned on their heads, he was beat.

The man who had met him at the terminal twisted around in the front passenger seat to face him. "Ever been to Moscow?"

"First time."

"It takes some getting used to. Cold, impenetrable."

"Like the people?"

"Naw, they're fine if you can get past their suspicion of foreigners and strike up a friendship. Problem is, I've never been very good at figuring out what they're really thinking."

"*Rossiyu umom ne ponyat.*"

"What?"

"*Russia cannot be explained by your mind*," Nick replied. "Tyutcheu."

"Who?"

"One of their great Romantics. The others are Pushkin and Lermontov."

"Impressive. Maybe you'll do okay."

"Would it be possible to swing by Red Square? I'd like to get a feel for the place."

Their car's diplomatic license plates allowed them to drive in the designated middle lane of the expressway leading from Sheremetyevo International Airport to central Moscow. They bypassed the thousands of boxy Zhigulis and Moskvich cars crammed together on the outer Ring road and arrived in less than thirty minutes.

Nick caught a glimpse of the Kremlin and the iconic domes of Saint Basil's cathedral through the roadblocks encircling Red Square. He wanted to get closer, but the police forced them to turn around. A huge dull-white tarp shrouded the main entrance of the GUM. Cleanup teams from the Fifth Guards Rifle Brigade in MOPP suits were still washing down the square with detergent and vacuuming up the contaminated water into special tank trucks before it froze—a nasty business. He prayed the process wouldn't have to be repeated in other cities.

Nick studied the rigid Stalinist monumental style that dominated the city's architecture as they crossed the inner ring road bound for the Presnensky District and the American Embassy. He found the effect oppressive, although he had to admit his fatigue and the gray overcast colored his assessment.

The driver slowed and wove through the concrete barriers fronting the embassy. He stopped in front of the heavy gate of the compound and rolled down his window for the security guard to verify their identities.

Nick pulled the edges of his coat together to ward off the blast of frigid air blowing into the back seat. He glared at the guard who seemed to be taking his time verifying their documents. *A civilian? Odd.* He wondered if the Marine guards had been pulled because of any lingering contamination from the bomb's plume. The guard handed back their ID's and they proceeded inside the compound where his escort ushered him to a secure conference room.

The CIA station chief rose to greet him. "Welcome to Moscow. Any problems with the flight?"

Nick rubbed the scruff on his face. "Went well enough. It's been a long day."

"Understood. We'll get you over to the Marriott Grand once we finish up."

"Has there been any movement at this end?"

"The Russians finally agreed to a meeting. They were tight-lipped about divulging any information until we told them we knew the origin of the nuclear material."

"When?"

"Tomorrow morning. Ten. The Lubyanka."

"FSB Headquarters?"

"I suppose it's as good a place as any," the Station Chief replied. He pulled a sheet of paper from his briefcase and handed it to Nick. "They gave us a name. Alex Grekov."

"We know anything about him?" Nick scanned the page.

"A complete unknown."

"Well, it's a start."

"Let me brief you on what we have, then we'll check you into the hotel. Get a good night's sleep. You'll need it."

THE LUBYANKA
HEADQUARTERS, RUSSIAN STATE SECURITY

Nick swayed as his sedan entered the roundabout fronting the Lubyanka precisely at 0950. He surveyed the imposing Neo-Baroque edifice from his vantage point in the back seat. He thought it fitting that the headquarters of the FSB used to be a prison. The car pulled to a stop in front of the main entrance. He swung open his door only to find himself eye-to-eye with a stern-faced security guard.

"This way," the guard said waving an arm toward the entrance.

He followed the man down a series of dim hallways into the bowels of the building. If the location of the office was an indication of the status of his contact, the chances of this person being some low level apparatchik were increasing with each step.

His escort didn't say a word until he stopped before one of the doors lining the barren corridor and knocked.

"*Da?*"

"Your visitor."

"Show him in."

The escort opened the door and stepped out of the way. He gestured to the void beyond. "Enter."

Nick took several steps and stopped. His suspicions were confirmed. The room had a faint musty smell, like an old closet. A closed door on the left likely led to the inner office. The receptionist stood and extended her hand.

"I am Aleksandra Kuzminova Grekov."

She grasped his hand in a firm grip and gave it a quick shake. "You have fifteen minutes."

Nick gathered his wits. *Aleksandra?* This was no reception-ist. Could this be Alek, not the male 'Alex' as he'd presumed? He took another look around the room. Sterile, unadorned except for a picture of Srevnenko and a scattering of drab wooden furniture. Nothing on her desk. No family photos, no memorabilia, nothing that would provide any indication of who this person might be. Was she even the contact?

So, what do I know? Her middle name—Daughter of Kuzmin. The "ova" indicated her father's family could have once held a position of distinction in Czarist Russia before the revolution. Dark gray, two-piece suit. Severe, with no hint of what was under it. He studied her face. Could be in her thirties. Black hair pulled back in a tight bun. She wore no makeup to speak of except for a bit of mascara and lip gloss. A small colorless scar ran through her right eyebrow. Deep-set brown eyes. Her mouth, a horizontal slash revealing no emotion.

She noted the inspection. "You were expecting something else?"

"Yes."

"I've been assigned as your contact."

"Your middle name indicates your father—"

She placed her hands on the desk. "Things are not always as they appear."

Nick noted her nails were manicured; clear polish. No wedding ring—that was something anyway. "So it seems."

Grekov pulled her hands back and watched his eyes. "What is it you want?"

"Answers."

"There are many questions."

Nick wondered if he should answer in Russian. He opted for English. "Yes, for the many unknowns we must confront."

Grekov gestured toward an empty chair. "*Vnogakh pravdy net.*"

"*Spasibo,*" he replied, recognizing the Russian saying—an invitation to take a seat. "There is no truth in the feet."

She opened a desk drawer, pulled out a dark brown dossier, and handed it to him. "We have retrieved pieces of the first explosive device."

"The one from the restroom?"

"We are familiar with the device. Gas chromatography and mass spectrometry analysis have identified the explosive as Triacetone Triperoxide combined with a binder of mineral oil and lecithin. Based on the force of the blast, the bomb contained approximately five hundred grams of explosive."

"Just over one pound," Nick said. "Easy enough to conceal in a large envelope."

"Correct. We are conducting a forensic examination of small fragments from the container, but have not found any fingerprints."

"Not surprising." Nick examined the pictures in the dossier. "And the other components?"

"The switch was a simple kitchen timer and the power source a standard nine-volt battery. There were no enhancers such as ball bearings or nails."

"So the intent of the first device was to be a diversion?"

"And to drive as many people as possible toward the main blast."

"Do you have any leads on the perpetrator?"

"We are reviewing security footage."

"Would the Ministry be willing to share those tapes?"

"I will ask."

"Thank you."

Alek grasped the arms of her chair. "Then we are done."

"No, we need to address the nature of the radioactive material used in the dispersal device." He waited for a response.

"There is a precedent," she said after a pause.

"Yes?"

"Chechen terrorists attempted to detonate a crude radiologic dispersion device using materials stolen during a raid of one of our radon waste deposal sites near Grozny."

Nick kept his face expressionless. The knowledge of that event in 1996 was open source. She hadn't given him a thing and she knew it.

"And we are working with the Ministry of Defense Twelfth Main Directorate to re-examine a case of a corrupt manager at Atomflot suspected of trafficking in radioactive material," she added. "Perhaps that is the source."

Still nothing. He knew that case had nothing to do with

the event in Red Square. *What was she holding back? And why?*
He decided it was time to play his strongest card. He pulled
three photographs from his inside coat pocket and slid them
across the desk. "You may find these of some use."

Alek's eyes widened as she examined the images.

"From one of your surveillance satellites?"

"We have several more photographs of the truck taken in
the vicinity of the ambush. Driver. Two more riding in the
back. Three men, maybe four, if there was an individual in
the passenger seat." Nick noticed her jaw tighten.

"Check the produce in the bed of the truck, the timelines,
and the direction the truck is traveling on each of the images."

Alek spread the photographs across her desk in sequence.
"The bed of the truck is empty in the last image."

"Except for that barrel. And they're heading south."

She pushed the images together and handed them back.
"It's probable the truck was stopped and searched at one of
the paramilitary checkpoints."

"I'd suggest we begin our search for an isolated farm
somewhere off the M-5 highway near Chelyabinsk."

"Our search?"

There was no mistaking the tone in her voice. She had no
intension of including him in any investigation on Russian
soil. He changed his approach. "Whoever committed this act
has set a very dangerous precedent."

"I don't disagree. I would suggest they have done what
they set out to accomplish."

"Perhaps, but that is a risk my government is not prepared
to accept."

"Do you have evidence he will act again?"

Nick ignored her question. "Have you considered the
possibility your terrorist is working with a transnational crime
organization?"

She stiffened. "It is not possible. The TCO's are
concerned only with profit, not terror. It is not possible."

"I would think—"

Alek pressed a buzzer on her desk, cutting him off. "Your time here is over."

The outer door opened, and his escort appeared before Nick could respond.

"Escort Mr. Parkos to his car."

What the hell? Nick looked from the escort back to Grekov. She ignored him, busying herself with a sheaf of papers on her desk. He had no choice but follow the escort out of the room and down the dim corridor. His mind reeled from the sudden turn of events. What was she hiding? And if she refused to cooperate? Then what?

Chapter Eight

CHELYABINSK
RUSSIAN FEDERATION
SATURDAY 15 NOVEMBER

Grekov's cryptic call to his room at the Marriott had woken him just after one in the morning. "We have found something. A car will pick you up in one hour. Dress warmly."

Now, Nick kept his eyes focused on the counter-terrorism unit advancing toward the farm buildings scattered across an open field.

"Stay in the vehicle," Alek commanded.

He didn't move. Two-dozen Special Forces troops of the FSB's Spetsgruppa poured out of the armored personnel carriers flanking them. The team split into smaller assault groups and approached a one-story house with a thatched roof and a large barn with weathered wooden siding. Three cupolas, each adorned with a Russian Orthodox cross, topped the barn. A silo and a small outbuilding with a sagging roof made the entire scene surreal, something akin to a Russian

Currier and Ives painting. It could have almost been beautiful. *Except for the troops and armored vehicles.*

The only sound was their car's idling diesel engine. A heavy snow that began before dawn blanketed the countryside. The snow enveloped the white camouflaged soldiers, who soon vanished from sight.

"We'll know soon enough if you were correct," Alek said in the silence.

"The evidence—" Nick stopped when Alek's right hand pressed against her earbud.

"The area is cleared."

"And the terrorists?"

"Gone."

They exited the car and trudged through the snowdrifts to the farmhouse. If there was a typical Russian country home, this was it. The home's front door was faced with a classic herringbone pattern of bleached boards. A blue gingerbread surround meant to ward off evil spirits defined each of the three frosted windows flanking the entrance.

Alek pushed open the door and entered. Nick took a step to follow her. A burly Spetsgruppa officer blocked his way. "*Nyet.*"

Nick tried to go around him.

The officer shoved him in the chest, sending him stumbling backwards. "Outside."

Nick caught himself before he fell. He backed away, afraid he might be detained and never heard from again.

Alek heard the commotion and spun. "What are you doing?"

"I have my orders," the Spetsgruppa officer said. "The American is not to interfere."

Alek advanced on the soldier, stopping within inches of his face. He towered a good six inches over her. "I give the orders here. Let him in."

The soldier glared at her but stepped aside.

Nick didn't wait. He slid by the man and positioned himself behind Alek. This wasn't the time to be caught in the middle of a battle of wills between these two Russians.

Alek ignored the officer and addressed Nick. "What do you see?"

He surveyed the room dominated by a simple wooden table and four chairs. His eyes came to rest on the only spot of color in the otherwise drab interior—a drooping bouquet of sunflowers set in the center of the table. A scattering of faded yellow petals lay around the base of the empty beet can that served as a vase. "Not much."

He fished around in his parka and pulled out his digital camera. He focused on the table and snapped off several pictures before putting the camera back in his pocket.

He walked over to a cast iron stove set in the far corner of the room and touched his hand to the flue. Cold. He grabbed a poker, opened the front grate, and stirred the coals. A solitary ember glowed with a remnant of life. Whoever had been here must have left just hours before. *Were they tipped off?*

He found nothing more of interest and headed for the back rooms. A forensic team already roved in the bedroom, bagging what personal belongings remained and dusting for fingerprints. Two, perhaps three, individuals had slept here.

Nick returned to the kitchen. Remnants of a half-eaten meal were scattered over the countertop. A wadded ball of paper lay on the floor beside a crate filled with trash. He picked up the paper and smoothed it out. At the top of the page were three typed lines of Cyrillic characters. At the bottom, someone had scrawled several sentences in longhand that he couldn't read.

"Hey, Alek, what does this say?" he asked, handing her the paper.

"It's the Chechen national anthem." She lifted her eyes. She had no need to look at the words to recite them.

"'We were born at night when the she-wolf whelped. In

the morning to the lion's deafening roar, they named us. There is no God, but Allah.'"

She dropped her hand to her side and turned away to stare out the window. The paper fell from her hand, fluttering to the floor.

Nick leaned over and picked it up. There had to be more "Can you make out the bottom lines?"

She didn't respond.

"Alek?"

"No, not this," she whispered.

He cocked his head. Her words hung suspended in the frozen air. "Not what?"

His question was met with silence. At a loss, he folded the paper and stuffed it in his coat pocket. "Let's check out the barn."

———

Nick grasped the handle of the sliding door and gave it a shove revealing the vaulted interior of the barn. Two Spets-gruppa sat on hay bales smoking cigarettes. One cast him a disinterested look. The other gestured to the row of stalls behind him.

"The only thing we found were the cows."

He looked at the stalls. From their fawn color and white patches, he identified them as Guernsey dairy cows.

"I'll take a look around anyway." Nick walked toward the closed end of the barn.

The cows emitted plaintive moos, following his progress with hopeful, soft brown eyes. Nick turned at their call and noticed their engorged udders. They hadn't been milked for some time. "Sorry, ladies. You'll have to wait a bit longer."

"You know cows, then?" Alek asked as she came up behind him.

"I spent some time on a farm," Nick replied. He stopped at the far end of the building. Something didn't look right.

He pointed to the bales stacked in front of him. "Help me move these."

"What? You are going to feed them?"

"No," Nick smiled. "You see these bales?"

"How can I not?"

"There's a mix of new and old hay. See the difference in color?"

He didn't wait for her answer and began pulling bales off the stack. "Ha, I knew it."

"What?"

Nick grabbed an iron ring set in the floor and gave it a heave. The trap door flung open and clanged against the wall.

"*Bozhe moi!*" Alek said over his shoulder.

Nick peered into the void. He placed his foot on the first rung of a wooden ladder and took a tentative step, testing its strength. He felt along the edge of the doorframe seeking a light switch. His fingers brushed against something and gave it a flick. Light from three banks of suspended high-bay florescent fixtures flooded the space.

He descended the remaining steps, astonished. Centered in the cut stone room was a large acrylic glove box with two inverted black-vulcanized rubber arms dangling from the front. On the floor next to the workstation stood a large beet can, exactly like the one on the kitchen table. Several cardboard cases were stacked against the right hand wall with more beet cans resting on them. *What are all of these cans doing down here?* His gaze swept over the rest of the room.

An aluminum pipe lay at the base of the far wall. It looked to be a good ten feet long. Next to it, a zirconium alloy fuel rod assembly. A three-foot-high container stood in the far right corner. He recognized the VIPAC containment vessel listed on the manifest of the destroyed transport truck. He yelled up to Alek. "You're going to want to see this."

He pulled out his camera and clicked off a panoramic series of photos. His eyes came to rest on a small table in the corner opposite the containment vessel. The viewfinder framed a scattering of metalworking tools. He snapped several pictures before Alek interrupted him.

"What have you found?"

Nick pocketed his camera. "Our evidence. We need to check out that fuel rod assembly."

They made their way over to the burnished aluminum tube, steering well clear of the VIPAC containment vessel.

"Let's see." He picked up one end of the fuel rod and tilted it to empty the contents. A half-dozen shiny ceramic-clad fuel pellets rolled onto the floor, each no bigger than a nickel. He shook the rod. Nothing else came out. That spelled trouble. There should have been hundreds.

He leaned over and picked up the scattered pellets. They easily fit into his palm. He clenched his fist around the tiny cylinders and turned to Alek. "This is bad."

Chapter Nine

Q asif felt the bead of sweat carve a ragged course through the layer of dust coating his face. He looked over his shoulder at the file of mujahedeen behind him. Their faces remained expressionless. Perhaps it was their fatigue, or the oppressive heat, but they showed no other signs of what they had just done.

He pulled out a plastic bag containing the meager remains of his khat. He stripped a few of the mottled green-brown leaves off the stem. The khat was old. They hadn't received a new supply from their brothers in Yemen. He stuffed them in his mouth and chewed a bit before pressing the leaves into his cheek with his tongue. The macerated leaves added to the small wad already there. In a few minutes he'd feel the mild amphetamine-like rush.

Four days before, he'd been one of the men chosen to protect their leader, Adbul Aleem for a visit to his ancestral home in the coastal city of Barawa. Aleem was the self-appointed leader of Harakat al-Shabaab al-Mujahida, the militant wing of the al-Qaeda affiliated Somali Council of Islamic Courts. He'd also chosen his own nom-de-guerre. "The Servant of the Omniscient." Qasif had concluded the name didn't fit, but he kept his opinion to himself.

On their third night in Barawa, the American SEALs struck. They emerged like apparitions from the surf near Aleem's house but were forced to retreat after a running gun battle. Aleem then ordered his own attack on the town to extract revenge on those he felt were responsible for betraying his location.

Aleem focused his wrath on one individual, Abdi Kareem Jawari. Jawari was from a rival clan and a past leader of the Council of Islamic Courts. Jawari had turned to piracy, siphoning support and money away from al-Shabaab. He was a rival, not to be trusted.

Qasif and his fellow warriors couldn't penetrate Jawari's defenses in the narrow alleyways of the town and retreated. But another group, the radical Amniyat branch of al-Shabaab, slaughtered dozens of innocents before they abandoned the city. Both groups made their way thirty miles inland to the Webi Shabeelie River.

Qasif helped conceal their Toyota pickup under a scattering of skeletal trees clinging to the river's western bank before joining the others for the trek to their base camp in the low hills above the town of Haaway. It was safer to travel the rest of the way on foot to minimize the chance of being detected and attacked from the air. He feared the American Predator drones. All of them did.

The previous leader of al-Shabaab had been blown to pieces before his very eyes. He suppressed the memory of the smoldering ruin of the minivan destroyed by a Hellfire missile. The Americans were closing in on their cell. They were becoming the hunted instead of the hunters.

He searched the empty sky. A vulture circled in the distance. He wondered if the bird was prophetic.

His temples throbbed. The temperature neared ninety-six, the cloudless sky bleached a pale blue by the blazing sun. A lone acacia tree cast a feeble shadow across the parched land-scape offering no relief. He reached up to adjust the black cotton Ghutrah covering his mouth and nose in a futile attempt to protect his eyes from the glare reflecting off the rocks.

A single gunshot shattered the silence of the desert.

Qasif startled at the sound and dropped to one knee, searching for the source. It appeared to come from the head of their column. He looked in that direction. Several men tossed a body off to the side of the trail. Aleem yelled some-thing at the two and shoved them back into line. Qasif adjusted the sling of his AK-47, feigning indifference as he approached the lifeless form.

Flies buzzed around the corpse, attracted by the pool of blood staining the dirt around its head. Qasif retched at the sight of Mahmoud.

A push from behind propelled him forward. "Forget him."

Vomit filled his throat. He turned his eyes away. Another eight hundred meters and he would be able to collapse in the shade of the mud-brick huts that served as their base camp.

He dared not look back. He willed himself forward. He could do nothing. Mahmoud's body would remain there to rot under the merciless sun. Qasif hoped someone would return under the cover of darkness to cover it with stones and mark it with a white flag signifying the final resting place of a martyr.

From his time in Somalia though, he already knew the reality that waited his friend. The vultures that inhabited this godforsaken place would attend to it.

He looked skyward. There were three of them now, circling, waiting. Soon there would be more. They would pick Mahmoud's bones clean.

Qasif staggered up the path. Over the past six months, he'd come to certain degree of acceptance of his fate operating from a premise the mujahedeen of al-Shabaab applied to their enemies. "As you kill, you will also surely be killed."

He stumbled on a loose rock. A hand reached out from behind to steady him. The hand tightened on his arm and spun him around. Aleem.

"Perhaps you question what I have done," he said.

"It was necessary," Qasif answered automatically.

Aleem's eyes narrowed. "Ah, but he was your friend, was he not? An American, like you. From Minnesota, yes?"

"I am a youth of al-Shabaab. Not like him."

Aleem thrust his face to within an inch of Qasif's, his breath, hot, foul. "Then you will prove it."

Qasif couldn't prevent his voice from breaking. "What must I do?"

Aleem released his grip and brushed the dust off Qasif's shoulder. "You fought well in Barawe."

Qasif tensed with fear.

"You will work with as-Sahab and be my voice to the infidels in your homeland."

Stunned, Qasif didn't answer. As-Sahab, the Clouds, was the propaganda branch of the movement specializing in open source Internet activity and the clandestine digital underground.

He had turned down a request by the leaders of the as-Sahab to join them shortly after he made his way from his home in the Minneapolis suburb of Cedar-Riverside to the horn of Africa. His choice did not sit well with the leadership and he was sent to the desolate southern part of the country where he could be watched and his resolve tested.

Aleem's merciless black eyes burned into him. "You refuse my offer?"

"No, no. It is most generous, Mahadsanid," Qasif answered, using the honorific title.

"You have made a wise choice, my friend," Aleem responded before pivoting and returning to the front of the column.

The encounter filled Qasif with dread. Aleem had no friends.

He completed the remainder of the march in a daze before staggering through the door of the hut he'd shared with Mahmoud. He dropped his rifle and collapsed on the dirt floor, wracked by sobs. He clasped his hands around his knees and curled into a ball, striving to shut out the madness surrounding him.

An eerie silence enveloped the camp when he woke. Prayers. The lilting voice of the muezzin called out in the fading light. "Hasten to prayer. Hasten to prayer. Come to salvation."

Qasif reached for his prayer rug, unrolled it, and bowed toward Mecca. The words flowed over him, calming his soul. "Allah is Great. Allah is Great. I bear witness that there is no divinity but Allah…"

After completing the fourth of the day's five prayers, the Maghrib, Qasif opened his Koran. He reflected on the written words, seeking answers to a life devoid of meaning. He knew he shouldn't question his beliefs, lest he give voice to his thoughts, and meet the same fate as his friend.

His breathing slowed. The answers came to him: *I will not know the time or place of my death, but I will not die of my own hand. I will find a way to return home, and there, die the death of a shahid—a martyr.*

Chapter Ten

NATIONAL COUNTERTERRORISM CENTER
McLEAN, VIRGINIA
TUESDAY 18 NOVEMBER

Nick finished his third coffee of the day while he watched the IT tech complete the setup of his computer. He'd just returned from Moscow and the jet lag was killing him. His eyes drifted to the window of his new office in building LX1. The upgrade included a view of the Capital Beltway paralleling the western side of the Liberty Crossing Intelligence Campus.

The tech tightened a white zip-tie around a bundle of cables that disappeared through a hole in the rear of the desk and straightened the monitor. "There you go, sir. All set."

"Thanks for the quick turnaround, Jim. I appreciate it."

"Anytime."

Nick turned his attention to unloading his few possessions. He opened one of the two copy paper boxes containing the items from his old office. He peered inside at the meager contents. On top of the pile was his *Pearls Before Swine* day calendar—a reminder of better days. Marty used to give him a calendar each Christmas, knowing it provided a bit of comic relief to his day. *Well, that was then and this is now…*

He picked up the calendar displaying a cartoon panel of *Larry the Crocodile.* The strip featured another one of Larry's ill-fated encounters with his Zebra neighbor. He smiled and placed the calendar next to his computer, feeling a certain affinity for the well-intentioned but bungling reptile.

He lifted a framed picture of Marty and Emma from the box. He held it, focusing on the face of his daughter. Thanksgiving was a week away and the department stores were already decorating for Christmas. She was a year older and he needed to find her something age-appropriate. And he needed a new picture. He debated if he should chance a call to Marty. His last call hadn't gone well. After a moment, he pulled out his iPhone and scrolled down to her number hoping she'd answer when she saw the caller ID.

"Hello?"

Nick noted the hesitation in her voice. "Are you busy?"

"What do you want, Nick?"

"Could you send me a picture of Emma? I've got a new office—"

"I'll see what I can do. Listen, I just got home and have to get dinner ready."

"Yeah, I—"

"Goodbye."

The line went dead.

Nick sighed, staring at his phone. The conversation went pretty much as he had expected. She rarely sounded happy. Work, the house, disagreements with her father. There always seemed to be something.

He set Emma's old photograph on the desk and finished unloading his boxes wondering if his new section was planning any office parties. *Probably not.* The agency wasn't exactly loaded with extroverts and he hadn't seen any fliers posted on the bulletin boards.

He didn't have any close friends or family in the area and concluded his best bet for Thanksgiving would be to open a bottle of Wild Turkey bourbon, warm up some leftovers, and watch the Detroit Lions get beat.

"At least that outcome is predictable," he told the empty room.

A flash of light prompted him to look out the window. The building's exterior floodlights. He looked at his watch: 4:56. *No sense in leaving.* He'd only sit in traffic, frustrated by the gridlock. Might as well work.

He opened his briefcase and took out the digital camera, connected it to the USB port, and transferred the files with the pictures of the farmhouse and barn to his computer.

The first sequence of photos showed the interior of the house. Nothing remarkable in the barren rooms caught his eye except the bouquet of sunflowers. If one of the terrorists had bought them at the GUM, they could identify him. What were the odds?

He moved on to the pictures of the root cellar. The first centered on the glove box. On the floor, next to the box's right-front leg, sat an open beet can. *Funny place for that to be.*

He scrolled to the next picture. Stacked against the cellar's stonewall were two cardboard cases with a scattering of loose cans sitting on top. A label on each of the four cans advertised its contents in English, BEETS in block letters along with a picture of the blood-red vegetable over a yellow background. *What else?*

There appeared to be two broken-down boxes underneath the stack. Each case would hold six two-liter cans—twenty-four cans. *So, what's with all the beets?*

He pressed the advance key, bringing up the picture of the workbench. The first thing he noticed was two more beet cans. He shook his head and enlarged the photo to examine the tabletop. Beside the cans lay a collection of miscellaneous tools: tinsnips, needle-nose pliers, tack hammer, can opener, spool of solder and flux, soldering iron, the top of a beet can... *Oh, crap.*

He touched his thumb to his fingertips counting off the cans. These two, plus the four on top of the boxes, six. No, there were two more—the one on the floor by the glove box and the one on the dining room table. That made eight. Presuming the broken-down cases had been full, there should have been twelve.

The missing fuel pellets.... *That's how he got them out.*

He brought up the previous picture, craning his neck forward trying to read the blurred print on the cases. *M, E — MEYCEK. Really?* An unlikely coincidence.

A blinking ALERT box appeared at the top-right corner of his monitor, interrupting his thoughts. There was a new message in his secure inbox. He closed the picture file, and with it, his question about the significance of Meycek Exports and the company's new parent company, the Novoroosiyk Business Group.

He typed in his password and clicked on the message. The routing code indicated the originator was the Station Chief at the Moscow embassy. The subject line read: Red Square Incident. His heart rate jumped as he scanned the two-page message. Alek had come through.

The first page contained the key to the investigation. One set of fingerprints obtained at the house matched those of a Chechen national.

Name: Bashir al-Khultyer

Born: 1974

Place of Birth: Grozny, Chechnya, Russian Federation

Nick skimmed the scant biographical information and focused on a student ID picture of al-Khultyer taken in 1994: Handsome, clean-shaven, no visible scars, slightly rounded head, intelligent eyes. He surmised the Russians would use their age-progression software to create an image of al-Khul-tyer at age forty-two. They could then search their surveillance tapes and see if they could place him at the GUM.

He scrolled down the page and stopped at a listing of al-Khultyer's degrees:

- Moscow Institute of Physics and Technology, BS/1994;
- Joint Institute for Nuclear Research, Moscow - Masters/Radiation & Radiobiology/1997;
- Université Pierre et Marie Curie, Paris – PhD – Process Engineering (incomplete)

Oh, man. There's no doubt this guy knew what he was doing. And the Russians sent him to Paris to get a PhD? Impressive, but why didn't he complete his studies? What the hell happened? Nick scanned the rest of the message looking for an answer. Nothing.

The guy just disappeared? He couldn't believe the Russians could lose track of someone in whom they had invested so much. *Did he return home? Why?*

Nick rocked back in his chair. *What would make a man drop out of school and disappear? Family?* He sat back up and typed "Grozny" into his search engine. A clue appeared at the top of the page: "Battle of Grozny 1999-2000."

He read through the Wikipedia summary. The January siege of Chechnya's capital city had been a nasty affair. After taking heavy casualties in their initial assaults on the city, the Russians pulled back and reverted to their old World War II modus operandi—they flattened the place. They entered the destroyed city, killing scores of rebels and civilians.

He scanned the remainder of the article until he came to a highlighted section: The Novye Aldi Massacre. On the 5th of February, special police troops looting that same neighborhood had slaughtered fifty civilians.

That's it! He grabbed his briefcase, pulled out the Center's language expert's two-page translation of the handwritten sentences from the piece of paper he had found in the farmhouse and scanned the first. 'I bought into their lies, and as a result, I have betrayed myself, my family, my people, my country.'

Whose lies? The Russians? "If al-Khultyer had returned to Grozny... Or, were there others he felt were complicit in the destruction of his homeland?"

He read the first verse of the Chechen national anthem titled, *Death or Freedom*, the translators had included in their report: 'We were born at night when the she-wolf whelped. In the morning, to the lion's deafening roar, they named us.'

Is there a clue hidden in those words? What had Alek said in the farmhouse? "No, not this." *What did she mean by that?* He set the first page aside and started to read the second. He stopped at the header.

The Jungle Book
Rudyard Kipling

"Good God. Emma's favorite story. Marty would read it to her almost every night." He moved on to the translation of the excerpt. "The Law for the Wolves."

'And the Wolf that shall keep *them* may prosper, but the Wolf that shall break *them* must die. For the strength of the Pack is the Wolf, and the strength of the Wolf is the Pack.'

These are the words the wolves told Mobli. He laid the translation aside and typed a message to the embassy: "What can you tell me about al-Khultyer? Married? Children? The fate of his family in Grozny? Where has he been the past fourteen years?"

The FSB—no, Alek, had to know more than what she sent

the Station Chief. He stopped typing, saved his draft, and brought up the file with his photos. He clicked through the pictures before stopping at the only one he had of Alek. She stood outside the barn, engaged in an animated discussion with the Spetsgruppa team leader. Nick zoomed in on her face, then pressed the print button. *So, Alek, where do you fit into my Venn diagram?*

Chapter Eleven

COMMITTEE BRIEFING ROOM A
NATIONAL COUNTERTERRORISM CENTER
FRIDAY 21 NOVEMBER

As Nick completed his brief detailing the events of the Russia trip, he paused to judge the body language of those in the room. Every seat was occupied this time including the one assigned to the DoD. There were no crossed arms and his team appeared receptive—with the notable exception of Taylor Ferguson. The CIA rep sat stone-faced at the end of the table, conspicuously spinning his pen in his fingers.

"Mr. Ferguson, you have a question?"

Ferguson laid his pen down. "Yes, as a matter of fact, I do. You touched on what is known about this Khultyer guy, but what leads do you have on his current status? There'll be hell to pay if you've managed to lose him."

Nick tightened his lips, not at all pleased with the repeated use of 'you.' He certainly didn't need any reminders as to the consequences if he failed.

"You presume he's gone underground?" Ferguson continued.

Nick glared. "Perhaps you have some information on al-Khultyer's probable whereabouts that you would care to share with the group?"

"No."

No? "No, I don't?" or *"No, I won't share?"* Nick wrote down NO and underlined it twice before answering. "Then I would say the operative word here is, 'presume.' At this juncture, I wouldn't assume anything. From what I saw in the farmhouse, al-Khultyer took off just hours before we arrived."

"Luck."

"I doubt it. Judging by the embers in the stove and our arrival time, he would have fled sometime around three in the morning. I'd ask, why would he leave at that hour? Was he tipped?"

"Maybe he had to catch a plane?" Ferguson whispered in an aside to the DoD rep eliciting a muffled chuckle.

John Elliot didn't appear amused. "Say again?"

Ferguson didn't respond.

"Was he forewarned?" Nick repeated. "Because that's what the director wanted to know when I briefed him yesterday."

Jessica Caudry put her hand to her face covering a smile. He had served an ace. She'd followed the give-and-take with Ferguson as if watching a tennis match. There was something about Ferguson that he couldn't put his finger on. Of course, Jessica did say the guy was a prick. He decided to move on.

"Has the Agency come up with a list of plausible scenarios?"

"I'll see what I can do," Ferguson replied through tight lips.

Game, but not match. Nick turned to his right. "Mr. Elliot?"

"Well played, Parkos," Elliot said over his shoulder before addressing the others. "Based on what we've just learned, it's probable al-Khultyer is the bomb maker, but he couldn't have escaped without help."

"What if he used a courier to transport the remaining nuclear material out of the country?" Caudry asked.

"Indeed, another variable," Elliot replied. "But, for now, we need to focus on al-Khultyer's probable escape route. His safest path would have taken him south through Kazakhstan and the Caucasus to the Black Sea. From there, he could make his way to Turkey, Pakistan, Afghanistan, or damn well anyplace else if he boarded a ship."

"Can we back up a minute?" the Treasury's Office of Terrorism and Financial Intelligence rep, Mark Arita asked. "This operation would require significant supporting infrastructure and financial backing. We need to look at what organizations could provide those."

"Nick, you're the expert on transnational crime organizations," Frank Garcia said. "Could it be one of them?"

"Why would they?" Coulter asked.

"It would be a mistake to focus on a Russian TCO. The risks would be too high."

"I concur," Ferguson said.

"Who said anything about the Russians?" Arita replied. "al-Khultyer is Chechen."

"But there is precedent for Russian criminal organizations being linked with international terrorists in the trafficking of nuclear material," Caudry said.

"It would also be a mistake to limit our analysis by thinking in terms of a traditional TCO whose sole motive is profit," Arita pointed out.

Nick finished making a note in the margin of his Venn diagram and looked up. "And that brings us back to motive. If we exclude profit, what else is there?"

"The obvious," Ferguson answered. "Terror, fear, revenge —the list goes on. We know the Chechen terrorists' history of threatening to use radioactive dispersal devices. Detonating one of in Red Square fits. They tried before. 1995. Buried a RDD in Gorky Park."

"For argument's sake, permit me to offer an alternative explanation," Elliot said. "Russia's economy is in shambles, the oligarchs are unhappy, and Svrevnenko is losing the support of the average Russian. Suppose someone has sensed an opportunity to destabilize the government and replace him?"

"Not likely," Ferguson said. "This was an attack against Mother Russia. If anything, it'll strengthen him."

Nick massaged his chin while he sorted through the pros and cons of each viewpoint. Perhaps Elliot and Ferguson were both correct? He picked up his pencil and jotted down several cryptic notes inside the MOTIVE and INTENT circles of his Venn diagram.

"The clock's ticking," Nick said. "We need to move on. I've been populating the Venn diagram I presented at our last meeting, penning in data for several of my headers including Device and Leader. The information required for each is incomplete. We've identified al-Khultyer, but is he the leader? If he's not, who is?"

"We have to know the nature of the device," Caudry said. "Hundreds, maybe thousands, of fuel pellets are unaccounted for. And this moves us from a discussion of motive to one of intent."

"Intent should be our immediate concern," Elliot said.

"Jessica, you're suggesting there's another bomb?" Garcia asked.

"Worst-case scenario." She nodded.

"And the target?" the DoD rep asked.

"Unknown," Nick responded.

"So we find al-Khultyer," Arita said.

"Can we go back to the pellets?" Elliot asked. "I have something that may pertain."

"Of course."

"We received a message from the Turks. They've detained an Armenian national crossing the border from Georgia carrying an unknown amount of radioactive material. We don't know if it's our missing pellets."

"We might have our courier," Garcia said.

"Maybe we can turn him?" the DoD rep added.

Nick held up his hand to suppress any more questions. "My gut tells me, this isn't our guy."

"Your gut?" Ferguson's hands tightened into fists. "What makes you so damn sure?"

"It's what I saw in the barn."

"What, those beet cans?"

"Yes, as a matter of fact. Those beets tie in to what Mr. Elliot said earlier about al-Khultyer's escape route."

"Perhaps you'd care to enlighten us," Ferguson said.

"The evidence in the root cellar suggests that al-Khultyer emptied the cans, filled them with pellets, and resealed them. The shipping boxes for those cans were stenciled MEYCEK EXPORTS."

"Okay."

"This company was recently acquired by the Novoroosiyk Business Group.'"

Ferguson waved his hand dismissively. "So?"

"So, the NBG is a known transnational crime organization. Meycek is one of their front companies. Those cases could be shipped from any of the Black Sea ports under a flag of convenience."

"Like Batumi or Novoroosiyk?" Elliott said.

"Yes."

"You're suggesting the NBG is backing our terrorist?" Arita said.

"That's certainly a leap," the DoD rep said. "I have to share Ferguson's skepticism. Why would they?"

"Mr. Parkos and I have been looking into the NBG," Arita answered. "Its leadership, networks… it's worth consideration."

"Again, why?"

Arita looked at Nick.

"The key is NBG's leadership."

Ferguson rolled his eyes and pushed away from the table. "You're wasting our time. Are we done here?"

Elliot's face reddened. He stared Ferguson back into his chair. "No, we are not. Mr. Parkos may be on to something. Unless you happen to have a better idea, Mr. Ferguson, I'd like to pursue it. We cannot dismiss the possibility of a causal link between al-Khultyer and the NBG. There's certainly a precedent for terrorists and TCOs working together.

"We'll start chasing down the shipping manifests of all merchant ships leaving a Black Sea port. Mr. Ferguson, your people will do the same. If there are any manifests listing Meycek beets, we'll track the shipment to a port-of-call, and the recipient. Don't expect the NBG to use one of their own ships. They'll use a flag of convenience."

Ferguson looked like he was about to protest. Nick preempted him. "Thank you, Mr. Elliott. Is there anything else we need to address before we adjourn?"

"Yes," Frank Garcia answered. "I'm not sure if it pertains, but just after al-Khultyer disappeared, we intercepted a number of messages from al-Shabaab in Somalia that included a new codeword. YLVA."

Ferguson's hand tightened around his pen.

Elliot challenged the CIA agent. "Mr. Ferguson, you've heard this word before?"

"No. No, I haven't."

"We haven't seen it either," Garcia added, "but it was used in the context of a statement about President Stuart's upcoming visit to Paris." He cleared his throat and quoted.

"'Our brothers in France, your salvation is only through Jihad. Mark the work of our Chechen brothers who bloodied Srevnenko and his running dogs. The French are next. They have rubbed your honor in the dirt of the Crusaders and the pig Jews.'"

"Who knows about this?" Elliott demanded.

"Mr. Gilmore and the Secret Service," Garcia replied.

"And the French?"

"Their Central Directorate of Interior Intelligence has been alerted."

Caudry waved her pen. "How did al-Shabaab know it was a Chechen?"

Ferguson appeared to have regained his composure and answered. "They're guessing. They're opportunists. Taking advantage of the Moscow incident to push their own agenda."

"Can we be sure?" the DoD rep asked.

"No," Nick answered.

Chapter Twelve

MARSEILLE
THE FRENCH REPUBLIC
THURSDAY 4 DECEMBER

B ashir stepped off the gangway of the merchant ship *Aquila* into a cold drizzle. Light from a hooded lamp on the adjacent warehouse reflected off the puddles scattered across the concrete expanse of the South Terminal. The quay was silent except for the oaths of a few crewmembers who pushed their way past him heading for the nearest bar.

He extracted a black Greek fisherman's hat from his pea coat and pulled it low over his head. There were bound to be security cameras. He scanned his surroundings. *There's one. And another on that light pole in the parking lot.*

The crewmen's voices faded into the night. He glanced at his destination, a seven-story administrative building fronting the main access road to the port. The safest route would be to work his way down the side of the warehouse stretching along the pier across from him. He slung his duffle over his shoulder and set off.

He kept to the shadows and crept between several parked

trucks to the end of the structure. A door slammed, but he didn't see anyone. He cast a final look at the rust-streaked hull of the Liberian registered *Aquila,* and slipped around the corner.

There was no sign of his contact's vehicle, a Renault Clio. No color or license- plate number had been provided in the cryptic message he received from his contact in Istanbul. Even if he'd had a disposable cellphone and a contact number, he wouldn't have dared use them. The danger of having his call intercepted and traced too great. He shrugged and crossed the empty marshaling yard, avoiding the prying eyes of the security cameras.

When he reached the front steps of the administration building, he dropped the duffle and sat. He fished in his shirt pocket for his last pack of Murads, the aromatic, small-leafed cigarettes he bought in Istanbul and settled down to wait for his contact. He was used to waiting. A few extra minutes, or hours, wouldn't matter.

He ran his hand over the scruff of the two-week beard he grew while onboard the *Aquila.* The ship made good time on its run to Marseille including the brief stop in Istanbul before they transited the Bosporus Strait into the Mediterranean. They only stayed in the Turkish city long enough for the stevedores to offload the containers in her aft cargo hold. Bashir personally supervised the loading of the pallets from Meycek Exports onto the truck destined for Karachi, Pakistan.

The brief stop was his second in Istanbul. He'd passed through the city fourteen years before on his own journey to Pakistan after escaping the horrors of Grozny. Unlike February of 2000, he now traveled openly, albeit under an assumed name as a registered agent for the Novorosiyk Business Group.

Bashir's thoughts turned to his relationship with the NBG. *Can they be trusted? There is no reason to believe they will betray me—*

they have too much to lose. But two questions lingered in his mind; their motive in assisting him and their ultimate goal.

He'd readily accepted the NBG's offer for the Moscow affair and his subsequent escape. He never shared his plan to smuggle the remaining radioactive pellets out of the country.

He blew out a column of smoke, watching it swirl out of existence in the mist. *In any event, they would do well not to trust me.* He chuckled, sharing his thoughts with the night.

Rain clattered off the metal roof above him, the only sound in the port. His mind drifted back to the midnight call he received at his safe house in Chelyabinsk: "Get out. Now. The FSB knows."

The caller hadn't identified herself and she hung up before he could ask any questions. He had no choice but to believe her. *But how did they know where he was? Worse, how did she get his cell number? Who was she?*

A single thread of water droplets falling along a chain suspended from the corner of the roof attracted his attention. Their brief life splattered to an end on the pavement. Each droplet represented a variable in his mind. There were too many unknowns, too many variables to contain.

He rubbed the base of his left third finger with his thumb, a habit he'd developed in Afghanistan. If he were to survive, he would have to abandon his support network and go off the grid. The monotonous sound of the dripping water transformed into that of a metronome—regular, predictable, comforting.

A car emerged from around the corner of the building. The flash of light from its headlamps startled him back to the present. The Renault Clio slowed, rolling to a stop.

"Monsieur, Chauvin?" a voice asked from within the vehicle.

"*Oui.*" Bashir stood, responding to his new name. "*Je suis* Chauvin."

The lid of the trunk popped open. Bashir walked to the

back of the car and threw in his duffle. He crushed the remnant of his cigarette on the pavement and climbed into the back seat.

"I am Hassan," the driver said. He jerked his thumb at his companion. "He is Ahmed."

Bashir nodded and slid across the seat. There was less legroom behind Ahmed, but it would be easier to kill him if it were a trap. Hassan looked no older than twenty-five, of average build, and North African descent. Ahmed appeared older, perhaps because of his beard, and stronger, with broad shoulders.

"We have been instructed to take you to our safe-house in the Rue Lonque des Capucins neighborhood," Hassan said to the windshield as he exited the port and headed north for the old quarter of the city. "Have you been there?"

"Once, many years ago," Bashir lied.

"We are members of the GIA," Hassan continued.

"I am familiar with the group." Bashir said, recognizing the French initials for the Algerian Armed Islamic Group.

"We are a small cell, but doing our part," Hassan added. "I, myself, have just returned from Syria where I sent many infidels to their deaths."

Bashir considered the implications of what the kid just said. *That means the French know about you. These two are going to be a problem.* He looked over his shoulder. The car he'd seen pull in behind them as they left the port was still there. "Do you see that dark Citroen sedan behind us? Behind the old Peugeot."

Ahmed jerked his head around searching for the vehicle through the rain-flecked rear window. "What?"

"I would suggest you lose him."

Hassan didn't appear to react, staying in the far right lane and maintaining the same speed. They passed a sign indicating the left hand exit ramp of an overpass.

Bashir observed the kid's face in the rearview mirror.

Hassan's eyes flicked from the rearview to the side mirror and back again. The kid slowed, allowing the Peugeot to close the distance. The Citroen slowed as well, maintaining its distance. When the Peugeot pulled up to pass, Hassan checked his mirrors again.

Bashir anticipated Hassan's next move and braced his left arm on the seat. The kid jammed his foot down on the accelerator, pulling ahead of the adjacent car. He spun the steering wheel to the left, sending them careening across the front of the Peugeot and toward the exit ramp. The trailing Citroen was blocked, not able match to Hassan's maneuver without ramming the other car.

Bashir caught a glimpse of their tail as they roared up the ramp. The Citroen spun one-hundred-eighty degrees to follow them.

The kid turned off the Renault's headlamps and kept accelerating, whipping around a small delivery truck. A hundred meters down the road, he slammed on the brakes and spun the wheel, the hard right turn sending them fishtailing on to the Rue André Allar.

Bashir looked over his shoulder. There was no sign of the Citroen.

Hassan made another turn in a couple blocks, flicked his lights back on, and wove his way through a warren of narrow branching streets. He drove for another fifteen minutes before pulling over in front of a dingy walkup covered with graffiti. A cobweb of electrical wires and television lines crisscrossed the building's façade, most of the apartment windows shuttered.

A GT Mobile store topped with a large red-lettered sign, ALLOD DO BLED occupied most of the ground floor. Hassan pointed to a recessed door to the right of the storefront. "We live here."

He got out of the car and popped the trunk. "Ahmed will take you up. The car's been made. I must ditch it."

Bashir collected his duffle and trudged up the rickety stairs following Ahmed to the third floor.

Ahmed unlocked the door of his apartment and pushed it open. He scanned the empty hallway before following Bashir into the living room. He closed the door, but didn't throw the deadbolt.

The apartment stunk. Takeout food boxes and dirty clothes littered a tattered couch and a dilapidated table. A bottle of cheap brandy sat in the middle of the table, an envelope beside it. Bashir noted the liquor. *So, these jihadists are not strict practitioners of the faith.*

Ahmed followed Bashir's eyes to the bottle. "It belongs to a friend."

"*Ah, oui,*" Bashir said. "One must be careful of the friends he chooses."

Ahmed picked up the envelope and handed it to Bashir. "I haven't opened it."

"Who gave it to you?"

"I don't know. The letter was in the mailbox, Monsieur Chauvin."

Bashir turned the envelope over in his hands looking for a postmark or any other indication of its source. He spoke softly, but the menace in his voice was clear. "If there is any hint that my identify has been compromised, you both will die."

He extracted the note and read the single typed line: "The DCRI and Americans are watching." The Central Directorate of Interior Intelligence he could understand. Those were likely DCRI agents in the Citroen. *But the Americans?*

He folded the note and stuffed it in his pants pocket. His fixed his eyes on Ahmed. "Do you have my kit?"

A flicker of fear crossed Ahmed's face. "Yes. All of the items that were requested."

"Get them."

Ahmed disappeared into a back room and returned carrying a cardboard box. He pushed the brandy bottle aside and set the box on the table. "Everything is here. I took the liberty of ensuring the remote had a good connection to the detonator. The signal is strong from well beyond four hundred meters. I also connected the detonator to the Semtex."

Bashir examined the PETN-based explosive. Several hundred grams of pentaerythritol tetronitrate was molded into thin 3x12 inch sheets. Two wires connected the sheets to a detonator that Ahmed had attached to a receiver with a plug-in for a nine-volt battery. The job was professional—as good as the ones Salim made. "Excellent."

He set the bomb aside and opened a small case containing a semi-automatic Beretta. Nested beside the pistol, a pair of fifteen round clips and a silencer. He removed the pistol and screwed the silencer onto the muzzle. He held the assembled weapon in his hand, judging its weight and balance, nodding approval as he tested the trigger pull.

"The clips are full," Ahmed volunteered. "Their weight offsets that of the silencer and keeps the weapon in balance."

Bashir picked up a clip, inserted it into the pistol grip, and retested the weapon's balance. "Yes, this will do very nicely."

He chambered a round and spun to his right, leveling the Berretta at Ahmed's head. He squeezed the trigger, the only sound a muted *phutt*. A hole opened in his target's forehead. He noted his aim was just a bit off-center.

The noise of an opening door caused him to spin. *Hassan.* He shifted his stance preparing to fire.

The kid entered the room and closed the door. "I bought some—" He choked on the remainder of his words, staring in disbelief at his friend crumpled on the floor. He looked at Bashir. Their eyes locked.

Hassan dropped his bag of groceries and tried to run. Bashir cut him down with a three shot grouping to his back, the impact sending the boy sprawling across the table. The brandy bottle clattered onto the floor, rolling to a stop against the couch.

Bashir froze, listening for any reaction from the adjacent apartment. Nothing. He stepped over Hassan's body and picked up the gun case. He pressed his thumb on the Berretta's safety to secure the weapon, removed the silencer, and placed both in their respective recesses in the case's black-foam cutouts. There were now two fewer variables.

He lit his last Turkish cigarette and tossed the empty pack into a trashcan before deciding to check out the bedroom. In the morning, he would shave off his beard and dye his hair. After breakfast, he would decide how best to get out of Marseille.

Chapter Thirteen

MARSEILLE
THE FRENCH REPUBLIC
FRIDAY 5 DECEMBER

Bashir woke to a beam of sunlight that had found its way through the shuttered bedroom window. He rolled away from the light, swung his legs over the side of the bed, and made his way past the corpses to the kitchen to brew a cup of coffee. Cup in hand, he returned to the bedroom to begin his preparations.

He turned on the radio that sat on the lid of the commode and spun the dial to the local classic radio station. Humming to Chopin's piano concerto number 1 in E minor, he lathered his face and shaved off his beard. Next, he trimmed and dyed his hair to match the pictures on his new IDs. When he finished, he folded and hung up his face towel, cleaned the black smears from his hair tint from the washstand, and slipped on the pair of faux black-rimmed Saint Laurent spectacles he'd bought in Istanbul. He studied the new face of Monsieur Chauvin that reflected back from the mirror. *C'est bon. J'ai un homme d'affaires maintenant.*

Bashir returned to the bedroom and laid his clothes out on the bed before crossing to the closet in search of a suitcase. Just inside, he discovered an exclusive Bottega Veneta wheeled trolley—a brand favored by international travelers and business executives. It had to be a knock-off made with imitation leather. He could think of no other suitable explanation why Hassan or Ahmed would have such an expensive item. A real one cost over five-thousand Euros.

He pulled the trolley out and examined it for defects. He found the suitcase quite suitable and set about transferring the remaining items from his own battered duffle, packing them around the components of the bomb, and the two remaining beet cans. He wondered if the pallets from Meycek Exports containing the other beet cans had made it safely from Istanbul to the warehouse in Karachi.

The sound of vendors setting up on the narrow street fronting the apartment caught his attention as did the aroma of freshly made baguettes filling the bedroom. The neighborhood coming to life. He crossed the room and closed the casement window. The stench from the apartment would soon be overwhelming.

He decided not to pack the Berretta and zipped the lid of the suitcase. Bartók's Second Suite played in the background. The suite was one of his favorites, so he left the radio on and walked to the living room. He sidestepped Ahmed's corpse, pausing at the front door to listen as the final measures of the suite played out.

Bashir was well past the city of Aix-en-Provence by mid-morning, driving north on the A7 under an azure sky. Traffic on the toll road, notorious for being heavy, moved swiftly. He would soon be in Avignon to drop off the rental and board the Eurail TGV express to Paris.

The scenic vistas of rural France, dulled by winter's cold, passed by his window. The last time he'd been in the south of France was during the summer and these same fields were colored with lavender blooms stretching as far as the eye could see. But the memory he treasured most was Katya's shrieks of delight as she pointed to the acres of yellow sunflowers. They had just stopped at a roadside park near the small village of Aurel for a picnic. Nadia held her hand as they—

An indignant honk from a passing truck shattered the memories. He fought the flash of rage sweeping through him. *It would not do to tempt fate and attract the attention of the Police de la Route.*

PARIS

Bashir exited the first class coach and descended the three steps to platform D of the Gare de Lyon train station. He moved to the center of the aisle allowing the other passengers to pass while he waited for the porter to bring his bag. His position by a support column allowed him to scan the length of the platform without attracting attention. Just one security officer. The patrolman, wearing the uniform of the Préfecture de Police de Paris, stood by the escalator leading to the Galerie Diderot and the taxi stands.

"Would you care for assistance to the taxi, Monsieur?"

Bashir peeled off a five Euro note from his money clip and handed it to the porter. "*Non, merci.* I can manage."

He extended the handle on his suitcase and blended into a knot of passengers making their way toward the exit. They halved the distance. No sign of trouble. He slowed his pace and drifted to the right of the crowd. *Uh oh. What is this?*

The policeman had shifted his stance in response to something he'd seen in the approaching crowd. Bashir's shoulders tensed as the man raised his right hand ever so slightly to his holster and cocked his head to speak into the radio clipped to his vest.

Could they know? He could not escape. He had no choice but to continue.

The distance narrowed—another twenty feet. Bashir kept his face expressionless, avoiding eye contact. Yelling erupted from the far end of the platform. The policeman took several steps forward, attention focused on the disturbance. Bashir lowered his head and hurried to the escalator.

————

The queue for the taxis wasn't long, but Bashir remained on edge. He swept his eyes across the sidewalk behind him.

"*Pardon, Monsieur? Voulez vous le taxi?*"

"*Ah, oui. Merci.*" Bashir turned to face the driver. "*L'Aligré s'il vous plaît.*"

He noted the question begin to form on the cabbie's face. The guy had no idea where to find the hotel. But then, very few people did.

Bashir wasn't about to take any chances. The last thing he needed was to end up wandering all over the Left Bank while the cabbie searched. "It is directly across from Saint Julien Le Pauvre. Take the Quai Saint Bernard past the Université Pierre et Marie Curie."

The cabbie raised an eyebrow but kept whatever thoughts he had to himself and set off on the fifteen-minute drive.

Bashir allowed himself to relax as they drove along the Seine, grateful the driver wasn't one who felt compelled to comment on the weather, which, in fact, was quite nice. *I still need to buy an overcoat—and a suitable leather satchel.*

He paid the cabbie and paused to admire the ancient façade of Saint Julien le Pauvre and the Gothic spires of

Notre Dame soaring above the Seine before crossing the cobbled street to the L'Aligré.

The receptionist looked up from his desk tucked away in a corner of the tiny lobby. *"Bonjour, Monsieur. Vous désirez?* I am the manager here."

"I have a reservation. Chauven."

Bashir surveyed the old limestone walls, ancient oaken beams, and the mismatched furniture while the man flipped through his registration book. A thick rope serving as the banister looped its way toward the upper floors. Everything as he remembered.

"Ah, yes, Monsieur. You plan to stay with us for a week?"

"Yes, but my plans may change."

A frown appeared on the manager's face, but he collected himself. "We have a very nice room for you facing Notre Dame. We've recently renovated and trust you will enjoy the intimacy and eclectic décor of your room."

Bashir pulled out his credit card. "I'm sure I will."

He knew the NBG would track him to L'Aligré if he used the Crédit Lyonnais bank card, but no matter. He planned to enjoy his time in Paris, even if this ancient hotel wasn't the Ritz.

"Your passport please."

"Would my national ID or driver's license do? I am visiting from Marseille."

"Pardon, Monsieur. Either will suffice," the manager replied studying the picture on the fake ID, comparing it to Bashir's face.

Bashir helped himself to copies of *Le Monde* and *L'Express* from the small stack of newspapers on the counter and tucked them under his arm while he waited. If nothing else, the manager was methodical.

The manager held out Bashir's ID and credit card. "Will you require one key or two?"

"Just one." Years before, he had requested two.

He accepted his key and ascended the narrow stairs leading to the first floor. Navigating a ninety-degree turn halfway up, he proceeded down a crooked hallway, and unlocked the door to his equally narrow room.

He tossed the newspapers on the bed and reached to open his suitcase when the headline on *Le Monde* caught his eye: *Un President d'États-Unis Visite.* Unpacking could wait. *The President of the United States is coming to Paris? When?*

He found the answer in the first paragraph—this coming Wednesday. Randall Stuart and his Secretary of State, Richard Valardi, were meeting with their counterparts, Jean-Phillip Lemaire and Claude Jannet, for a two-day summit addressing joint economic and security issues. He dropped into the chair by the window and finished reading the article. When he finished, his eyes traveled over the rooftops of Paris. *Should I change my plans?*

He reread the articles pondering his options. The columns held few specifics of the presidents' itinerary but he didn't find that surprising. Besides, only a fool would consider striking them. *But the wives?* That was an entirely different matter.

So, how would les Madames be spending their days? Was it possible? He leafed through the pages of *L'Express* and found what he was looking for.

Five days.

Chapter Fourteen

HOTEL L'ALIGRÉ
PARIS, FRANCE
MONDAY 8 DECEMBER

B ashir finished reading *Le Parisien* and set the newspaper aside. He pursed his lips and blew out a thin plume of blue-white smoke. He studied the tip of his cigarette before crushing it in an ashtray overflowing with cigarette butts. The room reeked of stale smoke. He reeked of stale smoke. After two days of research, the details of Madame Stuart's schedule were beginning to emerge. He lit another cigarette and continued his research.

Stuart's itinerary for Thursday appeared solid, including visits to an orphanage and a progressive school. No opportunity there. He would not risk harming the children. *But Friday?*

Friday's schedule was less firm, but from the information he gleaned from the papers, Madame Lemaire preferred to steer the Americans toward one of Paris's flea markets and, if time allowed, an art museum.

Would they actually lock down the Louvre or the Musée

d'Orsay? Of course they would. Nothing was impossible for the wives of the Presidents of France and the United States.

He snuffed out the remnant of his cigarette and reviewed his notes. Then again, perhaps something more intimate was being arranged?

Perhaps. Dianne Stuart minored in art history at Marietta College, a small liberal arts college in the state of Ohio, and she professed a fondness for the romanticists. *So, if I were scheduling an excursion, where would I go?*

He recalled his trips with Nadia to Clignancout, the *grande dame* of all Parisian flea markets. The market sprawled into alleyways and covered halls, always jammed with people.

Antiquing would be impossible. The Secret Service would insist on a venue where they could do their advance work and secure the site. *Where would that be?*

He clasped his hands behind his neck, pushing his chin to his chest to relieve the tension in his shoulders. His eyes fell on the copy of the women's magazine, *Madame Figaro,* he'd bought the day before. A picture of Madame Stuart and her daughter graced the cover.

Deep in thought, he tapped his pen on their picture. He studied the two women. The daughter had her mother's blue eyes. His fists tightened, the color leaching from his knuckles. With a crack, the pen snapped. The pieces fell from his hand.

Enough.

———

A towering Christmas tree in the main hall of Le Galeries Lafayette drew Bashir's eyes to the art nouveau stained glass dome soaring seven stories above. Multiple arched galleries faced by intricate wrought iron balconies were backlit by blue lights matching those on the tree. Seated to his right, a three-member ensemble added their music to the festive spirit of the store.

This was real, not the pretentious opulence of the GUM. But where to start? Chanel, Dior, Cartier? Maybe the Swarovski crystal? They were all listed on the store's directory. Nadia would—

He caught himself. *But she's not here. She's gone, isn't she?*

An elbow pushed into his side. He blinked. Something had changed. *No music.* The musicians were putting their instruments away. People shifted around him. A woman threw him a poorly veiled look of annoyance.

How long have I been standing here? He checked his watch. 2:37. Ten minutes, maybe less. *Another hour here, then I must leave.*

He made his way to the lift, taking it to the men's accessory department on the second floor where he selected a tasteful Le Tanneur brown-leather briefcase. The fashion cognoscenti of Paris would approve of his purchase, but not its use. He wasn't so sure what they'd have to say about his next item. The black Burberry trench coat would do very nicely for his stay in London where he planned to detonate his third device.

———

Bashir stood at the corner of Rue le Jacob and Rue de Furstenberg considering whether he had deduced correctly. The Place de Furstenberg, with its small shops and the Musée Delacroix, epitomized the charm and ambience of the Left Bank quarter of Saint Germain des-Prés. *And if I haven't...? So be it. There will be other opportunities.*

He proceeded down the narrow sidewalk toward the roundabout of the iconic square and the antique shop he wanted to investigate. He decided against a visit to the museum housed in Delacroix's old apartment. The security measures designed to protect the paintings would also prevent him from placing his bomb in one of the galleries. The antique shop situated just a few meters away on the corner was a different matter.

Before he reached his destination, the blue and gold sign of La Maison Du Chou beckoned him from across the street. He crossed the square and stopped in front of the window display. Before him were dozens of elegant creations: golden brown croissants, small cakes topped with strawberries, rows of pastel-colored macaroons.

He resisted the temptations and proceeded across the square. The welcoming tinkle of a brass bell suspended from the front door sounded when Bashir entered the artfully cluttered L'Antiquités. A woman's head topped by silver-gray hair appeared through the door of an adjacent room. She grasped a pair of half-glasses dangling on a thin chain hanging around her neck and set them on the bridge of her nose to assess her potential customer.

"Bonjour, Monsieur. May I be of assistance?" she said, satisfied that the gentleman's dress and manner justified her attention.

"Bonjour, Madame. I was drawn by your collection of wooden artist mannequins," Bashir replied while he scanned the tables and shelves for a suitable place to hide his bomb. "Such wonderful things."

"*Merci*, Monsieur." The woman handed him her business card.

Bashir accepted the card, memorizing her name before placing it in his wallet. His eyes fell on an old wheeled cart on the floor directly in front of him. "But this…"

"Yes, an excellent piece," she affirmed. "You have the eye of a seasoned *chineuse*, Monsieur."

Bashir searched his mind for the translation. "One who antiques." He nodded a polite reply to her compliment.

"It is a child's toy from the late eighteenth century," she continued. "We are pleased to have a such a unique object in our collection. The child would stand in the middle and push himself about. There, under the stuffed rabbit. Let me move these wooden balls from the tray."

Bashir shifted his satchel and leaned over to examine the interior. "May I?"

"But, of course," she replied, reaching for the toy rabbit and the wads of stuffing paper obstructing his view of the interior. "You see, there is a small seat for the child."

"It will be perfect."

The owner's eyes lit with anticipation. "Perhaps you would like to take it home with you today, Monsieur...?"

Bashir filled in the blank. "Monsieur Chauven. However, I regret that today will not be possible. I must make arrangements."

He noted the change in her face. He reached for his wallet. "*L'argent n'est pas un obstacle, Madame.*"

She appeared reassured by the sight of Bashir's alligator-skin wallet. "It is to be a surprise then?"

"Yes, I intend it to be," Bashir answered with an engaging smile. "Would a small retainer be acceptable to secure the piece?"

"That would be most acceptable, Monsieur Chauven. May I run your *carte de crédit?*"

He hesitated. The credit card would be traced. The risks of disclosing his visit to the shop, too great. "I'd prefer to use cash."

"Certainly. And would you like me to prepare the object for shipment?"

He hadn't thought of that. "Please do not trouble yourself. I will return later this week."

"I hate to impose, Monsieur, but could you come Wednesday or Thursday? Friday may be most difficult. I—"

"No explanation is required, Madame Dupreyon."

She responded with a smile. "But I feel I must. It is too

exciting. You see, I received a visit this morning from the authorities. They advised me to expect a special visitor this Friday. I may have to close the store."

"*Aux contraire*, Madame. The timing works out very well."

Chapter Fifteen

Nick found inspector Alain Gallet seated behind a plain gray-metal desk. The inspector motioned Nick toward an empty chair. "Please, Monsieur Parkos. Coffee?"

More coffee was the last thing Nick needed. "No, thanks. I'm good." He set his attaché on the floor and surveyed his host's office.

A boxy computer monitor dominated the right side of Gallet's desk. An unruly pile of papers stacked on the opposite corner threatened to overflow onto the floor. "Actually, maybe I will take that coffee."

"Black?"

"Yes, thanks."

Gallet poured a cup from a half-empty pot and handed it to Nick. "You have visited France before?"

"No, first time. The closest I've come was the one year of French I took in high school."

"Of course."

Nick detected the faint undertone of disapproval in Gallet's response. He'd been warned before leaving D.C. that he should expect a certain aloofness from his counterpart in the DCRI. He needed a mild reproof of his own to level the playing field. "*V gostyakh khorosho, a doma luchshe.*"

"*Pardon?*"

"Russian. I've found it useful." He didn't volunteer the translation of the proverb. 'Visiting is good, but home is better.'

The Frenchman pursed his lips. "No doubt."

Gallet set his coffee cup down, spinning it so the DCRI logo faced Nick. "I have investigated the al-Shabaab communications. They were directed to a small terrorist cell in Marseille. Our data collection programs tracked the key term, YLVA, every time they were logged on to the Internet."

"Do they present a threat?"

"They're amateurs, but we've kept the one who just returned from Syria under surveillance."

"Were you able to determine the significance of the letters: YLVA?" Nick asked.

"Not with certainty. It may be Scandinavian."

"It's a word?"

"Translates to: 'she wolf.'"

She wolf. To Gallet he said. "They're talking about al-Khultyer. He's the reason I came."

"*Qu'est-ce que?*"

"The al-Shaabab messages. They have something to do with Bashir al-Khultyer, the perpetrator of the GUM incident. He's here."

"In Paris?"

"I'd bet on it."

"*Santané*! Damn," Gallet repeated in English. "What do you know of this man?"

Nick spent the next ten minutes reviewing what he knew,

including al-Khultyer's enrollment at the Université Pierre et Marie Curie. He stated with certainty that al-Khultyer had escaped from Russia after the bombing, been secreted on board the *Aquila*, and had made his way to Marseille.

Gallet reached for his phone. "So you have reason to believe this terrorist will attempt to defile Paris with his dirty bombs?"

"I—"

Gallet raised his index finger. "*Allô?*... Françoise? Gallet. Bring me the full report from Marseille and pull anything we have on Bashir al-Khultyer... You can spell it, *oui*? ... *Répétez...* *Bon...* He was in the PhD program for Process Engineering at UPMC from '98 to early '99. Send a team immediately ... *Oui*, Françoise, *nous avons un grand problème. Présidente Lemaire. Sa vie est en danger.*"

He terminated the call and addressed Nick, "You were saying?"

"We—"

A rap on the door silenced him again. He gave a bemused shake of his head and took a sip of coffee.

"I had it on my desk. I was almost done ..." the man said, holding out a thick manila envelope.

This must be Françoise.

Gallet directed a reproachful stare at his assistant and snatched the envelope. He glanced at the header on the report's red cover. "*Merci*, that will be all."

"Take your time," Nick said to the top of Gallet's head. There wasn't anything else to do but wait for Gallet to finish reading. His mind drifted back to the significance of the code word YLVA. It made sense. The gray wolf was the embodiment of Chechen nationalism. What else is there? *The note from the cottage... Grozn... the Aldi Massacre?... al-Khultyer's family? Were they ...?*

Gallet ran his fingers through his hair and emitted a grunt. He closed the report and placed his hands over the cover as if to hide the contents. "We have a new development."

Nick gulped the remnant of his coffee and grimaced.

"Yesterday units of the SDAT, the Sous-direction de L'anti-terrorisme, conducted a raid on an apartment in the Rue Lonque de Capucins neighborhood of Marseilles. The cell members I mentioned rented it. They are dead. Murdered."

"When?"

"Two, maybe three days ago. A neighbor called because of the smell."

Nick nodded an acknowledgement, but his mind focused on something else—on Alek. Her most recent message confirmed what he already knew, that al-Khultyer was on the *Aquila*. But she also claimed he was heading for Amsterdam. *Why would she plant a false lead?* He barely heard Gallet's voice.

"... the team is conducting their forensic investigation, but there is one item they found in the apartment that is of immediate interest—an empty package of Murad cigarettes."

Nick refocused. "I'm not familiar with them."

"A popular Turkish brand. They found several butts scattered on the ground where our..." He stopped in mid-sentence, grabbed his phone, and punched in a number. "*Françoise, Gallet ,encore*...Do you know if they ran those fingerprints through Interpol?... Find out now. I want the results within the hour." Gallet dropped the phone back in its cradle.

"The ship stopped in Istanbul, yes?" Nick asked. "We must assume al-Khultyer is traveling under an assumed identity and has made his way to Paris."

"Are there other creditable scenarios to consider?"

"No," Nick replied. "We have to review the intercepts."

Gallet tapped the report. "There is something else here." He flipped through the first several pages and found what he was looking for. "Our Marseille unit observed someone slip a letter into the victim's mailbox. If they can identify that person, he may lead us to a collaborating cell."

Nick picked up on the possible implications of Gallet's new information. Al-Khultyer's sudden disappearance wasn't a coincidence. "This isn't the first time al-Khultyer's been warned."

"Oh?"

"He fled just hours before our raid on his safe house in Chelyabinsk. We were able to trace him to the Crimean port of Novorosiyk where he boarded the *Aquila*."

"Who's behind him?"

Nick stroked his chin. He had to trust his instincts. "A business called Meycek Exports. It's a front for the Novorosiyk Business Group, a known Transnational Crime Organization. In any event, we possess several intercepts sent to the NBG from an unknown using the handle Charal."

Gallet rocked back in his chair. "Is there anything meaningful in this handle, Charal?"

"Only if you're acquainted with American *Star Wars* movies."

"I am not."

"Charal's a character in the TV movie, *The Battle for Endor*." Nick explained. "She is a force-wielding Night Sister who turns her back on her sisterhood and … Good, Lord … Alek?"

Nick stared at the wall over Gallet's shoulder, unaware he'd been speaking aloud. "Could it be possible? Chelyabinsk? Amsterdam? She…"

Gallet was taken aback. "*Revenons à nos moutons*, Parkos."

Nick didn't respond.

"*Alors*, Parkos," Gallet shouted. "What is it? Who is this Charal?" His agitated questions worked their effect.

Nick looked up. "She's my contact at the FSB."

"What? Charal is your contact at the FSB?"

"No… No, Alek is."

Gallet's fingers rapped out an agitated staccato on his desk. "Who is this Alek? Parkos, you are not making sense. What does she have to do with a Star Wars character?"

Nick slowly exhaled. "Her name is Aleksandra Kuzminova Grekov. I met her in Moscow. When I returned to DC, I did some background. Grekov is the family name of an old aristocratic family prominent in Czarist Russia. Her middle name means daughter of Kuzmin. Count Kuzmin Grekov was a general in the White Russian army fighting the Bolsheviks during the 1918 Russian revolution. He was killed defending the Crimean enclave in the last days of the war, but some of his family managed to escape on an American destroyer, the *USS Overton*. She is his great-grand daughter."

"And how is this significant?"

"The old resentments still linger."

"Then, why would the FSB even consider bringing her in?"

"Unknown."

"And how does all of this pertain to al-Khultyer?"

"It's complicated."

"*Jamais de la vie! C'est impossible.* You can't mean to say the Russians are behind this?"

Nick made a mental note. Gallet reverted to French when he was agitated. "Not the Russian government. It's someone else."

Nick read the look of exasperation on Gallet's face and clarified his response. "The NBG's leadership is composed entirely of men from the old aristocracy. They are the ones backing al-Khultyer."

"To what purpose?"

"I believe their intent is to destabilize Srevnenko's government and re-establish the old order."

"What does this have to do with France?"

Nick didn't answer. *Good question. What* was *the relevance?* But

Gallet's question provided a clue. "He's cut his ties. We're dealing with a rogue whose motives are known only to him."

Gallet picked up his phone and dialed. "Françoise, drop what you're doing and get over here." He replaced the phone. "He will have changed his appearance. Do you have photographs?"

Nick opened his attaché and extracted several pictures. "Alek sent these. The top one is an age-enhanced photo of al-Khultyer taken when he was a student at the Moscow Institute of Physics."

"May I keep this? We need to make copies for the Gendarmerie Nationale and Service de Protection des Hautes Personalities."

"Certainly."

Gallet picked up the second photograph. "And this?"

"From a surveillance camera outside the Metro Station in Red Square. The time stamp indicates it was taken just minutes after the attack on the GUM."

Gallet scrutinized every detail of the photograph before sliding it across the desk. "He appears to be carrying a bouquet of sunflowers. Doesn't that strike you as a bit odd?"

Chapter Sixteen

HÔTEL D'ALIGRÉ
PARIS, FRANCE
THURSDAY 11 DECEMBER

B ashir pulled on a pair of rubber kitchen gloves to avoid staining his hands. He opened the top of one of his two-liter cans and poured the contents into the sink, then swirled his hand through the mix of ceramic pellets and sliced beets. The latter he dropped into the commode. He rinsed off the pellets that remained in the basin, scooped them into a plastic freezer bag, and zipped it closed. He repeated the process with the second can.

After cleaning the stains on the washstand, he peeled off his gloves and dropped them into a brown paper grocery sack with the other items he needed to dispose. The empty beet can and other items were simply garbage, but under them were his cut-up Crédit Lyonnaise bankcard, shredded IDs, and passport. There was no further need for Monsieur Chauven.

He'd considered the risks of dumping the sack in a

random trash container. His greatest danger at this point was being recognized. And in this, there was very little he could do. His plans would not be disrupted if a member of the Préfecture de Police happened to stumble across the discarded bag.

And what if some vagrant were to find these items and try to piece together and use the data off his credit card? A mental picture of the unfortunate being grilled by the Sécurité Intérieure formed in his mind. His hoarse laugh echoed off the walls of the tiny room.

Still smiling, he gathered the various components of the bomb from their respective hiding places and laid them out on the bed for final assembly.

Fifteen minutes later, he was done. He slid the assembly and the bag of ceramic pellets into his briefcase. He took great care not to dislodge the tiny red and black wires that led from the detonator to the Semtex sheets.

All that remained was to dress. He planned to dine at an upscale brasserie only a short walk from L'Antiquités, so he chose his attire accordingly.

He completed his preparations with a splash of *L'homme infini*, pondering a line he had read on the cologne bottle's insert. "Man has the infinite horizon of life before him."

He inhaled deeply, intrigued by the cologne's top notes of coriander and black pepper and, beneath those, the masculine undertones of cedar and oak with a subtle base note of amber.

Perhaps there is some truth in those words…

The strains of Brahms's Piano Concerto number 2 in B-flat major called from across the room. He capped the bottle of cologne and focused on the majestic notes of the Allegretto Grazioso. The master had just introduced a new element by the soloist restating the concerto's main theme in triple rhythm now being echoed by the orchestra.

Bashir's lifted and dipped his hand, following the piece before he sliced through the air with a dramatic downbeat at the concerto's conclusion. *C'est magnifique.*

The downbeat was appropriate. His time in the diminutive hotel was drawing to a close. He needed to go if he were to reach L'Antiquités before Madame Dupreyon closed her shop.

He reached for the gray-and-light-blue patterned silk scarf draped over the back of the armchair and wrapped it loosely around his neck. His hand lingered just above the silver eagle embossed on his Armani belt buckle. He admired the result in the mirror. *Parfait. Et l'charpe?* The scarf provided the perfect balance to his dark blue shirt and black wool and mohair blend sports coat. The ensemble was a statement of restrained elegance.

————

Madame Dupreyon turned at the sound of her store's bell, a bright smile forming on her face at the sight of her customer. "*Bienvenue*, Monsieur Chauven. You have come for your piece?"

"I can't today but would Monday be convenient?" Bashir said, inwardly relieved the cart was still on display. "There are some details I still need to attend."

"But of course. That would do very well. As you see, I haven't had the opportunity to move your piece to the back room."

"Preparing for your visitor?"

"*Ah, oui.* I received confirmation this morning from the Service de Protection des Hautes Personalities. It's all so very exciting. I have selected a small piece to present Madame Stuart as a reminder of her trip to Paris."

Bashir's smile was genuine. "Then I must let you resume your preparations."

"*Merci*, there is so much to do with so little time. My guests will arrive at ten o'clock."

The chime of the phone ringing from the adjacent room provided him the opening he required. "Please, you must take your call."

"Yes, excuse me."

Bashir opened his briefcase and set to work as soon as she disappeared into the adjacent room. He was well on his way to the café by the time Madame Dupreyon completed her call.

———

There were a few hardy souls scattered among the tables under the awning of Les Deux Magots, but Bashir opted to take a seat inside. Nadia would have insisted on sitting outside. She never wanted to miss the activity of the busy corner while she indulged in a steaming pot of hot chocolate.

He smiled at the memory and opened the door, permitting a young couple to leave before approaching the maître d. "*Bonjour, Monsieur. Je voudrais une table, s'il vous plaît.*"

The maître d made a rapid assessment of the man standing before him. He nodded a polite reply. "*Certainment, monsieur*. This way please."

Bashir followed the maître d to a preferred seat deep within the restaurant. The small square table was tucked into a corner beneath the two iconic Chinese figurines from which the café derived its name. The table's location provided him an excellent view of the entire dining area.

The maître d handed Bashir the menu. "Would you prefer an *apértif* to start Monsieur?"

Non, merci. I will be having wine."

"May I suggest our excellent Poully Fumé. It pairs very well with the comté and charcuteirie."

"*Merci*, that will do very well."

Within minutes his wine arrived. The waiter opened it

with a flourish before presenting the cork and a small pour. Bashir swirled the glass under his nose picking up the subtle notes of fruit and minerals. He held it up to the light to judge its color. "Magnificent."

He was about to take a sip when the stunning almond eyes of the woman sitting at the opposite table completely distracted him. Long, dark-brown hair flowing over her shoulders in luxurious waves, framed her face. And she was looking at him with obvious interest.

His glass remained suspended just above his lips before he recovered and lifted it in acknowledgement.

Her knowing smile left him further nonplused. He took an undignified gulp of the Fumé and set the glass down. He tried to appear nonchalant, but the woman distracted him even further when she motioned for her waiter and spoke a few words into his ear.

The waiter straightened and approached Bashir. "Madame noted that you appear to be alone. She would like to know if she could join you?"

Bashir was dumbfounded. He tried to read her face. She appeared bemused. A half-smile formed on her lips. His words escaped before he could stop them. "Please tell Madame, I would be honored."

"Forgive my impertinence,' the woman said as she approached, "but a handsome man such as yourself should not be dining alone." She offered her hand. "*Je m'appelle* Angelique."

Bashir stood, "*Enchanté. Je suis* Marc. Marc Arnaud." To the waiter he said, "Would you please bring another setting?"

Angelique raised her glass, her eyes sparkling with mischief. "*Enchanté*, Monsieur Marc Arnaud. "Do you come here often?"

Bashir returned her question with a grin. "Perhaps not enough. And you?"

"Les Deux is one of my favorite brasseries," Angelique said. "And now I have another reason to come."

Bashir continued their flirtatious dance. The words flowed easily between them, and with their second bottle of wine, she mentioned her love of skiing and a long weekend she planned at a ski resort in Bardonecchia, Italy.

Bashir picked up on the open-ended invitation. He leaned forward. "I have never been there, perhaps you—"

"Monsieur al-Khultyer?"

Bashir almost choked on the slice of soppressatta he was chewing. He stared in disbelief at the long white apron of the waiter standing beside his table. His eyes traveled from the man's apron, over the black waistcoat and bowtie, and stopped at the man's face. He struggled for recognition. "Excuse me, but you must be mistaken. My name is Arnaud."

The waiter looked skeptical but answered politely. "Pardon, Monsieur. I have mistaken you for someone who use to frequent Les Deux many years ago."

Bashir's sense of panic subsided, but he kept his eyes on the man until he disappeared into the kitchen. He shook his head, adding a bemused smile for effect. "Now, where were we?"

"I believe we were about to discuss my holiday," she said.

"Ah, yes. Will you be staying at a chateau?"

"I'll be leaving tomorrow afternoon," she said. "Perhaps you are free to see for yourself?"

Bashir couldn't believe the opportunity Angelique's unexpected invitation provided. *How better to hide, than with a beautiful woman at an Italian ski resort?*

He had discarded his plan to take the Eurostar to London after checking out of the L'Aligré deciding the risk of discovery was excessive. The problem was, he hadn't decided on an acceptable alternative. He reviewed his options. Unless things had changed, the security checks at the border for the major road leading from Chambery to Turin were essentially non-existent for French citizens. *And, if I crossed the border into Italy—then what? Didn't Ushiska mention he had friends in Bosnia? I can make my way to the port of Ravenna, and from there …*

Bashir reached for the bottle of wine to top off her glass. "I haven't been on the slopes for years. I'd break a leg."

Angelique looked into his eyes from over the rim of her glass. "Who said anything about skiing?"

Chapter Seventeen

HEADQUARTERS
DIRECTION GÉNÉRALE DE LA SÉCURITÉ
INTÉRIEURE
FRIDAY 12 DECEMBER

G allet looked up from the report he was reading. He waved Nick toward the coffee pot. "I've been reviewing the UPMC file."

Nick emptied the remnants of the coffee pot into the white ceramic mug bearing the DCRI logo and took a seat. "Find anything?"

"Possibly. And you?"

"Nothing new," Nick replied, eyeing the report from the University.

"Nothing from your Secret Service?"

Nick reached into his briefcase for his notes and a pen. "I sat down with them at the embassy this morning. They have a number of individuals under surveillance, but none that match al-Khultyer's description."

"How about your FSB contact?"

"Not a word." The brevity of his response reflected Nick's

frustration with Alek and his own lack of success in locating al-Khultyer. "And you?"

"Al-Khultyer lived with his wife and child in a—"

Nick's hand tightened around his pen. "He had a kid?"

"*Oui.* I believe a little girl." Gallet leafed through several pages of the UPMC report and found the reference. "Yes, a girl. Katya. Age four. They lived in a one bedroom apartment on Rue Visconte in Saint Germain des-Prés."

Nick scribbled a quick note to himself. This had to be more of Alek's duplicity. "Alek made no mention of a little girl. Or a wife."

"Knowledge the FSB most certainly has," Gallet said. "Why didn't she tell you?"

"I don't…" A picture of his daughter, Emma, flashed through Nick's mind. "My God… this could explain everything."

"Explain what, Parkos?"

Nick's mind raced. His daughter, his ex, Marty … He forced himself to refocus on the problem at hand. There were too many pieces of the puzzle that didn't make sense, but at least now he had the answer to what drove al-Khultyer. Alek and her probable connections with the NBG and al-Khultyer could wait. "I'm betting his wife and child were victims of the Nouye Aldi massacre."

Gallet threw his hands up in protest. "*Tant pis*, but the French had nothing to do with that. Why is he here?"

"Revenge. He wants to punish those he feels are complicit in his family's death—the ones that should have done more to stop the atrocities."

"What? Lemaire? Stuart?" Gallet waved his right hand in the air emphasizing each name. "He's going after them?"

Nick stared over Gallet's shoulder at the picture of a smiling Lemaire posed in front of the French tricolor. He was about to take a huge risk. And, if he were wrong … "No, he'll be going after a softer target—the wives."

"*Merde!*" Gallet snatched the sheet of paper with the presidential party's daily schedule off the corner of his desk and reread it. He looked at his watch. "It is 0953. They should be on their way from Élysée Palace to Place de Furstenberg. The tour is scheduled for 1000. They must be warned."

Gallet grabbed his personal cell, found the number he wanted, and punched the direct dial button for the Presidential Security Chief's office. "*Allo?*... "*Oui, c'est* Gallet, DCRI. I must speak with Monsieur Souchon immediately... *Non*, I cannot wait... It's a matter of extreme urgency."

Gallet rapped his fingers on his desk while he waited, then lifted the receiver for his desk phone. "Françoise, fax the picture of al-Khultyer to Luc Rollin, then bring the car around. We've got to get to Place de Furstenberg."

LE BAR DU MARCHÉ
SAINT GERMAIN DES-PRÉS

Bashir stopped at Le Bar du Marché and checked the time. 0955. He selected one of the wicker bistro tables lined up in two tight rows under the red and white striped canopy and took a seat. A waiter in blue denim coveralls appeared and presented a menu.

The restaurant prided itself on its bohemian atmosphere that attracted a loyal nighttime crowd of twenty-somethings who lived in the neighborhood. Le Bar du Marché also listed an impressive selection of wines. On the flip side, Bashir also knew from experience that, unless things had changed, the food was decidedly plebian and overpriced. He perused the menu and ended up ordering something safe, a *croque monsieur* and a glass of Chablis. He set the menu down and unfolded his napkin.

The tabletop was too small for the bouquet of yellow sunflowers he'd purchased on the short walk from Place de

Furstenberg. He tucked the bouquet well under his chair so the waiter wouldn't step on them, then reached up to adjust the brim of his blue wool ivy cap that had slid down over his forehead.

The cap complemented his mid-length black-leather coat, dark-gray slacks, and the light-gray and blue diamond-patterned turtleneck. He fit in very well with the locals seated around him, but not so much with the few tourists who looked completely out of place. He took an enormous risk being here, but he was now certain that Madame Dupreyon's guest was coming. If Stuart's schedule had changed and she'd gone else-where, he would have returned to the antique shop and retrieved his device.

Thirty minutes earlier, the taxi had dropped him off on Rue de'Abbaye two blocks above Place de Furstenberg. After paying his fare, he crossed to the other side of the street and walked toward Rue de Seine. He had no intention of visiting L'Antiquités, even if that were possible—which it was not. All three streets leading into the square were barricaded and several dozen men from the Gendarmerie Nationale patrolled the area. Each was armed with a French army FAMA semi-automatic rifle and there was no mistaking the look on their faces. Anyone who appeared the least bit suspicious would be stopped and questioned. Most of the citizens crossed to the opposite side of the road as Bashir had done.

He proceeded past the square, pretending to look at the various cafés and shops lining the street. He stopped in front of a promising flower shop just after he made the left turn onto Rue de Seine. One-meter high Christmas trees bound in plastic netting were propped around the front entrance and along the length of the shop's exterior display tables. Arranged on tables behind the conifers were dozens of containers of brightly colored flowers. Near the end of the row, he had found the sunflowers.

The conversation with the shop's owner still haunted him.

"They are beautiful, are they not?" she said, lifting a bouquet from its plastic container and handing them to him. "Perhaps they are for a child?" He had replied to her question with silence. "*Non?*" she'd continued unaware of his pain. "A pity. Children are such a blessing."

PLACE de FURSTENBERG

Luc Rollin, senior agent on site for the Service de Protection des Hautes Personalities, turned at the sound of rapid foot-steps approaching from behind. He stopped to allow one of the members of his security detail to catch up. The man was one of those assigned to protect Marguerite Lemaire and Dianne Stuart. The wife of the Secretary State, Chris Valardi, wasn't feeling well and had decided to not accompany the other wives and Stuart's daughter had opted to visit the Louvre.

This was the ladies' second stop of the morning and, much to Rollin's astonishment, they were only running six minutes behind. They were scheduled to be at the courtyard for a full hour, more than enough time to buy a croissant and visit the antique shop before taking a tour of the Musée Delacroix. His team had completed their final security sweep and had escorted anyone from the square that didn't possess the temporary ID card permitting them to be there.

"We just received this," the man said handing his boss the picture of al-Khultyer.

Rollin studied the photo. His jaw tightened, his only outward sign of emotion. *What the hell took them so damn long?* The motorcade was just minutes out. He barely had enough time. "Do you have any more of these?"

"In the comm van."

"Distribute all of them to the roving patrols. I'll start with the shops. He jogged across the square toward La Maison du

Chou as his man disappeared around the corner of Rue Cardinale, the small side street off the square where the security detail's vehicles were parked.

The staff of the pastry shop looked up in astonishment when Rollin burst through the door waving the picture. "Have any of you seen this man?" None of them had.

He ran across the street to L'Antiquités.

Madame Dupreyon stood outside of her shop waiting for her guests to arrive. "Monsieur Rollin what is the—"

"Have you seen this man?"

She startled at the sight of the picture thrust under her eyes. "Why, yes. That is Monsieur Chauven. Why do you ask?"

"What was he doing here?"

She turned and pointed to the antique cart. "He was here earlier in the week and purchased that wonderful cart. He's to pick it up Monday. It is to be a surprise. Is—"

Rollin didn't hear the rest of the question. He stepped around her and entered the shop. He approached the cart and looked inside. A toy rabbit blocked his view of the interior. He gently shifted the rabbit to one side with his index finger. "*Mon, Dieu.*"

He spun and slammed into Madame Dupreyon who had followed and stood directly behind him. He caught her by the shoulders to keep her from falling. "Run!"

She didn't move.

"There's a bomb." He gave her a push toward the door and bolted past her into the street. The three cars of the caravan were just slowing to a stop in front of the pastry shop. The doors of the two black SUVs bracketing the armored sedan carrying Mes Dames Lemaire and Stuart opened.

Rollin sprinted toward the vehicles. "*Bombe!* Get them out of here! There's a bomb!"

The Presidential Security Chief's frantic call from his headquarters to Senior Agent Rollin wasn't answered.

LE BAR DU MARCHÉ

Bashir glanced at his watch. 10:11. His calculations on the probability of success were based on the assumption that Stuart and Lemaire would first visit the pâtisserie and then cross the courtyard to L'Antiquités.

His intent was to catch the women in the open. If they were still in La Chou, so be it. They would still be severely wounded by the shards of glass exploding inward from the shop's display window. He pulled the cellphone out of his overcoat pocket and flipped open the cover. The signal was strong. He pressed the CALL button.

He feigned surprise at the muffled roar that followed, jerking his head around as if trying to locate where the explosion had come. Several people at the end of the block pointed to a plume of black smoke just beginning to show above the buildings a few blocks away. The wail of sirens soon pierced the air of the quiet neighborhood.

He reached for the bouquet of sunflowers and took a final sip of wine before walking back to the L'Aligré to finish packing. Angelique would pick him up at noon.

Chapter Eighteen

AMERICAN EMBASSY
PARIS, FRANCE
FRIDAY 12 DECEMBER

Nick's car slid to a stop in the crushed-stone courtyard fronting the American ambassador's residence. He looked out the window, hand poised to open the door.

Armed men swarmed the grounds. Most of them appeared to be from the embassy's Marine guard. The remainder, Secret Service.

"Alors!" Gillet exclaimed. "The place is crawling with *policier*." He opened the door. A Secret Service agent yelled before he took a step.

"You. Stand fast." The agent addressed Nick. "Parkos. This way." He grabbed Nick's elbow, almost dragging him through the front door into the foyer. "It's all we can do to keep the president secured. He's demanding to see Mrs. Stuart."

Nick recalled seeing the agent at the embassy just a few hours before but couldn't remember his name. "Have you heard anything from the ER?"

"Bits and pieces," the agent said over his shoulder leading Nick up a winding staircase to the second floor. "Possible neck injury. Nothing's been verified. From the pics we got from the scene, it appears the lead SUV took the brunt of the blast. Her vehicle was blown onto its side, almost halfway through the front of some shop."

"How about Lemaire's wife?"

"She was transported to a different hospital," the agent answered ushering Nick down a long marbled hallway. He rapped on the right-hand door of a gilded pair and entered without waiting for response.

Nick followed, his eyes darting over the chaotic scene. Embassy staff and Secret Service rushed about setting up computers and status boards, transforming the elegant reception room into a command center. Electrical cables snaked their way across the parquet floor. A crystal chandelier hung strangely out of place above a long folding table festooned with a bank of walkie-talkies resting in their chargers.

Stuart stood before a red-marble fireplace that dominated the far wall, deep in conversation with someone Nick didn't recognize. The president motioned to Nick's escort indicating that he should approach. Nick made to move but was halted by the Agent.

"Stay here."

Nick stayed put watching the president and the other man exchange words with his escort. The president nodded several times before all three men pivoted toward the center of the room. Nick froze. Their eyes were locked on him.

His first impulse was to bolt, but he couldn't move.

The individual the president had been talking to detached himself and walked across the room. He stopped in front of Nick, extending his hand. "Mr. Parkos, I'm Dan Lantis, President Stuart's Chief of Staff. The president would like a word with you."

Nick broke into a sweat. His vision tunneled. All he could

see through a swirl of tiny black spots was the blurred face of a large clock on the fireplace's mantel. His heart pounded in his ears.

Lantis guided him back across the room toward four Louis XV chairs that had been shoved into a corner. Stuart pulled two out and spun them around to face each other. "Please, have a seat."

Nick barely heard him. He took a deep breath and sat. "Yes, sir."

Lantis remained standing, positioned himself behind Stuart's right shoulder, further unnerving Nick. The president appeared to be studying his face. *Did he just say something?*

"Are you okay, son?" Stuart said.

"Yes, sir. Just a little faint. I missed breakfast."

"I see," Stuart replied in a knowing voice. He addressed Lantis. "Dan, could you see if you can round up some orange juice?"

Stuart turned back to Nick. "Mr. Gilmore briefed me on al-Khultyer before I left Washington. Was it him?"

"I believe so, sir. We had evidence he made his way to Marseille where he killed two men and disappeared. Sir, I'm sorry. We should have found him before—"

Lantis returned with a glass of orange juice and a plate of chicken salad, handing both to Nick.

Nick balanced the plate on his lap. "Thank you."

Stuart waited until Nick took a drink before he spoke. "It's likely he's already left Paris."

"Yes, sir. Just before the explosion, we had narrowed our search to several neighborhoods in the Left Bank. He lived there with his family while attending graduate school. The French national police are…"

Nick stopped. Stuart looked distracted. He decided to continue. "The French police are going through the neighborhoods with al-Khultyer's picture."

Stuart's eyes hardened. "I want you to find that son-of-a-bitch. Whatever you need, you'll get. From any agency. If I need to authorize a black-op, let me know."

"Yes, sir."

"Stuart looked at Lantis. "Dan, get him on my schedule."

The request stunned Nick. *Did I just get a summons to the Oval Office?* He followed Stuart's eyes to a young woman approaching from across the room. She stopped at a respectful distance and held out a cell phone. "Excuse me, Mr. President. I have Doctor Lewis."

Nick started to rise, but Stuart waved him back into his seat. He dropped into the chair trying to decide what to do next. He gazed hungrily at the chicken salad. *Am I allowed to eat in front of the president?*

Stuart accepted the phone and walked over to a window overlooking the residence's gardens. Nick caught his first words to the White House physician. "When can I see her?"

"You better eat that," Lantis said pointing to Nick's plate.

Nick consumed most of the salad before Stuart returned. He set the plate on the floor and pushed it under his chair with the heel of his shoe so the president wouldn't step on it.

Lantis cast an imploring look at his boss.

"She's okay. They want to watch her overnight."

"You agree?"

"I don't have a lot of choice in the matter. I need to get over there."

"I'm working that with PSD," Lantis said.

Nick understood Stuart would only be able to leave the compound once the Presidential Security Detail felt it was safe. They would have preferred to have him at thirty-five thousand feet flying back to the States, but Stuart had already vetoed any plan that involved leaving his wife behind.

"Doc said she's asking about her personal secretary and the agents assigned to her detail," Lantis continued.

"How is she?"

"Patti should be released in a couple hours. She still had her seatbelt on when the car flipped."

"And the others?"

"We lost three agents in the lead vehicle. I'm not sure about the French. We're putting together a casualty report."

Stuart looked at Nick.

"I know of at least one Frenchman, sir. Luc Rollin, their senior agent." Nick hesitated. "Sir, if I may …"

"Go on."

"Are there any reports of contamination at the scene?"

Stuart paled. He scanned the room, and then made a couple rapid flicks of his index finger to beckon a uniformed man who'd just walked into the room. "Ask him."

Lantis whispered in Nick' ear. "He's the senior military attaché at the embassy."

The soldier came to attention. "Yes, Mr. President?"

"Colonel, have you received any word on possible radioactive contamination at the site?"

"Yes, sir. Just a few minutes ago."

Stuart looked down, exhaling loudly. "How bad?"

"The contamination appears to be contained to the area around the square. The French are setting up monitors and evacuating the surrounding neighborhoods."

"What are we looking at?"

The colonel hesitated.

Nick decided to inject himself into the conversation. "Sir, if I may?"

"Go ahead."

"We're likely looking at a device with MOX ceramic fuel pellets identical to those al-Khultyer used in Moscow."

"MOX?"

"Mixed Oxide. The Russians were using a mix of reprocessed weapons grade plutonium and uranium to manufacture their fuel pellets."

"What happens to those who were exposed?"

"The worst case is acute radiation sickness. Initially there were few cases reported from the Moscow incident. Most of their casualties were from the actual explosion. Those individuals that survived the blast but had significant exposure manifested symptoms of acute radiation sickness within a few hours."

Nick stopped. "Sir, Mrs. Stuart was in her vehicle. Her exposure would have been very low."

Stuart responded with an irritable edge to his voice. "I understand that."

Crap, I just pissed him off. He collected himself and plunged ahead. "The greatest danger would be from aerosolized material."

"And the long-term risk?"

"That would be dependent on the amount of material she inhaled."

"How would we know?"

"The first symptoms of acute exposure would be headache, fatigue, and nausea."

"She hit her head on the window... had to have stiches..." Stuart said softly. He looked up. "A concussion would manifest the same symptoms."

Nick didn't know how to respond to this mention of the first lady. He decided to keep his response simple. "The ER can run a urine screen for uranium isotopes."

Stuart looked at Lantis.

"I'll call Doc Lewis." Before he could dial, another staffer approached.

"Excuse me, Mr. President. I have President Lemaire on the secure line. Can you speak with him?"

"Certainly, I'll be right there. Dan, I want Nick to ride home with us."

"I'll make the arrangements."

Lantis watched Stuart follow the staffer to a quiet corner of the room and then addressed the question on Nick's face.

"You did fine."

"I'm not so sure."

Lantis pulled out his iPhone and provided a bit of reassurance. "If he was angry, he wouldn't have invited you to ride with us. I'll need contact numbers."

Nick decided to start with his personal phone. "Three-zero-one, nine-two... No, three ... Nick's mind blanked. *Shit, I can't even remember my own cell number.* He started over.

Lantis appeared unfazed by Nick's gaffe. "One of the staff will be in contact and walk you through the process to obtain your clearance. Air Force One is parked at Villacoublay Air Base, about eight miles southwest of Paris. You need to be there no later than 0830."

Lantis pocketed his iPhone. "That should do it. I expect you have a lot to do."

Nick interpreted that as meaning he could leave. He felt compelled to say something. "If anything comes up, I'll call."

He left the room and made his way back down the hallway trying to sort through all that had just happened.

———

"Parkos. A moment."

Nick took a couple more steps before the sound registered. He stopped and looked in the direction of the voice. A man in a dark-blue suit stood in front of a doorway leading to a small anteroom. He motioned Nick to join him, then disappeared through the door.

Nick frowned but retraced his steps to the anteroom. Empty. *What the hell?*

"In here."

The voice, barely above a hoarse whisper, came from the adjoining room. Nick rounded the corner to find himself in the residence's formal dining room. The man waited for him at the far end of a long credenza.

Nick tensed. He heard footsteps. Judging from the sound, a woman in heels. The footsteps slowed but didn't stop. "What do you want?"

The man didn't introduce himself. "Certain information has come to my attention that pertains to YLVA."

Nick didn't reply. He wanted to hear what this guy had to say.

"This code word has been traced to your FBS contact, Grekov."

"I'm not surprised."

The man looked toward the door to the anteroom before continuing. "What may surprise you is that she has been collaborating with certain American assets and the Novoroosiyk Business Group. You are acquainted with the handle, Charal, yes?"

Nick tried to keep his face impassive. *How the hell does he know this?*

"It's her."

Nick's suspicions were confirmed. Someone on his committee had leaked the information. He needed more. "To what end?"

"Suffice it to say, your investigation has implications to national security that cannot be underestimated."

Nick wondered where this conversation was going but could only conclude it somehow linked to today's events. He ventured a guess. "Where does al-Khultyer fit in?"

The man shrugged. "That is for you to discover."

"What the hell's the matter with you? He just tried to kill the president's wife for God's sake."

The man appeared unmoved by Nick's outburst. "I would suggest you look closer to home for your answers."

Nick had heard enough of these riddles. *Why should I even trust this guy?* He turned to leave.

"Parkos."

Nick paused at the door.

"If anyone were ever to ask, this conversation never took place."

———

Nick descended the spiral staircase and spotted Gallet hunched over his iPhone in the far corner of the foyer. He looked up as Nick approached.

"Damn, Parkos. What were you doing up there?"

"Long story."

Gallet shrugged at the non-answer. "Anything new?"

"Possibly. What about you?"

"We have a lead."

Chapter Nineteen

VILLACOUBLAY AIR BASE
THE FRENCH REPUBLIC
SATURDAY 13 DECEMBER

Nick cast a sideways glance at his escort. She wore a tailored blue jacket with the presidential logo topped with the surround, *Presidential Flight Crew*, over her right breast pocket. Her name, Michelle O'Brian, written in white script topped her left pocket.

His eyes traveled the full length of the 747 before coming to rest near the aft cargo door. "Can we stop for a moment?"

Nick observed that his request didn't come as a surprise. Air Force One apparently had that impact on people.

She stood quietly by his side before speaking. "Impressive, isn't she?"

Nick nodded, awed by the massive plane. A squad of Marines in dress blues and white gloves formed up on the tarmac near the back of a large utility truck. They marched up a ramp leading into the bed of the vehicle in two files of four men each. They reappeared carrying a casket draped in an American flag. The voice of the color sergeant softly counting out cadence carried over the tarmac.

Nick concluded the casket must be for one of the three secret service agents who lost their lives in Furstenberg Square. He wondered why they weren't being transported by one of the support planes.

Michelle followed his eyes. "The president wanted to fly them home in his aircraft." She came to attention as did the others working around the plane.

They didn't speak again until the final casket was secured onboard. Nick was distressed at seeing the fourth. *Damn, another agent must have died.*

She broke the silence. "The White House is notifying the families so the president can speak with them." She sighed. "There's so little we can do. Perhaps it will help."

"Perhaps it will," Nick replied softly, coping with another pang of guilt at not being able to stop the attack. "Shall we board? I suspect you have a lot to do."

"We're pretty well set," she replied. "Let's use the forward boarding stairs. It's reserved for the president and his family's use, but he won't mind."

Nick looked at the Presidential Seal just forward of the steps leading to the private entrance. "I hope not."

"He's pretty good about letting folks take a look around when he's not on board," she said, leading him up the steps. "I'll give you the cook's tour."

He was more than happy to steer clear of the van parked by the 747's cargo door.

———

"This is where you'll be." Michelle guided him to a set of four seats, paired to face each other. "You're with the worker bees. The senior staff sits forward. The strap hangers are in the next space aft."

"Strap hangers?"

She smiled, her green eyes sparkling. "The guests and reporters along for the ride. Generally, they don't do anything but get in the way."

"I don't qualify?"

"Not yet. Your seat is assigned to someone who has to stay behind. Mr. Lantis wanted you to have it."

"I'll try not to make a nuisance of myself."

He was completely taken by Michelle's eyes and the scattering of freckles running across her nose and cheeks. Her red hair was cut short to meet military regulations. But it was to her eyes he returned. He pulled his own away, embarrassed. If Michelle had read his thoughts, she masked her reaction well.

"You're off to a good start," she teased. "If you need anything, just ask."

Nick settled into one of the first-class sized chairs and looked out the window. He wondered if he was being a nuisance or not.

He fished around and found the seatbelt. The Presidential Seal was embossed on the buckle. *Impressive.*

"Not exactly Delta is it?" a new arrival said as he settled into the seat across from him.

Nick dropped the buckle.

"The man offered his hand. "Mike Rohrbaugh."

Nick returned the firm grip. "Nick Parkos."

"I'd heard you were here. Catching a ride back?"

I heard you were here? "Yes."

Rohrbaugh read Nick's consternation. "Sorry, I've got you at a bit of a disadvantage. I'm one of State's reps on the NSC. I got word I might be assigned to your committee."

That was news to Nick. "I didn't get the memo."

Rohrbaugh countered the peevish reply with a disarming smile. "Doesn't surprise me."

"What do you do on the NSC?"

"Political-military affairs. My real job is with the Navy. I just spent the past couple days working counter-terrorism. That and firming up our basing agreement for Camp Lemonnier."

Rohrbaugh's iPhone buzzed. He pulled it out, read the message, and stood. "Gotta go."

Nick looked around the cabin after Rohrbaugh disappeared around the corner. His assigned seat was the one closest to the lavatory and a small galley. The four seats in his cluster didn't have a table like the other clusters, but he could hardly complain. He pulled out his MacBook, balanced it on his lap, and set to work.

He was lost in thought when Michelle stuck her head in from the main passageway. "If you want to get some work done, why don't you sit at one of the tables?"

Nick answered with a dubious look, not wanting to intrude on a regular's space.

"It's okay. Our departure has been moved back four hours. You have the place to yourself."

He rolled his eyes in feigned exasperation. "Do I get a free ticket if we're waiting on the tarmac for over six hours?"

"Nope. If you get thirsty or need something to eat, help yourself from the galley."

Nick glanced at the wide screen mounted on the forward bulkhead.

Michelle smiled. "Sorry, no movie service until we're airborne."

Nick moved to the nearest table. The first thing he noted was a black lacquer roller pen with *The White House* printed in gold letters along its length. Next to it lay a 4x3 pocket jotter with the Presidential Shield embossed on the cover. They would be a great gift for Emma. He placed both in his briefcase.

His could not wait to see his daughter again. He'd been awarded joint custody after the divorce, but Marty said flying Emma to D.C. for a visit was out of the question. His well-intentioned efforts to see visit her in Miami had fallen short. He shook the negative thoughts from his mind. He would get nothing done feeling sorry for himself.

He set to work on the outline of his after-action report. He reached into his briefcase and pulled out the file Gallet gave him just before they had left his office for the French Airbase. The French agent insisted on driving, saying he knew the way and could save him some grief getting through the main gate. Besides that, they needed to compare notes before Nick returned to the States.

Nick reviewed the report. The maître d and a waiter at Les Deux Magots recognized al-Khultyer's picture from when he dined there on Thursday. That wasn't particularly helpful at this point, but the other pieces of information they provided the French police were. Al-Khultyer used an assumed name: Marc Arnaud. And he left the restaurant with a woman. The waiter recalled her name—Angelique—but didn't have a credit card receipt for her drinks and food. Arnaud had picked up the tab for both of them and paid in cash.

The restaurant also caught pictures of al-Khultyer and Angelique on their security cameras. Gallet's men had the tapes and were preparing to release copies to Interpol. If they tried to cross the border, they would be detained.

Nick typed the woman's name in caps to begin a new header. *So, Angelique, who are you? Part of his network? ... or unwitting accomplice?*

Gallet would find the answers to the most basic questions: Full name, occupation, home, friends, criminal background, travel history. Nick leaned back in his chair. It would be up to him to figure out the link, if any existed.

His cell buzzed impatiently under a pile of papers in his briefcase. He pushed his files out of the way, snatched his phone, and glanced at the screen. Unknown caller. He slid his finger across the bottom of the phone to silence it. "Parkos."

"Nick? *C'est* Gallet. I took a chance to see if I could track you down."

"We're still on the ground. What do you have?"

"Our mystery woman has a last name. Fontaine. Single, lives alone, works at a local modeling agency. Nothing suspicious turned up in our background investigation."

"A dead end?"

"*Non*. We discovered where al-Khultyer was staying. He spent the week at L'Aligré, a small boutique hotel just across the Seine from Notre Dame. The police showed the manager a picture of Mademoiselle Fontaine. He saw a woman matching her description pick up al-Khultyer just after he checked out. Her car had a rack mounted on the roof with a pair of skis lashed to it."

Nick grabbed a roller pen and pocket jotter. "Do you have the make of the car?"

"We did better than that. We've got her license number, CF-485-JN, issued in Chambéry. And the car. 2014 Peugeot 406 Coup. She's got good taste in autos."

"I'll say, but not so much in men."

Gallet grunted his agreement. "*Tout à fait*." He switched back to English. "My agents paid a visit to the agency. Talked to a friend of hers."

"Boyfriend?"

"Not that the friend knew of, but she did said Fontaine planned on taking a long weekend to go skiing at a resort in Bardonecchia, Italy. We've alerted the Highway Patrol."

Nick had a hunch. "Where's Chambéry?"

"The Rhône-Alpes region. Five hundred kilometers from here. Why do you ask?"

"Perhaps she has family."

"I doubt al-Khultyer would let her stop. He's got to get out of France. There's no reason for him to delay for broken travel."

Nick considered Gallet's logic. Broken travel was the term

for someone using multiple stops to mask their movement. "How much time do we have?"

"It's a seven hour drive from Paris to the border town of Modane. They'd have to drive through the Fréjus Tunnel after crossing into Italy. We'll stop them there."

"Did the manager say when Fontaine picked up al-Khultyer?"

"Just after noon... *Merde*, they probably crossed the border into Italy hours ago. I'll alert the Italian authorities. I'll touch base with you later."

Nick stared at the blank screen on his phone. *Merde* pretty well summarized his own feelings at the moment, but he couldn't think of anything useful he could do to assist Gallet. *But there is something I can do, something tougher than chasing down al-Khultyer.* Out of the corner of his eye he saw Rohrbaugh enter the compartment.

"Trouble?" Rohrbaugh said as took his seat.

Nick nodded. "Yeah." He didn't bother to elaborate.

"You must be the new guy."

Nick closed his laptop and looked up at the intruder.

"Kevin Marks," the man said, dropping his briefcase with a thump on the table, "Assistant Deputy for Scheduling and Advance." He glanced at Rohrbaugh. "How ya doing Mike? You hanging in there?"

"I'm not taking your chair, am I?" Nick said.

"Nah, stay put. The others won't be here for at least another half-hour," Marks made for the galley. "You guys want anything? I'm grabbing a beer."

Nick was startled. *Alcohol on an Air Force plane?* "Maybe later."

Marks plopped down in the chair next to Rohrbaugh,

popped the tab of his Michelob, and took a noisy sip. "Man, I need to decompress. How about you, Nick?"

"Yeah, it's been a tough couple days."

"So, what do ya think?" Marks swept his arm around the compartment, apparently unfazed by Nick's reply. "Sure beats the hell out of travelling coach."

"Yeah, sure does," Nick said trying to figure out how to escape. He looked at Rohrbaugh who merely smiled.

"It can get old, though," Marks continued, "I mean, how many trips to Europe can you take?"

Nick wished he'd taken up Marks' offer for a beer. He couldn't figure out if the guy was serious or just kidding.

Marks looked over the empty seats and took another swallow of beer. "This sucks. I can't wait to get out of this place."

"Mr. Parkos, sorry to interrupt, but Mr. Lantis would like a word with you."

Nick recognized Michelle's voice. "Just a sec," he replied reaching for his briefcase.

"You can leave that," Marks said. "It's safe."

"Can't"

"Ah, that's right. Eyes only. I heard you were a spook."

Nick cocked his head at the comment. Even though Mark's comment annoyed him, he'd just given him an idea. "Say, Kevin, didn't you say you worked for the Advance Team?"

He answered with a suspicion-filled, "Yeah?"

"Do you happen to have any pictures of the Embassy staff?"

Marks looked surprised but recovered and began rummaging through his briefcase. "Matter of fact, I do. Here ya' go. Good hunting."

The comment earned a curious look from Nick. He held up his index finger to Michelle indicating he needed a moment. He looked over the pictures before stopping at the middle of the bottom row. The face of the Embassy's Deputy Chief for Economic and Environmental Development, William Lisle, smiled back at him. The title was likely a cover. *Well I'll be damned. Lyle's the CIA station chief.*

————

"Is he always like that?" Nick asked Michelle as they walked forward to the senior staff cabin.

"Kevin or Mike?"

"Kevin."

"Yeah, he's a little unfiltered," Michelle smiled. "He can be a bit of a challenge. Mike can take care of himself. He's a SEAL."

Nick was impressed. "He didn't mention it."

"He wouldn't." She stopped outside the entry to the plane's senior staff compartment. "Here," she said handing him a business card, "in case you need anything."

He glanced at the embossed card. "Thanks, I—"

"Nick," Lantis interrupted, "the president arrives in ten minutes. He'll want an update."

Nick stuffed Michelle's card in his pants pocket.

Lantis motioned for him to take a seat. "What do you have?"

Nick spent half of the time reviewing his phone call with Gallet, adding his own analysis while Lantis wrote down a few cryptic notes. Nick took a drink of water when he was done, buying time to think. Now was not the time to hold anything back. "Sir, something else happened at the embassy."

Lantis set his pen down and settled in to listen.

Chapter Twenty

CHALET DELLA PORSENA
BARDONECCHIA, ITALY
SATURDAY 13 DECEMBER

Bashir contemplated the fire softly crackling in the stone hearth. Several glowing embers floated lazily upward, disappearing into the flue. He swirled the ice in his glass, mixing the sweet vermouth, gin, and Campari of his Negroni and took a contemplative sip. He felt at peace for the first time in weeks.

He felt Angelique's thigh press gently against his, a subtle act of forgiveness. She had wanted to stop at her home in Cambéry but, at his insistence, drove on to Bardonecchia with only a brief stop for petrol and a bite to eat. He explained he didn't want to waste a minute of their long weekend. That, of course, was true—to a point.

He reached across her for the small platter of *Cicchetti*, brushing his arm against her breasts. He selected a deep-fried olive from the selection of Venetian-inspired savory snacks she'd ordered and held it up for her to nibble. She smiled and took a swipe of the cinnamon whipped cream topping her Caffè Coretto with her finger. She presented her offering.

His lips closed around her finger, lingering. The taste was bittersweet. In his heart he knew the moment wouldn't—no, couldn't—last. He saw the change in her eyes.

She withdrew her finger. "Is there something wrong my love?"

"I was just thinking of…"

She twisted away from him, following his eyes to the window. The flashing blue lights of two police cars bearing the logo of the Arma dei Carabinieri illuminated the snow-covered parking lot.

He stood. "I have a surprise for you. It's in the room."

He bounded up the stairs, taking two at a time, and ran down the hall to their room. He burst through the door, grabbed his suitcase, and pulled out the duffle containing his seaman's cloths, new IDs, and the remaining Ziploc bag of ceramic pellets. There wasn't time to collect anything else. He looked out the window facing the courtyard. Two policemen were heading for the front door. Another pair appeared to be circling around to the back of the chalet.

The two entering the lobby wouldn't find a Monsieur Arnaud in the guest register, but if they were smart, they'd inquire about a certain man who had checked in the evening before with a beautiful woman.

Bashir looked at the sign in his room posting the route to the fire escape. He closed the door behind him, walked to the end of the corridor, turned right, and jogged down the back stairway to the parking lot.

He scanned the lot for the Carabinieri. None were in sight. He crouched and worked his way down the line of five cars parked against the side of the chalet, testing the door handles of each, avoiding Angeleique's Peugout coup. The fourth, a Fiat Spider, was unlocked.

He'd opened the door and slipped into the driver's seat.

He reached under the floor mat and flipped down the sun visor searching for a key. Nothing. He cursed under his breath and turned the steering wheel. The column wasn't locked, but he'd still have to hotwire the ignition.

Just under the steering column he located the pigtail containing the wires of the four-post ignition system and set to work. A small spark from the black wire leading from the battery appeared on his third attempt. He depressed the clutch and touched it again. The engine turned over.

He shifted into first gear and slowly made his way toward the exit. With any luck, the owner wouldn't know his car was missing until morning. By then, he'd be in Ravenna. He slowed and eased onto the main road without tapping the brake pedal.

He turned on the car's headlamps just before entering the first curve and continued east toward the mountains. A few kilometers down the road, he pulled over and rummaged through the center console. He pulled out a tire gauge and a Phillips screwdriver. He dropped these on the passenger seat before turning his attention to the glove box. To his relief he found a map. Only a short distance to the on-ramp for the A2. His finger traced the toll road's route until it intersected the A1. From there, it would be another six hours to Ravenna— too long. By then, the car's owner would have notified the police.

But, what of Angelique? Bashir pushed any further thought of her to the back of his mind. There could be no regrets.

He checked the rearview mirror. No headlights. Petro? *Just over three quarters of a tank. Perhaps enough to reach to Parma.* He would ditch the car and take a bus the rest of the way to Ravenna. The rear wheels spit gravel as he accelerated back onto the road.

The traffic on the A1 was sparse and the kilometer markers swept by with monotonous regularity. A wave of fatigue washed over him. He yawned and felt on the armrest for the window button to let in some cold air. A set of head-lights flashed in the side mirror. They flashed again.

He looked in the rearview mirror at the car that had been driving in tandem with him for the past hour. It slowed and drifted to the right. He swiveled his head to look over his shoulder. An unmarked vehicle in the left lane was overtaking him. He took his foot off the accelerator.

The car, a dark Maserati coup, made no move to slow. It flashed by. He exhaled and released his grip on the screwdriver. The Phillips was a lousy choice for a weapon, but it did give him an idea. He accelerated to the speed limit of 100 km/h and passed through another toll plaza without difficulty.

He drove for another forty kilometers before he spotted what he'd been looking for. He pulled off the Autostrata onto the access road leading to a rest stop. In a few minutes, his erstwhile travel companion appeared and parked a short distance away. Bashir smiled, grabbed the screwdriver, and made his way to exchange plates.

Bashir strolled down the Via D'Alaggio, the tree-lined street fronting the upper portion of the Canale Candiano. The bright awnings, pastel colors of the shops, trattorias, and osteria bordering the canal and the laughter of children added a festive air to the day.

He paused in front of an osteria advertising *Prodotti Tipico* and read the menu held by the white-aproned mannequin set beside the front door. The menu was not elaborate but appeared promising. He selected one of the circular wrought-iron tables facing the canal and ordered the *antipasta della casa* and a bottle of Chianti. There was no need to rush. After lunch he would follow the waterway to the commercial build-ings and wharfs. He held up his glass up to the sun, judging the color of the wine. *Magnifico*. He settled into his chair to enjoy his meal and the afternoon. An hour later he was on the move.

The name printed across the front of a plain two-story concrete office building prompted him to stop: Spocca Adriatica S.R.L., Shipping Chandler. Taped to the front window was the information he sought. He adjusted the sling of his duffle and ran his finger down the first of several columns listing the names and registry of the ships scheduled to arrive over the next week, their departure dates and destination.

His finger stopped mid-way down the second column: MV *Zora*, 320 tons, Bosnia and Herzegovina, 13 Dec/16Dec, Dubrovnik, general cargo/automotive parts. *Perfect.* No bigger than a tramp steamer, she would have a small crew and would not attract the attention of the authorities. Now, he just had to get onboard. He made a note of the ship's berth and set off to find her.

———

Bashir kept his eyes on the *Zora*. He shifted his stance and leaned against the massive iron bollard at the edge of the pier. The floodlights set along the wharf flickered on providing some sense of the time. He lit a third cigarette and continued his vigil.

Movement at the top of the gangway caught his eye. The shadowy form of a man descended the ramp and began walking toward a narrow alleyway running between two warehouses.

Bashir straightened. *That has to be one of the crew and he appears to know where he's going.* He took a final pull on his cigarette, dropped the butt into the canal, and followed the sailor.

The alleyway emptied into a gritty street lined with a scattering of pawnshops, strip joints, and *birreria*. Halfway down the block, the man stopped under the flashing neon sign of the Café di Scarola. He looked over his shoulder, then disappeared through the door. Bashir tried to ignore the prostitute sauntering toward him with a seductive sway of her hips. He swatted away her hand as she made a grab for his crotch.

"*Vaffancuio!*" She spit the words at him. "*Testa di cazzo.*"

He didn't know what the words meant, but they were undoubtedly quite colorful. He smiled, filing the curse words away for further use, and entered the pub.

A single bank of dull red-shaded lamps lit the narrow interior of the *birreria*.

Cigarette smoke hung heavily in the air. No music. No food. A long bar ran along the left wall and a half-dozen tables lined the right. The pub's few patrons occupied several of these. Nobody bothered to look up. The bartender continued to wipe the inside of a shot glass with a filthy rag, ignoring him.

Bashir spotted the man he followed sitting at an isolated table near the end of the bar. He took a seat directly behind the bartender and scanned the meager collection of liquor bottles searching for something he recognized. The bartender's frown reflected from the smeared mirror topping the counter. He randomly selected something from the shelf. "Grappa."

The request prompted the bartender to stir. He reached for the bottle and poured a shot into the glass he'd been wiping. He set it down in front of Bashir without uttering a word.

Bashir hefted the glass and downed it. "*Grazie.*" He gave the empty a couple raps on the counter indicating he wanted another. Out of the corner of his eye, he saw the sailor looking at him. He lifted his glass in acknowledgment. The man jerked his chin toward the empty chair beside him. Bashir nodded and stuffed a ten euro note in the empty glass.

"You were following me," the man said when Bashir approached.

"Yes."

"What do you want?"

Bashir pulled out a chair and motioned for the bartender to fill the man's glass. "Passage to Dubrovnik."

The man eyed Bashir, then drained his glass. "You have trouble with the authorities. No?"

"I wish to return home."

"That is not always so easy."

Bashir lit a cigarette and signaled the bartender that he wanted the bottle of grappa. He refilled the man's glass, then his own. "Perhaps you are in a position to help?"

The man threw his head back, downing the glass's contents and held it out for another shot. "One thousand euros."

Bashir could easily peel off ten one-hundred euro notes from his clip, but knew he'd be setting himself up as an easy mark. He blew out a plume of smoke and countered. "Five hundred."

"Eight hundred."

"Seven fifty."

The man reached for the bottle. "I'm Barusik, the first mate."

Bashir recognized the last name. He was likely a Bosnian Muslim. He held out his hand. "Dragan Kovacevic."

Barusik polished off the last of the grappa. "Come with me, brother."

Chapter Twenty-One

NATIONAL COUNTERTERRORISM CENTER
McLEAN, VIRGINIA
MONDAY 15 DECEMBER

Nick shifted his briefcase and unlocked the door to his office. He pushed it open with his knee and flipped on the light. He felt a fleeting pang of guilt for not coming in on Sunday but rationalized that he deserved to take a day off. Besides, after a brief catnap and indulging in only one—well, maybe two—glasses of wine, he worked for most of the eight-hour flight home.

The upside of flying Air Force One was organizing his notes and knocking out his trip report. The downside? The plane landed at Andrews and he had to find a way to Dulles to pick up his car, a drill that added another two hours to his day. He hadn't arrived at his condo until after two AM Paris time —too late, or perhaps too early, to sit down in his recliner with a bottle of *Wild Turkey*.

He opened his briefcase while he waited for his computer to run through its startup program. On top, the pocket jotter embossed with the Presidential Seal, a pretty neat souvenir. Clipped to it, the black lacquer pen and Michelle's business card. He pulled out the pen and her card fell face down on the desk. He stared in disbelief. She had drawn a happy face and next it, her cell number and email address. He picked up the card, recalling her green eyes, the sound of her voice.

Beep. The computer asking for his password. He propped her card against the monitor and typed in his password and verification to access his encrypted email.

Fifty-three secure messages. Almost double what he'd usually get in four days. He scrolled through the headers deciding where to start. He paused at the third: a message from Gallet forwarded at ten AM Paris time by the embassy's communication section. Alain was working Sunday. He scanned down his screen. He rocked back in his chair, absorbing the content of Gallet's message. *Damn, I should have come in.*

Al-Khultyer had vanished, just managing to elude the Italian police. The bewildered girlfriend, Mademoiselle Fontaine, was still being interrogated, but she apparently had no idea about her acquaintance's real identity, what he'd done, or where he'd gone.

The only clue to his whereabouts had been another guest's report that his car had gone missing. The Italians made the correct assumption and reviewed their tollbooth cameras. They spotted the Fiat on their traffic cams heading east on the A21 before it turned southeast toward Parma. The Carabinieri found the car abandoned in a parking lot near the outskirts of the city. From there the trail went cold.

Nick typed in a search for Italian toll roads. Nothing in his files indicated al-Khultyer was familiar with Italy and his decision to use the woman suggested he didn't coordinate his movements with his facilitators. *He's cut his ties to his support network. He's freelancing.* The investigation just became much more complicated.

His fingers tapped out a thoughtful rhythm on the sides of his keyboard. There was a certain futility in analyzing an individual's motives and al-Khultyer didn't fit into any of the various accepted schools of thought he learned in his criminology classes. One thing was clear. Al-Khultyer was a survivor and very smart.

He re-read Gallet's message. Al-Khultyer used a new alias when he checked into the ski lodge—Dragan Kovacevic. The name was common enough in the Baltic, but this was no common man and now he was on the run. Nick reflected on a quote from one of his professors. "People act the way they do because of who they are." He sat up. *The note from the farmhouse.*

While ideology could be part of the equation, al-Khultyer appeared to be motivated by revenge and a desire to atone for his own perceived failure—a dangerous combination. Nick's fingers stopped their drumming. He recalled something else his professor had said. "Thinking is great, but at some point you need to act on your instincts." He refocused. *Where would al-Khultyer find safe haven?* Nick pulled on his chin. *He's heading to Croatia or Bosnia and Herzegovina. So, how would he get there?*

Nick considered a number of options, then slapped fist on the map. Al-Khultyer would take a ship. The closest seaport? Ravenna.

Before he could pursue this line of thought, his computer flashed an alert. He clicked on a cryptic message from the Moscow embassy. The Turks had apprehended a man carrying a container of nuclear fuel pellets trying to cross their border from South Ossetia, a breakaway province of the Republic of Georgia. They extradited the man to Russia where the FSB quickly linked him to the GUM bombing. His name: Ushiska Abkhaz.

That's it? Nick scanned the rest of the message. It appeared Abkhaz had met with an untimely death. He recalled his last principle's meeting. John Elliot mentioned the Turks had detained an Armenian trying to cross their border carrying ceramic fuel pellets. *The same guy?*

Nick clasped his hands, tapping his index fingers together. Ushiska Abkhaz? He was either Bosnian or a Croat, not Armenian. Could Abkhaz have been trying to link up with al-Khultyer? He had to figure out how to contact the port authorities in Ravenna for a list of ships and their destinations. *Crap. I don't even know who I'd call to get—*

"Gotta sec?"

Nick recognized Strickland's voice. He spun his chair and started to stand. Strickland waved him back down.

"I understand al-Khultyer's disappeared."

"Yes, sir. The message from Paris—"

"I saw it."

Nick skipped the details. "He's in Ravenna."

Strickland rocked back in surprise. "You sound pretty damn sure about that."

"He's headed to one of the Baltic States."

Strickland's eyes widened. "What—"

He didn't wait for the question. "I just read Moscow's message."

"What's that have to do with it?"

Nick realized his mistake. The reason Mr. Gilmore had assigned him the investigation. The DNI recognized his cognitive skill, his ability to link seemingly unrelated events to a common point. Others had difficulty grasping how he could make the leap from point A to point C without fully understanding how he managed to make the jump without point B. "We need to know where Abkhaz grew up."

Strickland looked puzzled. "Why?"

"My bet is al-Khultyer is in Ravenna looking for a ship. Once he makes it across the Baltic, he's planning to join Abkhaz."

"But Abkhaz's dead."

"He doesn't know that."

Strickland nodded. "We have a chance. You need anything?"

"I could use some help from the Port Authorities in Ravenna. We need to identify any ships heading to the Baltic ports. We could board it in international waters and grab al-Khultyer."

"I'll take care of it. You need to find out more about this Abkhaz guy." Strickland paused, his voice taking on a different tone. "I got an inquiry for the White House. They're doing a background check. Is there something I should know?"

Background check? "Ah, I don't think so," he replied. "The president did ask me to keep him appraised of my... our... investigation. They're going to notify me when I'm on his schedule... I was going to talk to you... Something wrong?"

Strickland crossed his arms. "We'll need to scrub your briefing notes before you go."

Nick wondered if his boss even heard him. He fingered the souvenir pen. "I did brief the president just after the incident. Maybe it was a spur of the moment decision."

"The president doesn't make flippant decisions."

Nick wasn't sure what to make of the undercurrent of anger in Strickland's voice. He didn't answer immediately, trying to make sense of the direction their conversation had just taken. *And did Strickland say, 'scrub'?*

"Yes, sir."

Strickland dropped his arms. "Right answer. Think about it." With that, he turned and left.

Nick stared at his computer screen. *What the hell was that all about?* His eyes fell on the pocket jotter where he had written a single cryptic note. "Look closer to home for your answer."

He pulled out his minutes from the Principles meetings, uncapped a yellow highlighter, and set to work. In a few minutes, a number of lines stood out:

- We need to think out of the box...

- Was he (al-Khultyer) forewarned?
- Greatest risk is from a network we haven't identified...
- Suppose someone has sensed an opportunity to destabilize the government?
- It would be a mistake to limit our analysis by thinking in terms of a traditional TCO whose sole motive is profit

The underscored lines reinforced his sense of unease. He studied them, questioning himself. He knew better than to take them out of context. Perhaps they just reflected an unconscious bias on his part. *Possibly, but the minutes didn't record everything.* He'd excluded the more contentious comments made by the CIA rep, Taylor Ferguson. *Perhaps Jessica was right and he was just being an ass, but...*

He rummaged through a desk drawer and found the tape recorder. He switched it on, concentrating on Ferguson's words: "Has your trip been vetted?... wasting our time searching for phantoms... wasting our time looking at the Novoroosiyk Business Group ..."

Nick turned off the recorder. *Am I chasing phantoms? What else had Lisle said at the embassy?* The code word, YLVA, had been traced to Alek and she was collaborating with American assets. The CIA. *And my attempt to access the NSA's Project Talon for SIGINT on Alek's handle, Charal?* Thwarted.

At the time, he chalked up the rebuff to the agency's paranoia due to Edward Snowden blowing the cover on a similar program, Project Stateroom, in 2013. Now, he wasn't so sure. He glanced at the words embossed along the length of his pen: The White House. *What have I stumbled on?*

His hand's trembled as he fed the highlighted minutes through his shredder recalling Strickland's words. *Could I be under surveillance by my own agency? Or the CIA? What are they hiding?*

He emptied the machine's contents into a red-hashed burn bag and stapled it closed. There was also the matter of his notes. He couldn't risk documenting anything in an electronic record, no matter how well encrypted. He'd have to keep an off-line written record. He slipped the pocket jotter into his coat pocket.

Who can I trust?

Chapter Twenty-Two

NEUM
BOSNIA AND HERZEGOVINA
SATURDAY 20 DECEMBER

Nick stared through the rain-streaked window at the empty street that wound along the waterfront. The skeletal branches of an isolated tree fronting the café framed his view of the chopped gray waters of Mali Ston Bay. *Where is everyone?*

Even the few tourists that ventured to the remote port of Neum were nowhere to be seen. In all fairness, though, the city was usually an attractive destination. Situated at the mouth of the Nevetra River, the majority of its buildings were packed along the shoreline of the harbor. Its whitewashed buildings and red-tiled roofs backing against limestone cliffs offered a refuge from the ethnically torn, war-ravaged interior of the country. Unfortunately, Neum was also beginning to attract less savory visitors, those representing a dangerous consortium of terrorists and transnational crime organizations.

Nick picked at the veal stew congealed on his plate. He

dropped the fork and pushed the plate away. Two émigrés from the former Soviet Republic of Georgia managed the place. FSB. They also did the cooking.

A young German couple was the café's only other patrons. They burst into a raucous laugh, downed the last of their bottle of cheap wine, and made a dash for the door. Nick watched them from his vantage point in the corner of the room wondering if they were going to have sex.

A solitary car, a rusted Yugo spewing exhaust, drove past without slowing. Alek was already over an hour late. He drained his beer. *Where the hell is she?*

He pulled out six euros and dropped them on the table, intent on going to her room in the Marista, a small hotel a few blocks away. A hoarse smoker's cough caught his attention. One of the Georgians. The man wielded a pocketknife, putting the final touches on a *Chichilaki*, a traditional Christmas tree from his homeland. A small pile of wood shavings cluttered the floor around his feet.

The man looked up, gesturing to his work with the knife. "You like?"

The tree, shaped from a branch of walnut and topped with a black ribbon, reflected the work of a skilled artisan. Nick nodded in affirmation even though it looked to him like a longhaired yeti that had been cast in a Muppet movie. He got up and refilled his beer from the tap behind the counter.

He'd give Alek another fifteen minutes. When he spoke with her the past Tuesday, she said they knew where al-Khultyer had gone—Neum. Nick surmised the information had been extracted from Abkhaz but didn't ask. Gallet provided confirmation the following Thursday.

The French frigate, FS *Surcouf*, had intercepted the MV *Zora* in the Adriatic Sea shortly after the freighter got underway from Dubrovnik bound for Istanbul. The boarding party of Commandos Marine did not find al-Khultyer, but the first mate did admit to accepting five hundred euros from a man in Ravenna in payment for passage to Croatia.

The mate recognized the picture of al-Khultyer but said his name was Dragan Kovacevic. He also informed the Frenchmen that the man they were looking for had left the ship in Dubrovnik and planned to visit his family in Neum. That was enough information to send Nick back across the Atlantic with a four-man team from the CIA's Special Operation Group.

President Stuart personally approved their mission to capture al-Khultyer and bring him to the U.S. The president used his authority under the umbrella of the States Secret Privilege ruling. By doing so, he applied a reverse logic to the Extraordinary Rendition program stating there was substantial evidence to believe al-Khultyer would be tortured by the Russians if they got to him first.

The SOG operated under the cover of a DEA unit on a covert drug operation. The DEA informed the embassy in Sarajevo they needed to grease the skids with the Bosnians for the mission's unmarked Gulfstream V to land in Mostar, twenty-seven miles from Neum. Not even the ambassador knew what they were doing. Nick thought sending a SOG team a bit of overkill, but they were trained in counter terrorism, hostage rescue, and personnel recovery. In the end he figured they might come in handy.

Nick took another sip of beer and grimaced. He tolerated the first glass of Tuzlanski, but it wasn't worth a second. He recalled one reviewer branding the pilsner as a "punishing product." He pushed away from the table and pulled on his overcoat. There was no sense waiting.

He exited the pub and turned right, bending into the cold, wind-driven rain coming off the mountains. He hadn't gone more than twenty feet when the old Yugo he'd seen before passed by and pulled to a stop against the curb. The back door opened. "Get in."

One of the SOG paramilitary agents slid over to make room.

"Figured you'd have enough sense to stay inside."

"Something doesn't feel right."

The agent gave him an odd look. "Care to elaborate?"

"Grekov was to meet me an hour ago."

"You were headed to her room?"

"Working a hunch."

The agent dropped his jaw, but bit off whatever he was going to say. Instead, he thumped his hand on the back of the front seat. "Drop us off at the Marista, then join up."

———

The unease in Nick's stomach grew as they approached the hotel. He threw his door open before the car came to a complete stop and ran inside.

When they reached Alek's room, he knocked, hoping against hope his suspicions were wrong. "Alek." She didn't answer.

He pounded his fist on the door. "Alek!"

The senior SOG agent grabbed his shoulder, shoved him out of the way, and leveled a kick at the door. It burst inward, splintering the wood around the cheap doorjamb. The second agent leveled his weapon, sweeping the barrel in an arc across the room. "Clear."

Nick drew his Sig 229 and followed the two. Alek lay crumpled in the middle of the floor. Blood stained the carpet around the back of her head. He holstered his weapon and knelt, feeling her wrist for a pulse. "Alek?"

He ran his eyes over her body looking for wounds. "Alek?"

A moan escaped her lips. She stirred. Her eyes flicked open. She tried to lift her head.

"It's okay."

Alek sat up, steadying herself on an elbow. She shook her head trying to clear the blurred image in front of her. "You."

Nick answered with a Russian proverb. "*Da, beda ne prikhodit edna.*" Trouble never comes alone."

"Help me up."

Nick grasped her elbow, assisting her to her feet.

She wobbled, leaning against him for support. "*Spaseebo.*"

"*Nezechto*—don't mention it. He led her to a chair. "What happened?"

Alek reached her hand for the back of her head and gave it a tentative rub. "We set him up."

"Who?"

"Al-Khultyer. He was planning to join Abhkaz."

"But he didn't know."

"Abhkaz served his purpose."

Nick pulled up a chair and sat across from her. That made sense, but why didn't al-Khultyer kill her?

She glanced at the two CIA operatives standing across the room. "I... I tried to stop him, but he—"

Nick followed her eyes. A burly man, likely FSB, pushed past the two CIA agents and crossed the room. "*Hvatit!*"

The FSB had used the Russian verb demanding someone stop talking. Nick looked from Alek to the agent and back, judging her reaction. She looked terrified. There had to be more.

The agent placed himself between him and Alek preventing him from asking any more questions. He glared at Nick. "You leave."

Nick didn't argue.

Alek gave a subtle jerk of her chin toward the corner of the room. On it was a plastic baggie filled with dark-gray ceramic pellets. There were easily enough for another bomb—the third. *Where had he intended to detonate it?*

He spoke so only she could hear. "*Berezhonogo bog berezhot.* God keeps those safe who keep themselves safe."

He stood and motioned for the CIA men to follow.

———

"You want to tell us what that was all about?" the senior agent demanded once they were back inside the Yugo.

"She baited al-Khultyer into a meeting."

"Why'd she freelance instead of staying with the agreed plan?"

Nick had been wondering that himself. *Was she afraid of what al-Khultyer might divulge if he ended up in the hands of the Americans? And why hadn't he killed her and taken the pellets?* He looked out the window at the falling rain, then turned back to the agent. "No idea, but it just about got her killed."

"I'd say. That FSB guy didn't look real happy," the other agent said.

Nick reacted to that observation with a sharp intake of breath. *Could the Russians know of her complicity? That's why al-Khultyer didn't kill her. He was trying to save her life.*

The agent stared at Nick. "What?"

The words slipped out of his mouth. "They thought we planned to grab her."

"So, where the hell is al-Khulter?"

Nick starred out into the darkness. "No idea. But there was a plastic baggie in her room with enough pellets to construct a third device."

"Well, the Russians have it now. That's a win."

Nick faced the agent. "He's still got enough for two more."

Chapter Twenty-Three

KARACHI
ISLAMIC REPUBLIC OF PAKISTAN
TUESDAY 6 JANUARY

Bashir recoiled at the stench. The remnants of the offshore breeze carried a nauseous blend of raw sewage, rotting fish, and God knew what else. He placed his hand to his nose and scanned the anchorage. His vessel was near the edge of an assorted clutter of ships waiting their turn to dock in the morning. He looked over the bow from his vantage point on the starboard bridge wing. The port of Karachi lay just over the horizon, its location betrayed by a toxic yellow-brown haze smudging the remnants of the setting sun.

He had hoped to rendezvous with his contact before nightfall, but that appeared to be out of the question. The bridge-wing lights clicked on. Within minutes, the vanguard of a horde of flying insects attracted by the glaring bulbs arrived. He swatted at them, turning to seek refuge within the wheelhouse.

"Passage, friend. Passage to shore."

He stopped in mid-stride and walked back to edge of the

catwalk, looking for the source of the call. A man clad in a dirty-white robe stood at the rail of a rickety dhow, his knees absorbing the rocking motion of the vessel. The man waved in the general direction of the city and yelled. "Passage? Yes?"

Bashir took one glance at the dhow pitching and rolling in the chop. He could wait until morning.

"One thousand rupees. Cheap."

He reconsidered the offer—about ten euros—a small fortune in Karachi. The man turned at the sound of metallic clanking coming from the side of the ship. The crew was rigging the accommodation ladder. Someone planned to go ashore. He shouted down a number. "Five hundred."

The man returned a brown-stained smile from his remaining teeth. "Five hundred rupees. Yes."

"Where is the dock?" Bashir said.

The man looked puzzled.

"The landing?" Bashir repeated.

"Ah, landing. Across from the Navy dockyard. West Wharf Road."

Bashir pulled out his burner phone but paused before entering the number for his contact. Something didn't fit. The man had dropped his heavily accented pidgin and spoken quite well. His thoughts on what that meant were conflicted, but he needed to make contact. He placed the call. After a moment, an agent at the À Souhat Travel Agency picked up.

Bashir reviewed the reservations made under the name of Jean-Luc Chéreau and arranged for a wire transfer from his Swiss account to cover the cost of the single supplement.

Unfortunately, the agent noted that he remained on the *Étoile de Mer's* standby list. The remainder of his itinerary was confirmed. Bashir assured him that he remained flexible and ended the call. He anticipated he would have no difficulty obtaining a stateroom on the French luxury yacht.

———

Bashir heaved his duffle onto the pier. He regained his balance and judged the pitch and roll of the dhow. Flotsam churned in the chasm separating the boat and safety. The gap narrowed. The bow began to rise. He crouched in readiness. His legs uncoiled as he swung his arms upward, launching himself off the narrow deck. He barely caught the edge of the pier and toppled backwards. A hand reached out and pulled him upright.

"*Deer wahkht wosho na khary*. It's been a long time, my friend."

Bashir glanced over his shoulder at the abyss, then gave his old comrade a tight hug, slapping him on the back. "And you have managed to save me once again, brother."

Batoor Abdali placed his hand over his heart and gave a slight nod.

Bashir inquired about Abdali's health and family in the Pashtun custom. He was well and his wife and family were safe in the tribe's enclave in North Waziristan. Bashir knew there was more. "I heard you were wounded."

"A lucky shot from a Pakistani militiaman, may he and his family be cut into pieces and devoured by dogs."

"And your son?"

Abdali's eyes took on new life. "He grows strong, God's blessings be upon him. He—"

Bashir held up his hand. He'd caught sight of something lurking in the shadows of the nearest warehouse. *The white-robed man from the dhow.* A young boy stood beside him. The kid looked at Abdali and quickly lowered his eyes. The man leaned over and said something to the boy. The kid took another look in their direction, then ran down the road.

"We need to go," Bashir said.

"Yes," Abdali answered, his gaze fixed on the robed man. "He probably wants to sell us a brick of hashish or offer us the boy for pleasure."

Bashir watched the boy disappear around the corner of a building. *Or is he reporting my arrival?* He picked up his duffle and caught up with Abdali. They turned south and followed a cluttered path running along the water's edge before encountering a set of stairs cut into the seawall. His plan to travel to London and detonate the third bomb had been thwarted in Neum. He had to improvise. Returning to Europe would be too dangerous. *But I still have enough material for two devices. Perhaps—*

"This way," Abdali said.

Bashir followed Abdali up the stairs to an open marshaling yard. They continued for a couple hundred yards walking parallel to an elevated rusted pipe set on a row of crumbling concrete pylons before encountering a row of dimly lit warehouses.

He pitched his cellphone into the bay just before they turned into a darkened alleyway. He'd taken an enormous risk using it, but he couldn't think of another way to contact Abdali except through their intermediary in Islamabad or to confirm his reservations. He'd memorized Adbali's number years before, and had used it just once, when he notified his contact that he was on his way to Karachi.

Abdali's head swung toward the sound of the splash.

Bashir noted his friend didn't comment. *Wise.*

They passed a row of shanties facing an unpaved street and turned onto a two-lane road lined with assorted business offices and small warehouses. They proceeded several blocks before Abdali stopped in front of coiling steel door secured with a large padlock. He pulled out a key, unlocked it, and gave it a heave.

The door slid into the overhead bin with a metallic screech before sticking halfway up. Abdali ducked under the door and waited for Bashir to follow before he rolled the door closed behind them. He pointed to the void beyond. "Your shipment from Istanbul is there, stacked against the far wall." His voice echoed in the darkness. He didn't ask about the pallets from Meycek Exports.

Bashir's eyes adjusted to the dark. The warehouse looked like any other he'd been in. He didn't see anything unusual that would alert the authorities. "And the ship?"

Abdali walked to a small office set under the stairs leading to the second floor. "We have identified two. The MV *Zemian Bay* and the cargo ship *Articus*."

Bashir settled on a crate. "Tell me about the cargo ship."

"The *Articus* is scheduled for demolition at a ship grave-yard in Mauritania. This will be its last voyage."

"Is there a scheduled departure date?"

"Sometime within the next week or two."

Bashir didn't want to remain in Karachi that long, but he wasn't ready to dismiss the ship. "Cargo?"

"There is none listed on the manifest."

"That means nothing."

"That is true."

Bashir noted the hesitation in his friend's voice. "What haven't you told me?"

Abdali shrugged. "There are rumors that agents from the Iranian Ministry of Intelligence are looking for a vessel."

Bashir wanted nothing to do with the Iranians. "Weapons?"

"I was told the ship would pass near Somalia. Arrangements can be made."

Bashir hesitated, wondering why Abdali had dodged his question. He stroked his beard as an idea formed. *It would be madness to take the Articus, but could it be used as a decoy?* If there were even a hint it carried clandestine cargo, the Americans would track its position, course, and speed... And if they suspected what it carried? What measures would they take?

"Brother?" Abdali questioned.

"I was thinking about the other ship, the *Zemian Bay*."

"It is scheduled to depart in two days for Lamu with a cargo of plastics and pharmaceuticals."

Bashir had never heard of the place. "Lamu?"

"A city on the northern Kenyan coast, not far from the Somali border. The port connects with a major transportation corridor leading inland."

"It would be best to find a fishing vessel to take me up the coast."

"True."

"I will use the *Zemian Bay*." Bashir saw the change in Abdali's face. "What is it?"

"The Master will insist on examining your documents."

"I have a set prepared." Bashir stood. He also had another set of documents under the name of Jean Luc Chéreau, ten thousand euros, and a Carte Bancaire credit card sealed in one of the cans. The CB card was linked to a Swiss bank account he'd opened to cover unanticipated contingencies. One such contingency—the reservation he made with the *À Souhait* Travel Agency in France. Equally important, neither Alek nor his NBG contacts knew of Monsieur Chéreau and his Swiss account.

"I need to examine my pallets."

"What are you looking for?"

Bashir stiffened. "Make arrangements to move them to the *Articus*.

"There will be questions."

Bashir smiled, confident in his ruse to ensnare the Iranians. They should not have interfered and now they would pay. "I'm counting on it."

Chapter Twenty-Four

KUMA
REPUBLIC OF KENYA
SATURDAY 17 JANUARY

Bashir kept a wary eye on the orange-hulled harbor patrol boat keeping station just off their port side. A sailor manned the pintle-mounted .50-caliber machine gun on the bow. The Marine Police had been shadowing them ever since they left the protected anchorage. The Kenyan authorities tolerated the presence of the Somali fishermen who sold their catch to the fish mongers of Kamu, but they held no love for them.

The sailor kept an easy grasp on the machine gun's twin handles, keeping the barrel moving in rhythm to the rise and fall of the patrol boat. Bashir remained squarely in the gun's sights. The standoff continued for another ten minutes before the patrol boat broke off with a roar of its engine reversing course back to Kamu.

Bashir took a deep breath and wiped the sweat off his face. He had to get out of the sun. The remnants of wind from the southwest monsoon did little to dissipate the blazing heat pounding his head and shoulders. He worked his way down from his perch on the peaked bow of the fishing boat and wove through the clutter of ropes and gear on the deck. He stopped under the slip of shade provided by the overhang of the flat roof topping the pilothouse and rubbed the ache out of his left thigh.

They were still hugging the shoreline about a kilometer off the coast, heading north toward Barawa. All he could see though the haze blurring the horizon was an unrelenting expanse of brown sand sloping into distant foothills. They'd passed the rusting hulk of a burned-out pirate mother-ship beached in the surf several kilometers back, but that was it. Nothing else since he'd debarked from the *Zemian Bay* in Kuma.

The crew, dulled by the heat, lethargically cast their lines over the side, paying him little attention. One of them stopped long enough to tell him that if they were a bit farther out, they would have better luck catching one of the few tuna that remained in the waters during the off-season. Bashir couldn't determine whether the fisherman blamed him for their misfortune.

A voice yelled in a dialect he didn't understand. Several of the men working near the bow responded to the shouts by pointing to something to their right. Bashir left the shade of the overhang to see what caused the commotion. He couldn't see anything at first, then he spotted the black speck just over the far horizon.

In a few minutes, the unmistakable WHUMP, WHUMP, WHUMP of a helicopter resounded off the surface of the ocean. The aircraft appeared to be well east of them, but as he watched, it altered course. Soon the helicopter would be overhead. He wasn't concerned. There was nothing onboard that would arise suspicion... *except me.* He stepped back under the overhang.

The helicopter passed down their starboard side, then

swung around and made another approach from out of the sun. Bashir recognized the aircraft—a Russian built KA-27. He'd seen several of them in Afghanistan. The aircraft's tail markings identified it as Indian. One of their ships must be working with the international anti-piracy force nearby. The helicopter dipped its nose and gained speed, heading out to sea, no longer interested in them.

Bashir surmised that the helicopter monitored the boat traffic coming in and out of Barawa. One of the crewmen slid up to his side and informed him that al-Shabaab had wrestled control of the port back from government forces that held the town since October. He whispered that wasn't a good thing. The helicopters and drones had returned.

Bashir weighed the comment. *Perhaps.* He also knew from talk on the dhow that the Somali pirates were preparing for a new raiding season. In past years, the relationship between the pirates and al-Shabaab was strained, but now the terrorist movement needed the ransom money generated by the pirates. The raiding would be tolerated.

He wouldn't bother himself with the difficulties of either group. What mattered to him was the renewed presence of al-Shabaab in the city would make it easier to link up with the group. He presumed someone from the organization would be watching for anyone suspicious coming ashore from the vessels of the fishing fleet.

Bashir turned his attention to the monotonous Somali shoreline. The dhow pitched and rolled in the trough of a small wave as the vessel made a slow turn. They were beginning their run-in to the beach. An ancient stone lighthouse marking the entrance to the small seaport slid astern and a jumble of whitewashed buildings lining the waterfront came into view. A scattering of gray-green date palms provided the only color to the desolate seascape.

The dhow coasted to a stop amid a half-dozen similar boats bobbing offshore. The faint odor of diesel fumes drifted over him, mingling with the other smells of the harbor: wood smoke, fish, brine. A flurry of activity caught his attention. The crew was reeling in the small dinghy tethered to the squared-off stern of the dhow.

"You will go now."

Bashir turned at the sound of the captain's voice and left to collect his duffle. He returned to the deck, slung the bag over his shoulder, and descended the rope ladder dangling over the side. He found a place to sit wedged between three wicker baskets full of salted fish and set the duffle between his legs. He unzipped the canvas bag when no one watched and reached his hand in, feeling for the reassuring solidity of the beet cans.

BARAWA
FEDERAL REPUBLIC OF SOMALIA

The fisherman guiding the dinghy cut the engine and tilted the propeller out of the water just as they ground to a halt on the sand several meters from shore. The other crewman in the boat jumped over the side and waited for the coxswain to hand him one of the wicker baskets of fish. He hefted the basket to his shoulder and set off.

Bashir grabbed his duffle, clambered over the side, and followed the barefooted man. He trudged out of the water, passing between two garishly painted skiffs before stopping to survey his surroundings. There was a significant amount of activity, but no one appeared to notice his arrival. Even the dogs sprawled around the boats didn't raise their heads. He didn't have a clear idea of what to do next, but if al-Shabaab controlled the city, one their members would likely spot him.

His feet sunk into the soft sand as he made his way toward the road leading to the town. A glint of light flashed in the corner of his left eye. He tensed in fear, prepared to drop. The

last time he'd experienced that feeling was when he saw the
sunlight reflecting off the scope of a sniper rifle just before the
bullet tore through his pakol. He still remembered counting
his blessings as he poked his finger through the hole in the flat
Afghan cap. The flash appeared to come from the concrete
block wall that bisected the beach halfway down to the water's
edge. He didn't see anything to harm him.

He resumed his trek only to be forced to a halt beside a
line of burlap grain bags stacked beside the road. A camel
laden with driftwood ambled by. The strange animal fascinated him. The last time he'd seen one was when his mother
took him to the Grozny zoo when he was a child.

"You."

Bashir spun. The command seemed to come from a youth
sitting on one of the stacks of grain bags. The boy wore jeans
and a faded camouflage field jacket that drooped off his
skinny shoulders. His hands were loosely draped over an AK-
47 lying on his lap. Bashir watched the kid's eyes.

The youth hopped down and approached. "What are you
doing here?"

"Are you al-Shabaab?"

"That is not what I asked."

Bashir assessed the youth. The kid had to be al-Shabaab.
Otherwise, he wouldn't be armed. He shifted his eyes to see
how the youth handled his weapon. Poorly. He could easily
disarm him, but then what? He noticed the kid moving his
tongue around in his cheek. Khat. That would make him less
predictable. "I wish to find Abdul Aleem."

"Do you have a name?" the youth asked.

"Dhi'b."

"That is Arabic. You are not."

"Yes, for wolf. In my country, the wolf has great
significance."

"What is your country?"

"Chechnya."

Bashir's response had the desired effect. Of all the foreign fighters, the ferocity of the Chechen fighters was legendary. The youth straightened and waved his hand toward the road. Two others appeared at his signal. They were heavy-bearded, hardened fighters, not to be trifled with.

Bashir placed his hand over his heart. "*As salamu 'alaukum,* Peace be upon you."

The nearest of the two men, apparently the leader, answered. "*Wa alaikum salaam.* And upon you peace."

"*Hal beemkani msa'adati?* Can you help me?" Bashir said.

"What is it you wish?"

"To speak with Adbul Aleem."

The man waved the kid toward Bashir's duffle. "Search it."

The kid pawed through the bag, then stopped. He pulled his hand out and turned the duffle upside down, dumping the contents on the ground. Two beet cans rolled to a stop at Bashir's feet.

The warriors swung their rifles, leveling the weapons at Bashir's chest. The leader pointed his barrel at the nearest can, motioning for the kid to pick one up. "What is that?"

"Beets."

The kid examined the label, turning it around in his hand before shaking it against his ear. He shrugged his shoulders and handed to it the leader. The man hefted the can, accessing its weight. He gestured to the other can next to the kid's feet. "Check it." To Bashir he said, "Why did you bring these things?"

Bashir didn't want to risk angering the man with a flippant response so he answered, "They are from my homeland."

The two men turned their heads away exchanging words. The conversation ended with the leader pulling out a cell phone and placing a cryptic call. He ended the call with a curse. "Come."

Bashir gathered his belongings and stuffed them back in

his duffle. Neither spoke until they stopped in front of a house a few blocks from the waterfront.

"Wait."

Bashir watched the two disappear through the decaying archway of the concrete block wall fronting the building. He looked over the other structures along the sandy street. Multiple bullet holes and divots from larger caliber weapons pockmarked their exterior. Several buildings, including one topped with a faded-green minaret, had gaping holes caused by RPG rounds. There'd been one hell of a firefight here not too long ago.

The second of the two fighters reappeared holding a plastic water bottle. He handed it to Bashir. "You will come with us."

Bashir twisted off the cap and took a drink. The offering was a good sign. He didn't bother to ask where they were going.

Chapter Twenty-Five

HAAWAY
FEDERAL REPUBLIC OF SOMALIA
SUNDAY 18 JANUARY

B ashir and his escorts pulled off the rutted road from Barawa and slowed to a stop. The senior fighter, who had identified himself as Najib, parked their Toyota pickup under a clutter of parched trees adjacent to the bank of a muddy river. Bashir peered out the small window of the rear jump seat. The shimmering red-orange globe of the setting sun cast long shadows over the barren landscape. The stagnant river snaked its way across the plain to the distant foothills.

Najib slammed his door and grabbed his rifle from the bed of the truck. "We walk from here."

Bashir followed, splashing across a shallow ford and up a cut in the far bank. He considered his experience in Afghanistan. Leaving the truck was a reasonable precaution, but the measure wasn't effective. The American drones were always there, circling above, unseen. The only warning they'd have of the laser-guided bomb would be a faint whisper just before it blew them to oblivion. He scanned the sky. A trio of vultures glided in lazy circles in the distance—waiting.

The three-kilometer trek to the camp was easy enough, but he remained unsettled. There was evidence of vehicle traffic along the route they'd taken. He could easily detect the tire tracks. The Americans surely knew of the path and had it under surveillance.

"This way," Najib said when they came to the edge of the encampment.

Bashir stayed at his side as they wove their way between a scattering of mud-brick huts to a berm of loose rubble fronting a small hill. The conical shape of some of the hovels reminded him of baker's ovens, an apt analogy considering the heat. The place appeared deserted. Then he spotted two women strolling across the compound. Both were dressed in the traditional Somali direh, one a dull red, the other black. He caught a glimpse of their brightly patterned petticoats billowing beneath their tent-like dresses. A lock of golden hair fell over the forehead of the one in red. She cast him a curious glance before turning her head away to say something to her companion.

Najib spotted the women. "Stay here." He walked around the far end of the berm and disappeared into the crumbling entrance of a tunnel.

Bashir noted the disapproval in Najib's voice but ignored him. He finished off his second bottle of water, watching the two women until they ducked into a hut. The woman in red struck a chord in his mind. He searched his memory. She resembled the young woman wearing the fur coat he'd encountered in the GUM.

He shook off the image, found a discarded crate to settle on, and surveyed the ground around him. The debris and scattering of shovels and picks strewn about the area was a dead giveaway. Someone was tunneling. He wasn't impressed with whomever was in charge.

Najib reappeared. "Follow me."

Bashir had to crouch to get through the narrow entrance, but after going a few meters he could almost stand upright. The tunnel zigzagged downward through the soft rock, a prudent measure that offered some degree of blast protection.

Bashir's heart pounded. His palms were moist. He knew tunnels. A laser guided five-hundred pound bomb would easily collapse the tunnel, burying alive anyone unfortunate enough to be caught inside—the death of a coward.

A gasoline-powered generator thrummed in the distance. The smell of exhaust tinged the cool air. The ventilation appeared adequate. A single strand of bare light bulbs dangling from the right side of the ceiling offered him a glimpse of several side rooms. These contained drums of fuel, munitions, food and water. And a sleeping chamber. He doubted he would be invited to stay, but if he were, he'd decline. He'd had enough of caves.

The tunnel ended in a large room measuring four by five meters. A wooden ladder leaned against the far wall, presumably leading to an escape hole. In the center of the space stood a solitary table with a laptop computer and several chairs, one of which was occupied.

"The Chechen," Najib announced.

"You may leave," the seated man replied. He continued to write in a ledger, not bothering to acknowledge his visitor.

Bashir suppressed a smile, amused by the power play.

The man set down his pen. "So, you wish to join us, Dhi'b." He adjusted the angle of the pen to form an unconscious barrier. "That is not your given name of course."

Bashir noted the man's right hand slide under the table, presumably reaching for a weapon. "It is what I go by."

"I could have you killed."

Bashir held his gaze. "Yes."

"You are not afraid to die?"

"I did not say that." Bashir saw the man's reaction reflected in his eyes.

The man waved Bashir to a chair and handed him a bottle of water. "I am Abdul Aleem."

"We heard of you in Afghanistan," Bashir said. He noted the hint of a smile on Aleem's face. The lie had its desired effect.

"What of Afghanistan?"

"There is little to tell. We lost many mujahedeen in the struggle against the infidels."

"You came from Karachi. Why were you there?"

Bashir considered his answer. How much did Aleem know? "My mission requires I fade from sight."

Aleem's eyes traveled to Bashir's duffle. "Is there something you wish to share with me?"

"No."

Aleem stiffened. "If you are requesting sanctuary, it would be wise to tell me. What is your mission?"

"We must all do our part." Bashir changed the topic. "I understand the fighters of Harakat al-Shabaab al-Mujahida have struck a blow against the Kenyans."

"They deserved to taste the bitterness of death."

"As must all infidels," Bashir answered.

"So, you have heard that I will re-establish the Sultante of the Ajuran Empire." Aleem said. He didn't wait for Bashir to respond. "I will be the father of the Somalis and rule from our ancient capital in Taleh."

Bashir knew nothing about Taleh or the Sultan of Ajuran. He told another lie. "I have heard of the Ajuran Empire."

"And I will have my revenge on the British, the brothers of apes and pigs who tried to bury the Somalis two centuries ago."

Bashir found something in that statement he could at least agree with—even if their motives differed. The British, like the French and the Americans, were complicit in permitting the atrocities in his own country. His plan to detonate a third device in London had been thwarted in Neum and the material for the fourth device was on the *Articus*, but he still had enough material for a fifth bomb. He chose not to divulge any of this to Aleem. "But you survived."

"My family survived," Aleem said. "We survived through hundreds of years. I have traced my ancestry to the ancients who ruled this land. I will smash under my thumb the usurpers in Mogadishu who dare to oppose me."

"And the Americans?"

"I wait for the Americans like the desert thirsts for the rain. My mujahedeen long to drink of their blood."

The sheer audacity of those pronouncements astounded him. Aleem was either delusional, a malignant narcissist, or a psychopath. He decided he was probably a mix of all three. He had known such men. He pushed back his chair. "I have taken too much of your time."

Aleem tightened his lips, fixing Bashir with a malignant look. "You will stay with Qasif, an American. His friend lost his way and was martyred. Perhaps the young Qasif will learn the discipline required of a mujahedeen from you."

Bashir was left at a loss on how to respond to this latest twist. "There is much I can teach him."

"You—" Aleem stopped and looked over Bashir's shoulder at someone who'd entered the room.

"Pardon, you are busy," the newcomer said. "I will return."

"No, stay," Aleem ordered. He gave a dismissive wave at Bashir. "We are done here."

Bashir rose and moved past the new arrival. Their eyes met as he passed. The man's face suggested he was Iranian, as did his accent. He also looked vaguely familiar. Bashir made his way back through the claustrophobic tunnel into the twilight. With no clear idea where he was to go, he climbed to the top of the berm. He needed to clear his mind and review his options. Remaining at this caustic place was not one of them. *Perhaps this American, Qasif, might provide something of use?*

The sound of voices coming from the tunnel entrance caught his attention. He recognized them. Aleem and the Iranian. He only caught snippets of their conversation and strained to hear more. They were talking about a shipment of weapons and the *Articus*.

Bashir understood something of the shifting alliances in Africa. The various factions in Somalia were struggling to determine with whom to side, either remaining with al-Qaeda or switching their allegiance to ISIS. *Was Aleem being courted by the Iranians?*

The Iranian stepped around the corner of the berm. He spoke into a satellite phone. Bashir pressed his back into the berm, blending in with the rubble. He closed his eyes, concentrating on the conversation. The man spoke in Farsi, a language he didn't understand. What the Iranian said was lost except for one word—Dhi'b. Then he heard his real name. The Iranian completed his call and disappeared into the tunnel.

How did he know my real name and why was he talking about me? Who was he talking to? Someone in Tehran?

Stunned, he worked his way down the incline and walked toward the mud-brick huts. *How much did they know?* One thing was clear. His stay here would be days, not weeks. He had to devise a plan to escape before he was killed.

A figure appeared out of the shadows. "I am Qasif. I was told to find you."

Bashir took measure of the gaunt, hollow-eyed fighter standing before him. He recognized the far-away look, the flat voice. "I am Dhi'b. We have much to talk about."

Chapter Twenty-Six

NATIONAL COUNTERTERRORISM CENTER
McLEAN, VIRGINIA
TUESDAY 20 JANUARY

"You've got a visitor."

Nick set his yellow highlighter down and turned toward the sound of Strickland's voice. "Good mor—" The rest of his greeting stuck in his throat. Standing behind his boss was the CIA rep from his committee, Taylor Ferguson.

Strickland stepped into the room so his voice wouldn't carry into the hall. "We have a situation."

Nick twisted to turn off his monitor while keeping one eye on Ferguson. He wasn't about to let him see his work and he had a pretty good idea of what 'the situation' entailed. His conversation in Paris with Lyle had been leaked. Ferguson came here to explain. "What's going on?"

"Tehran," Strickland replied.

The one-word answer caught Nick completely off guard. He'd been in the midst of analyzing a report from his contact in Treasury's Directorate for Terrorism and Finance Intelligence, Mark Arita. The report confirmed the link between al-

Khultyer, Meycek Exports, and the NBG, but Arita had also come across something else in his forensic investigation. There appeared to be another party involved.

Nick suspected Grekov was that party. He'd been going over Arita's report looking for something to confirm his suspicion, but after fifteen minutes, he'd seen nothing to confirm her involvement. His response to Strickland's pronouncement escaped before he considered how it would sound. "What do the Iranians have to do with this?"

Strickland appeared irritated by Nick's use of "this."

Nick realized his response didn't fit as soon as it left his mouth. His stream of consciousness had gotten him in trouble again. He'd vocalized only part of his thought process, a recurring problem of his and a continuing source of tension between the two of them. His boss had no idea he was thinking about Grekov's involvement with al-Khultyer's support network.

Strickland stepped to one side to expose his tight-lipped guest. "I'll leave that to Mr. Ferguson to explain."

"Are you staying?" Nick asked.

Strickland stepped toward the hallway. "No, I've got to explain this mess to the Director."

Nick watched his boss disappear. *Mess? What mess?* "Okay… I've got it." He motioned to Ferguson. "Could you get the door?"

Nick waited until the latch clicked shut. Ferguson had him at a complete disadvantage. He needed to level the playing field. "This about Paris?"

"In part."

"What haven't I been told?"

"Grekov's in Tehran."

Ferguson's reply left him reeling. This was no admission of maleficence. *What the hell was going on?* He could think of only one explanation. "There's a link between the Iranians and al-Khultyer?"

"That's the angle we're working."

"What's she doing?" Nick asked, wondering about the 'we' piece.

"It's complicated."

"Try me."

Nick saw the flash of anger in Ferguson's eyes. The CIA agent caught whatever he planned to say, then collected himself. "Did you know al-Khultyer is in Somalia?"

Nick tried to mask his surprise. "No."

"That's what we thought."

"We? Who's we?"

"Doesn't matter."

"It sure as hell does. Why should I trust you after what I learned in Paris?" The tone in Nick's voice reflected his mix of anger, frustration, and fatigue. Ferguson's answer didn't help.

"If I were you, I wouldn't."

"Why did you guys think this damn plan of yours would even work?"

"We miscalculated," Ferguson replied.

"No kidding."

"So what are we going to do?"

Nick stared at the CIA agent. He'd used "we" again. "Care to explain what happened?"

"Just over a year ago, a deep source within the FSB said we'd be able to turn Grekov. We were led to believe she held no love for Shrevnenko and wanted him deposed."

"Makes sense. Her family was part of the old aristocracy."

"The same family that owns Novoroosiyk Business Group," Ferguson added.

"Where does al-Khultyer fit?"

"She recruited him."

"He's murdered scores and damned near killed Dianne Stuart."

"True enough but this is where things get interesting.

What would you say if I told you the president signed off on a black op, code-named Blue Vector. Authorized us to work with Grekov."

"Shit."

"That pretty well summarizes what we thought after al-Khultyer targeted the GUM instead of the military installation we'd authorized."

Nick nodded. Ferguson's disclosures enabled him to connect the dots. No wonder Grekov tried to protect al-Khultyer, she was covering her own ass. *But what is she doing in Iran? What is the connection between the NBG and the Iranians?* Rather than voice these questions he said, "You've lost containment."

"It's Grekov. We don't know what she's doing."

"I do," Nick said. He reached for his secure phone and punched in a number.

"Mark? Nick... We secure? ... Good. You got a minute?... I've got your forensic report... Yeah, I've got some questions... Before we go any further, I want you to know Taylor Ferguson's with me... the CIA rep from our committee... Yeah, 'interesting' is one word for it. Is it okay to put you on speaker?"

Arita's disembodied voice came over the speaker. "What's up?"

"We're chasing down a lead in Tehran. Could you fill us in with what you have on the Iranian business owners of the office building you guys just seized?"

"The one in Manhattan? Ajman Corporation?"

"That's the one."

"It's a shell corporation masking the operations of Bank Shalmal. Shalmal is a front company for the Iranian government. Our indictment states Ajman is one of several companies using bank accounts with aliases that Shalmal taps to launder funds linked to Iran's nuclear weapons program, their Revolutionary Guards Corps, and its Quds Force. One of the transnationals they've used is the Novoroosiyk Business Group. This is all in the report."

"Yes, I know," Nick said. "In your research, did you come across the name Aleksandra Grekov?"

"Your FSB contact? She's involved?"

Ferguson interrupted. "Mark, this is Taylor. Grekov's in Tehran. We believe she's talking to a senior general in their Quds Force."

"What about?"

"We're not sure, but her family owns NBG," Nick said.

"Damn, I didn't make the connection," Arita responded.

"The other piece you don't have is she was one of our operatives," Ferguson said.

Arita's voice rose. "What do you mean, 'Was?'"

"We've lost containment," Ferguson repled. "She's…"

Nick leaned forward to say something, but Ferguson pushed the triangular desk phone out of Nick's reach.

"She ran al-Khultyer," Ferguson continued, "but he went rogue. We believe she heard that Iranian assets in Karachi were trying to obtain his nuclear material."

"Why would they do that? They can get those damned pellets in their own country," Arita said.

"Yes, they could. But if they used al-Khultyer's pellets in a RDD—"

"A what?" Arita interrupted.

"Radiation Dispersal Device," Ferguson explained. "And if the Iranians passed those pellets on to one of their proxies for use in a dirty bomb, we'd trace the radioactive material back to al-Khultyer, not them."

"Good, God," Nick said, "That's the key. She's trying to stop them just like…"

Ferguson slashed his left index finger across his throat indicating Nick should stop. "Thanks, Mark," he said,, reaching across Nick's desk for the button to end the call. "We have what we need."

"Why the hell did you do that?" Nick demanded. "I wasn't done."

"Because we have what we need, my friend. You made the connection. Now, what her colleagues in the FSB will make of all of this remains to be seen."

"I'm not your friend."

Ferguson smiled. "Yet."

Nick pushed back from his desk. "Are we done here?"

"No, I have a few more things for your meeting at the Oval Office tomorrow."

"How'd you know about that?"

"Suffice it to say, it's my business to know what you're doing."

The smug look on Ferguson's face set Nick off. He was being played. "You son of a bi—"

"Settle down," Ferguson said. "You really do need to develop a thicker skin if you're going to be in this business. Besides, I'm about to help you."

"How?"

"I'm going to tell you exactly where to find al-Khultyer."

Chapter Twenty-Seven

THE OVAL OFFICE
WASHINGTON, D.C.
WEDNESDAY 21 JANUARY

"The president is ready to see you now."

Nick pushed down his coat sleeve covering his watch. He made a pretense of adjusting his tie, embarrassed he'd been caught checking the time. His nerves were completely frayed. He looked at Stuart's Executive Secretary. She'd introduced herself simply as, MaryAllus, when she seated him in the small alcove just outside her office.

She gave him a reassuring smile. "You'll do fine."

He pushed himself out of the chair and returned her smile with a weak one of his own. He took a deep breath and followed her into the Oval Office.

"Mr. Parkos, sir."

Stuart looked up from his desk. "Thank you, MaryAllus."

Nick's eyes swept around the room. Was he really standing in the Oval Office about to have a chat with the president? He took a step, then froze unable to grasp this new reality. Everything was gold. Gold- and-beige-striped wallpaper, wheat-toned carpet, light-mustard colored fabrics. The colors were calming. He recognized Dan Lantis, the only other person in the room.

Lantis stood and offered his hand. "Good to see you again, Nick." He motioned to the other sofa. "Please have a seat."

Nick settled onto one of a pair of sofas facing a marble-topped coffee table. Everything else was a blur.

"Good tie," Stuart opened. "Scarlet and Gray. You know I'm a Buckeye?"

Nick adjusted the pillow angled at his side so he could face the president. "Yes, sir. My daughter gave it to me for Christmas."

"What's her name?"

"Emma."

"Well, tell Emma she has good taste."

"I will, sir. Thank you."

Stuart flipped open a black leather-bound notebook and uncapped his fountain pen, signaling it was time to get to down to business. "I understand you've had a busy couple of days."

Nick wondered if Stuart knew what he'd been doing. He looked at Lantis who merely nodded. He presumed that meant he needed to say something. "Yes, sir."

Silence. He looked at Lantis again.

"Why don't you start with telling us what you have on al-Khultyer," Lantis said.

"Our latest—"

Nick stopped as the door across the room opened a crack. Justin Brown, poked his head through the opening.

"Come on in, Justin," Stuart said. "We're just getting start-ed." To Nick he said, "I believe you know the NSA?"

Nick started to stand, but Lantis waved him back down as Brown took a seat. "Yes, sir. We met in Paris."

"Good. You were about to say?"

"al-Khultyer's in Somalia."

"How solid is your information?" Brown asked.

"We have visual confirmation. He was spotted three days ago in Barawa..." Nick noticed Lantis cock his head. "It's a small coastal city north of the Kenyan border."

Lantis leaned forward. "How'd you get his picture?"

"Are you familiar with operation Celestial Balance and the Cardinal Device?" Nick replied.

"No."

Nick looked at Stuart.

"It's okay," he said.

"Celestial Balance is the name of a surveillance program. The Cardinal Device is a high-tech camera that's been placed in cases designed to look like a cement block, a rock, even a tree trunk. A SEAL team installed one of the devices in a seawall in Barawa this past November, one of twelve they placed along the Somali coast. Al-Khultyer was added to Poison Scepter, the southern target watch list. Defense used their facial recognition software to match his picture with one they have in their Biometrical Watch List."

"What's he doing?" Brown asked.

"I can't say with certainty, but—"

Stuart set his pen down. "A couple weeks ago, some fishermen stumbled across one of the Cardinal devices on an island 350 kilometers south of Barawa. Then I learned this morning the Iranians are involved. The system's compromised. I want to know if there's a connection."

Crap. Nick wanted to ask who told the president about Tehran, but managed to hold his tongue. Probably the DNI. The evidence for any Iranian involvement with al-Khultyer was circumstantial at best. "I believe the link is tangential, sir."

Brown cocked an eyebrow at Stuart. "Tangential?"

"After al-Khultyer disappeared, we picked up his track in Karachi. Several pallets of beets—"

Lantis scrunched up his forehead. "Beets?"

"It's how he smuggled the fuel pellets out of Russian. He

put them in beet cans. The pallets were offloaded from a ship in Istanbul and transported to Karachi. He went there to retrieve them."

"And you have information that suggests Iranian agents made a play to obtain this material?" Brown said.

"Yes, sir."

"Were they successful?" Stuart asked.

"I can't say for certain. The CIA believes they were," Nick replied.

"What are you sure of?" Brown asked.

"We have intercepts of several conversations that confirm information obtained by HUMINT in Karachi. One was a call made by an Iranian agent from a terrorist camp in Somalia to Tehran. In it, the speakers talk about beet cans and a man named Dhi'b."

Brown's forehead wrinkled.

"Dhi'b is Arabic for wolf," Nick clarified. "Based on the context of the conversation, I believe that person is al-Khultyer."

"Where's your link?" Brown asked.

"We've been monitoring the internet activity of a person using the handle, Charal."

"And?"

"Charal is the handle of my Russian contact in the FSB, Aleksandra Grekov."

Brown looked puzzled. "Where does she fit?"

"Grekov's in Tehran," Nick said. "She met with a senior general in the Quds Force."

"Why?"

Nick spent the next several minutes explaining the connection between al-Khultyer and Grekov. He then provided the information Mark Arita had on the Iranians, the NBG, and al-Khultyer.

Stuart stiffened when Nick touched on the bombing of the GUM and how the CIA had lost containment of their operation. Nick realized his mistake. "The Iranians found out about the pellets and Grekov went there to stop their operation."

"Back up a minute," Brown said. "Why would the Iranians go to all the trouble?"

"Our operating premise is they'd give them to one of their proxies to construct a dirty bomb. If one were detonated, we'd trace the radioactive material back to al-Khultyer, not Tehran. There's no other plausible explanation."

"Have you been in contact with her?" Stuart asked.

"No, sir. Not since Neum."

Nick glanced at Brown. The NSA looked exasperated.

Lantis gave a shake of his head. "So we don't know what happened?"

Damn. Nick realized his circuitous thought pattern had gotten him in trouble again. He hadn't been able to piece together his findings in a way Stuart and the others could understand. He'd lost them, but apologizing would be a mistake. "Let me go back to what happened in Karachi."

"Please," Brown said.

"A member of ISI, the Pakistani Directorate of Interservices Intelligence, informed one of our agents that the Iranians were asking about the pellets. When our source asked the Pakistani to provide specifics, he would only say that several pallets of material were loaded onto the cargo ship MV *Articus*. When pressed, he said the ship carried a clandestine shipment of small arms, ammunition, and explosives."

Stuart nodded. "Knowing the Iranian's track record, that ship could be going anywhere. What more do you have?"

"It was purchased by a broker representing the Amjan Corporation—a company fronting for the Revolutionary Guards Force. The ship used to be registered under a Marshall Islands flag of convenience, but there's no documentation that it's been re-flagged."

"That's odd. I'd think the Iranians would use a second party to mask their ownership," Brown said.

"It's scheduled for demolition," Nick said. "The last information we have is its headed for a ship graveyard in Mauritania."

"It's left Karachi?" Brown asked.

"Four days ago."

Stuart closed his notebook and rapped a staccato on its cover with his fingers. "This ship could simply vanish."

"Yes, sir."

Stuart nodded. "Are we tracking it?"

Nick couldn't answer with certainty. "The Navy may be, but ..."

"Find out." Stuart punched the button of his intercom. "MaryAllus, could you track down Bryce Gilmore and Admiral Lawaon? I need to speak with them." To Nick he said, "You're flying to McDill this afternoon. I want you to talk with General Iverson's people at SOCOM. Give me a plan to neutralize that ship and take out al-Khultyer."

Nick could only nod.

Stuart turned to Brown. "Parkos is going to need someone to run interference. Call Captain Rohrbaugh and tell him to pack his bags."

Nick thought that was a really good idea.

Chapter Twenty-Eight

BARAWA
FEDERAL REPUBLIC OF SOMALIA
THURSDAY 22 JANUARY

Bashir looked out the window of their four-wheel drive Toyota as they bounced their dusty way down the sloping hill toward Barawa. The dark-blue waters of the Indian Ocean sparkled in the distance just beyond the white-washed buildings of the town. His thoughts were on the young woman with the blond hair and red direh. He'd asked Qasif about her. He'd said her name was Maryam and she and her companion, Halima, were Canadians. Like him, they'd come to Somalia to seek martyrdom, to fight the Kuffar—the disbelievers.

The Toyota dropped into a large pothole with a loud thump, bouncing him out of his seat. He tightened his arm around the canvas haversack on the seat beside him to keep it from falling on the floor. The haversack contained his beet cans. Someone, likely the Iranian, had pulled them from their hiding place on his second day. He would not make the mistake of leaving them unattended again.

Today marked his fourth day in Aleem's compound. Four days too long. His time hadn't been wasted, though. He quizzed the youth, Qasif, on all manner of things pertaining to Aleem's organization and what he knew of his plans. The information he gleaned convinced him that he must leave. The night before, Qasif had provided him with an idea on just how.

He focused on the fishing dhows dotting the harbor. A number of them were gliding past the fortress-like buildings of the old town and the stone lighthouse toward open water. One of the few boats remaining at anchor caught his eye.

The vessel, larger than the others, had a broad white stripe streaked with rust running along the full length of its black hull. The ship's design was typical for a Somali fishing boat: sharp up-thrust bow and forward raked mast. Another tripod mast topped with a marine radar towered over the aft deckhouse. Unlike the other boats, a dull-white canvas tarp obscured the vessel's deck.

Qasif told him the ship still made forays to capture and hold for ransom any merchant ship not accompanied by an armed escort. Qasif had also given him the name of the vessel's owner, Abdi Kareem Jawari. Bashir had to find this man.

He cast a sideways glance at Najib. He was certain Najib had orders from Aleem to not let him out of his sight, that Dhi'b could not be trusted. In this, Aleem was correct.

"Stop."

"But—"

"I will walk the rest of the way." Bashir grabbed the door handle. "Pull over."

Najib hesitated, not sure what to do. He had his orders. The foreign fighter must not be left alone. When Bashir opened the door, Najib compromised. "Qasif will go with you."

Bashir jerked his head toward the youth, laughing. "What? This child is to protect me?"

"You would do well to have me as your escort," Qasif said. "You can't speak a word of Somali. How do you expect to find—"

Bashir cut off the youth. "Come then, my little wolf. We shall see what you will do to keep me safe." He grabbed his haversack and jumped out. He left the door ajar and strode down the hill.

Qasif grabbed his rifle, slid across the seat, and scrambled after him. When he caught up, he asked, "Why did you call me your little wolf?"

"My name is Dhi'b, yes?"

"It means, Wolf."

"The wolf is the symbol of my country," Bashir said. "I have decided to call you Sirhaan, little wolf. Like the wolf, you have shown the strength and tenacity to survive this place."

They walked on in silence, weaving their way through a cluster of thatched-roofed, mud-wall houses. A cane fence around one home held a small herd of bleating goats. They passed a young boy sitting on his haunches watching several more goats grazing on the tuffs of parched-brown grass covering the hillside.

"You decided. Why?" Qasif asked.

The young American's brashness amused him. He'd only known one other American, a fellow fighter in Afghanistan. He wondered if they were all this way. "I have decided to trust you."

Qasif scoffed. "Seriously. You have decided to 'trust' me? Why should I trust you?"

"Because loyalties can never be certain in these times. You need to leave this place as much as I."

Qasif didn't answer. Bashir knew he'd hit a cord. "Take for example, the Iranian."

"Ahmad Farhaadi?"

"Yes, he is an agent for MOIS." Bashir said.

"What is that?"

"Iran's Ministry of Intelligence and Security.

"It makes sense," Qasif said. "They want to have a network and foster their intelligence sources."

"Indeed, but why so much interest in me?" Bashir asked.

"Beats me."

"Because I possess something they want," Bashir answered. "And that is why we must leave."

"We?"

"Aleem doesn't trust you. Not any more than he did your friend, Mahmoud."

Qasif grabbed Bashir's sleeve pulling him to a stop. "How do you know about Mahmoud?"

"I listen and I observe. That is how I survive." Bashir jerked his arm free and his voice hardened. "You would do well to do the same. If not, you will share the same fate as your friend, Mahmoud... to be shot and left to rot in the sun. Aleem values your life no more than that of a cockroach. Now, let us find this man, Jawari."

"He will be near the bazaar," Qasif said as he made for the road paralleling the beach.

Bashir spotted the Toyota near the breakwater where he'd come ashore earlier in the week. Najib stood on the far side of the vehicle talking to several men, gesturing toward the road and then the slope. He dropped down to one knee. "Hold."

Qasif crouched beside him, swiveling his head looking for danger. He unslung his rifle. "What is it?"

"We need to lose Najib. See him? ... No, over there. We'll circle around."

They backtracked around the goat pen and made their way to the far side of the town before turning down a sandy street. Bashir stepped behind one of the buttresses supporting a crumbling wall to let a two-wheeled donkey cart pass. Qasif sidestepped the cart and joined him.

Bashir surveyed the length of the street. A number of unarmed men crisscrossed the open area. Several others, dressed in the traditional white robe of the region, strode by, intent on joining a group bunched together further down the street.

"This way. The Iman will know where to find Jawari." Qasif pointed to another cluster of men. They were gathered around a man sitting in the shade of a date palm. The man's prayer hat, a koofiyad, identified him as an elder.

They had covered half the distance to the Iman when Bashir noted several of the men turn. One disappeared into a narrow doorway. The other studied Bashir before joining his companion.

The street was quiet. A sense of danger permeated the air. Bashir wondered if the kid felt it.

Qasif slowed and handed his rifle to Bashir. "You should wait."

Bashir swept his eyes across the second-story windows of the buildings lining either side of the street. He didn't see anything, but he knew they watched. He answered. "I will come if something goes wrong."

He leaned against a low wall, pulled out a piece of flat bread from his haversack, tore off a piece and chewed on it while Qasif paid his respects to the Iman.

The two spoke for some time before Qasif touched his heart, bowed, and took several steps back. He returned to Bashir with another man wearing a plaid wrap-around macawiis and a white-cotton shirt favored by the local fishermen.

"This is one of Jawari's men," Qasid said. "He will show us the way."

Bashir followed them to the end of the street where they turned into a narrow passageway between the cramped buildings leading to the waterfront. They emerged from the tunnel-like passage onto the road fronting the bay. Bashir blinked at the bright light reflecting off the water. A skiff, laden to the gunwales with a mishmash of food, crates, and fishing gear was being pushed off the beach. Another skiff, empty, had just moved away from the side of the pirate mother ship, making for shore.

"Here."

Bashir turned to see his guide pointing to a storefront. Nothing identified what lay beyond the door.

"Jawari will see you now."

Bashir followed the man into the building. The room reeked of cigar smoke and the fetid odor of unwashed men. His eyes readjusted to the dark. The far wall featured a mural of a solitary fish painted over a peeling background of faded blue paint. A woven reed mat covered the dirt floor. A table pushed into one corner was piled high with small bundles of khat. In the other corner he saw the muzzle of a high caliber weapon poking out beneath a blanket. Bashir recognized the weapon—a Russian 12.7mm heavy machine gun.

Bashir knew Aleem felt that Jawari posed a threat to his leadership and had tried to kill him. That would explain the machine gun. He knew with certainty other weapons were hidden on the street ready to be manned at a moment's notice.

He studied the three men seated in the room. The one in the middle sat on a white molded-plastic armchair. The remnant of a cigar hung from the corner of the man's mouth, his feet splayed out over the mat in a pose of nonchalance. He removed the cigar and pointed it at Bashir. "You come to me. Why is that?"

"To discuss business."

Jawari studied Bashir's face for a moment before waving one of his men out of his chair. He pointed to it with his cigar butt, indicating Bashir should sit. He looked at the haversack. "What do you have that would interest me?"

Bashir ignored the implicit question and took his seat. "I need passage to Tanzania or Mozambique."

"That does not interest me."

"No, but the information I possess should."

"What information?"

"A ship carrying arms to Aleem will be nearing the coast in three days."

Jawari pulled himself upright. "How do you know this?"

"I was in Karachi. A friend made inquiries."

"And the name of this ship?"

"The *Articus*."

Jawari said something into the ear of the man seated to his right, who left the room. He turned back to Bashir. "Perhaps you would like some tea?"

The question didn't require an answer. The standing man disappeared and returned with a black ceramic pot and matching cups. Jawari poured. "These are interesting times. One must be prepared for all eventualities."

Bashir accepted some sweet milk and sugar and said 'Thank you' in the only Somali word he knew. "*Mahadsanid*."

Jawari prepared his own tea, raising it to his mouth. "You have found our country interesting?"

"Yes, what little I have seen of it."

The two continued their polite exchange until the first man returned and whispered his message to Jawari. Jawari gave several affirmative nods before facing Bashir. "One must never be too careful."

Bashir took a sip of tea. "Perhaps you would also be interested in the French yacht *Étoile de Mer?*"

Jawari set his cup on a rickety table. "What of this yacht?"

Bashir had done his research, unlike the pirates who would trust their luck to happen upon a vessel. "The *Étoile de Mer* will be leaving the Seychelles tomorrow. Two years ago, two million euros were paid for the release of her sister ship."

Jawari smiled. "I believe we can do business."

Chapter Twenty-Nine

CAMP LEMONNIER
DJIBOUTI
SATURDAY 24 JANUARY

"Djibouti tower, this is Marine Executive 1636. Over."

Dead air greeted Marine Major Brian Stahl, the pilot of the military-configured version of the Gulfstream passenger jet. He rolled his shoulders to loosen the knot in the base of his neck and ran his hand through his hair. They'd been in the air for over eighteen hours and he was beat. His only respite had been two brief stops to refuel at the Royal Air Force base in Lakenheath, southwest of London and Aviano Air Force base in northern Italy.

Stahl was a member of the Marine Air Support Detachment flying the C-20G aircraft out of Joint Base Andrews, the sprawling airbase sited on the outskirts of Washington. He'd gotten the call for a short-fused special air mission the day before. Two passengers, a navy captain assigned to the NSC and a civilian spook were to be transported to Camp Lemonnier, Djibouti.

A twin-engine Ethiopian Airlines turboprop making its

final approach to the airfield passed below Stahl's left wing. He looked at his fuel gage. *Unsat.* In another fifteen minutes, he'd be forced to land despite the lack of permission from the air traffic controller.

He sighed and left the base behind, flying over the blue waters of the Gulf of Aden. Suspended dust from gusting winds blowing off the desert blurred the shoreline as the east coast of Africa passed below. He tried contacting Air Traffic Control again. "Djibouti tower, this is Marine Executive 1636. Request landing clearance."

Nothing. Stahl twisted so he could see the passenger cabin through the open cockpit door. He addressed the man seated in the first row. "Captain?"

Mike Rohrbaugh looked away from the window. This was his second trip to Camp Lemonnier and he'd been studying the changes to the base. The Navy had completed a considerable amount of construction to improve the place since his last time here. The former outpost of the French Foreign Legion now spread over nearly six hundred sun-scorched acres. The single runway of Djibouti-Ambouli International Airport defined the northern edge of the joint French/U.S. facility.

A six-story control tower, the source of Stahl's growing anger, anchored the end of the terminal. He motioned for Rohrbaugh to approach.

Mike pushed out his chair and walked the few steps to the cockpit. "What do we have, Major?"

"Damn ATC isn't responding."

"Not much of a welcome."

"Par for the course. We have to use the locals. Besides being marginally competent, they don't care much for our Reaper and Predator ops. It's how they show their displeasure."

Mike was familiar with the horror stories. Things were different on his previous trip years before when his team had staged a mission to capture an al-Qaeda operative in Somalia. "How we set for fuel?"

"Enough for another forty minutes."

"That—"

Stahl turned down the volume of his radio to dampen the screaming voice on the other end: "What do you want? Don't you Americans know we are busy? Look over your wing. Can't you see..."

Mike shook his head and returned to his seat leaving Stahl to deal with the aggrieved ATC.

Nick leaned across the aisle from his second row seat. "What's up?"

"Pilot's catching some flak from the tower. We'll be on the ground soon."

"Hope so."

Mike caught a snippet of Stahl's conversation coming from the cockpit. "... runway zero-nine-left. We have a clear deck."

Mike settled into his seat, saying under his breath, "Be careful what you wish for, my friend."

"How's that?"

"Nothing," Mike answered as the jet banked to begin their approach.

Nick pulled off his earbuds and stuffed them into his canvas carry-on. He glanced out his window as the jet braked to a stop at the end of the runway. He couldn't believe he was in Djibouti. *Djibouti. This was completely nuts.* Three months ago, he'd been sitting in his office researching transnational crime organizations in the Balkans.

His eyes fell on a coil of concertina wire strung along the

side of the runway. Tied to the wire was a hand-painted sign: KILL THE DRONES, NOT INNOCENT PEOPLE.

Nick suppressed a wave of anger. *Well, within thirty-six hours, some not so innocent people are going to die.*

The jet completed a 180-degree turn and the sign slipped from view. The buildings of Naval Expeditionary Base, Djibouti passed by as the C-20 rolled down the taxiway paralleling the main runway. They came to a stop in front of a large hangar. Several Predator drones were parked inside surrounded by their maintenance crews. The whine of the Gulfstream's twin engines wound down and went silent.

"We'll take care of your bags, Captain," the crew chief said to Rohrbaugh. "You have some folks waiting for you on the apron."

Nick unclipped his seatbelt and followed Rohrbaugh down the steps to the tarmac. A three-man welcoming committee left the shade of the hangar and approached. Two wore desert cammies; the third, a sand-colored safari suit.

One of the two, with a pair of black eagles sewn on his collars, approached Rohrbaugh and gave his hand a vigorous shake. "Welcome back to Djibouti, Mike." He turned to Nick and shook his hand. "Bill D'Angelo. I'm the CO. I'll let these two introduce themselves."

The first stepped forward. "Commander Steve Dreyer, General Mattingly's 'Three.' Good to have you on board."

The third person hung back. Nick studied him: Close-cropped hair, floppy hat, *Under Armour* sunglasses, tight-lipped.

"Chuck Sanders, AFRICOM's Agency rep," the man said after a moment.

Nick extended his hand, then dropped it. Sanders appeared distracted. "Nick Parkos."

Nick looked at the others. If any of them noticed the interaction, they weren't letting on. The other piece he tried to figure out is what agency Sanders referred to. If he were NSA, he should have known about him. *Must be CIA.*

D'Angelo's voice intruded on Nick's thoughts. "Mike, the General wants to see you guys. Steve will take you to the task force compound. You can get settled in the Q later. I've got something else on my plate that can't wait."

Sanders hung back with Nick as Dreyer led off with Rohrbaugh at his side. In the distance, Nick could see a long double row of shipping containers topped with solar panels.

"CLU's, Container Living Units," Sanders volunteered. "They're primitive, but sure beat the hell out of the tents that used to be here. The entire housing and support area is called CLUville."

Nick spotted a sign. NEX CLU-mart and beneath it, Barbershop. He could hear the metallic sounds of clanking weight machines in the distance. *Navy Exchange, gym—all the comforts of home.* He picked up his pace to catch Rohrbaugh, his feet stirring up puffs of finely powered dust that coated his loafers and pants legs. Beads of sweat appeared on his forehead. *Man, I'm not dressed for this.*

Sims came to a halt in front of a windowless concrete structure, the SCIF.

Nick recognized the initials: Sensitive Compartmented Information Facility. He and Rohrbaugh were going to meet with the planning team. Getting settled in and grabbing something to eat could wait. They only had a few hours to finalize the joint operations to neutralize al-Khultyer and intercept the *Articus.*

A plaque mounted on the wall to the right of the door advertised the major command represented on the base: USAFRICOM—U.S. Africa Command, and below it, another: JTF-HOA—Joint Task Force-Horn of Africa.

Nick took a step to follow Rohrbaugh into the building, but stopped at the sound of Sanders's voice. "Parkos, a moment."

Nick turned to face the agent. The last time someone used those words was in Paris.

"We've got a problem."

Nick's jaw tightened. "We" again. *Why is it every time there's a problem* … He tried to get a read on Sanders. All he saw was his own reflection in the guy's sunglasses. "Will it impact the mission?"

"Possibly."

"If that's the case, I'll need to alert Captain Rohrbaugh."

"I've been instructed not to divulge this information to anyone but you."

"That's a non-starter," Nick said. He noted Sanders appear conflicted.

"What you choose to do is your own business."

"I'm listening."

"We've infiltrated an agent into Aleem's organization. Goes by the name, Mahmoud. We haven't been able to contact him. His last transmission was in early November. Worst case, he's been killed."

"Or tortured," Nick said.

"If he was interrogated …" Sanders stopped and cleared his throat.

Nick noticed Sanders tighten his lips, fighting for control. He obviously knew the agent. "Real name?"

Sanders took a deep breath. "Ali Abdulahi Hassan… We assigned him the code name, Butterfly, after the boxer Mohamed Ali's axoim: 'Float like a butterfly, sting like a bee.' The guy's tough…" Sanders paused to collect himself. "Our last visual was captured by the Cardinal device. You're familiar with the op?"

"Yes."

"Besides planting the device, the SEAL team left behind an encrypted communications system."

"Did he recover it?"

"We have no indication the system was ever activated."

"When was your last transmission?"

"A com check on the sixteenth."

"Was any information passed to indicate we knew about al-Khultyer?"

"No."

Nick wasn't convinced. "His cover was blown. Someone tipped them off."

"My guess is Aleem acted on his own. The guy's a psychopath."

Before Nick could rebut, Rohrbaugh called out from inside the building. "Hey, Parkos. We're waiting on you."

Nick yelled over his shoulder. "Be right there." He looked at Sanders. "We'll need a picture."

"You'll have one by this evening."

"Good." Nick took a step toward the door, then stopped. He turned to face Sanders. "If Hassan's there, we'll find him."

Sanders nodded. "There's another piece you need to know."

Nick braced himself. He mission could very well be compromised, there could be an American agent still alive in the compound, and now Sanders was going to spring something else on him. "What?"

"Ali said there was another American in the camp. A kid from Minneapolis. Goes by the name of Qasif."

Nick filed the information about the kid, not sure if he represented a threat. He needed to focus on the op to take down al-Khultyer. *And now, what to do about Hassan.*

"What's up?" Rohrbaugh asked.

"Things just got more complicated."

Chapter Thirty

GULF OF ADEN
SATURDAY 24 JANUARY

Bashir stood near the bow of Jawari's black-hulled dhow, his gaze fixed toward the east. The other ship was out there. Somewhere.

His thoughts were unsettled. The horizon dipped and rolled as the dhow plowed through the swells of the quartering sea. He likened the motion to the tumult raging in his mind.

Would they be intercepted by the Greek frigate, *Psara*, patrolling for pirates off the coast? Would they even be able to find the yacht? Would Qasif be able to return home without being caught by the Americans? Would his audacious plan even work?

Then there was Neum. Why did Grekov 'out' the American, this Parkos? What were her motives for telling him? Did he know too much about what she'd done? Nothing made sense.

Bashir frowned. There were too many variables to consider, too many things he couldn't control, too many chances for failure. He clenched his jaw, angered at himself. *Enough of this*.

His escape from Aleem's camp went as planned. Jawari's men waited at the river crossing as promised and they boarded the dhow as soon as they arrived in Barawa. He would have to trust them.

Bashir cast a sideways glance at Qasif. "You need to shave that off."

Qasif touched the remnants of his beard. "You want me to board the yacht?"

"No. Neither of us will. The risk is too great. Any pictures taken by the crew or a passenger will be sent to the DCRI."

"But the French know nothing of me," Qasif protested.

"Do you think it wise to make such a presumption?"

Qasif gave an indifferent shrug. "I guess not."

Bashir's hands tightened around the wooden rail. "This is not the time to behave like a petulant child." He glared at Qasif. "Do you understand?"

Qasif paused, then looked Bashir in the eyes. "Yes."

"Good. Now go."

With Qasif out of sight, Bashir calmed. He recognized his flare of anger reflected his own uncertainty. He only had himself to blame if his mission failed. He hadn't told the kid of his designs for the American, Parkos. Grekov warned him of the American agent during their botched rendezvous in Neum.

His plan was complicated, wrought with opportunity for failure. Was it even necessary to threaten Parkos's wife and child? He knew the answer. The American had to be stopped. And what better way to shatter a man's mind?

The horizon vanished as the dhow shuddered into a deep trough. A spray of cold water, thrown into the air by the impact, slapped his face. Dark storm clouds were rolling in, driven by an approaching gale. The French luxury cruise yacht, Ètoile de Mer, would soon encounter the same weather.

Bashir stood fast, maintaining his vigil.

ÉTOILE DE MER

The *Étoile de Mer* maintained a steady ten knots despite the deteriorating weather. The First Officer cast an anxious eye at the barometer. The barometric pressure continued to fall. He had a schedule to maintain. They could not afford to get stuck in the queue of ships waiting to pass through the Suez Canal. The approaching storm was going to be a problem.

The *Étoile de Mer* was underway for her next destination, the Italian port of Civitavecchia. She'd kept well clear of the Somali coast after departing the Seychelle Islands the day before, staying within the recognized shipping route seven hundred kilometers from the pirate den of Barawa.

Many of her two-hundred and twenty-four well-heeled passengers had gathered in the main lounge located at the stern. They downed flutes of champagne after indulging in another magnificent meal. Several couples wobbled around the dance floor. The more practical guests clustered around the white-enameled grand piano, chatting with the Captain and Chief Engineer.

All of them looked forward to their next port of call, a short drive from Rome. The ship was ablaze with lights reflecting the festive atmosphere and their collective *joie de vie*.

The *Étoile de Mer's* Captain shared their good humor. He hadn't received any mariner's warnings. They were far from the coast and he hadn't thought it necessary to post a security watch or dim his lights. They were also scheduled to rendezvous with the French frigate *Guépratte* in six hours.

PIRATE MOTHER SHIP

Bashir stumbled. He gripped the hatch combing to keep from falling off the ladder, waited for the dhow to complete its roll, then made his way up the remaining steps to the darkened bridge.

"The sea, she is lively tonight, yes?" the captain greeted him.

Bashir chose not to reply. He had no interest in the sea. "Have you found our target?"

The captain motioned for Bashir to approach. He stood to one side so Bashir could see the radarscope. A wedge of green fluorescent afterglow lagged behind the sweep line. But each time the line swept around the scope, two bright dots remained a moment before dimming out of existence.

"This dot is the *Étoile de Mer.*" The captain said pointing to the first blip. "This one, the Maersk Line container ship, *Ebba.* There are no others."

Bashir was impressed with the captain's navigation skills, but the information raised further concerns. "What is the radar's range?"

"Eighty kilometers."

"Does the container ship present a danger?"

"No, she is making fifteen knots. The sea state does not bother her," the Captain replied. "The Frenchman has slowed and changed course."

"Is that a problem?"

"He is trying to keep his guests comfortable. He decreased speed and pointed his bow into the waves. My men will benefit."

Bashir's anxiety prompted him to ask another question. "What of the Greek frigate? The *Psara?*"

"The Greeks are too far away to interfere."

"No others?"

"No."

If the Somali was irritated by all of his questions, Bashir

couldn't detect it in his responses. "And—" Bashir cut himself off. "Then I will prepare my package."

He made his way to the cramped cabin below. Qasif was curled in a corner, loudly retching in a bucket. He would be of no use, which Bashir thought just as well. He opened his duffle and pulled out a rucksack and the components of his device. He set the beet can with the uranium pellets to one side. The other, containing his passport, credit card, the last of his money, and his custom itinerary from *À Souhait* remained in the duffle.

He arranged the bomb's components on a small table and set to work. First, he tore off lengths of duct tape and secured four half-kilogram blocks of C4 explosive around the beet can. Next, he clipped off four lengths of detonator cord, each capped with a cylindrical booster charge. He took out his pocketknife, made a nick in the Mylar wrapping of the blocks. After inserting a charge in each of them, he attached the cords to a receiver and battery pack. Finally, he checked all the connections and secured them with more duct tape. The entire device measured twenty-six by twenty-four by twenty centimeters and weighed about twelve kilos—bulky, but small enough to be hidden on the cruise ship.

Bashir picked up a pair of Mercedes key fobs. One he would keep. The other he would give Qasif. The kid would be his backup in case something happened and he couldn't detonate the device himself. Juggling the fobs in his hand, he smiled and stuffed them in his pants pocket. He hefted the rucksack with the device secured inside and climbed up the narrow ladder to the deck. He waited a moment to allow his eyes to adjust to the dark, then made his way to the lee railing. He looked over the side.

The dhow's eighteen-foot open boat banged against the ship, pitching in the chop. Two Yamaha 40's idled on the boat's transom. A grappling hook rested on a coil of rope in the bow. Eight heavily armed pirates were crammed into the small vessel. Several draped belts of ammunition across their chests for their PK-74 machine gun. Another had a PRG-7 anti-tank launcher propped between his legs.

Bashir's eyes stopped on a pirate seated on the middle thwart. The man held a rusted two-liter can, bailing water over the side. Bashir was not pleased. The boat could easily swamp and sink. He wasn't concerned about the safety of the pirates. Their lives meant nothing to him. *But if his device was lost?* He hesitated, then lowered the rucksack to the outreached hands of one of the pirates.

The pirate flashed a white-toothed grin, giving Bashir an enthusiastic thumb's up. Then he yelled a command. The twin Yamaha outboards roared to life and the boat swung away from the ship, gaining speed. It raced into the night, slamming over the waves toward the *Étoile de Mer.* The captain spun the dhow's wheel, assuming a heading toward his next destination—an isolated beach north of the Tanzanian city of Dar es Salaam. The fate of those in the skiff was in their own hands. He had his orders from Jawari: If they were able to find their way back to the ship, good. If not, so be it.

Bashir noted the change in course. All was going according to plan. He remained at the rail until he could no longer hear the skiff's engines. There was nothing more to do. If everything went according to his plan, he and Qasif would soon be relaxing at the Ibo Island Lodge in Mozambique.

ÉTOILE de MER

"Sir?"

Étoile de Mer's First Officer turned to face the watch officer. "Yes, Ándre?"

"I have a contact at 341 degrees, 3.7 nautical miles."

The First Officer suppressed a yawn. He should have known better and resisted the advances of that femme fatale the night before. "Our satellite data indicates nothing in the area transmitting on the AIS except the container ship. We're picking up sea clutter."

"It's not clutter. The contact is closing on a steady bearing at twenty knots. Our course intersection is fourteen minutes."

"Then it's a fishing boat, the First Officer admitted. "Any vessel less than three hundred tons isn't required to have AIS."

"We know all about fishing boats, don't we? And twenty knots? What about the *Vie Aquatique?*"

The First Officer did indeed know of the company's three-masted sailing yacht. One of his friends was among the thirty crewmembers captured in these very waters. They'd been held for nearly two months before being released. "Okay, we'll play it safe. Change course to 30 degrees and ring up fifteen knots."

"Should we notify the Captain?"

"No need. We'll be clear of the contact within fifteen minutes."

The attack came just after ten o'clock. The captain's first hint of the coming nightmare was a piercing scream from one of the women. He spun. A flood of black-hooded pirates burst through the door leading from the lower deck. He yelled at his engineer. "They boarded from the jet ski ramp. Get down to the engine room and lock the doors."

A roar of automatic rifle fire from an AK-47 sent the passengers scattering like so many flushed quail. In the confusion, the Captain bolted from the room. He ran down the line of passenger cabins on the forth deck and up the forward stairs to the bridge. He grasped the door handle. Locked. He slammed his fists on the door, screaming a warning. His actions gave the First Officer just enough time to radio a distress call.

"Mayday, mayday, this is the French motor yacht, *Étoile de Mer*, call sign FIGV, AIS source 247. We have been boarded by pirates, I repeat, boarded by pirates."

He looked down to verify his position. "Our position is South 2 degrees, 17 minutes, 4.38 seconds; East 54, 40, 46.8. Heading 30 degrees true, speed 15 knots. Wind, 16 knots, 52 degrees northeast. We—"

The remainder of his call was cut off by the sound of gunstocks pounding on the bridge door. Bullets riddled the door, shattering the lock. The door burst open.

The First Officer dropped the microphone, staring at the barrel of a PK-74 machine gun. Three more pirates followed the first onto the bridge. One pushed the bloodied captain ahead of him, throwing him onto the deck. Another pointed his rifle at the crewmembers and herded them into a corner. The third approached the ship's control panel and took a seat.

The forth pirate, a rucksack slung on his back, surveyed the scene. "No one will die if you follow our instructions."

Chapter Thirty-One

SECRET COMPARTMENTED INFORMATION
FACILITY
CAMP LEMONNIER, DJIBOUTI
SATURDAY 24 JANUARY

Nick scanned the room from his vantage point in the right rear of the SCIF. He sensed the change.

Sanders' final slide, showing two photographs of his operative, Ali Abdulahi Hassan, lingered on the projection screen. On the left, Hassan stood grim faced, in tribal costume, with a heavy black beard and long unruly hair. On the right, a picture from better times. Smiling, dressed in a sports shirt, clean-shaven, with close-cropped hair.

Nick studied the contrasting pictures. He sensed the focus of the operation had shifted to a new reality—one that resonated with these warriors. These men were going in to save a life, not take one. They understood the chances of finding Hassan alive were minimal, but the assault force would find him and bring him home.

Nick considered another reality. The mission, designated Amber Dawn, had become considerably more dangerous.

The option of simply flattening the entire compound with an airstrike was off the table.

A picture of Aleem's compound replaced Sanders' slide. The picture amazed him. He'd been briefed on the U2, but he couldn't recall ever seeing what the plane could do. Seven different bands of visual and infrared imagery taken from the aircraft were blended to produce a picture that looked like a high definition 3D photograph.

An Army colonel stepped up to the podium to continue the mission confirmation brief. The patch on his left arm bearing an upright sword crossed by three diagonal lightning bolts identified him: Special Forces. He swept his arm toward the slide.

"Neutralizing Bashir al-Khultyer and his nuclear material remain the primary objective of this mission. Our secondary objective is to locate and extract Mr. Hassan, codename, 'Butterfly.'"

Nick noted the colonel didn't add the caveat to his statement about Butterfly. "If he's still alive."

"From our analysis of the surveillance photos, Butterfly is likely being detained in one of these mud huts near the far edge of the compound, here." The colonel pointed his laser designator to a scattering of huts surrounded by a low stone wall.

"We have reason to believe there's another American in the camp. We don't have anything on him except a name. Qasif. We'll have to presume he signed on to al-Shabaab. He is to be considered a hostile. Next slide."

A graphic overlay of the camp appeared. Nick was impressed. He'd heard of the automated tactical target graphic but had never seen one. The overlay showed the location and disposition of forces, structures, defensive positions, and significant geographic features. The colonel pointed out two Russian heavy machine guns he identified as a KPV and a Dushka. The Dushka was mounted in the bed of a Toyota pickup, the KPV emplaced above a cave entrance. Both presented a significant risk.

"Intel's updated their estimate of the number of fighters in the camp. Based on activity detected by yesterday's U2 mission and Butterfly's—"

Nick cocked his head. *Activity?* He began to raise his hand, then dropped it. The soldier was focused on the immediate threat. Made sense. He turned his attention back to the presentation.

"... reported the arrival of eleven fighters from Amniyat, al-Shabaab's intelligence branch. These folks were behind the slaughter of civilians following our raid in Barawa last November. The Kenyans have also provided intelligence that implicates Amniyat in the massacre of one hundred forty-seven students at Garissa University.

"That said, two pickups with approximately ten men on board left the camp at daybreak for Barawa. That leaves sixty-eight hostiles including two women."

The colonel moved on to the next topic in his Mission Tasking Packet.

Nick couldn't shake his sense of unease. Why had those ten left? There had to be more. *Could they be after al-Khultyer?* He looked across several empty seats at Rohrbaugh. The SEAL, like the others in the room, was focused on the presentation.

He caught a few of the colonel's words. "ESG-1, 31st MEU(SOC)." He was reviewing the assets available for the mission. Nick had learned enough military shorthand to translate these: Expeditionary Strike Group One and the 31st Marine Expeditionary Unit (Special Operations Capable). The names and location of the various units assigned to Amber Dawn were transposed on another slide. He caught the names of several units of ESG-1. The Expeditionary Strike Group was built around the big-deck amphibious ship *Bonhomme Richard,* LHD 6. The destroyer, USS *Truxtun,* DDG 103, and the fast attack submarine, USS *Tucson,* SSN 770 provided the muscle—tomahawk cruise missiles to destroy the camp if that became necessary.

Nick blocked out the colonel's voice. He needed to think. If al-Khultyer planned to escape, how would he do it? And where would he go? What unfinished business did he have?

Look for the unexplained—what others would dismiss. He began to construct a scenario based on al-Khultyer no longer being in the camp. He sorted through the possibilities. There were no airfields, crossing overland into neighboring Kenya would be very difficult ... *Of course, the harbor.*

He looked back to the slide. Someone's got to have surveillance shots. They could check to see if any dhows were missing. And the Navy? They're tracking the *Articus*. He didn't know if the Navy was using a P-8 patrol plane flying out of Diego Garcia or their Triton drone, or both.

Nick had no idea how broad an area the Navy's search pattern covered. Would it be large enough to monitor any fishing dhows coming out of Barawa? He thought about the Navy's aircraft. He doubted their patterns would include the coastline. *Damn.* Trying to re-task the aircraft would be impossible.

He shook his head. He was getting way out ahead of himself. Other than his hunch, there was no reason to believe al-Khultyer had managed to evade him again. He could try to anticipate and prepare for every contingency, but there were no certainties.

"Parkos?"

He turned toward Rohrbaugh. He didn't look pleased.

"Where's your head?"

Nick realized he looked distracted. Not good. Rohrbaugh must think I'm daydreaming. He didn't try to explain. He mouthed, "Okay" and turned his attention back to the brief. The colonel was presenting the order of battle.

"A platoon from B Company, Operational Detachment Alpha from the First Battalion, Fifth Special Forces Group, will be the initial assault group. They are part of our crisis response element and are currently in isolation at Arta Beach prepping for their mission. They will be inserted by an Air Force MC-130P Combat Shadow special mission aircraft and conduct a high altitude airdrop from ten thousand feet. They will free fall to four thousand, pull out, and deploy their high-glide parachutes. The teams will then form their stacks and maneuver to the drop zone. Once on the ground, they will rendezvous and proceed to their assigned objectives."

The colonel pointed to the mud huts. "An eight-man element will approach this area from the north. The second element will take out the Dushka and secure the LZ. The last element will neutralize the KPV and assume a blocking position on the rise behind the cave. They have five minutes to execute their mission before the main force sets down.

"Echo Company, Second Battalion Fourth Marines will stage on the *Bonhomme Richard*. They will embark on four V-22 Osprey from VMM-161. Fox Company is the designated reserve force. Two Super Cobra attack helicopters will ride shotgun. A 'Spooky' will be airborne and on-call if the situation warrants."

Spooky? Nick cast a questioning look at Rohrbaugh.

Rohrbaugh supplied the answer, "AC-130U gunship."

"The assault will take place at 0400 hours local. 2100 hours Washington time. A Global Hawk drone will provide the president and the NSC with a live feed. If there are no questions, that concludes my brief."

Nick made for the exit and saw Commander Dreyer pull Rohrbaugh off to one side. Rohrbaugh scanned the room, then motion for him to approach.

"What's up?" Nick asked, convinced he was going to get an ass chewing.

"Just a FYI," Rohrbaugh replied. "A French passenger ship was boarded by Somali pirates this morning."

"Anybody hurt?"

"No, but they scared the shit out of the passengers. Relieved them of their valuables before taking off," Dreyer said.

"Don't they usually hold them for ransom?"

"Usually," Dreyer answered. "They took a big risk for not much reward." He shrugged. "Hell, who knows with those guys."

"Is there a link to the *Articus*?" Nick asked.

"Unknown."

Dreyer and Rohrbaugh turned to leave. Conversation over.

Nick didn't believe in coincidences. "Mike, you got a sec?"

Chapter Thirty-Two

THE WHITE HOUSE
WASHINGTON, D.C.
SUNDAY 25 JANUARY

"How ya doin' boss?"

President Stuart looked up from his desk in the Oval Office. "I guess we'll know in a couple hours."

"Roger that," the Chairman of the Joint Chiefs said.

Stuart smiled. His relationship with Robert Lawson stretched back many years to when he was a nugget, the Navy term for a newly commissioned Ensign in the pilot training program. Lawson had been his flight instructor at Naval Air Station Pensacola. The Admiral was now his closest advisor. He could also count on him to share a good bottle of Scotch whisky at Camp David.

"I spoke with Jim Mattingly at AFRICOM before coming over," Lawson said. "The mission's on track."

Stuart nodded. "We've got a moment before we go downstairs. Have a seat. I want to run some thoughts by you."

"Sure thing." Lawson settled on the couch, trying to get a sense of Stuart's mood. "What's on your mind?"

"Iran and the *Articus*."

"How come I'm not surprised."

"Their duplicity never ceases to astound me." Stuart shuffled] through a stack of papers on his desk. "Here it is. Let me quote their UN rep: 'Iran denies any knowledge of an arms shipment to al-Shabaab in violation of UN prohibitions. These are baseless allegations and ridiculous fabrications.'"

"Well, we know better," Lawson said. "The intel from the Pakistanis is solid. That ship is carrying components for a WMD."

"Are we set?"

"We've detached the *Tucson* and transmitted the *Articus*' bearing, projected course, and speed. She'll intercept in a couple hours."

"Have we picked up transmissions from an AIS transponder?"

"Nothing."

"Is that unusual?" Stuart asked.

"Not really. There's any number of reasons for not receiving a broadcast—their transponder is down, the signal is not strong enough."

"Could they be broadcasting false information to mimic another vessel? I don't want us taking out the wrong ship."

"It's not without precedent. We caught the North Koreans trying that trick."

"How sure are you?"

"We've been tracking the *Articus* since it left Karachi and this morning. A P-8 conducted an over-flight a few hours ago. Another thing in our favor is they weren't in one of the normal shipping lanes."

"So for all intents, nobody knows that ship's out there?" Stuart turned to look out his window as if seeking affirmation for the decision he was about to make.

"Except the bad guys," Lawson said.

"I don't think it would do any good to go back channel

and confront the Iranians with what we know," Stuart said to the window. He spun his chair around. "They'll deny any knowledge of the ship."

"You can't make friends with a hornet. If we smack them, they'll get the message. If Tehran raises hell, then it'll be our turn to disavow any knowledge of what happened. Just another old ship running into trouble with a storm, lost a sea. That, or we'd say the ship must have been carrying a shipment of unstable munitions and the cargo spontaneously detonated."

"There's a storm in the IO?"

"Convenient, yes?"

"One final question," Stuart said. "Will you have another visual before the *Tucson* fires?"

"She's carrying the new Sea Robin vertical launch UAV. It's equipped with an electro-optical system and a repeater to detect an AIS. We can patch the data so you can personally authorize her to release weapons."

"No need. ComFifthFleet can do it."

"You want to proceed?"

"Yes. I just needed to clarify those few points. I've signed the Executive Order. Sheldon's greasing the skids."

"I'll notify Fifth Fleet."

Stuart paused. "This doesn't fit, but there's been another hijacking off Somalia. Bryce got a call from the French ambassador this afternoon. One of their cruise ships, the *Étoile de Mer,* managed to get off a distress call. Paris is pretty worked up."

"I hadn't heard. Do we need to re-route the *Truxtun?*"

"No need. Their ambassador said they'd handle it. They've got a frigate proceeding to the area."

"Must be the *Guépratte,*" Lawson said. "She's part of CTF-465. The Greek frigate HS *Psara,* and the German frigate *Rhienland-Pfalz* are also in the area."

Stuart looked over his notes, then pushed back from the desk. "Let's get downstairs."

Stuart paused at the door of the Situation Room. He suppressed a frown. Bodies packed the tiny space. The men had removed their jackets and loosened their ties. The women looked comfortable. A scattering of half-empty Styrofoam cups dotted the conference table between the computers. He surveyed the faces and concluded everyone had a legit reason to be there.

The first to see him, Richard Valardi, the Secretary of State, voiced his acknowledgment, "Mister President," and moved out of the way.

Stuart approached his spot at the head of the table and placed his hands on the back of his chair. He addressed the Secretary of Defense, Sheldon Payne. "We good to go, Sheldon?"

"General Mattingly's on secure with AFRICOM. He's confirmed the mission's on schedule." Payne gestured toward a large flat screen mounted on the far wall. "And the live feed is up."

Stuart looked at the Global Hawk's light-enhanced and thermal imaging of the camp. He had a ringside seat of the mission about to unfold in a few minutes. A scattering of structures and a pickup truck were visible in the quarter moon's light. He couldn't detect any activity. "Looks pretty quiet."

"Yes, sir." Lawson answered. He glanced at the wall clock. 2049. "The drop is scheduled for 2100. We'll have boots on the ground at 2110. Echo Company will touchdown at 2115.

Stuart nodded. "Provided there are no mishaps."

"Yes, sir."

Stuart poured himself a glass of water and started to pull out his chair. A voice stopped him.

"Mr. President?"

Stuart set the glass down. Payne sounded hesitant. Something was wrong.

Payne held out a red-hashed Top Secret folder. "CYBERCOM just sent this over." He looked at Lawson. "Bob, I don't believe you've seen this."

Stuart accepted the folder and looked at the single page.

"Tenth Fleet's detected a network intrusion," Payne confirmed as Stuart read. "Someone's trying to access AFRICOM's secure net."

"The Chinese again?" Stuart asked.

"Unknown. Considering our op, I'd place my money on the Iranians."

Stuart motioned to Bryce Gilmore. "Bryce, you need to hear this. Someone's tried to penetrate AFRICOM. Sorry, Sheldon. You were saying?"

"We've got a—"

"It's the Iranians," Gilmore said.

Payne pivoted to face the DNI. "What makes you so sure?"

"Their track record. It's a natural extension of Solvent Rain, their op we blocked last year. Hell, their Quds chief is on record for saying that we're a tempting target."

He also said his forces didn't want to get involved in acts of adventurism," Valardi said.

Gilmore shot Valardi an annoyed look. "You believe that?"

Valardi ignored him. "You're taking that statement to mean they're behind this? Don't you think that's a bit of a leap?"

"No. Just keeping things within context," Gilmore said. "They have an agent on the ground working with Aleem. He—"

Stuart wasn't pleased. He was already under enough stress

and didn't need to listen to these two squabbling. He cut Gilmore off. "We'll talk about this later." He addressed Payne. "Were they successful?"

"CYBERCOM's assessing the situation," Payne answered. "We've shut down the secure network and rerouted their coms."

Stuart turned to Gilmore. "Is there anything hard from NSA to collaborate Iran's culpability?"

"We've detected several suspect transmissions from Aleem's compound linked to the Iranian agent's Sat phone. We have to assume there's a network intrusion."

"I agree," Stuart said. "Bob, what's the risk?"

Lawson looked at his watch. 2053. He studied the live feed on the flat screen. He thought he saw a flash of light. He saw another. "What the…?"

Stuart knew Lawson well enough to read his body language. "Bob?"

Lawson continued to stare at the feed. He didn't answer. A shadowy form exited the cave complex and ran across the compound. Several more followed, moving toward the pickup truck. "We've got a problem. Dim the lights."

Stuart followed Lawson's finger. He saw the same thing and took several steps toward the flat screen. He echoed Lawson's command. "Someone dim the lights. Now." The wall clock read 2055. He faced Lawson.

Lawson didn't need to hear Stuart's question to provide the answer. "Someone's tipped them off. We've got to abort."

"Isn't it too late?"

"I hope not." Lawson grabbed the secure line to AFRICOM. "Jim? … No? Who is this? … Commander, do you see what I'm seeing on the feed? … We've got to recall. Those guys are jumping into a hot LZ. Get General Mattingly."

The time. 2059.

BARAWA

"Aw Jawari." The man used the honorific title for his leader. He whispered again. "Aw Jawari."

Jawari stirred in the darkened room. He rubbed his eyes and looked at the florescent dial of his watch. 3:59. "Yes?"

"I heard helicopters."

"Where?"

"To the east."

Jawari rolled off his sleeping mat and stepped into the empty street. Helicopters did not make the sound he heard. He pivoted, scanning the sky. He spotted them just as they passed out of sight to the west. Highlighted by the setting moon, he could make out the outlines of four aircraft. They looked like pictures of American V-22 Ospreys that he'd seen on the Internet. Marines. And they were on a heading that would take them over Haawa.

Jawari smiled. By tomorrow night, his own men will have captured the *Articus* and its cargo of weapons. Soon, there would be no Somali capable of challenging his rule. "Aleem has overplayed his hand. The Americans are about to eliminate him and his nest of vipers."

Chapter Thirty-Three

JOINT OPERATIONS CENTER
CAMP LEMONNIER DJIBOUTI
MONDAY 26 JANUARY

Commander Steve Dreyer's red bat phone clamored in AFRICOM's command center. He terminated his ship-to-shore satellite link with 2/4's op boss on the *Bonhomme Richard* and picked up the direct line to Washington.

"Commander Dreyer. How may I help you, sir? ... Yes, Admiral ... No sir." Prompted by Lawson's questions, he stared at the live feed from the drone. His hand tightened around the receiver. The situation developing on the ground was deteriorating. His eyes shifted to the digital clock on the screen: 0402.

"Yes, sir. I see them. Hold one." Dreyer covered the mouthpiece with his palm and yelled across the room to General Mattingly. "General. It's Admiral Lawson. He needs to speak with you, sir. He's ordering a recall."

"Say again?" Mattingly yelled.

"Sir, the chairman's on the line. We've been ordered to abort."

———

Nick knew something was wrong even before Dreyer called to the General. A moment before, the military staff had been focused on the opening phases of Operation Amber Dawn. Murmured voices. Professional. Then a few hands pointed to the live feed. Their scattered voices of alarm turned to stunned silence when Mattingly ran across the room to take Lawson's call. *Abort?*

———

The Special Forces colonel knew it was too late. He'd received confirmation his teams had egressed the aircraft. In less than a minute, they would be pulling out from their free-fall and deploying their high-glide parachutes. Their jump was configured to minimize chute time, but it would still be several more minutes before they were on the ground. An eternity.

The colonel starred at the live feed. *Damn it.* His twenty-four soldiers were in their stack, likely adjusting their formation to land in a predetermined pattern. They were about to drop right into the middle of an ambush. He didn't want to think about the fate of any man who overshot the drop zone.

He turned to his Forward Air Controller, a Marine major. The FAC was a F-18 fighter pilot and a graduate of the Corp's Weapons and Tactics Instructors course. He was an expert in combat management. They didn't come any better. "How far out are the cobras?"

"They're holding at five clicks, sir."

"Do you have coms?"

"Yes, sir."

"We've got a change of plans. Get the flight leader on the horn. The A-teams will need fire support. They're about to land in a hot drop zone."

"Sir, we were just ordered to recall."

"It's too damn late for that, Major. Those gunships need to be there right now."

The major recalibrated to this new reality. There could be no recall. "Sir, the cobra's downwash will catch any open chutes. I'd recommend we vector the Spooky. She's maintaining a five mile arc, orbiting at twelve thousand."

The colonel studied the screen, assessing the deployment of the terrorists. "You're right. If someone doesn't get a quick release on their harness, the wash could blow them into a kill zone."

The only positive the colonel could see in the deteriorating situation was there appeared to be no coordination to the terrorist's movements. They didn't know what was happening. He'd lost the element of surprise, but he still might be able to give his men an edge. "Call Dragon Flight. Tell them to concentrate their fire on the west side of the encampment. We need to take out that KPV and their leadership element."

"Dragon Flight, Dragon Flight. This is—" The rest of the Marine's transmission was drowned out by a shout from the staff's communication officer. He'd been scanning the known terrorist radio frequencies, searching for any indication the operation might be compromised. "I've got something."

The colonel spun toward the officer. "Who's transmitting?"

"The bad guys. They've spotted the drop."

———

"Nick. Over here," Rohrbaugh yelled over the mounting noise.

Nick pushed away from his console and ran to Rohrbaugh's station.

"Listen," Rohrbaugh said.

Nick leaned over Rohrbaugh's shoulder, listening the words coming over the speaker of Mike's computer. He couldn't understand a damn thing. The words were masked by static. He strained to hear. Were they speaking Somali?

"What the fuck are they saying?" someone yelled.

"Hang on. I'm running it through the translator," the command's linguist said. "I'm feeding now."

Nick focused on the computer-generated translation. The computer's monotone voice made it impossible to tell how many speakers there were:

"Can you hear me?"

"Yes."

"Can you see them?"

"One just landed. He's…"

"What the hell's going on?" Nick said.

Rohrbaugh held up his hand.

"Gunfire," the linguist yelled. He pressed his earphones against his head so he could hear the live transmission. "I've got different voices."

Nick pulled up a chair so he could catch the computer's translation. He looked at the live feed. Several green dots traversed the screen going in the direction of the drop zone. The Global Hawk had detected the heat signature of bullets. There was something surreal to the detached voice coming from the computer and the action unfolding on the screen— like watching a video game. And that was the disconnect. This was very real.

"They're gathering on the ridge."

"Attack, with the help of God."

"God give us victory."

"God is great."

"Shoot the sons of shit."

Nick gripped the arms of his chair. More rounds were visible. Some in singles, others in clusters. They were beginning to converge on the same point on the ridge. The terrorists must see something.

Rohrbaugh leaned forward. "They've made our guys. Come on. Come on, get the hell out of there."

Several long streams of pale-green beads snaked their way across the screen.

"Shit, heavy machine guns," Rohrbaugh said to himself. He twisted to address Nick. "They're firing blind, but they can still get lucky and hit something. Our guys should all be on the ground by now... there. See those small white ovals? Muzzle flashes. We're returning fire. They're aiming for the muzzle flashes. There goes a group of our guys right there, deploying left toward those huts. They're going to flank those assholes."

Nick wouldn't have been able to pick out anything if Rohrbaugh wasn't providing the running narrative.

Another four shadows zig-zagged across the open ground taking cover behind one of the huts.

"I've got the team leader," the comm officer said. He'd been working the link with the team's AN/PSC radio, frantically searching for the team's narrow-band satellite signal.

"Put him on speaker," Mattingly ordered.

"Covey, this is Blue Knife. It's getting pretty sporty down here. We—"

The team leader's understated words were his last. A white light blazed a long trail across the flat-screen in the direction of the hut. The trail ended in a brilliant flash.

"Fuck! PRG. Get out of there."

"Captain's down. We're taking heavy weapons fire."

Fragments of conversation followed: "...can't see anything... damn... not good ... Where? Coming from that truck... Got it."

Rohrbaugh saw a solitary figure dash toward the pickup truck chased by a green stream of rounds from the Dushka.

The figure dove for cover behind a hut. Heavy-caliber bullets from the Dushka chipped away at the mud brick wall around him. The hut disintegrated under the hail of fire from the heavy machine gun. A chunk of wall collapsed.

Rohrbaugh yelled at the shadowy form of the soldier projected on the screen. "Move, move, move… Get the hell out of there."

Another figure stood, exposing himself to the machine gun's fire. The stream of green beads shifted.

"God damn it. Get down," Rohrbaugh yelled at the flat-screen.

The soldier stood his ground and fired at the pickup. The truck erupted in a blinding white burst. The first figure bolted from his hiding place, weaving his way to another hut where he dropped out of sight.

Rohrbaugh gave a fist pump and jumped out of his seat. "Awesome!"

Nick saw the flash. The flicking light from the burning vehicle. The burst of secondary explosions. "What was that?"

"That guy just smoked the truck with a Javelan anti-tank missile," Rohrbaugh answered.

"Who—"

The top left portion of the flat-screen erupted with multiple flashes.

"Ah, right. The cavalry's arrived," someone whooped.

"Is that the Spooky?" Nick asked.

Rohrbaugh's eyes didn't stray from the sight. Hundreds of rounds of 30mm cannon fire impacted around the cave entrance and KPV machine gun. Every few seconds, larger explosions from the aircraft's 105 and 40mm cannons tore up the hillside. He finally answered.

"Yeah, it's Dragon Flight. Most of the flashes are impacts from their Bushmaster Gatling gun. It's spitting out eighteen hundred rounds a minute at predetermined coordinates. Area saturation. Nothing down there stands a prayer in hell."

General Mattingly's voice rang out. "Eagle Talon has touched down."

The four V-22's were now on the ground. One hundred

and twenty Marines joined the fight. They swept down on the encampment.

"You gotta love those guys," Rohrbaugh said. "Frontal assault."

The muzzle flashes from the advancing Marines increased. The distinctive clatter of a M-60 machine gun could be heard. The sound of gunfire rose to a roaring crescendo.

Aleem's remaining fighters were overwhelmed. The few that survived the onslaught threw down their weapons. There was no place to flee. A Marine's laser designator illuminated a pocket of holdouts. A hovering Super Cobra unleashed a torrent of fire from its 20mm Gatling gun, destroying the position. The cave was tougher to neutralize but fell to four special forces soldiers.

With the encampment secured, the search for Amber Dawn and Butterfly commenced. Inside the main room of the cave complex, the soldiers side-stepped the carnage and started comparing faces with their photographs of al-Khultyer. Other Special Forces teams began a systematic search of the huts for the missing CIA agent.

General Mattingly's first concern was his men. He radioed the A-Team's second- in-command. "Gunner, have you accounted for all your team?"

"Yes, sir. We have three wounded. One critical. They're being lifted to the *Bonhomme Richard*. The gator's surgical team is ready to receive them. The..." The warrant officer's voice trailed off.

"Gunner?"

"The captain's flying out with them, too."

"I'll call the Commodore. They'll take care of him, Gunner. You'll want to select several members of your team to accompany him home."

"Thank you, sir."

Mattingly refocused on the mission. "Do you have confirmation of Amber Dawn?"

Nick's breath whistled inward at the mention of al-Khultyer's code name. *Did they find him?* He stood and bumped into someone. He didn't hear the Gunner's answer. He regained his balance in time to hear Mattingly's response.

"Roger that," Mattingly said. "And Butterfly?"

"No joy, sir," the Gunner answered. "We need to finish securing the site. We may have better luck after daybreak."

"Understood." Mattingly said. He saw Nick approaching. He tightened his lips and gave him a brisk shake of his head. "No luck. There's no sign of al-Khultyer or any of his radioactive material. I'll arrange for an aircraft to get you and Captain Rohrbaugh over there. The president will want a report."

Chapter Thirty-Four

THE WHITE HOUSE
WASHINGTON D.C.
MONDAY 26 JANUARY

President Stuart's fingers tapped out a gentle staccato on his desktop. Amber Dawn had cost the life of a brave man, maybe two, if Butterfly couldn't be found. There were also the wounded. He heard a cough and raised his head.

Payne and the others waited for him to finish reading General Mattingly's after action report. He couldn't allow himself to dwell on the casualties. He needed to focus on Mattingly's final words: "The whereabouts of the primary objective remain unknown."

He stopped his drumming and read the last page of the report containing Parkos' analysis. His eyes came to rest on the third paragraph. Parkos suggested al-Khultyer escaped before the raid. To support his theory, he'd reviewed the surveillance photos of Barawa's harbor. A known pirate mother ship was absent. He didn't agree. Al-Khultyer's body was somewhere in that compound. Parkos was a smart guy, but he was dead wrong. *How could al-Khultyer have known of the impending attack? It wasn't possible.*

His thoughts drifted back to the human cost of the operation —the operation he'd authorized. He closed the report's cover and set it aside. "Bob, do you have an update on the wounded?"

"They'll make it," Lawson answered. "The critically wounded soldier was in surgery for three hours, but the Fleet Surgical Team has him stabilized. All three of them will be airlifted to Camp Lemonnaire this afternoon. A C-17 from the 183rd Airlift Squadron has been dispatched from Ramstein to pick them up."

"What about the Marines?"

"A couple sustained minor wounds. They insisted on remaining with their unit."

"And the team leader, Captain Santos?"

"He's coming home on the C-17."

"Has his family been notified?"

"Yes, sir."

"Any children?"

"Two girls, three and six."

Stuart sighed. A picture of the family formed in his mind. Lost in the image, he cast a vacant stare over Lawson's shoulder. *Damn.* He shifted his eyes to his Chief of Staff. "Dan, I'd like to speak to his wife. Will you set it up?"

"Of course."

Stuart squared his shoulders and addressed Lawson. "Bob, our window's closing. What's the status of the intercept?"

"Fifth Fleet has the execute on hold."

"Oh? What's going on?"

"The Iranians have thrown a curveball. The *Articus* changed course and has begun broadcasting on S-AIS. Their move works in our favor. We've tasked a SARSAT to track the ship. It'll collect the tactically relevant data. Speed, course, and image the ship's wake for verification."

"I recall you said their transponder may have malfunctioned."

"Yes, sir. The problem is, the AIS identification number we detected is assigned to another ship, the motor vessel *Salaha*."

"Have you verified identity?"

"The *Salaha*'s legit. She's headed to Yemen. The owners filed her projected course and destination with the International Maritime Bureau. The ship's manifest indicates she took on a load of eighty-five tons of charcoal at the Somali port of Obbia."

"Does this relate in any way to Amber Dawn?"

"It might," Lawson said. "If the Iranians know Aleem's been eliminated, they could be looking for another customer for their arms shipment."

"The Houthi," Gilmore said.

Stuart's hands tightened into fists. "There's no way I'm going to permit another bunch of terrorists getting their hands on those pellets. Can you imagine the consequences if the Houthi decided to set off a WMD in Riyadh and the Saudis traced the device back to the Iranians? I'm still trying to work that treaty with Tehran."

"We can't let that happen," Lawson affirmed.

"Are those ships near each other?" Stuart asked, steering the discussion back to the *Articus*.

"No, sir," Lawson answered. "They're separated by nearly seventy-five miles, running roughly on the same course and speed."

Stuart considered the implications. They still had a chance to take out the *Articus*. "Are there other ships in the area?"

Lawson paused before answering. His left hand brushed his chin. "Nothing. A P-8 is scheduled for another surveillance flight in a couple hours."

Stuart thought Lawson might be holding something back. He knew the admiral's mannerisms and picked up the hand gesture. No one else in the room noticed. He wondered what Lawson could be leaving out. Another ship? He set this question aside and tapped his index finger on the desk, sorting through his options. The one he would not accept was letting the *Articus* escape. "I want the *Tucson* to take out that ship. As soon as Fifth Fleet's confirmation is solid, he may provide the authorization."

"I'll get the message out," Lawson said.

"Okay. Now, do we have any loose ends?" Stuart said. He looked at Gilmore and the Secretary of Defense. "Bryce? Sheldon?" They shook their heads.

Stuart faced Lawson. "What about that cruise ship, the *Étoile de Mer*?" He noted Lawson shift in his seat.

"She's safe. Commandos from the French frigate *Guépratte* boarded her. All the passengers and crew are accounted for. The frigate's escorting her to the Suez Canal."

"What about the pirates?"

"*Étoile de Mer's* captain reported they were long gone before the boarding party arrived."

"Have the French found the mother ship?"

"Possibly. We've provided an assist and re-routed one of VUP-19's Triton drones to broaden the ocean surveillance. The Triton picked up a large dhow well to the south. Off the coast of Kenya. The dhow matches the picture of a known pirate mother ship operating from Barawa."

"What the hell is it doing down there?" Gilmore asked. "You'd think they'd make a run back to their safe haven."

"They probably figured the coalition would be looking for them. They tried a feint," Payne said.

Gilmore scoffed. "If I were them, I wouldn't take the risk. They've got to know the coalition ships are after them. If they made it to Somali territorial waters, they'd be home free."

"That's all well and good, Bryce," Payne answered, "but I don't believe—"

Stuart didn't want to spend any more time on this discussion. "Whose ships can do the intercept?"

"The Germans, Greeks, and French all have warships in the area," Lawson answered. "The German's have a boarding team on the *Rheinland-Pfalz*. It's my understanding, though, that the French have waved everyone off. They want to handle this themselves. I suspect…"

Stuart didn't catch the rest of Lawson's response. His mind was on what Parkos said in his analysis. The dhow. Could al-Khultyer be on it? That would explain why his body hadn't been found. *So, where the hell was he?* "Hold one, Bob."

"Sir?"

"Contact the French and send them al-Khultyer's picture."

"You've lost me," Gilmore said. "Is there a link I've missed?"

Stuart picked up Mattingly's report. "Parkos suggested al-Khultyer may have escaped. It's a long shot, but there's a chance he's on that dhow."

"I'll divert the *Truxtun*," Lawson said.

"No, let the French handle it. After Paris, the interrogations… No, we need to concentrate on Haaway. I want Parkos and Rohrbaugh to personally go over every inch of that camp. If they can't find al-Khultyer, we'll have to presume Parkos was correct in his assessment."

Chapter Thirty-Five

HAAWAY
FEDERAL REPUBLIC OF SOMALIA
TUESDAY 27 JANUARY

The CH-53E Super Stallion bumped and settled on the ground. Nick pulled out his orange earplugs only to be assaulted by the high-pitched shriek coming from the helicopter's three turboshaft engines. He molded the earplugs back into a cone, reinserted them, unclipped his lap belt, and twisted to look out one of the small oval side windows. The helicopter's seven rotor blades stirred up a huge cloud of dust. He couldn't see a damn thing.

The Marines of first platoon, Fox Company; 2/4, were undeterred by the noise or the dust. They stormed down the aft ramp of the aircraft and deployed across the slope leading to the compound. Nick stood and checked the quick release holster for his M-9 Beretta. He recalled Rohrbaugh's admonition. His finger could hook around the trigger when he drew the weapon and if he wasn't careful, he could literally shoot himself in the foot. He also recalled Rohrbaugh's dubious look when he'd asked for the sidearm. He double checked the Beretta's safety and set off.

"O'er... ere."

Nick spotted Rohrbaugh standing off to his left. He jogged over to him, making sure he stayed well clear of the 53's spinning tail rotor.

"eens.. ot...er...hut ..."

Nick couldn't understand a word. He pulled out his earplugs. "What?"

Rohrbaugh's lips kept moving, but the helicopter's roar drowned out most of what he said. "The Marines... ave to... ear the... uts. We'll... art o'er... ere."

Nick followed Rohrbaugh's finger and nodded. He clapped his hand over his floppy hat and took off in the direction of a low mud-brick wall.

"Hey! Hey, hey, hey."

Nick looked over his right shoulder. A Marine was yelling and waving his arms at a lump of vultures. The birds were clustered around something on the ground, pecking and quarreling with one another.

"Hey, hey. Get the hell away from there," the Marine yelled again. He picked up a rock and heaved it at the birds. Most of the scavengers ignored him. A few agitated birds hopped away before returning to their feast. One that went airborne settled back down. The Marine lowered his M-16 and fired off a couple rounds hitting one. The remainder scattered, taking to the air to find a safer meal.

Nick walked over to check out what had set off the Marine. *Oh, crap. A body.* Or what was left of one. The corpse had no eyes. The remnants of its face grinned at him through lipless teeth. He retched at the sight, choking on the bitter taste of bile welling up in his throat. He stumbled backwards.

The Marine jumped out of the way. "Fuck this."

Nick thought the Marine's statement summed things up pretty well. A second Marine came over to see what was going on. He took one look at the corpse and grabbed his buddy's arm, pulling him away. "Leave that shit, man. Come on."

Nick closed his eyes, recalling something he'd heard about vultures preferring to eat the eyes first. Whatever that... person... body?... had done in his life, God had assuredly found a place for him in hell. Another disjointed thought entered his mind. He needed to make sure someone got a DNA sample from the remains.

He spotted Rohrbaugh talking to Fox company's CO, a Marine captain. At least they had the good sense to keep their distance.

Rohrbaugh waved him over. He shook his head to clear the sight of the corpse and jogged over to the two men.

"Nasty, huh?" the Marine said when Nick came within earshot.

He could only nod in response.

"We're good Captain, thanks," Rohrbaugh said. "You'd better check on your troops." He addressed Nick. "The first huts are clear. Let's take a look at that pickup." He called out to a Marine standing a short distance away carrying a portable gamma dosimeter/chemical agent detector. "Corporal. With us."

———

Nick approached the burned-out shell of the Toyota with considerable trepidation. He wasn't too keen on the idea of encountering any of al-Khultyer's fuel pellets. Corpses were one thing. Being contaminated or being exposed to a toxic chemical was something entirely different. Those things could hurt him. His assessment of the situation changed as they neared the pickup.

The first thing he noted was the barrel of the Dushka machine gun pointing toward the empty sky. Then he saw the charred body draped over the side rail of the truck. That was just before his nose was assailed by the stench. He recoiled at the smell, covering his nose and spinning away. His eyes caught something moving by the edge of an adjacent hut. *What the… ?*

He dropped to one knee, and in a smooth continuous motion, pulled the Beretta from his holster, pressed his thumb on the safety, chambered a round, and fired three times.

The ejected shell casings from of the weapon tumbled out of sight. His brain registered the sight of an AK-47 slowly flying from the terrorist's hands, the man spinning from the impact. Everything happened in slow motion. There wasn't any sound.

He stared in disbelief at the body sprawled face down in front of him. Gray pakol, dirty brown jacket, tan pants… He'd just killed someone. No, he corrected himself. He'd just killed a terrorist who was about to shoot him. Rohrbaugh's voice jarred him out of his trance.

"Damn, Parkos. Where'd you learn to shoot like that?"

Nick detected the disbelief in Rohrbaugh's voice. He un-cocked the hammer and holstered his weapon. He left the safety off. There was no telling if he'd have to use it again. "Quantico. I've spent some time at the range."

Rohrbaugh walked over to the terrorist and kicked the rifle away from the body. Two Marines joined him. The first rolled the terrorist over. The second pulled a photograph of al-Khul-tyer from one of the pockets of his armored vest and compared the faces.

Nick already knew it wasn't a match. The Marine put his photo away and marked the corpse with a casualty tag and moved on. Three more Marines ran over and formed a protective triangle around him and Rohrbaugh. More men moved hut to hut, checking bodies, taking pictures, tagging them. Their work was methodical, seemingly without emotion. Nick knew better. The Marine's silence told the larger story. They would remember today, just as he would.

He pulled off his floppy and wiped the sweat from his face with his sleeve. He was soaked. And dizzy. Rohrbaugh tossed him a plastic water bottle. He downed the entire thing in thirsty gulps, dropping the empty by his feet. "Thanks."

"Let's move on to the cave," Rohrbaugh said as he beckoned the two members of their Explosive Ordinance Disposal Team to join up. "We may have better luck there."

Nick followed without saying a word. The vista before him was one of total destruction wrought by Dragon Flight's guns. The sight reminded him of the pictures he'd seen of the moonscapes of the Verdun and The Somme battlefields of World War I. But those had withstood months of artillery fire. Dragon Flight's Gatling gun had spent mere seconds on this site.

His eyes scanned the churned ground dotted with craters from the gunship's 105mm cannon. There was nothing left of the KPV machine gun placed on the hill above the cave. He recognized a few body parts, just bits really, men cut apart by the merciless fire of the plane's 30mm Gatling gun.

Rohrbaugh halted at the berm that once protected the entrance to the cave complex. "Wait here until you hear me call. There may be 'stay behinds'."

"What?"

"IEDs."

Nick didn't argue, although he didn't want to be left alone. He watched Rohrbaugh and the EOD team disappear into the cave, before dropping down on the remnant of the berm. He tried to focus on al-Khultyer, trying to think of anything really. Just something to block out the mental picture of the man he'd just shot.

"Okay, it's clear," Rohrbaugh called from the cave entrance. "You're going to want to see this."

Nick made his way through the zigzags of the tunnel wondering what "this" could be. He passed side-chambers containing sleeping quarters, supplies, munitions. They all needed to be checked. He stopped at the entrance to the main chamber. A body slumped across a small wooden table. An outstretched hand still grasped what appeared to be a satellite phone. Rohrbaugh stood to one side of the corpse poking around the shattered remains of a computer. He held up a picture ID.

"Figure this may be your Iranian. Looks like he was trying to call someone." He pocketed the phone. "The intel guys should be able to lift the numbers. It'll be interesting to see who he's been talking to."

Nick pointed to another blood-soaked body lying on the floor beside the table. "Looks like Aleem."

"Seems we're finding everyone but your guy."

Rohrbaugh turned the shattered computer upside down. "Maybe we can get something out of this. The hard drive's still in one piece."

Nick heard him but was distracted by something in the far corner of the room. Another body. He'd mistaken her red direh for a blanket that had been discarded on the floor. Then he saw the spray of blond hair—the same honey-yellow as Marty's. He closed his eyes to block out the image of his ex-wife and made his way out of the cave.

He'd seen enough.

Chapter Thirty-Six

IBO ISLAND LODGE
QUIRIMBAS ARCHIPELAGO, MOZAMBIQUE
WEDNESDAY 28 JANUARY

"*Pardon,* Monsieur Chéreau. Would you care for something from the bar?"

Bashir shielded his eyes with the hotel's photocopy of *Le Monde Diplomatique* and looked at the beach attendant. "*Non, merci. Ça va.*"

The attendant gestured toward the adjacent beach chair. "And your companion?"

Bashir had no idea if Qasif wanted anything. The kid had wandered off looking for something to do. Bashir presumed he wouldn't return any time soon. "*Il va bien.*"

The attendant gave a short bow and made his way to the next cabana.

Bashir reached up to adjust the beach umbrella and settled back into his lounge chair. *Yeah, the kid. What to do about him?*

He actually knew very little about the young American. In fact, he didn't even know if the surname Qasif told him, Dalmar, was even real. None-the-less, he'd contacted his bank in Switzerland and arranged for a credit card to be issued in that name.

He fixed his eyes on the horizon, watching the waves break over the distant reef. *Had he made a mistake?* The kid had no depth and appeared to be just another disaffected youth drawn by the allure of al-Shabaab. *Like those two young women in Haawe.* He remained puzzled by that. There weren't any women among the fighters he'd known in Afghanistan. The men were the ones dying in the mountains for their faith, their tribes, their honor, something tangible. He'd asked Qasif about his family, but he said very little. The kid's sole motivation appeared to be returning to his homeland and becoming a martyr. He paused to consider his own motivation. Maybe that was enough.

He turned his attention to the article he'd been reading about an American drone attack in Somalia. Was he the intended target? Had the American agent, this Parkos, managed to find him?

'An airstrike targeted the local leader of the Harakat al-Shabaab, Sheik Abdul Aleem. According to Barawa elder, Akeem Jarawi, dozens of fighters were killed on the strike near the small village of Haawe.'

Sheik? Bashir was incredulous. The psychopath must have gotten a promotion to ease his way to the afterlife. He flipped over the page of *Le Monde* and continued to read. The Council of Islamic Courts spouted their usual vitriol in response to the attack:

'This cowardly attack will not deter us from our holy war against the infidel. You have left us martyrs and those Abdul Aleem trained will avenge his death, targeting the very heart of the Crusaders.'

Perhaps Aleem was the target. He'd certainly done enough to justify the American's attention. There was nothing in Jawari's statement that concerned him. He skipped to the next article. This one held his interest.

The paper reported French commandos boarded the luxury yacht *Étoile de Mer* hijacked by Somali pirates this past Saturday. The authorities confirmed that all the passengers and crew were safe and the yacht was now under escort, proceeding to the Suez Canal. From there, the ship would continue to its previously scheduled call at the Italian port of Civitavecchia.

The report made no mention of finding his device hidden in the forward lounge. Of course, he cautioned himself, would the French admit to finding the explosives? *And if they hadn't found his device?* Would the yacht's owners insist on conducting a more thorough search of their vessel once it arrived in Italy? Doubtful. Why would they suspect anything?

All things considered, he couldn't have hoped for a better outcome. That is, until he read the last paragraph. His hands tightened around the newspaper.

The article said the French Navy also located and destroyed the pirate mother ship responsible for the hijacking. The dhow's crew would be interrogated. He could care less about the fate of the pirates. They'd served their purpose and he felt no remorse at their loss. If Jawari's men were careless enough to be captured, that was their problem. But if one of the pirates told the French about the foreign fighters who'd been on board? A Chechen with the nom de guerre, Dhi'b, and an American named Qasif?

He cursed under his breath. The French would also know the two foreigners were gone, set ashore on a remote stretch of beach north of the Tanzanian city of Dar es Salaam. He smoothed out the newspaper, set it aside, and began to identify the flaws in his plan.

His greatest concern was the French showing a picture of him to the pirates. He considered this. Why would the French have any reason to suspect the man responsible for the Paris bombing was aboard a fishing dhow in the middle of the Gulf of Aden?

And what would the French do with the information they obtained from the pirates? Would they bother to share any of this with the Americans? They did share the base in Djibouti. What was the worst-case scenario? He backtracked and reviewed his and Qasif's movements after they were dropped off by the pirate's skiff in Tanzania.

They'd made their way from the beach to the city's airport where he searched for a suitable airline. He'd decided on Mozambique Air, in part because it was a small regional airline, but primarily because they weren't linked to the international airline reservation system. He paid cash for two tickets for the flight to Pemba. They were met by a staff member from the lodge who escorted them to a four seat Cessna for the short hop to Ibo Island. The terminal facility in Pemba was primitive and Ibo's, with its grass landing strip, even more so. The authorities conducted a cursory check of their passports and didn't ask questions. *Yes, the passports.*

There'd been some risk of being detained at the airport in Dar es Salaam. Not for him, though. He was confident in his new identity. But Qasif still used his American passport. That remained a problem. He hadn't been successful in finding someone who could forge a new identity for the kid. *Should he just abandon him to his own devices?* Perhaps. The kid did ask what their plans were after leaving the lodge, but his answer was vague. Yet, he could not afford to be vague if the next steps of his plan were to succeed.

He'd discarded his own travel agent's suggestion to fly Air France or KLM to Rome, opting instead for Emirates Airlines. The Europeans would have a larger database to run his passport. He felt confident in his own travel plans, but he still needed to work through his options on how to get Qasif back to America without being detained. Amsterdam's airport, long a favored waypoint for terrorists, was improving its security. He did find a flight to Rio de Janeiro via South Africa. And from Rio, the kid could connect with—

"You planning to stay here all day?" Qasif said, dropping into the empty beach chair next to Bashir's. He reached for Bashir's tube of sunscreen and squirted a long white line down his leg.

Bashir eyed Qasif with annoyance. The kid was wearing a new blue T-shirt. Emblazoned across the front in large white letters was: "*Life is a Beach, Then you Dive.*" *An interesting choice.* "I've decided you will go to Rio."

Qasif stopped rubbing in the sunscreen and faced Bashir. "What? Like Brazil Rio de Janeiro? Why?"

"Amsterdam's airport isn't safe."

"I went through Schiphol on the way to Somalia. I didn't have a problem."

"Now you're in the TSA's database."

"But—"

Bashir didn't want to have a debate. "I've decided." He looked at his watch and swung his legs over the side of the beach chair. "I'm going to the spa."

Qasif returned to rubbing in the sunscreen. "Have fun."

Bashir strode off, leaving the kid and his attitude on the beach. There was no sense getting worked up. Besides, what better way to spend the rest of the morning than to have a body rub with coarse sea salt and lemon grass followed by a coconut oil massage?

In the distance, near the infinity pool, he heard a burst of laughter. His thoughts turned to Angelique. She'd made him laugh. She would have enjoyed this place. A half-smile formed as he walked up the steps of the main building. He paused on the wide veranda to admire the view of the surrounding trop-ical garden and the turquoise sea beyond. Who would possibly think of looking for him at this isolated resort in the middle of nowhere—even if they were still looking? *And what of the Articus?*

He wasn't surprised the paper contained no word about the ship, but had the American's take his bait? Perhaps they had and destroyed the last of his fuel pellets. *Perhaps I've done enough? Do I have to continue?*

"*Bonjour, Monsieur* Chéreau. I hope you are finding your stay a pleasant one?"

"*Très agréable, merci.*" Bashir answered as he crossed the lobby. His eyes traveled to a huge bouquet of sunflowers set on the counter behind the man. He'd never seen anything like the variety. The colors dazzled him: mahogany, brilliant yellow, orange, a splash of red. He switched to English. "Would it be possible to have such an arrangement in my room?"

"*Certainement, monsieur.* They are beautiful, are they not? Did you know that Mozambique is one of the world's leading exporters of sunflower oil?"

He did not, nor did he care. He was thinking of his little Katya. He could hear her laughter.

Chapter Thirty-Seven

CAMP LEMONNAIRE
DJIBOUTI
THURSDAY 29 JANUARY

"Up and at 'em, Parkos. The day's not getting any younger."

Rohrbaugh's voice boomed inside Nick's head. He pulled his pillow over his ears and rolled away from the noise.

"Come on, man. The sun's going to be shining in twenty minutes."

"Humph."

Rohrbaugh switched to an Irish brogue. Wha t'are ya wait'in for, boyo? Some more o that Killian Red ya loved so dearly lass night?"

Nick opened his eyes a crack and peered at his alarm. 0610. And it was dark.

"That's a boy, signs of life."

He gave up and rolled over. Rohrbaugh was clad in sweat-soaked PT gear. He'd already been on a run. Nick's brain recoiled at the mere thought of movement, but he managed to prop himself up on his right elbow to confront his tormentor. "Damn."

He dropped back down, giving a tentative feel to an ugly bruise running the length of his right forearm.

Rohrbaugh smiled. "Ya took a mighty spill to starboard last night."

"What happened?"

"I'd say ya had a might too much liquor."

"Are you guys always that nuts?"

"Just on special occasions."

Nick massaged his throbbing temples. "Just how many such occasions do you have?"

"Depends."

"And last night?"

"The guys took a straw vote. They thought you needed to be initiated into the brotherhood."

Fragments came back. The straws. He'd lost. The FAC. Yeah, the Marine Forward Air Controller, the F-18 guy. He'd yelled something about the nugget needing to complete his first Cat Shot.

That suggestion signaled the beginning of the end. He recalled being handed a large beer mug, maybe several. Something about topping off his tanks. Tables being lined up end-to-end. Four guys grabbing his arms and legs. Launching him off the end the tables?

Really?

He groaned at the recollection. He touched his arm. *A carrier catapult shot? What on earth...?*"

Rohrbaugh provided the answer. "Clean sweep, fore and aft, boyo. You were in bad need of recalibration."

Nick considered the statement. True enough. He'd spent the previous day shifting aimlessly through the raid's after action reports and a few translated documents collected from Aleem's compound. He'd accomplished nothing. Amber

Dawn, his operation, was dead in the water. Rohrbaugh's voice broke through his gloom.

"And you need something to eat."

Nick was hit with a wave of nausea. His stomach turned at the thought of the mess hall's half-cooked scrambled eggs and greasy sausage. "I'll take my chances with coffee."

"Nope, you need the protein. And the carbs. You're also dehydrated."

Nick didn't answer. Rohrbaugh obviously spoke from experience.

"You all right?" Rohrbaugh asked.

He looked around the barren room. "Yeah, nothing that a couple of Tylenols won't fix."

"No. Are you all right?"

The face of the terrorist he'd shot flashed in Nick's mind. Dark, deep-set eyes. Beak nose. Black beard. Likely Arab, not Somali.

Rohrbaugh's voice softened. "It's okay, man. Word of what you did got around. You saved my ass. Probably your own as well."

Nick closed his eyes. He just wanted to go to sleep and forget.

"Look, Nick, you'll never forget what happened. What you saw. Over time, you'll learn to deal with it. Last night was a start. The guys understand. You've been accepted in the brotherhood. You're a warrior. Not many are. We'll always be there if you need us."

Nick nodded. *We.* Different context. Different meaning.

Rohrbaugh extended his hand. "Come on."

Nick winched as a wave of pain coursed through his injured arm.

Mike pulled him up.

"Parkos, you really need to be more careful."

Nick smiled. "Must be the company I'm keeping."

Rohrbaugh dropped his hand and placed it over his nose.

"Man, you really stink. You're in desperate need of a shower and a shave."

Nick reached up and massaged the scruff of his three-day beard. "Yeah, seems I do."

"Right answer. Next step, we're going to get you back up to full battery. First stop, the showers, then we'll rustle up something for you to eat."

'We' again. Different context, different meaning. *We.* The word resonated.

He climbed out of bed, grabbing the bedpost until the pounding in his head subsided. He collected his kit and followed Rohrbaugh out the door to the shower facilities.

———

To Nick's surprise, he survived breakfast. He took another sip of coffee, almost feeling human again. He pushed away from the dining table and made his way to the Operations building and his assigned cubicle.

A new stack of reports was piled to one side of his cluttered desk. Two yellow sticky notes clung to the frame of his computer monitor. He chose one at random. His department said Alek wanted him to contact her. He resisted the urge to crumple the note. The last thing he needed right now was more of her intrigue. He pulled off the other note. "Call your office—ASAP."

The message didn't have a contact name or a time, but he recognized the number—the DNI's personal line. He looked at his watch. 0702. Midnight Washington time. *Oh, well.* He picked up the secure phone and dialed. An unfamiliar voice answered on the second ring. "Mr. Gilmore's office. How may I help you?"

"This is Nick Parkos. I'm in Djibouti. I have a message to call Mr. Gilmore."

"He's expecting your call. Hold one."

Nick cradled the receiver between his ear and shoulder and leafed through several reports. He stopped at one whose header caught his eye. 'French intelligence sources—'

Gilmore's voice roared over the phone. "Parkos, where the hell have you been? I've got to brief the president in seven hours."

Nick dropped the report and grasped the receiver. "Yes, sir. I'm preparing a message summarizing what we've found. Did you receive my report on Haawa?"

"Have you gotten anything off that hard drive?"

Gilmore had seen the report. "No, sir. The cryptologists are still trying to crack the encryption."

"Do you have any leads on al-Khultyer? The president isn't happy."

Nick glanced at the report he'd begun to read. *There*. He scanned the second paragraph. "Yes, sir. The French believe he may have been on the pirate mother ship they intercepted. The one responsible for hijacking that cruise ship."

"You just used the past tense," Gilmore said. "Where the hell is he?"

"I don't know."

"Find out." The line went dead.

Nick stared at the receiver feeling nauseated again. Another line on his phone blinked. *Crap.* He ignored it.

"Oh, man. Sounds like that didn't go very well," the occupant of the next cubicle, a navy lieutenant commander, said.

Nick hung up the receiver. "It could have gone better."

"I'd say—"

"Hey, Parkos," another voice interrupted. "You got a call on the other line. Can you take it?"

"You know who it is?"

"No idea. Sounds like a Brit. Says he's a Commodore in the Royal Navy and has something that might interest you."

Nick sighed. "Okay." He picked up the receiver and punched the lighted button. "Nick Parkos."

"Guid mornan, sir. Commodore Patrick McClung, Royal Navy, here. Deputy Director of NATO's Sea Center of Excellence."

Nick had no idea what the Sea Center of Excellence was. "Good morning, Commodore. What can I do for you?"

"I say, oh chap. I had the devil's own time tryin to fine ya'. Finally got an assist from the Frogs. Chap named, Gallet. I believe you're acquainted."

Nick rolled his eyes. He loved the Brits, but damn... "We've worked together."

"I dare say. Well, I 'eard you two 'ave been looking for some bloke named Bashir al-Khultyer. I stumbled across something that ya' might fine useful."

Nick grabbed a pen. "Yes?"

"It's a bit of a round-about."

Nick spun the pen around the desktop with his finger. "Of course."

"To make a long story short, our man in Mozambique may 'ave spotted him."

"What? Where?" Nick heard McClung chuckle.

"We thought that'd be your response."

Nick wasn't amused. "What do you have?"

"As I was saying, our man was in Tanzania was waitin' to catch a plane home from Julius Nyerere International Airport—"

"Never heard of the place."

If McClung was irritated at the interruption, his voice didn't betray him. "Dar es Salaam. About midway down the Tanzanian coast. Our man was standing in the queue and spotted someone at the counter buy'in a ticket. The man resembled the picture of a terrorist he'd seen in the *Times*. The one responsible for the Paris incident."

Multiple questions rolled through Nick's mind, stopping at the ticket counter. "Did your man happen to catch where al-Khultyer was going?"

"Sorry, no."

Nick wasn't happy. Why didn't McClung's man have enough sense to follow a suspected terrorist?

"There's another thing you should know," McClung said. "There was a young lad with him. Looked to be in his twenties."

Nick made a mental note of the other person, but didn't ask McClung for details. "I don't suppose your man took a picture?"

"Blimey, mate. I nearly forgot. He sent us a couple from his iPhone. Do ya' 'ave a good address?"

Chapter Thirty-Eight

CAMP LEMONNAIRE
DJIBOUTI
THURSDAY 29 JANUARY

Nick set the receiver in its cradle and powered up his computer. He stared at the message he'd begun to draft to Gilmore. The words blurred. He felt dizzy, but it was more than just the aftermath of last night's bender. Could that Brit in Tanzania have really spotted al-Khultyer?

He leaned around the partition separating him from the next cubicle. He addressed the occupant, Sean Miller, the Navy lieutenant commander. "Hey, Sean. You have a moment?"

Miller's fingers paused on his keyboard. He spun his chair to face Nick. "Sure. What's up?"

"Aren't you the point for coordinating our anti-piracy ops?"

"Sure am, JTF-151. I'm also the liaison with CTF-465, the European Union guys. What's on your mind?"

"I just got a lead on the terrorist I've been chasing."

"The call you took?"

"Someone may have seen my target at the airport in Dar es Salaam," Nick said.

"Tanzania? I thought you guys took out al-Khultyer?"

"We never found a body."

Miller gave a shake of his head. "Not good. You trying to figure out how he got out of there?"

"My hunch is he escaped on a dhow. I went over the surveillance shots of the harbor in Barawa. A known mother ship went missing just before our assault."

"The one that went after the *Étoile de Mer*," Miller said. "You're thinking al-Khultyer—?"

"Exactly. Can you tell me where the French made their intercept?"

"I can do you one better, I can show you. Pull up a chair."

Nick pushed his chair around the corner and settled in over the commander's shoulder.

"Give me a sec to close this out and open my ocean surveillance program."

Nick watched Miller enter the keystrokes to bring his system online. "Weren't they found way to the south?"

"Yeah, that was odd. Here, take a look. This is the dhow's position at the French intercept."

Nick saw a blue field crisscrossed with longitude and latitude lines but no coastline. An X designated the intercept point, near a horizontal line marked 2.5 N and a vertical line marked 42 E. "Is that off the coast of Kenya?"

"Sure is. Let me back off." Miller gave his keyboard a couple clicks. He pointed to an indentation on the coast just south of the Somali border. "They were east of this bay. The city is Lamu." He clicked back to the original image. "The dhow was on a north-east heading when the French spotted them."

"You'd think they'd have been trying to get back home."

"We suspect their intent was to link up with the *Articus*."

"The *Articus*?"

"Another op. The ship carried an arms shipment for al-Shabaab."

"Could they have made it as far south as Dar es Salaam?"

"Who? The pirates or the *Articus*?"

"The pirates."

"Let me check." Miller ran his curser over a track from the ship's last position to the Tanzanian city. "About 650 nautical miles. The cruise ship was hijacked on the 24th at approximately 2000 hours. The French boarded the dhow late on the 27th. The dhow would have had to be making close to fifteen knots."

"It's possible then?"

"Maybe. Fifteen knots would really be stretching it."

"Damn."

"There's another possibility. They could have dropped your guy at Lamu. It'd make more sense."

Nick's hopes faded. "Okay, thanks."

He slid his chair back to his cubicle and signed on to his computer. The screen flashed just as something else occurred to him. The French. They would know. He poked his head around the corner. "Sean, do you happen to have an after action report from the French?"

"Haven't seen one." Miller paused. "Nick, I hate to keep pointing out the negatives, but if the French had found your guy, we'd know about it. I can't imagine they'd keep quiet if they'd just captured the terrorist responsible for the Paris and Moscow bombings. That'd be quite a coup."

Nick thought about that. Gallet would have said something. Miller was probably right. He searched for an explanation. Al-Khultyer had to be somewhere. He tossed out an idea. "He could've been hiding on the dhow."

Miller looked dubious. "If he was, he's toast. After the French took off the crew, they turned their 100mm cannon on it for a little gunnery practice. Sent it to the bottom."

Nick wasn't prepared to dismiss McClung's report. Al-Khultyer wasn't on the dhow when the French captured it, but he had to be somewhere. Tanzania was as good a possibility as any. And McClung was going to send the photographs. He still had a chance. "Sean, can you give me a good POC for the French?"

———

Grasping the slip of paper with the phone number of the French POC, Nick spun back to his desk. He felt energized, focused on the steps he needed to take to finally capture his quarry. He reflected on his word choice as a new realization came to him. An intangible he hadn't considered. Al-Khultyer was a worthy adversary. He'd developed a certain respect for this man he knew so little about. He wondered what he'd do if they ever came face-to-face. He had no idea.

Rohrbaugh stuck his head in Nick's cubical. "How you doing shipmate?"

"A bit better, thanks to you," Nick answered over his shoulder. "And a Brit."

"A Brit? I didn't know there were any around."

"I don't think there are. I got a call this morning from a British Commodore with NATO, Patrick McClung. You know him?"

"Nope."

"He said his man in Tanzania might have seen al-Khultyer."

Rohrbaugh grabbed a vacant chair and pulled it up. "How the hell did he get down there?"

"That's what I'm trying to figure out. I'm thinking he may have been on the mother ship the French boarded a couple days ago."

"I remember you saying that. Thought you were nuts. I hate to admit it, but it makes sense now. If al-Khultyer was dropped somewhere along the coast, it'd explain why the French found that dhow so far south."

Nick screwed up his lips. Rohrbaugh just connected the dots. "Commander Miller thinks he went ashore in Lamu."

"Naw, he wouldn't chance going to Kenya. My money's on Tanzania. That is, if your Brit's source is legit."

"Just a sec. Let me check my e-mail. McClung said he'd send a couple pics of our perp taken at the airport."

"Perp? Interesting word choice."

Nick ignored him and scrolled through his email. There. He clicked on the message, glanced at the note from McClung, then went to the attachments.

"Well, I'll be damned," Rohrbaugh said looking at the screen. "That's your guy."

Nick went to the other picture. "We have to get down there."

Chapter Thirty-Nine

JULIUS NEYERRE INTERNATIONAL AIRPORT
DAR es SALAAM, TANZANIA
THURSDAY 29 JANUARY

"Welcome to Tanzania, Nick," Chuck Sanders said as the unmarked CIA special mission aircraft braked to a stop. He scrolled through the messages on his iPhone. "Good. There's a vehicle waiting to take us to the embassy."

Nick grabbed his overnighter and followed Sanders into the terminal building. The place was empty. A few chairs were strewn about and a column of rope-linked stanchions was set to one side of a red carpet leading to the center of the room. Unnerved, his eyes darted around. *A setup?*

"We're in the VIP terminal." Sanders' voice echoed within the empty space. "The embassy pulled a few strings. Figured you'd want to keep a low profile."

"Where's—?"

"Hey, Chuck."

Nick dropped what he was going to say and looked in the direction of the voice, then back to Sanders.

Sanders pointed to a man and woman coming through the

far door. "Our welcoming committee." He approached the man who'd called out. "Hey, Tyvis."

Tyvis swung his arm around in the general direction of Nick and two other men standing off to his side. The two wore sunglasses and each had an aluminum case tucked by their side containing the team's weapons. "This everyone?'

"We're it."

"How about the aircrew?" Tyvis said as they crossed the room toward Nick and the two Special Activity operatives.

"They're staying with the aircraft."

"Any idea how long you'll be in-country?'"

Sanders pointed to Nick. "Ask him."

Tyvis extended his hand. "You must be Parkos. I'm Chuck's counterpart down here, Tyvis Powell." He gestured to the woman waiting by the far end of the roped stanchions and walked in her direction. "You'll be riding with Ms. Conti, our Deputy Chief of Mission. Chuck, you and the others will be with me in the Suburban."

Nick checked out the DCM. About five-six. Short, brown hair. Maybe mid-forties. Intelligent eyes. He grabbed the handle of his bag and followed Powell down the red carpet. They came to a halt in front of Conti, forming a rough semi-circle.

"Mr. Parkos. I'm Anne Marie Conti, the DCM." She ignored the others, turned, and started for the door. "We'll talk on the way."

He stared at the back of her gray suit coat. *Oookay. That went well.*

———

Nick barely got settled in the back seat of the embassy's armored sedan when the door slammed. They accelerated out the airport exit and turned northwest. Conti spoke first.

"The ambassador got a call from State a couple hours ago

saying you were coming. He was told that we are to provide any support you need. The ambassador's really spun up." She locked her eyes on him. "What the hell's going on?"

Nick was taken aback by her tone. *Wow, she's not a happy camper. Well, Ms. DCM, I've had better days too.* "I've been tasked to find the terrorist responsible for the Moscow and Paris bombings."

"What does that have to do with us?"

He pulled his briefcase onto his lap. "I have intelligence that confirms this individual was in Dar es Salaam several days ago." He extracted a copy of the photos taken at the airport.

"Under whose authorization?" Conti's voice had a sharp, accusatory edge.

On one level, Nick could understand her anger. He'd just totally upset their applecart with this no-notice drill. There was a terrorist in their back yard and they had no idea. How could they? He studied her face and decided apologizing was a non-starter. There wasn't time for it—or for hurt feelings. "The president's."

Condi's expression didn't alter, but Nick saw the change in her eyes. There would be no more attitude.

"I see." Her voice was business-like. "What do we need to do?"

"I'd suggest we start with the airline."

"May I?" Conti reached for the photos. She studied the pictures. "There's a fragment of a logo in one of them just visible behind the counter, but I can't make it out. The second picture has a pillar with some advertisements plastered on it. That should help identify the location. I'll have one of my staff check it out."

She turned her attention to the people in the pictures. "There were five adults lined up in the queue. Another at the counter. Which one's your terrorist?"

"The one at the counter."

"Who's he looking at?"

Nick chastised himself. He'd been so focused on al-Khultyer, he'd neglected the other person. "My contact mentioned a kid in his twenties."

She pointed out a partial figure to al-Khultyer's left. "That might be him." She handed the photos back. "I'm calling the office."

Nick studied the image. There wasn't much to go on, just a partial view of the unknown individual. He considered the implications. With the exception of the French woman, al-Khultyer had always traveled alone. *So, why the change?* What possible use would a second person be to him at this point?

Conti broke into his train of thought. "Do your pics have a date-time stamp?"

The question startled him. He hadn't noticed. "Let me check." In the upper left corner was a faint imprint. He could barely make it out. "Yeah, 0933 on the 26th."

"Can I see those again?" She grabbed the pics. "Thanks."

Nick watched in disbelief as she took out her smart phone, took a couple pictures, and hit the send key. "What the hell did you just do? That device isn't secure."

"No, it isn't."

"Where'd you send those?"

"The embassy." She handed the photos back. "These were taken three days ago. Do you really think he's still here?"

Nick considered her statement and shook his head. He looked out the window. They were now traveling due west into the setting sun. A red neon sign flashing by the side of the road, EMA's BAR, came and went. Where the hell was his head? He'd been wasting his time speculating about the second person in the picture. Conti was focused on al-Khultyer.

"If you have a better idea, let me know," Conti said.

He didn't. "You're right."

"Has he developed any patterns?"

Before Nick could answer, Conti's phone sang out a line from Bruce Springsteen's, *Born to Run.* "Hello, Jim," she said. "What do you have? … You're sure? … Smart move. A check of the international reservation system won't show anything … I agree, the counter's probably closed, but get over there anyway. See what you can dig up. … Yeah, it sure is, thanks."

"You found something?"

"The counter belongs to Mozambique Airlines. My guys are heading there." She swiped her finger over the screen of her iPhone.

Nick started to comment, but Conti held up a finger. "Give me a sec."

That was fine with him. He'd been thinking about what she'd said before taking her call: 'Has he developed any patterns?' Good question. He hadn't found any. Not yet, anyway.

"Okay, got it." Conti closed her phone. "There were only two flights on the twenty-sixth. The last left at three-thirty for Maputo. The other left earlier in the day. Pemba."

"I don't know the cities."

"Maputo is Mozambique's capital. Pemba's on the northern coast."

That didn't help. "I heard you mention the international reservation system."

"Your guy is either lucky or very smart. Mozambique Air isn't connected to the international reservation system. We won't be able to trace any connecting flights once we've figure out where he went."

"Damn."

The sedan slowed and made a right turn toward the gate of the embassy compound.

"When's the last time you ate?" Conti asked.

"Breakfast."

"Your brain will work better once we get some food in you."

Conti was right. He felt better after downing a cheeseburger
and fries from the embassy's canteen. He would have felt more
so if he had something to go on and if he knew what kind of
meat he'd just eaten. Zebra? He refocused. Chuck Sanders
hadn't been able to come up with anything either. Al-Khultyer
had vanished.

"I thought you might like some good news," Conti said,
entering the room she'd set up for him. "Does the name Jean
Luc Chéreau mean anything?"

Nick drew a blank. "No."

"It's the alias your guy used to buy his tickets. Paid in
cash."

"Tickets? So we know the next two stops."

"No. They were both one way to the same destination. I'd
say you source was correct about the kid."

Nick's brain spun with questions. What about this kid?
Why was he with al-Khultyer? Why...? His questions stopped
at the immediate problem. "Where'd they go?"

"Pemba. I've already spoken with my counterpart in
Maputo. He's rounding up his folks to pay a visit to the
airport."

"They'll be able to check the security cameras."

"I wouldn't count on it. They haven't gotten around to
installing them in their smaller airports"

"Great."

Conti unfolded a small piece of notepaper she'd pulled
from her jacket pocket and handed it to him. "We had to
apply a little arm twisting and call in a few favors, but my guys
got the names of the other folks in the queue. All of them
checked out but one traveling on an American passport, a guy
named Qasif Dalmar."

He looked at the paper. The name didn't register. Then he

remembered what Sanders told him the previous Saturday. "Holy shit."

"I take that to mean the name means something," Conti said.

"Chuck Sanders had an undercover agent in the terrorist camp we took down. He said his agent befriended an American kid from Minneapolis."

"Dalmar?"

"Probably. First time I've heard a full name."

"Has al-Khultyer traveled with anyone before?"

"No. Wait. After the Paris bombing, he... My God... Your question."

"What question?" Conti asked.

"There may be a pattern. Are there any resorts near Pemba?"

"They're several scattered along the coast. Why?"

"After the bombing in Paris, he ended up at an Italian ski resort with a woman he'd befriended."

Conti pulled out her smart phone. "Let's take a look." She tapped in her search words and scrolled through the results. "Okay, Pemba has quite a few... this one looks promising." She showed him the results on *TripAdvisor*.

Nick looked at the reviews of a small resort on Quilalea Island just off the coast. "Upscale private island."

"What's your guy like to do when he's not blowing things up?"

Nick thought about the profile he'd put together for al-Khultyer and the evidence that Gallet found in Paris. "I'd say, we need to take a look at that resort."

Chapter Forty

IBO ISLAND LODGE
QUIRIMBAS ARCHIPELOAGO, MOZAMBIQUE
FRIDAY 30 JANUARY

Bashir lingered over breakfast, listening to the muffled roar of waves breaking over the distant reef. A soft offshore breeze stirred the palms fronting his veranda. His bags were packed and the plane back to Pemba departed in an hour. He was in no hurry.

The flutter of tiny wings caught his ear. He tore off a piece of his croissant, tossed it on the wooden deck, and waited for the little bird he'd befriended. The staff informed him that it was a lilac breasted roller, one of the island's most beautiful. In a moment, a blur of brilliant color darted down to the deck and flew off with his offering.

He topped his coffee cup from the silver warmer and took a reflective sip. Yes, he could get used to this lifestyle. The night before, he even considered abandoning his plans and extending his stay. There was more than enough money in his Swiss account and he hadn't used the Credit Suisse card. And there was no indication the American, Parkos, had any idea where he was.

But he also understood he had to complete his mission. He would exorcise the demons threatening to consume him. He'd experienced brief moments of peace, like now, but they were rare. The memories of that day in Grozny, the 5th of February, haunted him. The anniversary. Just six days. Fifteen years. His body trembled, rage boiling to the surface. Katya would be a teenager, a young woman, full of life. And his Nadia…

Coffee sloshed over the edge of his cup. The red-brown liquid spread in a pool over the deck, like so much blood. He recoiled at the sight: Nadia, dead… His Katya dying in his arms, her brown eyes pleading. Her last words… *Ñaña*, daddy… His little angel. Gone. He could do nothing… A friend dragging him away...

"You ready to go?"

The sound startled him. The voice seemed to come from far in the distance. The coffee cup clattered onto the saucer.

"Sorry, man," Qasif said.

Bashir grabbed his napkin and leaned over to the mop up the mess covering the deck. The act gave him time to gather himself. He straightened, dropped the soaked napkin on the table, and looked at his watch. They didn't have to leave for another thirty minutes. "No, you're good. It's my fault." *Indeed*, he thought. It was his fault so many years ago and he would atone for his mistake.

He pushed the other chair away from the table with his foot. "Here, take a seat. We need to review our plans."

"We're going together then, Dhi'b?"

Bashir was gratified the kid still used his old name from the compound. Perhaps he hadn't picked up his new alias. All-the-better if he were to be captured and interrogated by the Americans. "No, after we get to Dar es Salaam, you're to continue to Rio by yourself."

"You're not coming?"

"No, I have made other arrangements."

"Where are you going?"

"It's best you don't know."

"But what am I supposed to do when I get there?"

Bashir suppressed a wave of anger, managing to keep his voice calm. "I've arranged a room for you at the Hotel Fasano on Ipanema Beach."

"Wow, like the song?"

"What song?"

"Man, you don't know? *The Girl from Ipanema.*" Qasif hummed a few bars. "It's a really famous song from the sixties."

Bashir chose not to answer. He didn't need to be reminded he was still dealing with a child. "There will be a Credit Suisse bank card in your name waiting for you at the hotel."

"But—"

"Once you are settled, you will contact me for additional instructions."

"But I—"

"Permit me to finish," Bashir said, anger now evident in his voice. "You will need to acquire a burner in Rio. And make sure it has international roaming." He reached into his pants pocket and extracted two slips of paper and a Mercedes car fob. He set the fob on the table and handed the papers over.

Qasif eyed the fob. "What about that?"

"Later."

Qasif unfolded the first slip of paper. On it, a single word: Parkos. "What's this?"

"The name of the man who has been chasing us. He must be eliminated. Since that may be difficult, I want you to find out all you can about his family. I've been told they live in Miami."

Qasif nodded and unfolded the second piece of paper.

"That is my contact number," Bashir said. "Memorize it.

When you call, just leave the number of your burner. No conversation. I will contact you."

"Okay."

Bashir fixed his eyes on Qasif. The kid was hard to judge and what he'd observed over the past several days had done little to instill confidence in the kid's ability to carry out his part of the mission. "Once in Rio, you will destroy your passport and obtain new travel documents. You will then check into a different hotel using your new identity."

"Any place I want?" Qasif asked.

"You may hang out in Rio. Use your new identity to buy an airline ticket to Canada, then cross the border. Do not go to your home in Minnesota. The Americans will be watching. Take a bus or train to Miami. Use cash and do not rent a car. You must be there no later than the 8th of February. Under no circumstance will you call me again. Do you understand?"

He paused, not sure if Qasif understood. He repeated his phone instructions. "You will call me only once and leave your contact number. I will call you. Can you do this?"

"I—"

"You told me you want to return to the United States to become a martyr. Has that changed?"

Qasif shook his head.

Bashir pushed the fob across the table. "Then listen very carefully to what I'm about to say."

Chapter Forty-One

PEMBA IINTERNATIONAL AIRPORT
PEMBA, MOZAMBIQUE
FRIDAY 30 JANUARY

A gust of wind rocked the single engine Cessna, jostling
the four passengers crammed into the small cabin.
Bashir grasped the attaché case resting on his lap, not happy
with the turbulence. He looked at the rapidly narrowing space
between the white centerline runway markers through the
open cockpit door. The horizon dipped to the right. The pilot
compensated. The plane bounced and settled on the ground.
The pilot taxied to the end of the strip, made a one hundred-
and-eighty degree turn, and proceeded toward the terminal.

Bashir happened to glance out his window just as a dull
gray two-engine Gulfstream touched down. Another rich
Arab. He turned his attention back to the contents of his
attaché case.

He extracted a pair of ticket packets and handed them to
Qasif. "We won't be sitting together on the flight to Dar es
Salaam. When we land, proceed directly to the gate. The
second packet is your confirmation for South African Airlines.

Your plane is scheduled to depart at 1430 for Johannesburg. From there, you will catch the connecting flight to Rio."

The Cessna slowed to a stop. Bashir glanced at the cockpit, noting the pilot flip several switches on the instrument panel. He closed his attaché and snapped the latches. He liked the finality of the sound. Soon, the kid would be on his own. If he got caught, so be it. He tucked in his elbow to allow the pilot to crabwalk his way down the aisle to open the rear exit door.

Bashir got up and followed him to the tarmac where he waited with Qasif and their bags. He nodded to the other two passengers, the young German couple he'd seen a couple times at the lodge. The husband spoke to Qasif.

"Did you get a chance to go diving on the reef? It was just—"

The whine of jet engines drowned out the rest of the German's sentence.

CIA SPECIAL MISSION AIRCRAFT
N30LX

Sanders leaned around the seat in front of him while their Gulfstream taxied to the terminal. "Well, if this is Friday, it must be Pemba."

Nick returned Sanders' remark with an irritated look.

"Jeez, loosen up, Parkos. It's a joke. Haven't you ever heard of the movie: *If It's Tuesday, This Must be Belgium?* Came out in the late sixties."

"I wasn't born yet."

Sanders exhaled, shook his head, and looked out the window at the whitewashed concrete terminal. There were only three planes parked on the tarmac, a Mozambique

Airlines Embraer e190, a two-engine turboprop, and a small four-passenger Cessna. "Step away, sir," he muttered under his breath, "There's nothing to see here."

"What?"

"Nothing," Sanders replied, unclipping his seatbelt.

Nick shot a glance outside as the Gulfstream slowed and made a right turn. He was afforded a momentary view of the Cessna before a flash of sunlight reflecting off the plane's windshield caused him to turn away. "Any bets that's our plane?"

Sanders leaned over Nick's lap to peer out the window. "I don't see anything else small enough to land on that postage stamp. Let's see what the embassy people have to say."

Nick looked at the tarmac. There were four people standing around the tail of the Cessna, their backs turned to him. He leaned over and pulled his carry-on from under the seat. "Maybe they've lined up a helo?"

"I'd rather take my chances in the Cessna," Sanders replied.

———

Bashir looked over his left shoulder at the Gulfstream. The jet had no markings except the aircraft identification number stenciled across the engine—N30LX. It nosed into the vacant spot next to them. He caught a glance at the faces looking out the jet's windows. *Westerners? It can't be.* He ducked his head, keeping his back to the jet.

"I believe this is yours," the pilot yelled over the noise.

"Yes, *merci*." Bashir collected his bag and caught up with the German couple placing them between him and the jet. Another few meters and he'd be out of sight. His mind was in turmoil. *How could they possibly know? No, it's not possible.* He walked through the door into the small reception area without looking back.

A small knot of men, definitely not tourists, stood off to one side watching the door. One glanced in his direction. He had no choice but to keep going. He couldn't run, where would he go? He turned his head as if talking to the German couple, using them to shield him from the three men. Six more steps and he'd be in the corridor.

He was so distracted by the men in the reception area, he almost ran into a khaki-clad security officer standing on the far side of the door. "Pardon me."

The man gave him a disinterested look.

Bashir exhaled and continued walking. He swung his eyes from side to side, alert for danger. Qasif was ahead of him. The kid disappeared into a restroom. Did he suspect anything? He had no way of knowing and he wasn't about to stop and ask.

The overhead speaker came to life. "This is the last call for Mozambique flight 1097 to Dar es Salaam, departing Gate 3."

Bashir looked at the number of the waiting area to his right. Gate 4. He willed himself to remain calm, fully expecting to hear a barrage of angry shouts from security personnel running to stop him.

He made his way to the counter, smiled at the agent, and presented his ticket. Moments later, he located 13A, took his seat, and looked out the window. A baggage trolley was pulling away from his plane. He spotted his luggage on the tarmac, then looked at the Gulfstream. Two men in sunglasses carrying aluminum hardshell suitcases were just entering the terminal.

He fastened his seatbelt and looked down the aisle. He spotted Qasif making his way toward the rear of the aircraft. They didn't make eye contact.

Chapter Forty-Two

PEMBA INTERNATIONAL AIRPORT
PEMBA, MOZAMBIQUE
FRIDAY 30 JANUARY

Nick followed Sanders into the terminal. He ignored the airport's overhead speaker blaring the last call for another flight. Three men stood along the bank of windows, facing the tarmac. Two of them broke free and crossed the room. The third remained by the windows, keeping a watchful eye on their surroundings. Nick saw Sanders give the man a nod of recognition and motion the team's special operatives to join him.

"Welcome to Mozambique, Mr. Parkos," one of them said when the flight announcement ended. "I'm Kevin Morales from the embassy. If you and your party will give your passports to Greg, he'll take care of the formalities."

Greg stepped forward, accepted their passports, and headed to customs.

"Do you need anything?" Morales asked.

"No, we're good," Nick answered. "Were you able to contact the resort manager?"

"He said one of his guests matched the description of your man, but his name didn't."

"An alias," Sanders said.

"Did he say anything about another person who may be traveling with him?" Nick asked.

"Nothing, but you'll be able to check that out yourself. I've arranged for a helicopter to take you there."

"How about the Cessna?" Sanders asked.

"Quilalea doesn't have a strip like some of the other island resorts."

"There're more?" Nick asked.

"Yeah, probably a dozen scattered across the Quirimbas archipelago: Vanmizi, Indigo Bay, Ibo Island Lodge—"

Nick cut him off. "Did you check them out?"

"No. Just the one you asked about. We assumed you knew."

Nick tightened his lips. He couldn't do anything about the misstep. But if al-Khulyter were on one of the other islands, he'd have a tough time getting off—unless he took a boat. *Damn.* They had to capture al-Khultyer before he could make a move. "Can you start calling them?"

Sanders spoke. "Are there any other airports around here?"

"Several," Kevin answered, "but keep in mind there are plenty of small time operators flying single-engine bush planes. They can land just about anywhere and most of them don't bother to file flight plans. There're also a number of seaplanes that serve the resorts."

"Can you cover them?" Sanders asked.

"It'll be tough. I'll contact the local authorities and see what we can do."

"We also need to set up a net just in case al-Khultyer tries to reach the coast by boat." Nick said.

Morales screwed up his lip at this latest twist. "Our best bet, then, is the FADM, the Armed Forces for the Defense of

Mozambique. There's a small Coast Guard station down the road. They've been rather successful in deterring the local smugglers. I'll have our military attaché give them a call."

Nick shuffled his feet, anxious to get going. He looked over the water. *Damn.* "How soon can we leave?"

Kevin pulled out his iPhone and entered a number. "Greg? ... Kevin. Can you meet us at the heliport? ... Right now ... Good." He spoke to Nick. "We've got a Bell 206 reserved for the entire day. We can get more time if you need it."

Sanders cocked a skeptical eyebrow.

"We've used these folks before. Parent company's German. Very reliable. No questions."

"Does the resort know we're coming?" Nick asked.

"No. It's a privately owned island, and they don't take kindly to drop-ins. The pilot will radio an in-flight emergency when he's five minutes out. There's a very nice putting green next to the main lodge."

"God damn it!" Nick crumpled the piece of paper in his hand. The manager at the Quilalea Lodge hadn't been happy at seeing the Americans literally arrive on his doorstep, but his anger couldn't match Nick's. The guest at the lodge didn't come close to resembling al-Khultyer's picture. *What the hell was that guy thinking?*

He let the balled-up piece of paper fall to the floor of the suite Morales had secured in a local hotel. He'd just blown hours on a wild goose chase. Written on the paper was a list of island resorts. Each had a check beside it, except one—Ibo Island Lodge.

Morales cringed at the display of anger. "The manager at the Lodge identified your man. He said Chéreau, that is al-Khultyer, and another guest named Qasif Dalmar checked out just before noon. They were on the Cessna that came in just before you arrived."

"Where are they?" Nick demanded.

"Not here," Morales replied.

"How do—?"

Morales continued before Nick could finish his question. "Two other aircraft departed shortly after the Cessna landed, both Mozambique Air. The turboprop went to Nampula, an inland city. The jet flew to Dar es Salaam."

Nick couldn't think of any reason why al-Khultyer would fly to Nampula. But Das es Salaam? Only ninety minutes flight time.

"A Mozambique Air agent identified both of them," Morales said. "I've called Anne Marie. She's sending a team to Julius Nyerere."

Nick looked at his watch. 1512. "How long ago did you talk with her?"

"Just before you touched down. Twenty, maybe twenty-five minutes ago."

"There's still time," Sanders said.

———

Nick chewed on the tip of his pen. An untouched sandwich lay on the desk beside the yellow legal pad he'd jotted down the flight schedules of the aircraft leaving Dar es Salaam. Had he made the correct decision? He'd taken a gamble and asked Conti to ignore the regional airlines and focus on the major carriers.

There were lines drawn through Delta, KLM, Air France, Turkish, and EgyptAir. They all reported no one with the names of Chéreau or Dalmar were booked on any of their flights. He was still waiting to hear South African Airlines and several from the Gulf States.

He set down his pen. "Chuck, you got anything new?"

Sanders' phone rang before he could answer. "Sanders ... You're sure? ... 2:35? ... Have you contacted Pretoria? ... Yeah, I understand."

Nick waved his hand to get Sanders' attention. "Ask them about Emirates and Qatar Air."

Sanders' nodded. "How about Emirates and Qatar Air? ... Just now?" He lifted the receiver away from his mouth. "Qatar's clear." He gave a throat-slash with his free hand. "He is? ... Okay, thanks. We owe you."

"They've found them?"

"We may have found Dalmar. South African Airlines has someone by that name on a flight to Johannesburg. He's got a connecting—"

"Forget about him. Have they found al-Khultyer?"

"They're still looking."

Nick stared at his legal pad. He'd made a mistake. "Call them back. They need to start checking the regional airlines." Another thought occurred to him. "No, wait."

His fingers ran over his keyboard typing *Orbitz.com*. When the site came up, he refined his search to Dar es Salaam and Emirates Air. *There it is.* DAR to DXB. Dar es Salaam to Dubai. Flight 722. One stop. Nairobi. Regional partner, Precision Air. Flight time: 1hr 20min to Nairobi. 5 hr to Dubai.

"He took Precision Air. He's flying to Dubai on Emirates Airways."

Sanders picked up his phone. "Tyvis? Check the manifest for any Precision Air flights to Nairobi ... Yeah, I know. We said not to. Listen, Parkos thinks al-Khultyer's connecting to an Emirates flight to Dubai ... How the hell should I know. Just do it."

"They think I'm nuts?" Nick asked.

"I suspect they think we're both nuts," Sanders replied. "So, where are we?"

"If I'm right, al-Khultyer will be in Dubai in three hours."

"We've got time. As soon as Powell gets us verification, I'll call my contact at the Embassy. The Emirates counter-terrorism police can arrest him at the airport."

Nick eyed his sandwich. He was suddenly starving.

———

Nick woke to a hand touching his shoulder.

"Sir?

He shook his head to clear the cobwebs. Greg, the embassy staffer, held a secure satellite phone. "Yes?"

"Sir, I have Pretoria. Can you take the call?"

He took the phone. "Parkos."

"Mr. Parkos, this is Mike Delaney in Pretoria. I'm afraid I have bad news on your man, Dalmar."

Nick braced himself. "Okay, what do you have?"

"The South Africans detained him as soon as he got off the plane, but they've released him."

Nick was incredulous. "But didn't you tell them he's on our terrorism watch list?"

"Somebody screwed up and released him. Said he had a valid passport, cleared security."

"His passport was—?" He stopped himself. He couldn't think of anything that he or the embassy in Pretoria could do. "Where is he now?"

"On a SAA flight to Rio de Janerio. If you'd like, we'll notify the embassy."

"Mr. Parkos?"

Another voice. Greg's.

Nick frowned at the interruption. He couldn't keep the edge from his voice. "Just a moment, Greg. I'm finishing up."

Greg held out another phone. "It's Washington. You need to take this."

"Nick, take the call," Sanders said.

Nick startled at the command in Sanders' voice. He looked at him. "I—"

"I'll finish up with Pretoria," Sanders said. "Your boss is on the line."

Nick relented. He handed his phone to Sanders and took Greg's. "Parkos."

"Nick, this is Ed Strickland."

"Hello, sir. It's—"

"Listen, Nick. I just got a call. It's not good."

Nick's hand tightened around the receiver.

"You have to go to Miami. There's been an accident."

A feeling of dread swept over him. *Miami? His family? Emma?* His heart began to pound. "Accident?"

"Marty called—"

"Marty?"

"She couldn't find you," Strickland said.

Find me? He tried to remember the last time she'd called him. "What happened?"

"Emma's been admitted to Nicklaus Children's Hospital's intensive care unit. She almost drowned. I don't know the details."

"I need—"

"Nick. We'll take care of everything. Let me talk to Chuck, okay? You need to call Marty."

Dizziness washed over him. He grabbed the edge of the desk. Strickland's voice faded... nothing more than buzzing... someone else spoke... Sanders? Someone eased the phone from his hand.

Chapter Forty-Three

BOSCOLO EXEDRA HOTEL
ROME, ITALY
SUNDAY 1 FEBRUARY

"*Mi scusi, signore.*"

Bashir moved his cocktail to one side so his waitress could set down his antipasto.

"Will you need anything else?" she purred.

"*No, grazie.*"

He cast a glance at his waitress, admiring her long legs, then turned his attention to his plate. Choosing a large green olive, he popped it into his mouth and carefully nibbled around the pit. *Magnifico. Such a simple thing, yet such perfection. Like so many things Italian.*

He took a sip of his Campari Spritzer and surveyed the bustle of activity in the Plazza della Repubblica. The city was so vibrant, the Italians so full of life. He would have to return one day.

A crowd of locals emerging from the metro station caught his eye. Some carried signs and these joined a larger group congregating in front of the building to his left. The building, paired with his hotel, formed half of a monumental semicircle fronting the piazza. Three police vans drew up. He tensed, placing his hands on the edge of the table preparing to push away.

He caught a snippet of conversation from the next table. The sign wavers were protesting unfair labor practices and the *polizia* were from the *Vigili Urbani*, traffic control. He watched the uniformed men exit their vans and begin to block off the square. The protestors paid no attention as two of the *polizia* herded several of their compatriots back onto the safety of the sidewalk.

He continued to eavesdrop, fascinated by the choreographed event unfolding before him. Apparently, this sort of protest was a common occurrence. In another hour, the crowd would disperse, having exercised their civic duty. Soon the traffic would flow and the taxis would be able to enter the roundabout. Nobody in the square seemed bothered by the temporary inconvenience and, in truth, he was planning to walk to dinner.

He'd stumbled across the *Ristorante Rinaldi al Quirinale* the day before while exploring the side streets branching off the Via Nazionale. When he perused the dinner menu, the melted snapper intrigued him. He had no idea what to expect but, based on what he'd eaten for lunch, it would be spectacular.

The dinner wasn't the only thing spectacular. The setting sun cast a golden hue on the buildings surrounding him. Floodlights lit the Fountain of the Naiad that dominated the center of the piazza. Beyond the fountain lay the ancient basilica of Santa Maria degli Angeli e dei Martiri, designed by Michelangelo.

An elegant woman in a black designer dress slipped by his table, her hips swaying seductively. A hint of her expensive perfume lingered in the air as she passed. Such beauty. Should he not avail himself of such an opportunity? He pondered his own question. And what opportunities would present on the *Étoile de Mer*?

He held his Spritzer up to the light. The remaining bubbles of Prosecco drifting to the top of the glass sparkled. He caught the scent of the boutonnière cologne he'd purchased that afternoon in the Brioni boutique. What had the salesman said of the under-tones of the fragrance? "An undisputed sartorial detail?" He finished his Spritzer and set the glass aside. Yes, he should not neglect the details.

CICITAVECHIA HARBOR
MONDAY 2 FEBRUARY

Bashir peeled seventy-five euros from his money clip, counted out another twenty-five, and handed them to the limousine driver. "*Mille gracie*".

He'd made his own reservation with the limo company, not wanting to risk leaving his name and destination with the hotel's concierge. There remained a remote possibility the Americans could track him to Rome. But to Civitavecchia? *Impossible.*

The only link remaining to the *Étoile de Mer* was through his travel agency, À Souhait. He'd destroyed the credit card and closed the Swiss account he'd used to pay for the cruise, but his current name and passport information were on the reservation. That remained a potential problem. On a positive note, his new iPhone and prepaid Europe SIM card were registered under the assumed name, Jean Luc Prévost. They would be very difficult to trace.

A ruckus coming from the drop-off lane broke into his train of thought. He turned to see a handsome woman in fashionable stiletto heels standing beside two large suitcases.

She was quite animated, gesturing vigorously with both hands at a hapless taxi driver. He would have thought her Italian, except she spoke English with an American accent.

"What do you mean there is no transport?" she said, spinning around to point down the line of huge cruise ships tied up to the quay. "I can't even see my ship. Surely I'm not expected to drag my suitcases all that way? It must be at least a quarter mile."

The taxi driver shrugged. "Perhaps you can call the ship, Signora."

"How am I supposed to call the *Étoile de Mer*? I don't have the number." The woman swung her arm across the front of an ancient castle bordering the drop-off area. "Do you even see a kiosk?" This is unaccept—"

Bashir smiled at the spectacle. She would do very nicely and, as a bonus, she had beautiful eyes. "Pardon, Madame. Perhaps I may help."

The startled woman dropped whatever she was going to say and faced Bashir. "Why, thank you. Maybe you can. She gestured at the retreating taxi driver. "That man—"

"The taxi driver is correct," Bashir interrupted. "We must all walk."

"But ..."

"I couldn't help but overhear you say you wanted to go to the *Étoile de Mer*. That is my ship as well. If you will permit, I can pull your largest trolley."

She relented with a sigh and offered her hand. "Marilyn."

"Jean Luc," Bashir answered accepting her hand with a small bow. "You are an American then?"

"Yes, I live in Miami. I thought it would be a nice change to take a ship home."

ÉTOILE de MER

Bashir and Marilyn made small talk until they reached the canopied boarding ramp of the *Étoile de Mer*. A liveried porter approached from the shade. He eyed the green tag affixed to the handle of Bashir's hang-up bag. "May I assist you with your luggage, sir?"

"Yes, thank you."

The porter lifted the tag and read the pre-printed label. "If you would please proceed to registration, Monsieur and Madame Chéreau and—"

"We're not travelling together." Marilyn pointed to her bags. "Those two are mine."

The porter checked the tags. "Yes, I see. Very good, Madame. Your luggage will be waiting for you in your stateroom."

Bashir tried to catch Marilyn's last name on her tag but was unable to do so before the porter whisked her luggage out of sight. He wasn't concerned. His eyes followed her up the ramp. There would be ample opportunity to learn her name, and perhaps much more, during their ten-day voyage.

———

Bashir popped the cork of the complimentary champagne, filling the crystal flute to the brim. He took a sip and walked to the counter beneath the room's flat screen TV. Below the TV was arrayed a personalized greeting packet, a bowl of fruit, and a satellite direct line telephone. He picked up the greeting package and sat on the sofa to familiarize himself with the ship's phone, WiFi setup, and Internet access. He didn't have his own laptop, so he'd need to use the ship's Internet café... or perhaps Marilyn had an iPad he could persuade her to let him use? The American's beauty fascinated him.

He reached for one of the chocolate-covered strawberries

arranged on a plate next to the champagne bucket. *Yes, Marilyn. You are such an interesting creature.*

His lips closed over the fruit, lingering a moment savoring the sensation before he bit down. The brittle chocolate coating snapped, melting on his tongue. *Where will you fit in my plan?* He dropped the green-leafed remnant on the plate, downed the last of his champagne, and headed out to explore the ship.

His first stop was the main lounge aft on the second deck where the pirates had gained access to the ship. He looked across the ballroom floor to the piano bar, visualizing what had taken place eight days earlier. He spotted a solitary bullet hole in the ceiling the crew had missed in their repairs.

A blast of the ship's horn signaled their imminent departure. He made his way forward to the Panoramic Lounge to join the other passengers. The expansive space overlooking the bow was just as the pirate had described it. He wove his way through a cluster of oversized chairs and past the piano to the wrap-around bench in the corner of the room. This is where the pirate said he'd placed the rucksack containing the explosives. *Excellent. And the pirate? Dead?*

A ship's steward carrying a tray of champagne and another holding a platter of hor d'oeuvres for his inspection stopped by his side. He was about to select a liver pâte, when he saw Marilyn enter the lounge. She'd changed into a short, emerald-green evening dress perfectly complementing her long auburn hair. He ignored the pâte, lifted two flutes of champagne, and walked across the room.

"Good evening," Bashir said, offering her a flute. "I was just going outside. Would you care to join me?"

"*Comment vas-tu, mon ami?*" she said, accepting the champagne.

"You speak a little French, then?"

"That's about the extent of it," she answered with a laugh. "I memorized a few other survival phrases. 'I'm lost.' 'Where's the bathroom?'"

"Then we shall stay with English," he said, joining her in another laugh. He swung open the glass door leading outside. "Shall we?"

He placed his hand lightly on the small of her back, guiding her to a place by the rail. They stood without speaking, absorbing the beauty of the pastel-colored buildings of the city.

"The view is spectacular, *oui?*"

She held up her champagne and clicked his flute in a toast. Her eyes held his. "To a wonderful start."

Bashir had the odd sensation sweep through him that they were the only two people standing on the deck.

Chapter Forty-Four

MIAMI INTERNATIONAL AIRPORT
MIAMI, FLORIDA
SUNDAY 1 FEBRUARY

Nick couldn't think. He'd barely slept, consumed with worry about Emma. Worry was just part, though. Marty also surfaced in his jumbled thoughts. *How could she have left Emma alone?* He caught himself. He'd left his daughter too, hadn't he? He hadn't even found the time to visit. He'd always had some excuse. *And now?*

"Pardon me," said a middle-aged woman behind him.

He stepped out of the way and looked at the overhead signs. *There.* He lifted his leaden feet and followed the arrows to baggage claim. Twenty-six hours and counting. There simply hadn't been any better way to get Miami. Dar es Salaam to Amsterdam to Atlanta to Miami. Marty's first update reached him in Amsterdam. "Emma is still on the ventilator. The doctors will know more in another twelve hours." Her second call had found him in Atlanta nearly four hours ago.

He pulled his bag off the conveyor, apologized his way

through the crowd, and made for the open space by the exit doors.

"Nick. Nick!"

Marty ran toward him. She threw herself into his arms, almost knocking him over. His arms went around her, more to keep his balance than in any form of greeting. Then slowly, his arms tightened in a comforting embrace. Sobs wracked her body.

"Oh, God, Nick. I'm so sorry. I'm so sorry. It's all my fault. I... I wasn't watching. She was only in the water a..." She choked off a sob.

"It's okay," he said over and over again. He stroked her hair until she calmed.

"Mom and Dad are at the hospital. Dad..."

He released her. He didn't want to hear about her parents, especially her father. He looked at her for the first time. She looked terrible. "How's Emma?"

Marty pulled a tissue from her purse and dabbed her red, swollen eyes, leaving a dirty smear of mascara over her cheeks. "She's stable. The doctors said she made it through a critical period. She's still heavily sedated. I'll tell you more in the car. We should go."

———

A nurse gently ushered Nick into the curtained room. "Emma's sedated and won't be able to respond to you, but she's been showing signs of improvement. The doctors ..."

He nodded. He understood her words, but nothing she said could have prepared him for the first sight of his daughter.

"Boy, you could sure use a shave."

What?

"Nick, we're so glad you're here."

The second voice belonged to his mother-in-law, but the

other? Nick clenched his fists, the anger born of worry, fatigue, and guilt boiling to the surface.

Nick glared at his father-in-law. They never did get along. Jim blamed him for the divorce, for everything. Was that his way of breaking the ice? Some sort of joke? His "humor" was always a bit off, never quite appropriate to the situation. Even now. He'd always had a talent for making a bad situation, worse.

He managed to force his hands to relax and addressed his mother-in-law. "Thank you, Ann. I appreciate you being here."

He faced his father-in-law. "Could you give me a moment alone with my daughter?" It wasn't a request. He looked at the nurse who'd escorted him to Emma's bedside.

The nurse took a step forward to guide the two grandparents from the room. "Mr. and Mrs. Heckler, why don't you come with me?"

They were almost out the door when another nurse appeared. She carried a large vase of red roses. "We waited to bring these, Mr. Parkos," she said, placing the vase on the bedside table. "We don't ordinarily allow flowers in the patient rooms, but in this case, we're making an exception." She didn't explain why.

Nick couldn't react. The mechanical sound of the ventilator was all he heard. Phuff-uff, phuff-uff, phuff-uff. Phuff-in, uff-out. In-out, In-out, In-out. He looked at his daughter. Her eyes were closed as if she were sleeping. She looked so fragile, so … He didn't know what to think.

A clear plastic tube, angling out of her mouth, led to the ventilator. The sheet covering her chest moved up and down. Phuff-uff, phuff-uff, phuff-uff. He couldn't accept the reality of what was happening. *Why?*

There was too much going through his mind to comprehend what the nurse said. He just wanted to hold Emma in his arms, as much to comfort her as to seek his own comfort from her. A moment from years ago flashed in his mind. She was almost three. He'd been fussing about something—a football game? Emma watched him, obviously thinking. Then she'd left and returned with her pacifier. She handed it to him. *Now, Daddy, just calm down.*

Was that her favorite stuffed bear next to her pillow? The one he'd given her? Tears welled in his eyes. He needed to sit. The only chair, a recliner, beckoned from the far corner of the room.

The nurse held out an envelope embossed with the gold Presidential Seal, like the ones he'd seen on Air Force One. "They're from President and Mrs. Stuart."

He took the envelope and slowly extracted the hand-written card. "Nick and Marty, please know that Emma and you both are in our prayers." They'd signed it. Randal and Dianne. He caught a glimpse of Jim's face. His father-in-law stood slacked-jawed in disbelief. Nick ignored him and sat on the edge of the bed. He took his daughter's hand.

"Honey?"

He looked up at the sound of Marty's voice. She hadn't called him that in years. A woman in a long white coat, a stethoscope wrapped around her neck, stood next to her.

"Honey, this is Emma's doctor."

The doctor stepped forward, extending her hand. "I'm Dr. Norwood."

Nick accepted her hand. "How is she?"

"Emma's doing very well. It was a near thing but your wife's actions saved her life."

"What about the respirator?"

"A precaution at this point. Emma's pulse ox, her blood oxygen level dropped, but has returned to normal. Often in near drownings, there is a delayed inflammatory reaction in the lungs. She's past that point, so we'll be extubating... removing the tube today."

Nick's shoulders slumped in a mixture of fatigue and relief. "Thank you, Doctor. Thank so much."

MONDAY 2 FEBRUARY

"Will you be staying?" Marty asked.

"A few more days, then I'll need to get back," Nick said. He felt a pang of guilt, but al-Khultyer was still out there, somewhere.

Marty's face remained expressionless. They'd had a long talk over dinner. There was no animosity, no finger pointing, no recriminations. They'd remain friends, but both understood reconciliation wasn't possible. They'd matured and grown apart, each building a new life. He'd told her what he could of his work. She professed to be happy with her new job, but he read something different in her eyes.

"Daddy?" Emma croaked.

Nick reached for her hand. Doctor Norwood had removed her endotracheal tube allowing her to talk. "Hi, Munchkin. How are you feeling?"

"My throat hurts."

Marty handed Nick a small plastic cup containing a yellow Cepacol lozenge.

"Here Munchkin, suck on this candy. It'll make it feel better."

"Daddy, can you stay with us?"

He couldn't answer. "Open wide."

———

Nick flicked on the light of his room in the Marriott Residence Inn and dropped onto the couch. He reached for the remote, turned on the TV, and flipped through the stations looking for something to help him decompress. All that seemed to be on were infomercials and sitcoms. He looked at his watch. 9:48. It seemed later.

He hit mute and wandered over to the counter of the small kitchenette. He selected a water glass from the cupboard and poured two fingers of Wild Turkey bourbon from the bottle he'd purchased. He returned to the couch and stared at the TV. *Damn, I'm a mess.*

He turned his attention to his bourbon and polished off the glass with a gulp. *What now?* He pulled out his iPhone and scrolled through his messages, stopping at one from his boss. It said simply to call when he had a moment. He'd better call.

———

"Strickland."

"Mr. Strickland? This is Nick. I saw your message."

"How are you doing?"

"Well enough, sir. My daughter's going home tomorrow."

"She's okay then?"

He skipped the details. "Her doctor said she'll make a full recovery."

"Good. I don't suppose you can get back to DC?"

"I hoped to stay for a couple more days."

"I see… Well, then, I'll need to arrange for a place for you to work in Miami. We haven't been able to find your target. I've got a hunch he's on the way to the States."

"Hunch?" Nick's response slipped out before he could stop it. "Don't you think you're being a bit paranoid?" Nick noted a pause before Strickland responded. The room did a slight spin. *Crap, the Wild Turkey.*

"I'm paid to be paranoid. So are you."

He detected the reproach in Strickland's voice and sought to make amends. "Sorry, sir. My brain hasn't been working all that well."

"Understood. Get some rest and get your head on straight."

"Yes, sir."

"I'll call Homeland Security's bureau in Miami. If I remember, they're only a short drive from the airport. You have a rental?"

"Yes, sir."

"Good. Touch base with me tomorrow after you're set up."

The connection went dead. Nick stared at his phone, not quite sure what to do. He was supposed to help Marty with Emma's discharge, and…

He poured another four ounces of bourbon, took a swallow, and fished out his wallet. He found what he was looking for behind Gallet's business card. He pulled out the card Michelle had given him on Air Force One. He turned it over, looking at her handwriting, the smiley face. He needed a smile, to hear her voice. Work could wait.

He entered her number in his iPhone and pressed the call button. It rang several times then cut off. He redialed. This time, she picked up.

"Hello?" Her voice sounded hesitant.

"Michelle, this is Nick. Nick Parkos. From Paris."

"Oh! Hi, stranger. I didn't recognize your number, so I hung up. Sorry about that."

He heard voices in the background. "If this isn't a good time—"

"No, no. We're good. I just have a few friends over. They can take care of themselves. How've you been?"

"I've been better."

Chapter Forty-Five

HOTEL FASONO
RIO de JANERIO, BRAZIL
MONDAY 2 FEBRUARY

Qasif stood at the curb outside his hotel studying the map he'd picked up at the concierge desk. The concierge explained the best way to get to Complexo do Alemão was by taxi, but she added a warning: He must be very careful. Despite being one of the supposed pacified areas cleared for the upcoming Olympics, the favelas was not a place for tourists, let alone for an unwary local. Just the week before, she emphasized, a policewoman was shot to death there in broad daylight. Qasif considered that. He'd have to take his chances.

He flagged down one of the city's blue and yellow taxis and climbed into the back seat.

"Destino por favor?"

Qasif showed the driver his map where he'd circled the address.

The driver reached up to the console and turned off his meter. "Special fare. Two hundred real."

Qasif wasn't surprised at the request, but the demand was exorbitant. The driver wanted three times the going rate. He countered. "One hundred."

"One-hundred fifty."

Qasif relented. "Half now, half later."

The driver held out his hand. "Okay."

Qasif handed him seventy-five and settled into his seat as the driver headed north along the bay for the thirty-minute drive. He didn't focus on the passing beaches and the bikini clad women strolling along the ocean's edge. He'd managed to find a source that could provide him with a new identity— NeedaPassport.com. The problem was, he'd lost a day making the connection with the company. Then after making contact through the unlikely website, he'd been instructed to go to the beach across from his hotel and wait by the concession stand. Someone would meet him. True enough. He looked out the window. He'd made it this far, but yesterday's experience had been nerve-wracking.

He'd been blindfolded and driven somewhere in the city. In a makeshift photo office, they'd taken his picture and relieved him of his down payment. Before dropping him at his hotel, they'd informed him they needed additional time to procure the necessary items. Qasif presumed that would be a stolen passport. That was reasonable, but he remained concerned he wouldn't be able to be in Miami by Dhi'b's deadline. Then again, the whole deal with NeedaPassport could have been a set-up. He might be headed to God knows where, already out several thousand dollars.

The cabbie slowed and made a left-hand turn away from the waterfront. The neighborhoods became increasingly shabby. He found himself agreeing with the concierge. This was not a place any tourist in his right mind would go. But then, most people thought he wasn't in his right mind. The memories only increased his resolve.

The driver turned right and headed up a narrow street.

Ramshackle buildings and shanties were crammed together, spilling down the mountainside in a haphazard heap. Piles of trash filled the gutters. The cab slowed to a stop.

Qasif checked his map. As best as he could determine, they were still blocks from his destination. He leaned over the front seat and pointed to the circled address. "Here."

The driver shook his head. "*No mas. Tu esta louco.*"

Qasif understood the "no and loco" parts. He looked out the window. They were idling at a corner across from a shuttered building; Farmacia do Trabaloador. A pharmacy? He spotted a couple of shirtless teens strolling toward them, likely sensing an easy mark.

The driver saw the threat. He reached around trying to open Qasif's door. "*No mas.*"

Qasif sized up the two toughs. He didn't see any weapons and doubted they'd be expecting a fight. He could take them. He handed the driver the remaining seventy-five reals and pushed open the door.

"Hey gringo," the shorter one wearing plaid board shorts said. "You lost, eh? Maybe we help you." His partner took several steps, blocking Qasif's way back to the taxi.

Qasif turned toward the blocker, judging the distance. He waited for the kid to close the distance. His right leg whipped out in a vicious snap kick. The ball of his foot impacted on the outside of the blocker's leg with an audible crack. The tough screamed and collapsed holding his dislocated knee. Qasif spun, took one step forward, grabbed the smaller one's shoulders, and drove his knee into his groin. The kid let out a grunt and collapsed, writhing on the sidewalk.

Qasif looked around. The cab was gone and so were the few locals who'd been standing around watching. A lone kid ran up the street, dodging around a junked car. Qasif pulled out his map and got his bearings. He looked up the cluttered street where the kid had disappeared and followed him.

The place stank of urine and rancid garbage. Graffiti

covered the building fronts. Wanted posters with the header, *Procurados*, shared a decaying wall. Several of the faces on the poster were X'd out. *Dead?* A dog growled. He moved on, side-stepping a pile of dog shit swarming with flies.

"You don't belong here."

Qasif stopped. The voice came from what appeared to be a bistro across the street. Two small tables were placed outside, one empty. Four men gathered around the other, two standing, two perched on tiny wooden stools. All were bare-chested except one wearing a yellow muscle shirt. Five brown quart-sized beer bottles crowded the space between the seated men.

Qasif caught a glimpse of the kid he'd seen run up the street peaking over the shoulder of the shirted man.

Muscle Shirt picked up one of the beer bottles, took a swig, and then waved it vaguely in the air. "It is best you leave, gringo."

Qasif decided to take a guess. He had to be somewhere near the right address. "I have business with Cezinha."

Muscle Shirt set the bottle on the table, stared at Qasif, then pushed the kid toward the door. "Tell Cezinha he has a visitor." To Qasif he said, "Come, my friend. Share a beer with us. You are either brave or very foolish." He grinned, exposing a large gold-capped tooth. "Both, I think."

———

Qasif didn't get back to his room until well after midnight. He flopped down on the bed and turned on the TV, then turned it off, got up, and went to the bathroom. He stared in the mirror, running his hand over his face. He'd have to shave again so his picture bore a closer resemblance to that of Ahsan Habib, the man whose identity he'd stolen. Beyond the absence of his beard, he didn't dwell on what other changes were reflected in his face. He dropped his hand. His eyes stared back at him from the mirror. Habib's were blue, not uncommon in the people of northern Afghanistan. In the morning, he'd have to see if he could find some contact lenses.

There was one more item he needed to attend to before going to sleep. On the way back to the hotel he'd passed a twenty-four-hour Internet café. He flipped off the overhead light and headed back out to do some research. He pulled out the first slip of paper Dhi'b had given him and unfolded it as the elevator door closed. What would he be able to find on this Parkos?

―――

He woke just before eight the next morning after a deep sleep. He wasn't pleased he'd slept so long, but he had to admit he felt better. After taking a shower and downing several strong cups of black coffee, he made his way to the lobby.

"Good morning, sir. How may I help you?" the man behind the registration desk asked.

"I'm expecting a package. Could you please check?" Qasif answered. "Dalmar. Room 1326."

"I will see." the clerk turned away. He appeared to be looking at the street.

Qasif flicked his eyes toward the front door, not knowing what to expect. A woman with an oversized purse was just leaving.

"Yes, one just arrived by messenger for you." the man lifted a brown mailing envelope off the counter and handed it over.

Qasif felt the shape of his new passport and reached for his wallet to provide his ID.

"That won't be necessary sir."

Qasif made his way back to his room, ripped open the envelope, and reached inside for the passport. His hand touched something else and pulled out a second, smaller white envelope. He opened it and extracted Ahsan Habib's BMO

Harris Bank card and his driver's license. He recalled what Cezinha had said: "Good for you, amigo, but maybe not so good for Señor Habib, eh?"

Habib had apparently met with an unfortunate accident while traveling alone to the *Christo Redentor* statue. Cezinha said the accident would provide Qasif enough time to get out of the country before someone notified the authorities that Habib was missing.

He put the credit card and license in his wallet and flipped through his new passport. He was now a Canadian citizen from Hamilton, Ontario—wherever the hell that was. Cezinha's forger had done an excellent job, but it had come at a price. The transaction cost Qasif most of his cash reserve. The credit card alone had set him back four thousand reals, over one thousand dollars.

He set the passport down and opened the room's safe, counting out his remaining cash. There was barely enough to purchase his tickets. He closed the safe, reminding himself he'd hardly been in a position to negotiate the cost with Cezinha and his toughs.

In any event, now that he had his new identity, he could check into a new hotel and make his airline reservations. The hotel was the easy part. He'd located a likely place on a tree-lined avenue not far from the Fasono—the Lasarito Hostel.

The plane reservations proved to be a bit more difficult, in part because he'd made some wrong assumptions. The first was assuming Air Canada would have a direct fight to Montreal, or any major Canadian city. All of the Canadian airlines routes had two stops in the States and the total trip would take nearly thirty hours. That would barely leave him enough time to reach Miami by the eighth. He still had no idea why Dhi'b made such a big deal about the eighth. He shrugged. *Whatever.*

He picked up the room phone and placed his call. His ticket on Delta for the seventeen-hour flight to Toronto involved only one stop in Atlanta where he would have to change planes.

This arrangement left him with a number of concerns. The first: he hadn't wanted to use an American carrier. While the odds were small, Ahsan Habib could be on Homeland Security's watch or no-fly lists. He also had no idea if he'd have to go through customs in Atlanta. He suspected he wouldn't, but if he did? His picture would be taken by one of the cameras in customs and his photo would be run through TSA's facial recognition database.

He stared out the window, a blurred image of his face reflecting back at him. He looked enough like the real Habib that he might just be able to pull it off. Maybe he could go to a salon and buy some makeup?

He flopped down on the bed, feeling a bit better. He fished around in his pants pocket and pulled out his burner, staring at it for several minutes while he ran through his plans. Maybe he could just cut his ties with Dhi'b? After all, once he was in Atlanta, he could simply disappear. *Maybe.* What were the chances of ever seeing him again? It didn't help his state of mind knowing Dhi'b wanted him to kill Parkos' family.

He decided he was wasting his time worrying and entered the phone number he'd memorized. He had no idea where Dhi'b was, or in what time zone. It didn't really matter. He heard the ring tones, then the standard, "Leave a message at the beep, if you'd like more options ... yadda, yadda." The seemingly endless monolog always set him on edge.

He pulled the phone away from his ear and cursed. *Shamoodo!*

Beep.

"Dhi'b, this is Sirhaan. 011-55-21-6812-3761." He hung up, then realized he hadn't followed his instructions, "Just leave the number."

Oh, well. How could it hurt?

Chapter Forty-Six

HOMELAND SECURITY BUREAU
MIAMI, FLORIDA
TUESDAY 3 FEBRUARY

Nick thanked his escort from Homeland Security and
settled in behind his temporary desk. The Bureau had
done a commendable job setting up the space for him on such
short notice. He unfolded his short To-Do list and set it to one
side. He rested his hands on the keyboard, recalling Strickland's words. "Get some rest and get your head on straight."

The rest part had not gone particularly well, even after
talking with Michelle. He'd tossed and turned most of the
night, worrying about all manner of things as they flashed,
one after another, through his mind: How would he get his
rent payment in? Would his car start after sitting in the
parking lot for weeks in the cold? Like most of the numbing
nights he'd been experiencing of late, none of what he
thought about resulted in anything useful.

The nightmares were the worst thing, though. They'd jolt
him awake, heart pounding. He kept reliving variants, fragments, of the same scenes, unable to suppress the horrors of

what he'd seen, what he'd done. The vultures picking at the face of the dead terrorist, the lipless grin laughing at him. Then in his dreams—the snake slithering out of the corpse's mouth, striking at him. Blood oozing from the two punctures on his arm. Falling. Falling.

He massaged the dull ache in the base of his skull. The bottle of Wild Turkey back in his hotel room? Almost empty. *Yeah, that was a problem.* A problem that would require more to fix than just stopping by the liquor store. Strickland's words returned. "Get your head on straight."

He knew he needed to talk to someone, but whom? A shrink? No way. And Marty was out of the question. Marty. *Oh, shit.* He'd told her he'd pick something up for dinner. God, he didn't even know Emma's favorite meal. *Don't blow it. Think.*

Emma, the only positive in his life. She was home and improving. Her cognitive abilities didn't appear to be affected and she was talking more. He and Marty were both terrified at what Dr. Norwood had said the day before. "Up to one-third of near drowning survivors had neurologic sequelae." *Would Emma be one of them?*

Neither of them ventured to the backyard pool still surrounded by drooping yellow crime scene tape. Marty was completely shaken by the limited investigation that implied she might be guilty of child neglect.

Damn it. Focus. He glanced at his To-Do list. The first item? Yellow Tape. He'd promised Marty he'd inquire about removing the tape since no charges had been filed. Finally reaching someone at the police department who gave his approval, he called Marty, and turned his thoughts to work.

He'd left Tanzania three days ago, but it seemed like an eternity. Except for the brief call to Strickland, he'd had no contact with the agency. He had no idea where the search for al-Khultyer and his probable associate, Qasif Dalmar, stood. He discarded any thought of calling Taylor Ferguson in Washington even though the CIA agent had been right about

Aleem's compound. If al-Khultyer was heading to the U.S. as Strickland suspected, the CIA would not have jurisdiction. He'd be collaborating with the FBI and Homeland Security.

First things first, though. He looked at his watch, calculating the time in Djibouti. Six-thirty in the evening. Sanders picked up on the third ring.

"Sanders."

"Chuck, this is Nick. You free?"

"How's Emma?"

"She's doing better. We took her home this morning."

"Outstanding. So, how are you doing?"

"About as good as can be expected."

"Roger that. What's on your mind?"

"I'm hoping you have something on al-Khultyer and Dalmar. I've been completely out of the loop."

"I do, but you're not going to be happy."

"My boss thinks al-Khultyer may be headed here."

"That would be as good a guess as any. Emirates Airlines confirmed a first class passenger by the name of Jean Luc Chéreau on their flight from Dar es Salaam. We contacted our embassy. They placed an alert to Dubai's security police."

"I take it he managed to elude them." Nick jotted down a few notes.

"Not exactly. The police just took their time getting to the airport."

"How long?"

"Six hours."

"Six hours? What the hell happened?"

"Short answer, we got screwed. The Dubai authorities sat on our request until they were sure al-Khultyer was out of the country. Turns out some minor sheik related to the ruling family had to bail out of the country after being stopped by LAPD for racing his Ferrari through an upscale Bel-Air neighborhood. In any event, some royal was miffed and stonewalled us.

"Do we know where he is?"

"Rome. And before you ask, by the time we found out and contacted the Italians, he'd disappeared. A security camera caught him walking out of the terminal. The NOCS, their Central Security Operations Service, is trying to find out what happened next. We're coordinating with Interpol and have sent out a Fiche S notice. I'll send you the names of our Italian points of contact."

"What about Dalmar?"

"The last I had on him was a cryptic follow-up from Pretoria. They sent their alert to Brazilia, but for some reason they didn't copy the consulate in Rio. The report got buried. They were dealing with a delegation from the CDC investigating reports of polluted water in the boating venues for this summer's Olympics."

"So, we lost him?"

"Can't say. You'll have to chase that down."

"You happen to have any contacts?"

"No, sorry."

"That's okay." Nick's head throbbed. Everything was far from okay. There was nothing more to say. he decided to end the call. "I'll take it from here."

"One final thing," Sanders said.

"What's that?"

"You take care of your daughter, now. Ya hear?"

"Will do. Thanks."

Nick terminated the call, accessed his government account on the computer, and opened two new files, one for al-Khultyer and the other for Dalmar. He looked over his notes. There was precious little to go on and he was at a complete loss as to their intentions or where they were heading. While dwelling on that grim assessment, he consoled himself with something he'd learned at the agency. "The absence of evidence is not evidence of absence." With that in mind, he decided to approach his research by focusing on the worst-case scenario—a coordinated attack on a U.S. city.

He looked at his To-Do list and added three more lines. Italian POCs. Call Rio. Set Up Conference Call. Under the latter, he wrote three names from his COBRA workgroup, Mark Arita—Treasury, Jessica Caudry—FBI, and Frank Garcia—Homeland Security.

He chewed on his pen top thinking of what he needed from each of his associates. Mark needed to chase down every one of al-Khultyer's credit card transactions. Frank—

His secure phone rang before he got any further. He grabbed the receiver.

"Parkos."

"Nick. Strickland. We got a lead. We were using the new program for PRISM screening all international satellite calls from Europe and Brazil tracking al-Khultyer's known aliases and got a hit on Dhi'b."

"When?"

"Yesterday afternoon."

"Could you trace the originator?"

"Not yet. The caller was probably using a burner. There's not much to go on, but the originator left a phone number with a Rio prefix and referred to himself as Sirhaan. That name ring any bells?"

Nick began typing *Sirhaan* into his search engine. "No, but we've tracked Dalmar to Rio. Can you tag the number in case this Dhi'b calls back?"

"Already done."

The answer to Nick's query popped up on his screen. "Got it."

"Got what?" Strickland asked.

"Sirhaan. It translates to 'little wolf' in Urdu."

Nick caught himself before proceeding. He might lose Strickland again with his tangential thinking. "Here's the connection. Al-Khultyer is Chechen. Chechnya's national symbol is the wolf. It's a long shot, but we may have the key to locating al-Khultyer."

"It's plausible. You need anything?"

"I'm good for now. I just have to sort out all the pieces to identify the common elements. I'm working a conference call with some of the members of my work group."

"You drawing one of your Venn diagrams again?"

Nick didn't detect any sarcasm in Strickland's voice, unlike other times when his boss would aim some caustic comment at his use of the diagrams and algorithms. In fact, Strickland almost sounded respectful.

"By the way," Strickland went on, "the DNI spoke with the president yesterday. He confirmed you're to remain the lead. He's also looking at the jurisdictional issues in case al-Khultyer targets something in the States. Once he sorts that out, he'll present his recommendations to the president."

These revelations confirmed Nick's thoughts about the CIA dropping out of the investigation, but he hadn't even considered the possibility of a turf war. Homeland Security? The FBI? Governors? Local law enforcement? His pursuit of al-Khultyer just got a whole lot more complicated.

"Let the DNI sort this out," Strickland continued. "You need to keep focused on finding al-Khultyer and his sidekick."

Nick hung up and commenced to chew on his pen. *Man, this is going to get interesting.*

Chapter Forty-Seven

ÉTOILE de MER
ATLANTIC OCEAN
WEDNESDAY 4 FEBRUARY

B ashir made his way to the Panoramic Lounge intent on catching the setting sun before it dipped below the horizon. But there was also something else, something deeper in his subconscious that drew him forward. He paused just inside the double glass doors, disappointed at what he saw. The lounge was almost empty.

He turned his attention to the map of the Atlantic mounted on the wall to his right. Inscribed on it was a black line leading from Civitavecchia to Miami. The ship's position, marked with a red star, indicated they were now well clear of the Strait of Gibraltar on a course that would take them just south of the Azores. He counted off the time zones. By the time he made his call, there would be an eleven-hour differential.

"I thought I might find you here."

Bashir turned, pleased by the sound of Marilyn's voice. "Am I so transparent?"

"Perhaps." She took his arm, guiding him to the bar. "I'll buy. What will you have?"

Like the day before, she'd managed to catch him off guard. "I'll—"

"No, let me guess," she teased, tapping her finger on her lower lip. She motioned for the bartender. "Do you have a cask strength scotch? Perhaps A'Bundadh?"

"Sorry, no Madame, but we do have a nice selection of other Scotch Whiskys."

She pouted in feigned dismay, then scanned the row of bottles lining the back counter. "Then my friend will have a Rob Roy with the Laphroaig 10."

"Sweet or dry vermouth?"

"Sweet," she answered casting a coy look at Bashir.

"And for you, Madame?"

"A dirty martini, vodka. Two olives."

Bashir had no idea what a Rob Roy was, so he watched the bartender pour a mix of the Laphroaig and vermouth. He finished the cocktail with a dash of bitters and a twist of orange. *This woman doesn't fool around. That was one stiff drink.*

His thoughts turned to Paris and the last time a woman offered to buy him a drink. Angelique. This woman seated next to him was entirely different. She was dangerous, a predator, like him. And he would use her, just as she was using him.

If Marilyn picked up on his thoughts, she wasn't letting on. He decided to drop a line he remembered from one of the Bond films. "Stirred or shaken?"

"Stirred. In martinis, I prefer the traditional way." she dipped her finger in her drink and gave it a swirl. She circled the tip of her tongue over her lips before raising her glass. "But in other things, not so much."

———

Bashir waited until Marilyn was asleep, then eased himself out of bed and made his way to the sitting room of her suite. The sliding door made a soft click as it closed behind him. Enough ambient light filled the room that he didn't need to turn on a lamp. The moon illuminated a trail of clothing strewn across the floor discarded during the opening act of their torrid love-making. At the head of the trail was her phone.

During dinner he'd casually brought up the topic of long distance calling from the ship, mentioning that he was having difficulty linking to the satellite net. She replied that she was not having any problems and offered to let him use her phone for a brief call. Her request for payment in kind hadn't been at all difficult to agree to.

He slid his finger across the iPhone's face, tapped the phone icon, and entered the number Qasif had given him. It was only a moment before the kid picked up.

"Hello?"

"Hello yourself."

"Where—?"

Bashir cut him off. "I told your mother I'd call. You know how she is."

"Well, you can tell her to stop worrying. I'm fine."

"When are you coming home?" Bashir asked.

"Tomorrow."

"Do you need anything?"

"No, I'm good."

"She wants to know if you're planning to visit family?"

"I hope so. I just have to check to see if they'll be home."

"I'll tell her. Give me a ring when you find out."

"Listen, I've got to go," Qasif said. "Is there anything else?"

"No. Say 'hi' to uncle."

Bashir terminated the call, a bit surprised the kid handled it so well. No names, his answers were vague, and he'd given no indication of where he was going or what he was planning to do. He was certain the Americans were monitoring the international calls, but it would be nearly impossible to track the kid. The issue was, could his call be traced to Marilyn's phone? And if they did trace it, would it lead them to the ship, her home in Coral Gables, or both?

He replaced the phone and slipped back into bed. Marilyn reached out to him and purred. "Do you need to make any more calls?"

Chapter Forty-Eight

HOMELAND SECURITY BUREAU
MIAMI, FLORIDA
WEDNESDAY 4 FEBRUARY

So, where was he? Or more accurately, where were they? Nick tapped his index fingers on the F and J keys of his laptop pondering how best to structure the upcoming video-teleconference with his workgroup. At least he had some idea of where Dalmar was. Or had been, he cautioned himself. He checked his watch. Three minutes.

He glanced at the camera perched on top of the HD screen as the vtel system flicked on. He ran his fingers through his hair, noting the slight delay beaming back from the upper left quadrant of the split screen. Mark Arita waved at his camera from a seat in one of the Treasury Department's conference rooms. In the right lower quadrant of the screen, Jessica Caudry typed furiously, her head bent over her laptop. The remaining screen shot focused on an empty table some-where in Homeland Security. Half a body appeared from the left side of the picture. A hand pulled up a chair. Frank Garcia sat down and reached for the remote control to swing the camera in his direction.

An IT tech entered Nick's room through the far door. "Is everyone up, Mr. Parkos? I have you down for the FBI's National Security Branch, Homeland, and Treasury?"

"They're all on-line, thanks. Can you run an audio check?"

The tech leaned over the microphone and switched on the sound. "Sound check. One-two-three."

All three of Nick's group responded with an affirmative, "I hear you."

"You're good to go. We have you scheduled for an hour. If you need more time, give me a ring and we'll extend your session."

"Will do."

Caudry spoke first. "Hey Nick, what gives with Miami? You down there checking out South Beach?"

He hesitated before answering. He didn't want to say anything about Emma that would put Caudry on a guilt trip. His second thought? South Beach held absolutely no appeal for him. At this point in his life, he simply couldn't fathom the pretentiousness of a life-style based on a foundation of alcohol and drug-fueled parties.

"Hardly," he answered. "I'm chasing down some leads, then I've got to get over to McDill to debrief CENTCOM."

"You have something new on al-Khultyer?" Garcia asked.

"He vanished after eluding the Italians in Rome. Our current thinking is he's headed to the States."

"Any idea where?"

Nick evaded the question. "We have an intercept of a call made from Rio de Janeiro to a person named Dhi'b, the alias al-Khultyer used in Somalia. The caller was a Somali-American, a known al-Shabaab sympathizer named Qasif Dalmar. The two of them escaped Aleem's camp just before we attacked. We've tracked Dalmar to Rio."

"You're thinking Dalmar's heading back home and is going to pass through Miami?" Garcia said.

"Yes."

"Do you have actionable intelligence?" Arita asked.

Caudry leaned forward, about to pile on. Nick grimaced.

"I concur," Caudry said. "Why would he pick Miami? Do you have alternative scenarios?"

Nick screwed up his mouth. This wasn't going well. He knew he'd be sticking his neck out assuming the kid would go through Miami. His own probability data barely supported his assumptions. Then again, he'd gone with his gut before and he'd been right. "No, that's it."

He noted the look of consternation cross Caudry's face. He withdrew into the protective shell he armored himself with this past week. He braced himself wondering what else she had in mind.

"Nick, we—"

"Thanks to the alert we received from that embedded CIA agent, we've already got him in our TIDE and TSD data bases," Garcia put in before Caudry could finish.

"Hassan." Nick said, his voice edged with anger.

"Pardon?" Garcia said.

"His name is Ali Abdulahi Hassan."

Nick's eyes suddenly glistened. The emotional toll of the past few days had caught up with him, stripping away his defenses. *What the hell?* He looked away from the camera reeling from the unexpected assault on his psyche—the horrors of what he'd seen and experienced in Aleem's camp, the report of finding Hassan's remains.

"His friends called him Butterfly ... after the boxer." His voice cracked. "He didn't make it."

"Damn, man," Garcia responded. "That sucks. I'm sorry."

Nick swiped his shirtsleeve across his eyes, working to gather his composure. He faced the camera. "Sorry for snapping at you, Frank. A friend of mine warned me this sort of thing might happen."

"Pretty rough over there?" Mark Arita asked.

Nick nodded. "I had no idea. You know, what really sucks is that nobody will ever know what he did."

"We will, Nick," Caudry said as she opened a folder lying next to her laptop. "How about I give you what Frank and I have on Dalmar?"

Nick's eyebrows shot up in surprise. How did the two of them even know about Dalmar, let alone know enough to brief him? *What the hell was going on?* "Let's have it."

He jotted down a few notes as Caudry reviewed Dalmar's FBI file. Most of what she presented he already knew or could have surmised: born and raised in Cedar-Riverside, a suburb of south Minneapolis. A loner. No known problems in high school. Briefly attended Ridgewater College before dropping out. His father immigrated in the early 90's. Physician. Limited his practice to the local Somali community. Social activist with no known radical affiliations...

Nick's mind drifted to thoughts of Emma. He planned to buy her a cute spotted unicorn he'd seen in a store window before heading to Marty's for dinner. Perhaps he would call Marty and see if she needed anything from the grocery. Anything to break the tension that still existed between them. He wondered how much of this was his fault, not sure he was prepared to deal with whatever the answer might be.

"Nick?"

Caudry's voice startled him. He looked at the camera. Garcia and Arita also had quizzical expressions etched on their faces.

"Is anything wrong?" she asked.

"Ah, no," he said, trying to recover. "You just caught me in one of my tangential thought processes. If he's learned anything—"

"Dalmar?" Arita asked.

"Yes. If he's learned anything from al-Khultyer, he'll be travelling under a new identity." He focused on Garcia. "Frank, if he goes through Miami using an alias, can you guys identify him using your facial recognition programs?"

"Let me double check. I know we have his picture in our Terrorism Screening Data Base. State will also have his passport photo on file. I'll call my contact at the National Bureau of Customs and Border Protection."

"We have several photos," Caudry said. "I'd suggest we work up some composites with easy-to-change features like hair color, beards, glasses. Could you get them into the system?"

"We might end up detaining some poor guy who looks like him, but that's the breaks," Garcia said.

Mark Arita broke into the discussion, his voice causing his quadrant of the screen to enlarge. "I agree with what y'all are saying, but we need to front load this and get Rio engaged. I'd be asking them how Dalmar would go about getting a new alias and fraudulent passport."

Nick welcomed the input, but he was puzzled how Caudry had so much on Dalmar including the photos. He couldn't recall mentioning Dalmar's name when he set up the vtel. Hell, he was having trouble remembering much of anything lately. "You have something specific in mind?"

"The Brazilian authorities should have some indication who the players are. I'd suggest we ask the embassy to query their counterparts and ask if any of their citizens have reported losing their passport or having one stolen."

"Or, if anyone has been reported missing," Caudry added. "Lifting a dead person's identity and changing out the passport photo would be one way to go. Dalmar would also have access to the victim's credit cards. If the vic was traveling alone, Dalmar could easily be out of Brazil before anyone submitted a missing person's report. And Nick... there's something else."

Nick detected the hesitation, the change in her voice. She was about to add something he didn't want to hear. He braced himself. "What?"

"We ran a MOSAIC threat assessment after our guys detected searches using your name on the Internet and several social media sites."

Nick was familiar with the assessment. Developed in the late '80's, it was an analytical system used by law enforcement agencies to screen the veracity and danger level of any given threat to any individual, be it a member of the Supreme Court or a victim of spouse abuse. He'd used the system several times himself gathering input from experts to populate his own computer models. Anything above a five on the standard one to ten scale he took very seriously.

She pressed on before he could say anything. "You and your family may be at risk."

"What's the threat score?"

"Based on the standard scale, we scored you at a two."

"And my family?"

"A six."

Chapter Forty-Nine

HARTSFIELD-JACKSON INTERNATIONAL AIRPORT
ATLANTA, GEORGIA
THURSDAY 5 FEBRUARY

Q asif rolled the stiffness out of his neck and stuffed his
Bose earphones and iPod into his backpack. He
eased his way out of the middle row near the rear of
the aircraft without making eye contact with his seatmates.
The Canadian was a nice enough guy, but Qasif had deflected
his attempts to strike up a conversation. There were two other
passengers who shared the middle four seats of row 39. The
one to his right, a Brazilian who'd been harmless enough. He
couldn't get a read on the third passenger in the far isle seat
who hadn't said a word to anyone. The man had given him a
hard look when they first boarded and he'd caught the man
watching him throughout the flight. What were the odds of a
Federal Air Marshall sitting in the same row? Maybe he
was DEA?

He exited the tunnel into the open concourse of the
international terminal and stopped to read the overhead. He
spotted Departing Flights and weaved through the crowd of

passengers clustering around the baggage carrousel. He slowed his pace and slid over to the far wall searching for the man who'd been in seat G. He spotted the guy talking on his phone, heading straight for him. *Crap.*

There was nowhere to go. He made a show of pulling his Canadian passport and ticket pack for the next segment of his flight from the side pocket of his backpack and flipped up his wrist in a partial wave. The man scowled and kept going, only to halt at the entrance to customs. He turned back toward Qasif, his stance broad based, arms crossed over his chest, challenging.

Qasif took a step toward the man, his eyes boring into him. *"Sharmauda."* The Somali swear word escaped with a hiss. *This will end now. I will kill you with my bare hands, you bastard.*

"Hey, Ahsan. You heading for the gate?"

Qasif halted in mid-stride. The voice belonged to the Canadian. He hesitated, working to control his rage. "Yeah, man."

"I've been through here before. We need to go upstairs."

"Thanks, man."

Qasif replaced his documents and followed the Canadian up the escalator leading to the departure level. Another checkpoint. He took a deep breath, and joined the line. Would he be stopped by TSA?

MIAMI STATION

Qasif looked at his watch. Close to midnight. There'd been a mishap somewhere on the line and they were almost four hours late. But at least he was in Miami. The four hundred dollars he shelled out for business class and a sleeping compartment had made the thirty-eight, no, the forty-two hour trip bearable. Almost. There'd been no WiFi for the entire last leg down the east coast. At least Amtrak provided access to the Internet on the New York segment, and he'd managed to connect and reserve a motel room.

The rental car could wait. He hadn't driven since leaving the States two years before and he only had a vague idea how to get to his motel. Besides, he'd heard horror stories about tourists taking a wrong turn and ending up in a bad neighborhood.

He looked around. The station appeared to be in the middle of nowhere. His heel strikes resounded off the arched overhead as he walked down the deserted platform toward the exit. He emerged into a well-lit entrance area and flagged down one of the two dented yellow taxis idling outside the station.

He tossed his bag and backpack into the rear of the first and slid across the stained seat. A faint, yet heavy, herbal scent hung in the confined space.

Seriously, weed?

"Where to?" the driver asked, studying Qasif in his rearview mirror.

Qasif looked over his shoulder through the tinted rear window. The other cab pulled away from the curb. He'd have to take his chances. "Tropical Sands."

The driver punched the address into his GPS while he mumbled something to the dispatcher over his microphone. He set the meter and turned up the volume of a old CD player balanced precariously on top of a pile of discarded food cartons and God knew what else. Rap music boomed as they left the light of the station and wove through increasingly sketchy neighborhoods. The cab slowed at a corner where a crowd of toughs loitered. One of them gave the cabbie a nod of recognition.

Gang Bangers. Qasif avoided eye contact. He wished he had a gun.

Why not? He raised his voice so he could be heard over the music. "Where can I get a gun?"

The driver didn't respond.

"Hey, man—"

"I heard you. Wha kinda piece you lookin fo?"

"Nine millimeter."

The cabbie drove another block and pulled over in front of a row of decaying one-story houses. Their windows were encased with metal bars, like jail cells and their lawns were overgrown with weeds and strewn with trash. A couple of juveniles dressed in black and topped with sideways baseball caps sat on the stoop of one of them, eyeing the cab with apparent disinterest. The cabbie opened his door. "Stay here."

One of the toughs tossed his cigarette and approached the cabbie, giving him a complicated fist bump. The cabbie said something to him and pointed to Qasif before both disappeared into the house.

Qasif looked around. A solitary streetlamp with a pile of garbage around its base cast its feeble light across the cracked sidewalks. Behind the pole stood a boarded up apartment complex. Graffiti covered the front, ending below a sign that read Avalon Heights Manor. When he looked back, the other tough stood by his door, hand resting on the handle of a semi-automatic pistol stuck through his belt.

Qasif looked away only to spin his head back around at the sound of a gun barrel tapping on his window. The tough jerked his head toward the house. "We got business to conduct."

———

Just after one in the morning, Qasif settled back into the cab, heading south on I-95. The Ruger SR9, crammed inside his backpack along with a box of ammo and two extra clips, offered some security. He breathed a sigh of relief amazed he was still alive and still had all of his cash—minus the five-hundred he shelled out for the weapon. All in all, he couldn't complain. In the morning, he'd get something to eat and set to work.

The cab exited the freeway and passed through several residential neighborhoods. He looked out the window at a row of houses. On the spur of the moment, he decided to get a start on his assignment. The cab would be good cover. "I'd like to swing by 603 23rd Avenue Southwest."

The driver nodded. "Whatever, man. It's your money."

Chapter Fifty

603 23rd AVENUE, SOUTHWEST
MIAMI, FLORIDA
SUNDAY 8 FEBRUARY

N ick emptied the last of his wine and looked at his watch. 1:20. Even Taz, asleep in his wicker dog bed in the kitchen, had given up.

"I'd better go," he said, his voice tinged with a note of regret. They'd been talking ever since Emma went to sleep. Nothing of importance, just an easy conversation between friends. He hadn't mentioned the FBI's MOSAIC Threat Assessment. He didn't have enough to go on and didn't want to alarm her. He did make a mental note to ask if he could trim the front hedge. Far from providing a safety buffer, it increased her risk.

"Yeah, it's way past our bedtimes," Marty answered.

Nick detected an unexpected softness in her voice. Perhaps it was the wine. He stood and started to make his way to the kitchen with their glasses and a couple of dirty plates.

"I'll take care of those in the morning," Marty said.

He ignored her and walked to the kitchen, setting the dishes in the sink. "It is morning."

Marty pushed off the couch and joined him in the kitchen.

"Do you have to go in tomorrow?" she asked.

"Yeah, there're some loose ends I need to clean up."

She hesitated and gave him a quick kiss on his cheek before giving him a small shove in the back to propel him toward the front door. "Let me know when you're coming over."

"Will do."

He was almost to his car before he noticed the yellow cab across the street. He didn't think much about it until he reached for the door handle. He stopped. The cab's lights were off, the motor idling. Was there someone in the back seat looking at him? The cab's lights flipped on and it pulled away from the curb slowly heading down the street. He could just make out the characters on the license plate before the cab's taillights disappeared around the corner of the next street.

Something didn't feel right. He jerked open the door, grabbed a discarded McDonald's bag off the seat, and found a ballpoint pen in the center consol. He began to write, but his pen skipped over a grease spot. He scribbled on another part of the bag until the ink flowed, then jotted down: Yellow Cab 444-8888, followed by the plate number: T52-90... He wasn't sure of the last character. It could be a B or an 8. He wrote both. 'B/8?'

He ripped off the piece of bag with his information and stuffed it in his shirt pocket. In the morning he'd call Jessica and get a point of contact in the FBI's Miami Field Office. He turned over the ignition, drove to the end of the block and parked so he could watch the house. He stayed there for almost an hour after the last light went out, then drove back to the Marriott.

———

"Special Agent Caudry. How may I help you?"

"I can think of a lot of ways."

"Nick?"

"Yeah. I'm glad there's someone out there as nuts as I am working on a Sunday."

"It's not even seven-thirty. What's going on?"

"Someone's watching Marty's house." He heard Jessica's sharp intake of breath.

"What makes you think that? I haven't gotten any updates to suggest an increased threat."

"There was this cab sitting outside the house when I left her early this morning."

"Have you talked to Frank?"

"No. He's my—"

"We need to find him. Can you set up a conference call?" Caudry asked.

"Not in my skill set."

"I'll see what I can do. Give me your number."

"305-228-3982."

"I'll call you." The line went dead.

Nick dropped his head on the back of the chair and stared at the random perforations in the ceiling's acoustical tiles. So much for getting the name of someone in the FBI's Miami Office to set up surveillance and getting an assist to run down that cab. Maybe he was just being paranoid, but he couldn't ignore what he'd seen.

Maybe he just obsessed about Dalmar because he had no clue where to find al-Khultyer. The trail had gone cold since the sighting at Rome's airport a week ago. He picked up a pen and made a note to call Mark Arita at Treasury. Maybe he'd had some luck tracing al-Khultyer's Carte Bancaire credit card data they'd obtained from the manager of the Ibo Island Lodge.

He shook his head. No. Screw al-Khultyer. He needed to

focus on the threat to Emma, to Marty, from some psychopathic jihadist.

The phone rang. He picked up. "Parkos."

"Nick," Caudry said, "I've got Frank on the line. He's got something."

Nick put the phone on speaker. "Morning Frank. What do you have?"

"A possible lead. The Canadian embassy in Brazilia told us one of their citizens went missing in Rio. A young guy on holiday with friends. He took off by himself to visit the Christ the Redeemer statue. He never returned.

"Do you know when?"

"His friends called the Embassy on Tuesday. They haven't found him, but they gave us a name. Ahsan Habib."

"Have you run it?"

"Yeah. He booked a flight on Delta this past Thursday. Toronto via Atlanta."

Nick leaned over the phone's speaker. "Was he on it?"

"Don't know. We're checking with Delta and the Canadians. I directed Atlanta TSA to review their surveillance footage and check with passport control. We should know something by tomorrow."

"Not good enough," Nick said. "Can you speed it up?"

"Ah—"

Caudry cut in. "Frank, I didn't explain. Nick thinks someone is watching his family."

"Oh, crap."

"That sums it up pretty well," Nick said.

"And you think it's Dalmar?" Garcia asked.

Nick wasn't so sure anymore but pressed on. "I'd rather play it safe."

"Understood. You want me to operate on the presumption Dalmar's lifted Habib's identity?"

"I know it's a long shot," Nick said. "If he was on that flight…"

"Any idea how he could have made it down to Miami?"

Nick pressed his lips together. "No idea."

"Do you have anything on the cab?" Caudry asked.

"Yellow Taxi. Phone number on the side. 444-8888. I got a partial plate—T52-90 something. I'm not sure of the last digit. It could have been an 8 or a B."

"I'll get in touch with Carlos Castellanos," she said. "He's the Special Agent in Charge for the Miami Field Office. He'll work with the locals to set up a protective detail and run down the cab."

"Thanks, Jessica. I really appreciate it," Nick said. "Do you guys have my number?"

"Yes," both of them answered.

"Give me a call this afternoon, will ya?"

Nick hung up and started to write his notes. Organizing his thoughts had a calming effect. He had gained back some measure of control. Then his thoughts turned to the cab. He needed to secure a weapon.

Chapter Fifty-One

ROOM 213
TROPICAL SANDS MOTEL
MIAMI, FLORIDA
SUNDAY 8 FEBRUARY

The air conditioner in Qasif's second-floor room rattled to a stop. Streams of light from the morning sun shone through holes in the room's curtains, throwing a pattern of dots over him like miniature spotlights. Within minutes the room began to heat up, going from too cold to too hot. He kicked off his sheet and rolled away from the window, then gave up. He swung his legs over the side of the bed and walked over to inspect something he'd noticed in the flowered draperies.

You've got to be kidding me. He poked his finger through the center of one of the flowers. Some pervert had cut out holes in the middle of the large faded-yellow daisies so he could peep into the room.

Disgusted, he pulled his finger out of the hole and walked to the bathroom. He flipped on the overhead light, sending a large cockroach scurrying for cover under the vanity. He cursed and aimed a futile kick at the fleeing insect before turning on the faucets. He watched the sink's overflow, ready to strike, but no bugs emerged.

He thought about his accommodations while shaving. He couldn't do much about the bugs short of buying a can of Raid. His options were to change rooms or move to another motel. The latter made the most sense. Maybe he could manage a room at the nearby Fontainebleau?

He washed the remnants of shaving cream from around his neck and ears, inserted his blue-tinted contacts, and tossed his kit on the bed. He absently scratched several red dots that had appeared on his thigh sometime during the night. Perhaps Allah would provide him with a taste of what He would provide in the after-life. Then again, perhaps Allah was just tempting him with impure thoughts.

He decided his path to the Fontainebleau would be in accordance with Allah's will. Nonetheless, he would ask for guidance and assurance during his noontime prayers.

After dressing in tan slacks, a Brazilian World Cup soccer jersey, and green loafers, he emptied the contents of his backpack onto the bed. He unraveled the cord leading from his iPod, inserted the earbuds, and selected one of his Brazilian downloads. The gritty mix of funk, hip-hop, and electronic music the locals called Mangue Bit flowed into his ears, bringing a smile. He'd missed music. Considered a heresy, it was one of many things forbidden in Aleem's camp.

Bobbing his head to the driving rhythm of the artist Nação Zumbi, he picked up his SR9. The weapon was almost new, the burnished black barrel set off by the light gray-green polymer frame.

The pistol had a nice weight, about two pounds, and the narrow, checkered grip felt good in his hand. He pushed the button release, dropping the eighteen-round magazine, and pulled back the slide to inspect the chamber to make sure no round was seated. One more hole in the curtains wouldn't matter, but a shattered window would be difficult to explain.

He sighted the weapon on one of the daisies and tested the trigger pull, firing off several notional three-shot groupings. He would have preferred something with a shorter travel, but it would do. Finishing his preparations, he loaded all three of his magazines and disassembled the pistol, giving it a thorough cleaning and oiling. Al-Shabaab had taught him well.

He wrapped the pistol in one of the room's face towels, placed the weapon in his backpack, re-packed his carry-on, and headed to the motel's office. He'd decided he would lock the weapon and ammunition in one of the Fontainebleau's safety deposit boxes until he needed them. He walked down the stairs to the front office just as the Enterprise courtesy van pulled into the parking lot. He waved at the driver and pointed to his suitcase and office indicating he'd be right back.

———

Qasif leaned on the balcony rail of his third floor Deluxe Bay room in the Chateau Tower taking in the broad vista of Biscayne Bay beyond the huge pool directly below. The view beat the one he'd had of the ocean from Barawa. He was only slightly disappointed the cheaper City View rooms were booked. At this point though, money was the least of his concerns.

He'd paid the bill for the motel room in cash as he had his Amtrak tickets, but decided to forego caution and used his—well, Habib's—Harris Bank card when he registered at the hotel. He'd also used it at Enterprise, acknowledging the risk if someone put an alert on the card. He had no idea how long it'd take for someone to report that Habib was missing, but the odds were good someone would have noticed by now. It'd been a week since he'd been murdered.

He wiped the negative thoughts from his mind. There was

no use in worrying about things out of his control. He returned to his room and unfolded the city map he'd picked up in a tourist shop off the lobby. It only took a moment for him to locate and draw an oblong circle around 23rd Avenue SW. With the location fixed in his mind, he collected his wallet and rental car keys and headed out the door in search of a computer. He figured the hotel's business center would have one.

———

Qasif drove past the Parkos' pink stucco home without slowing, continuing down the street a couple more blocks to a small shopping mall. He parked his white Kia Rio in one of the stalls and walked back, retracing his route. The quiet, palm-lined residential neighborhood had a completely different feel in the daylight. The homes were all well-kept, single stories with one-car garages and neat lawns. The neighbors were out and about and appeared to know each other. They would notice a strange car parked on their street.

He felt a bit conspicuous strolling down the sidewalk and made an attempt to blend in by giving an occasional wave and calling out a friendly "Hi" as he passed someone working on their lawn. He slowed his pace when he neared the Parkos house. An orange extension cord snaked its way down the driveway and over the sidewalk, connecting to an electric hedge clipper. A man trimmed the overgrown bushes fronting the house—the same guy he'd seen from the cab. *Parkos?*

The guy stopped and hefted a pile of clippings into a blue trashcan that hung over the curb. He straightened and glanced down the sidewalk in Qasif's direction. *Shit.*

Qasif made a half turn, dropped to a knee, and reached for his shoe pretending to remove a rock. He waited until he heard the sound of the hedge clippers start up and reversed course back down the street.

Qasif returned to the Fontainebleau in the evening and ordered room service. He'd had enough of being around people, of watching every cop car, of reliving the memories of his home in Minneapolis. He ate in silence on the balcony, watching the fiery sunset, nursing his bitterness, and thinking.

What were the odds of Parkos even being in Miami? That was an unexpected problem. Then he thought about seeing him leave the house at one-thirty in the morning. *Yeah, what was that all about?* He decided he'd drive back in the morning and watch the place. When Parkos left, he'd tail him. Then what?

No, he'd remain at the house and eliminate Parkos' family as Dhi'b instructed. And a security system? He doubted the woman would arm it while she and the kid were home.

He would've liked to have a silencer, but his SR9 didn't have a threaded barrel. He'd have to resort to muffling the sound of his gunshots some other way— provided he could get into the house undetected. Those bushes would have been helpful.

Chapter Fifty-Two

FBI SOUTH FLORIDA HEADQUATERS
MIAMI, FLORIDA
MONDAY 9 FEBRUARY

"Sir, Mr. Parkos is here to see you."

Special Agent in Charge, Carlos Castellanos, rose from his chair and walked around his desk to greet Nick. "Welcome, to Miami, Mr. Parkos." He waved toward an empty chair. "Coffee?"

"No, I'm good," Nick replied, giving the office a quick scan. "I'm glad you were able to work me in."

Castellanos looked him over before speaking. Nick figured must look like hell. He knew his face was pale, etched with fatigue and stress, and his eyes were bloodshot from the lack of sleep. He wondered if Castellanos would guess he'd also been drinking.

"You've got a good friend in D.C. backing you up," Castellanos said. "I've known Agent Caudry for years. We went through Quantico together." He took a sip of coffee from his mug. "You sure you don't want any? I just made a fresh pot."

"No thanks."

Castellanos shrugged and opened a folder on his desk. "Agent Caudry briefed me on your situation. We don't have a lot to go on, but I'd say your concerns are legit."

"Have you found anything?"

"We tracked down the cab. The company's log says their driver had nine fares during his shift. We're focusing on the one he picked up at the Amtrak station just after midnight. He dropped the passenger off at the Tropical Sands motel around two."

"Amtrak." Nick repeated. "So that's how he got down here."

"Pardon, me? Who? Dalmar?"

"Yes. Did the cab company have a name?"

"No. And the guy paid in cash."

"Amtrak should have a passenger list," Nick said.

Castellanos made a note in his folder. "I'll call Homeland and ask them to work that angle."

"I'll save you the call. They set up an office for me while I'm in Miami. I'll talk to them."

"Okay."

"How about a description?"

"Negative. The company tried calling the driver, but he didn't answer. They weren't surprised. He's not supposed to come in until six this evening.

Nick nodded. "Well, we know he had at least one stop. How long would it take to drive from the station to my family's house?"

"At that hour, not more than thirty minutes. And before you ask, the dispatcher told us he has no record of any other stops. They're going to pull the GPS to double check. I've got an agent going over to the cab company's office and two more heading to the motel. It'll be easy enough to identify someone checking in at that hour."

"And detain him?"

"If he's still there."

"What about my family? I don't want that son-of-a-bitch coming anywhere near them."

"A detail's setting up surveillance. I've also notified MPD. They're going to step up their patrols of the neighborhood."

"Can you issue me a weapon?"

"You authorized to carry?"

"By NSA?"

"Or anyone else for that matter."

Nick chewed on his lower lip. The thought never crossed his mind. He'd had to sign for an Agency 9mm, but that was for Somalia. He had no idea if NSA assets were even authorized to use a weapon in the States. "Not in writing."

Castellanos tapped the tip of his pen on the desk. "That's a problem. How about your wife? Florida's a 'No Duty to Retreat' state. She have a handgun?"

"Actually she's my ex, but to answer your question, no. When she moved down here after our divorce, she turned it over to the police."

"She know how to use?"

"She's had some training."

"Something you might want to talk to her about."

"She doesn't know anything about Dalmar."

Castellanos frowned.

"She's been through enough. I don't want to drag her into this mess."

"I'd say it's a bit late for that."

Nick crossed his arms and turned his head toward the window.

"Look, I understand," Constellanos continued, "but if she and your daughter are going to be under our protection, she deserves to know why."

Nick gave a slight nod and looked back.

"Do you want to tell her or should I?"

"I will," Nick said. "I've got a conference call with my team this afternoon. I'll go over after I finish up."

Constellanos moved on. "Agent Caudry also filled me in about al-Khultyer. Is there any chance he's coming to Miami?"

"We're working on the assumption he's heading to the U.S."

"That doesn't answer my question."

Nick took a deep breath. "Actually, I don't know where the hell he is."

"You need any help?"

"If he's heading here, I will. My biggest concern is navigating through the overlapping areas of jurisdiction. FBI, Homeland, MPD ..."

"Who's your reporting senior?"

"POTUS."

Castellanos's eyes widened with surprise. "The president? Damn, Parkos. You don't mess around."

Nick smiled for the first time. "He's been able to pull a few strings."

"I guess."

"I should know more after the conference call with my team. If there's any indication al-Khultyer's heading to Miami, I'll bring you in."

Chapter Fifty-Three

HOMELAND SECURITY BUREAU
MIAMI, FLORIDA
MONDAY 9 FEBRUARY

Nick ended the call to Washington with a frustrated sigh. He hadn't received authorization to carry. Strickland hadn't made any promises, but had at least said he'd see what he could do. He reached for the half-eaten six-inch tuna-on-wheat he'd picked up at Subway after leaving Castellanos's office. His frustration burst into anger. How in the hell did they expect him to protect his family? His fist tightened around the sandwich, sending a thick blob of tuna and mayo onto his desk. "Damn it."

"You okay?" Kevin Jacobs asked, peering into the room.

Nick looked at the Homeland staffer who'd been assigned to assist him. "Tough morning."

Jacobs looked at the mangled sandwich. "I'd say. Well, maybe I can make it a little better."

Nick wadded up the remnants of the sandwich in its wrapper and dumped it in the trashcan. "What d'ya have?"

"Garcia called. The Canadians came through. Long story,

short, they confirmed Dalmar used a fraudulent passport to enter their country."

"Name?"

"Ahsan Habib."

"The guy reported missing in Rio?"

"Yeah, the Brazilians found his body in a landfill."

Nick wasn't interested in the details. "Does the FBI know?"

"Not unless Garcia called them."

"Have a seat." Nick reached for his phone and punched in a number. When the ring tone sounded, he put the phone on speaker.

"Castellanos."

"Carlos, this is Nick Parkos. I've got Kevin Jacobs from Homeland on speaker with me."

"Pretty good timing. I was just about to call you. We—"

"I've got a name," Nick interrupted. "Dalmar's using the alias Ahsan Habib."

"That doesn't match the name the motel's manager gave us."

"Doesn't surprise me," Nick said. "From what I learned about that place, they wouldn't be asking their guests many questions."

"The manager verified that a middle-eastern looking male checked in around two o'clock in the morning on Sunday, then checked out about eight hours later. Paid in cash."

"Did the manager have any idea where he went?"

"No, but we've got something that lashes up with your information. The manager said an Enterprise shuttle picked the guy up. Guy named Ahsan Habib rented a white Kia Rio, Florida plates. BSA-516. Gave them a Canadian passport, driver's license, and used Habib's credit card."

"Does it have GPS?"

"Yeah, they tracked it to the Fontainebleau. The hotel

confirmed they have a guest by that name. I've got agents on the way."

"Hotel security?"

"If they spot him, they're to keep your guy under surveillance and not take any action to detain him."

Nick had to get to the hotel. Telling Marty about the threat would have to wait. Besides, if they caught Qasif, she'd never have to know. "I'm on the way."

"Nick, it's best you stay put."

"But—"

"You ever been there?"

"No..."

"I don't want to be a hard ass, but it's our turf. Let us handle it. MPD's setting up checkpoints along Collins Avenue and at the entrances to the bridges. I'll call you when we've got him."

"God damn it, Carlos, you can't expect me to just sit here."

Nick's protest was met with silence. He looked at Jacobs who merely shrugged and gave his head a defeated shake.

"All right," Castellanos said. "I'll send an agent for you. But don't do anything stupid."

HOTEL FONTAINEBLEAU

Qasif thanked the desk clerk and handed her the safety deposit key from the empty box. He adjusted the straps of his backpack and headed across the lobby to retrieve his rental car. He'd planned to return to the Parkos house the next morning but decided to move up his timeline after terminating his call with Dhi'b. It didn't make much sense hanging around waiting for him to call back to find out what to do with the Mercedes fob. Besides, he just wanted to get the hell out of Miami.

He stopped in midstride, about to push through the front door when two black Suburban SUVs pulled up under the portico. He caught a glimpse of a white government tag on the first as the doors of both flew open. He pivoted and headed back into the lobby. A pair of hotel security guards at the front desk looked in his direction. He had several options. He took off for the elevators near a cluster of restaurants and the bar.

He slowed near Gotham Steak and cast a cautious look over his shoulder. One of the security guards crossed the lobby, intercepted the two agents, and pointed in his direction. He cursed under his breath and resumed walking, seeking an alternative way out of the building. The exit leading to the ocean front pools was the closest.

A crowd of noisy conventioneers coming through the door prevented him from going outside. He decided going out by the pools was a bad idea, anyway. He turned and caught up with the crowd, mixing with them as they headed up the broad stairs leading to the upper level conference center.

He worked his way through another group of convention-eers milling around a table of refreshments. He helped himself to a can of Coke from an ice bucket and continued walking. Halfway down the hallway, he spotted three elevators. He rode the second to the ground floor.

The conference center's exit let out on Collins Avenue, the main street fronting the hotel. He scanned the busy street. He couldn't get to the Kia. *What about that row of luxury yachts tied up across the street? Maybe I can hide on one of them?* He dismissed the idea.

Several MPD patrol cars passed by and slowed by a line of taxis to make the left turn into the hotel's entrance road. *That's it.*

He polished off the Coke, tossed the can into the shrub-bery, and proceeded down the sidewalk. He stopped at the first cab.

The driver leaned toward the open window. "Where to?"

Qasif didn't have a clue. Then he remembered a place he'd passed while driving around the day before—a shopping district only a short distance from the Parkos house. "The Miracle Mile."

"Okay, get in."

The driver pulled away and made a U-turn one block up and headed south. Qasif looked out the tinted window as they passed the Fontainebleau.

"Something must be going on," the cab driver volunteered. "I can't remember the last time I've seen so many cops around here. Dispatch told me they're even setting up roadblocks at the bridges. I'm taking the exit for 95. With any luck, we'll be across before they stop us."

"The traffic doesn't seem any worse than usual. They'll probably not screw up rush hour too bad."

"You local?"

"No, I'm visiting from Canada. I'm heading home tomorrow."

The driver nodded his head toward the window. "There's another Suburban. Third one I've seen."

Qasif spotted the black SUV crossing the bridge going the opposite direction. "Who are they?"

"Feds. Seems your last day in Miami's going to be interesting."

"Yeah, that's what I'm thinking."

THE FONTAINEBLEAU HOTEL

Nick caught a partial glimpse of the license plate when they rounded the driveway for the portico. BSA-5—something. "My God, that's got to be it."

"Got to be what?" his escort, Agent Emmitt Ross asked.

"The rental car." Nick unclicked his seatbelt and jumped

out the door. He pushed his way past several gawking tourists dressed in matching flowered shirts and ran to the rear of the Kia. He spun around, looking for Qasif. Nothing. He ran to the driver's side window and looked in. *Map on the front seat.*

He reached for the door handle but before he could open the door, a large hand grabbed his shoulder.

"Whoa there buddy. Just where do you think you're going?"

Nick turned and found himself staring into the chest of a burly MPD officer. "I've got to search this car."

"No good. Show some ID."

Nick fumbled for his wallet and pulled out his NSA ID card just as Ross arrived, holding up his FBI badge suspended on a lanyard around his neck.

"Hold up," the policeman ordered. He scrutinized the new arrival. "He with you?"

"Yeah. This car's rented by the guy we're after."

The policeman took a closer look at Ross's ID and backed away. "It's all yours."

Nick opened the door and snatched the map. He saw the oblong circle drawn around 23rd Avenue. "That son-of-a-bitch."

"What's going on?" Ross asked.

Nick pointed at the map. "The bastard's targeted my family."

Ross waved over one of the valets. "Have you seen the driver of this vehicle?"

The valet shook his head. "No, he hasn't shown."

"How long's it been sitting here?" Nick asked.

"I don't know. Maybe fifteen minutes."

Nick took off at a run toward the hotel's front doors. "He's still got to be here. We've got to lock this place down."

Chapter Fifty-Four

ÉTOILE de MER
MID-ATLANTIC OCEAN
MONDAY 9 FEBRUARY

Bashir watched his cell phone tumble through the air before disappearing into the turbulence of the ship's wake. There was no muted protest from the device. It just vanished into the depths without so much as a splash. Gone.

He stared at the wake. Qasif's call had arrived a little over an hour ago: *Visiting family tonight.* There was a certain finality in those three simple words.

There would be no more calls from Qasif. That, of course, was obvious. Qasif could no longer contact him. But Bashir understood the deeper implications of the message. There would be no turning back. Odds were, Qasif would be killed. If not tonight, then later. Bashir felt a brief pang of remorse. For all his faults, Qasif wasn't such a bad kid and there was no doubting his courage.

Bashir had felt these same feelings during his last moments with Azad at the GUM. Bashir wasn't a devout man, but he'd been raised in a household that adhered to the tenants of the

Koran. The guiding principles of Islam were not lost on him. He also knew he would never have peace, even in death, until he purged the demons haunting his soul.

He stood at the rail for several more minutes. His thoughts turned to his brothers: Azad, Ushiska, Salim. They had chosen their fate, as he had done years before. And Qasif? He too had chosen.

———

Bashir finished his appetizer, relishing the last bite. The Pointrine De Canard Fumée was magnificent. He reached out his hand, then pulled it back, resisting the temptation to swipe his finger across his plate to mop up the last of the Calvados sauce. Instead, he took a sip of wine. The Clos de Vougeot Pinot Noir's earthy *sous bois* paired perfectly with the smoked duck breast.

"Caught ya." She held out a piece of roll and laughed. "This would work better my love."

He held up his glass and looked at Marilyn through the ruby-red color of the wine. "Is there nothing I do that does not escape you?"

She reached for his hand. "Nothing," she whispered.

"Then I must do better at concealing my intensions."

"Then I shall be on my guard, Monsieur Chéreau."

Bashir lowered his glass, feigning a look of bewilderment. "But my intentions are pure, Madame."

"Such a pity," she replied. She lifted her wine glass, and cast him a sultry look over its lip. "Though perhaps mine are not. Will you be needing my phone?"

Bashir was instantly on guard. *Could she know?* She disarmed him with a beguiling smile. "The phone, no. However…"

———

Bashir's breath caught at the sight of the vision before him. Marilyn's red hair cascaded in waves over her shoulders. The moon silhouetted her body, the soft glow bathing her ivory skin. She touched her finger to his lips, silencing him before he could say a word. She tugged on the sash of her silk robe. The sheer fabric clung a moment, then fell open.

He took a step toward her, hands eager to possess. She drew away with a smile. She shrugged the negligee off her shoulders, easing it downward until it gathered in turquoise folds around her ankles. Her breasts rose and fell with each breath. She turned, allowing him to take in every inch of her perfect body. She began to sway, hips, breasts, hands, hair flowing in serpentine movement, beckoning.

He reached for her again, grabbing her arm before she could elude him a second time. She pulled him close, pressing her lips to his. He quivered as she parted her lips, her tongue seeking his. Her breath whispered against his neck as she pulled him down to her bed. "Now I am ready for you."

Her fingertips explored his body, tracing lines, seeking permission, revealing secrets. He eased inside her. They made love slowly, pursuing a shared rapture, the rhythm of their hips giving way to urgent demand. There was no outward world now, only their intent remained.

A moan escaped his lips, a primal call of emotion no longer constrained by the barriers of his mind. The thoughts that came between his thoughts, the thoughts deep within, no longer denied. Pleasure consumed his being. Doubts swept away. He only knew this moment with this woman. Nothing else mattered.

———

Bashir lay on his side, watching her eyes as her fingers drew spirals down his back. He reached over to stroke her hair but flinched when her right hand found the deep scar on his left thigh.

She rose on an elbow for a closer look. "You were injured."

"Many years ago. I try not to think about it."

She traced the outline. "Does it still hurt?"

"Only rarely, when it is very cold."

"It must have been awful."

"Yes."

"May I ask what happened?"

Bashir hesitated. Only a few knew, and they were likely dead. He tensed. *Except those who'd killed his family.*

Marilyn pulled her hand away. "I'm sorry. I should not have pried."

He felt for her hand. "No, it's all right. It was many years ago… sixteen. My wife, my daughter… we were in an accident. They were killed."

"Oh, God. I'm so sorry."

Bashir saw the pain, the anguish in her eyes and reached for her hand. "There are moments when the memories return to haunt me, but I have come to terms with their loss. Those who were responsible—"

He stopped himself. She could not know. He pulled her close. "If Nadia is watching, she will be comforted that I have found you."

Chapter Fifty-Five

THE MIRACLE MILE
CORAL GABLES, FLORIDA
MONDAY EVENING 9 FEBRUARY

The taxi dropped Qasif near a three-tiered fountain at the corner of 37th and Coral Way. The shopping district of The Miracle Mile stretched from the fountain along a four-block landscaped corridor of high-end retail shops, galleries, and restaurants. Hardly a place he'd choose to go. The calming sound of cascading water drew him to the fountain. He sat on the concrete surround and spent a moment getting oriented.

The Parkos house was only a short walk away and he didn't want to delay too long. It would only be a matter of time before someone found the map on the front seat of his rental and determine his intentions. His thoughts turned to Dhi'b, wondering where he might be and what he could be doing.

He'd called him just before leaving his room at the hotel and didn't expect a return call. He also didn't know if the two earlier calls he'd made could be traced using any data saved in his phone. He fished out the burner from his rear pocket. It would be wise to not take any more risks than necessary.

He waited for a young mother pushing a baby carriage to pass and then walked over to a green trashcan by an arched gateway. He dropped his burner in the receptacle and trotted across the street to check out the shops. The decision wasn't one of his best. A seemingly endless line of bridal boutiques crowded the north side of the street. And the memories flowed back.

Memories. All the things he'd done as a dutiful child. All the right things. Played sports, been a good student. Everything was okay on the surface, but he could feel the suspicious looks when he'd leave the Somali enclave in Cedar-Riverside. He could sense the judgment behind their eyes, the words implied, but left unsaid. Damn foreigner. Probably a terrorist. Watch him. Even the Somali Justice Advocacy Center did little to help him. The final blow was falling in love during his first year at Ridgewater College. He'd walked by the church on her wedding day.

He'd become a loner after that, choosing only to be with his own kind, those who would accept him for what he was, for who he'd become. Ultimately he accepted the fact that he would never find a place in this world. Soon enough, he would find his place in Heaven. Perhaps not with the promised seventy-two virgins, but with those who'd shared his pain, those who understood.

He passed an upscale Italian restaurant, the smell of freshly-baked bread and roasted garlic enticing him to enter. He resisted the temptation and kept going. At the end of the block, he crossed to the other side of the street, backtracked to 37th, and headed south to 23rd Avenue.

Qasif stopped on the far side of a maroon Ford F-150 parked on the gravel medium separating the street and sidewalk. He kneeled and slipped off his backpack, checking over his shoulder to make sure no one was behind him. A clump of bushes shielded the oncoming traffic and a blue trashcan partially hid him from anyone who might be looking out their front window.

He ignored the sharp gravel digging into his knee, pulled out his SR-9 and the three clips of ammunition. He inserted one magazine into the pistol. The other two went into the front pockets of his cargo pants. He pushed the backpack under the pickup and inched forward, crouching behind the trashcan. Peering around the plastic bin, he looked up and down the street. Nothing.

He stood and walked to the Parkos' driveway. A green and white MPD cruiser making its way down the street caught his eye. He ducked out of sight behind the line of trimmed shrubs fronting the house. The cruiser crossed over the centerline and stopped. Another cruiser pulled up to the curb just down the street. They knew.

He dropped to the ground and chambered a round. The door to the house opened and the wife appeared. A small mutt at her feet spotted him and jumped in front of her. The dog bared its teeth, emitting a fierce growl.

The woman screamed at the sight of the gun. She tried to grab the dog's collar, but it escaped and ran toward him. She took a step forward, then ran back inside the house, slamming the door behind her. Qasif pulled the trigger a fraction too late. The bullet impacted the doorframe. His second round hit the dog, sending it tumbling to the ground. His shots could have been mistaken for a backfire, but the police recognized them for what they were.

"Police! Drop your weapon!"

Qasif stood and emptied his magazine at the nearest police car, stitching an irregular line of holes down its side, shattering the windows. He inserted a new magazine and spun toward a policeman zigzagging across the street. He fired three rapid rounds. The policeman cried out in pain, grabbed his leg, and fell to the ground.

Nick heard the gunfire as they neared Marty's house. "Pull over!"

Ross slammed on the brakes. Nick jumped out and ran down the sidewalk. Ross sprinted by him, pulling out his pistol. A bullet whizzed by Nick's head. Another tore through the fabric of Ross' left shirtsleeve. He staggered as the bullet ripped into the flesh of his upper arm, but he kept going.

Nick saw Dalmar shift his aim and cut down a neighbor's driveway. He vaulted over the chain link fence separating the backyards, ran past the pool, and burst through the kitchen door and ran to the living room. He couldn't see Dalmar but that didn't mean the bastard wouldn't burst through the front door and try to take his family hostage. He had to get them out of the house. "Marty. Marty. Where are you?"

"In here."

He couldn't locate her voice. "Where?"

"The hall closet."

He yanked open the door. She and Emma cowered on the floor, wide-eyed with terror. He pulled Marty off the floor, scooped up Emma, and ran back outside, depositing both behind a small aluminum storage shed.

Another burst of gunfire came from the front of the house. "Stay here. Don't move until I come back to get you." He grabbed a shovel leaning against the shed and took off for the garage.

Rounding the corner, he ran headlong into Dalmar. Both of them staggered backwards from the impact. Nick recovered first. He swung the shovel, striking Dalmar across the arm.

The pistol fell from his hand, clattering to the edge of the driveway.

Dalmar lunged for the shovel, jerking and twisting it for control. Unable to wrestle it from Nick's grasp, he yanked the handle, driving the edge of the blade into Nick's forehead.

Stars exploded in Nick's eyes. Blood trickled down his temple. He spotted the gun and lunged.

Dalmar dove at the same time. Dalmar's hand closed around the weapon. He rose to a crouch, changing his grip to depress the trigger and fired.

Nick's ears rang from the gun's discharge a split-second before a sharp sting in his chest knocked him off balance. His mind registered the surprise on Dalmar's face as the kid's body contorted from an unseen blow that sent him sprawling forward onto the walkway.

Through blurred eyes, he stared at Dalmar's inert body, bleeding from several wounds in his back. Then he noticed the blood soaking his own white shirt. He felt light-headed. Sirens wailed in the background. He needed to find Marty and Emma. He tried to stand. His legs wobbled and gave way.

"Parkos!"

He heard Ross yelling his name but couldn't respond. He tried to push off the ground. His arms wouldn't work. He felt Ross roll him onto his back and jam two fingers into the side of his neck. *Checking for a pulse?*

He attempted to tell Ross he was okay. Ross's face swam out of focus. He saw several buttons fly as Ross ripped open his shirt.

"Shit."

Ross's voice?

The spotted world in front of his eyes faded to gray. He felt Ross press his hand against his chest before he fainted. "I need an EMT back here."

Chapter Fifty-Six

SURGICAL WARD
CORAL GABLES GENERAL HOSPITAL
THURSDAY 12 FEBRUARY

Marty sat by Nick's bedside holding his hand. She'd spent the night in the past three nights in the hospital despite his vehement protests. Marty insisted on staying and had dropped Emma off with her parents.

Nick felt better after his transfusion, but his head and side still hurt like hell. He shifted his weight and grimaced.

Marty looked at him, concern etched on her face. "Are you okay?"

"Just a bit sore. I'll be better once they let me out."

"You can stay at my place."

Nick thought about her offer. She still didn't know the truth about Dalmar. She thought he was just some crazy who happened to get cornered in her front yard. He had to tell her. "Marty, I need to tell you about that guy. There's more to it."

She drew back, the sharp intake of her breath clearly audible.

"He was one of the people I was chasing."

"Chasing…? How did he…?"

"I don't know. I wanted to tell you, but …"

"How could you not tell me?"

Nick reached for her hand, but she pulled away from his grasp. He'd failed again. No matter what he tried to do, it never seemed good enough. "I had no idea he was coming here. Or how he even knew about you."

"Nick, he killed Taz."

Nick's mouth dropped open. He rocked back against his pillow, his hands clutching at the blanket covering his legs. "Taz? He didn't—?"

Whatever else he was going to say was cut off by his surgeon coming through the door. Dr. Laszlow nodded at Marty, then leaned over and lifted one edge of the dressing on Nick's chest. "You were lucky. The bullet didn't hit anything major."

He poked around the wound with his index finger, gave the bandage a sniff, and listened to his lungs. "Good. Good. No signs of infection and you've got good breath sounds."

Laszlow stood. "You were lucky. The bullet glanced off your rib. It fractured, taking most of the impact. Your lung collapsed and was severely bruised." He paused at the look on Nick's face. "It's not a bad as it sounds."

Nick looked at the chest tube protruding from his chest.

"I'm going to pull that. And if the x-ray in the morning shows your lung's still expanded, I'll send you home. I'll need to see you in my office in a couple days."

Nick looked at the blood staining the underside of the dressing.

"The nurses will be in and change that. Do you have any questions?"

"No." Despite his show of bravado, he was not at all assured. "Thanks for patching me up."

"No problem." Laszlow stopped typing a note into his

iPad and cast a knowing look at Marty. "He'll need to take it easy for the next couple weeks to let that rib mend."

Nick didn't miss the nonverbal piece of the message. He had no intention of taking it easy. As soon as Laszlow disappeared out the door, he pulled himself up in bed unable to suppress a grimace. "I think it's best I go to the Marriott."

"Nick, I—"

"No, I'll come over tomorrow afternoon. I've got—" Before he could finish, Emmitt Ross popped his head in the door.

"I'm not interrupting anything, am I?"

A smile lit Nick's face. "Hey Emmitt, come on in." His eyebrow's knotted at the sight of Ross' sling. "What's with the arm?"

"Dalmar winged me. Nothing much." Ross focused on Nick's forehead. "That's some goose egg. You really need to watch where you're going."

"Yeah, I'll do that. Hey, the doc said I can go home tomorrow."

"Good news, buddy. You going to be taking it easy?"

Nick hesitated and looked at Marty. "Al-Khultyer's still out there."

Chapter Fifty-Seven

"I'm fine. Really." Nick protected his left side and wove his way through a row of good intentioned people to get back to his temporary office. Both Ross and Marty thought he was nuts, although Marty had relented, and against her better judgment, dropped him off at the Homeland Security Bureau immediately after his discharge.

Jacobs cast him a dubious look. "I'm not convinced."

Nick picked up a white message slip once they'd made it to his office. "Mark called?"

"Yeah, this morning. He's traced the Carte Bancaire credit card al-Khultyer used in Mozambique. Turns out that back in early January he made a charge to the French travel agency, À Souhait. Mark said Interpol's providing an assist, but they haven't gotten back to him."

"What?" Nick spun his chair around, wincing at the stab of pain in his chest. "Screw Interpol."

He pulled out his iPhone and tapped on the directory,

scrolling down his list of contacts. He ignored the throbbing in his side and picked up the secure phone. "What time is it in France?" he asked over his shoulder.

"Beats me."

Nick looked at his watch and answered his own question. "Almost nine. He'll be home."

"Who'll be home?"

"Alain Gallet." Nick punched in the agent's home phone number. "He's my contact in French security." He held up his index finger to silence Ross.

"*Salut?*"

"Alain, this is Nick."

"*Quelle surpise. Comment va-tu, mon ami?*"

"I'm fine. Look, I need your help."

"Al-Khultyer?"

"Yes. His trail's gone cold, but we traced the credit card he used in Mozambique. We linked it to a transaction he made with a French travel agency. I need to know what he purchased. We've already crossed off all the charges he made related to his stay at the Ibo Island Lodge."

"*Il a fait ça? C'est vraiment stupide de faire une chose pareille!*"

"Alain, English please."

"Ah, pardon. That was not very smart of him. What of this card?"

"He used a Carte Bancaire under the name Jean Luc Chéreau in early January. The travel agency's name is À Souhait."

"I know of them. Very select clientele."

"Do what you can. It's most urgent."

"Of course."

"There's something else. We tracked down Dalmar and took him out. He targeted my family."

"*Fils de salaud!*"

Nick had no idea what that meant, but from the inflection in Alain's voice, it wasn't complimentary. "We have a phone intercept, but it didn't make any sense. There's got to be a connection to whatever al-Khultyer's planning."

"Where are you?"

"Miami."

"And you think he's headed there?"

"Possibly."

"And how would he manage that?" Gallet asked almost to himself. "A plane would be out of the question. He'd have to use a ship and he wouldn't be using an elite travel agency to book a ride on freighter. Gallet took a swift intake of breath. "A cruise ship."

Nick rocked back in his chair. "My God. Of course. I've gotta go. Call when you have anything."

"Of course. *Bonne chance.*"

"No sense waiting for your friend," Ross said. "I'll notify the Port Authority and Coast Guard. They can run all the passenger ships coming in this week from Europe."

"We'll need to expand the search to the entire East coast," Nick said. "Limit it to those leaving France, Spain, and Italy. Al-Khultyer wouldn't have enough time to get to another country."

"I'd add Greece."

"Good point."

"You want me to do that?"

"No, I'll call Frank and have him put his guys on it. I tell you what you can do, though. Set up a meeting with the Coast Guard, FBI—"

"We've got an emergency response team that has all the major players. I'll round them up."

Nick lay his head down on his desk once Jacobs was safely out of sight. He should have listened to Marty and gone to her place.

Chapter Fifty-Eight

ÉTOLE de MER
ATLANTIC OCEAN
FRIDAY 13 FEBRUARY

B ashir lay on his back, staring at the ceiling. The ship would dock in the next morning. Moonlight reflecting off the ocean dappled the overhead, like Rorschach prints. He couldn't read anything into the varying patterns. Like so much clutter, they didn't matter.

He knew nothing of the events in Miami but, whatever their outcome, they wouldn't alter the decision he must make. *Should he detonate the bomb in place or try to retrieve the device and carry it ashore? Should he even go through with his plan? Would this final act of revenge, at last, drive away the demons?*

He rolled over and looked at Marilyn. Her face was peaceful in repose, a wisp of red hair falling over her forehead. He would miss her. This was their last night together and their lovemaking had been gentle, a soft goodbye that both communicated without having to voice their feelings. He eased himself off the bed and wandered out to the balcony.

The disc of a half-moon shone brightly in the night sky,

illuminating a narrow wedge of turbulent sea. He contemplated the white-capped waves stretching endlessly to the horizon, toppling over one another before sliding back into the ocean—like the jumble of thoughts tumbling through his mind. *Is there any point in continuing? Maybe I should make a new life—maybe with Marilyn?*

He adjusted the cushions on the lounge chair and sat down, permitting his mind to drift to the sound of water whispering down the side of the ship.

———

He woke to Marilyn's hand on his shoulder.

"Is there something troubling you, my love?"

He smiled. "It's beautiful, is it not?"

She stood silently by his side before speaking. "'The meeting of two lonely souls is the meeting of the dark sea with the moonlight.'"

"So true."

"It's a fragment of a poem."

He slid to the side of the chair and eased her down so she could sit next to him. He kissed her gently on the lips. "I looked through the book on your nightstand."

"Julian Barnes?"

"You are what you have done," he quoted. "What you have done is in your memory. What you remember is what defines you.'"

"And defines what you can do to make yourself whole," she added. "You can be more than your memories, Jean Luc. You can be what you strive to be. Find what you have lost, my dear, and get it back through love."

The course he must take became clear at that moment. He stroked her hair, letting the ends slip through his fingers. Beautiful as she was, he only had one choice. And he could read in her eyes that she understood. She could see into his soul.

Chapter Fifty-Nine

HOMELAND SECURITY BUREAU
MIAMI, FLORIDA
FRIDAY 13 FEBRUARY

Nick drummed his fingers on the conference room table, barely conscious of the murmuring voices around him. He was exhausted but had no choice but to press on. Jacobs sat to his right, checking off his list of participants as they filed into the room and settled into their assigned places. They knew something was up because of the short-fused summons, but Jacobs hadn't explained why the urgency. What little the participants knew came from a press release the day before:

"Federal authorities yesterday killed a member of an extremist cell with suspected ties to al-Qaeda. A source familiar with the FBI investigation said the individual had been under surveillance and was about to be charged with conspiracy to sell stolen goods and the illegal possession of firearms. There was no intelligence to indicate a current threat..."

"Everyone's here," Jacobs said.

Nick nodded and stood, quieting the room. "Good morning. Thank you for coming on such short notice. My name is Nick Parkos. I work for the National Security Agency. For the past four months, I have led the effort, along with the FBI's National Security Branch, DHS's Office of Analysis and Infrastructure Protection, and other Federal agencies, to find and eliminate the mastermind behind the Moscow and Paris bombing incidents. We have reason to believe that this individual, Bashir al-Khultyer, is on a cruise ship destined for the Port of Miami."

Nick's information was accurate up to a point, but his next statement would require a leap of faith. A couple hours earlier, he'd left a message with the President's Chief of Staff, Dan Lantis, but he hadn't heard back from the White House or the Director of National Intelligence authorizing him to lead this task force.

Strickland cautioned him that no formal authority existed under the current statues of Title 10 or any other existing interagency agreements for him to do so. That was the bad news. The good—he finally received authorization to carry. Strickland had given him verbal authorization to do whatever was necessary to contain the threat. He'd also admonished Nick not to do anything stupid. If something went wrong, he might not be able to protect him.

Nick hoped he wasn't about to do something stupid. He paused to let the outburst of surprised exclamations diminish. "I've been authorized to direct and coordinate any and all efforts by local, State, and Federal agencies to find and eliminate this threat. To that end, I took the liberty of inviting the Assistant Director for Seaport Safety and Security for the Port of Miami, Mr. Richard Doherty."

"Excuse me."

Nick looked in the direction of the voice. The placard in front of the man and his uniform identified him as a Deputy Chief in the Miami Police Department. "Yes?"

"Can you tell us what led you to that assumption?"

"Certainly. Without going into specifics, we have intercepts and collaborating information from a number of Federal and foreign intelligence services that strongly suggest this individual is coming here. DHS is working with Mr. Doherty and the Coast Guard to identify all potential vessels scheduled to arrive within the coming week."

"So we don't know what ship he's on?"

"No. Not yet. But there is another unknown we must address. Al-Khultyer's intent may well be to detonate a RDD, a Radiologic Dispersal Device."

"You have hard intelligence?" a Coast Guard captain asked.

"Enough to make the threat credible."

"What do you intend to do?" a woman seated at the end of the table asked.

"I'm sorry," Nick said. "And you are?"

"Laurie Fields. FEMA."

"You're the local lead?"

"Yes."

"Then I'll leave the specifics of how to respond to a RDD to you. It's my understanding your agency would prioritize the resources and coordinate the Federal, City, and State EMS response if such an event were to occur. You have a nuclear response task force, yes?"

"Don't you think you're being a bit of an alarmist?" Doherty said.

"You want to take that chance?" Nick shot back. He was beginning to lose his patience. This wasn't an organizational meeting. These people needed to step up to the plate. He looked at Jacobs, who for some reason had remained quiet. *Didn't DHS usually chair these meetings?* He should have asked. *Crap.*

He shifted his gaze to Castellanos who tightened his lips and gave a slight nod of agreement. The Coast Guard captain picked up the nonverbal cues.

"We'll ramp up our off-shore surveillance of all incoming traffic and provide a consolidated operational picture through our SIMON system. That'll keep everyone in the loop. We'll also address various scenarios such as the ship being hijacked and transmitting a false location on its AIS beacon."

"And if this nut case transfers his weapon to a fishing boat?"

Nick ignored the question. "Can you be prepared to board?"

"I'll place our Maritime Security Response Team on high alert and get our Cutters underway. Our best bet will be to interdict the vessel at sea."

Chapter Sixty

TERMINAL J
PORT OF MIAMI CRUISE TERMINAL
FRIDAY 13 FEBRUARY

Nick grasped the overhead strap, grimacing in the pain from his damaged rib. Castellanos spun the Suburban's steering wheel. They lost traction on the rain-slicked asphalt, still damp from a late morning shower, and fishtailed off Biscayne Boulevard onto to the access road leading to the cruise ship terminal. Two other SUVs followed.

He'd received his call from Gallet thirty-five minutes before. Al-Khultyer had purchased a cabin on the *Étoile de Mer* under the name of Jean Luc Chéreau.

He pounded the dash, furious with himself. He should have recognized the name of the ship. He'd been too tired, too distracted. That and the Oxycodone. The night before, DHS and the Coast Guard had narrowed the possible cruise ships to six vessels. He was informed one of those was scheduled to arrive on Friday the thirteenth. The significance of the date was lost on him.. He hadn't even thought to ask what time the ship would arrive.

Castellanos counter-steered, correcting their skid, and rammed his foot down on the accelerator. The SUV roared down the road, leaving two strips of burnt rubber and a cloud of blue smoke hanging in the air. They swung around several cars and a passenger van, crossed the center strip, and headed the wrong way down the exit road, horn blaring. They screeched to a stop in front of Terminal J.

They sprang out of the car. Castellanos lead the way as they burst through the doors leading to the three-story concourse, weaving through a crowd of debarking passengers toward customs. Al-Khultyer was nowhere in sight.

Nick spotted a porter stationed at the bottom of the *Étoile*'s gangway. Behind the man, American and French flags flapped in the offshore breeze blowing toward metropolitan Miami.

Nick pointed the porter out to Castellanos. "That guy should be able to identify him."

They sprinted across the lobby onto the quay. Castellanos left him behind and got to the man first. He flashed his badge. "FBI."

Nick caught up, gasping for breath, and pulled out a photo of al-Khultyer. "Have you seen this man?"

The porter took the photo and studied it before handing it back. "*Oui*, that is Monsieur Chéreau. He was travelling with Madame Slade. They were first to debark."

Nick took a step back, a look of consternation on his face. *Who the hell was she?* He recovered. "How long ago?"

"Perhaps fifteen minutes."

"Have the bags been off-loaded?" Castellanos asked.

The porter gestured toward several neat lines of suitcases arranged on the pier. Perhaps a dozen passengers were clustered around them, checking tags. Others pulled their luggage toward the terminal. "*Oui, Monsieur.*"

"Crap." Castellanos grabbed his radio and set off for Customs at a run. "Team One. Converge on Customs. Shut down the lines. Nobody goes through. Team Two, secure the taxi and limo areas. Stop any vehicle trying to leave the terminal."

Nick pulled up at the sight of a pair of escalators leading to the second floor. They terminated at an exotically land-scaped atrium replete with tropical flowers. *Flowers!*

He yelled at Costellano's back. "I'll catch up."

Costellanos shot him a look, but didn't slow.

Nick ran to the atrium, intent on going up the escalator, but slowed to a fast walk. A roped barrier with signs reading: WRONG WAY, DO NOT ENTER, blocked his way. Behind the rope several Port Authority security staff paced around the base of the escalator. He stopped and pulled out his ID. "NSA. Is there a flower shop on the second level?"

The guards exchanged incredulous looks. Neither responded.

"Is there a flower shop on the second level?" Nick repeated, making a motion to step over the barrier.

One of the men stepped forward to block him. "Sir—"

"I don't have time to screw around. Answer my question. Now."

"Well, yes."

Nick looked at the guard who'd answered. "Come with me." He stepped over the barrier and started up the escalator without waiting for the man.

Taking two steps at a time, the guard caught up with him at the top, chest heaving. He managed to gasp a question. "What's going on?"

"Where's the flower shop?"

The guard pointed down the hall to Nick's left. "Fourth shop."

Nick took off, ignoring the pain in his side. He spotted al-Khultyer exiting the shop, a woman at his side. He carried a bouquet of yellow sunflowers, the stems wrapped in green floral paper. He drew his Beretta. "Halt. Federal Agent."

Al-Khultyer stopped in mid-stride. The woman grabbed his arm.

Nick took several steps toward al-Khultyer, leveling his weapon at his chest. "On your knees. Hands on top of your head."

Al-Khultyer pushed the woman out of the way and slowly knelt on his left knee, laying his bouquet across his right. He smiled. "You are Parkos. How is your family?"

"You son-of-a-bitch."

"So, they are not well?" al-Khultyer replied, slipping his hand into his right pants pocket. He looked at the sunflowers. "These are for my family, but then you must already know that. How else could you have found me?"

"Jean Luc, what is happening?" the woman cried.

"Face down. Hands on top of your head," Nick commanded. He swung the barrel of his pistol toward the woman, not knowing if she was an accomplice.

The woman covered her mouth stifling a scream and stumbled into the shop, distracting him for an instant. When he looked back, al-Khultyer held a Mercedes car fob.

"Don't do it."

"Would you shoot me?"

"Drop it."

Al-Khultyer pointed the fob toward the *Étoile der Mer's* bow. His thumb moved to cover the UNLOCK button. "I have no choice."

Nick hesitated.

The sound of a gunshot exploded in the confined space. Al-Khultyer spun from the impact to his chest. The fob fell from his hand, tumbling across the tile floor. He raised himself on all fours, trying to stand. A second round struck him, driving him onto his left side. His right hand moved, his fingers stretching for the fob. A third shot rang out. His hand jerked, then he was motionless.

"Tough bastard," Castellanos said, holstering his weapon.

He leaned over to pick up the fob. "I didn't know if he was going to press this damn thing again. Whatever he was aiming at didn't detonate."

Nick stared at al-Khultyer's inert body and the blood spreading toward the bouquet. His confrontation with Dalmar flashed through his mind. He'd been lucky. A few more inches.... "He was reaching for the sunflowers."

"The flowers?"

Nick knelt to pick up the bouquet and placed them in al-Khultyer's outstretched hand. "They were for his family."

"His family? That's just great," Castellanos said. "Well, think about this. We just stopped this sick bastard from destroying the lives of a lot of innocent families."

Nick dropped the bouquet. He stood, turning away from al-Khultyer. "It's complicated."

"Yeah, it always is with you NSA guys."

———

"Hey, man. Great job," Jacobs said as he popped into Nick's office at Homeland Security. "So much for Friday the thirteenth. You took out that A-hole."

Nick stopped typing and swung his chair around. "Yeah, we did. I appreciate your help. Thanks."

"No problem."

Nick changed the subject now focused on Friday the thirteenth and how close they'd... he'd...almost came to disaster. "You got anything on Slade?"

"The woman with al-Khultyer?"

Nick nodded.

"Nothing yet. She's still being interrogated."

"Let me know as soon as you hear anything. I've got to clean up the loose ends before I call DC."

"Will do." Jacobs pivoted to leave, then paused at the door. "You need anything else? Coffee?"

"Coffee would be great."

Nick returned to his keyboard. *Great job?* Not so much. There were too many loose ends he couldn't find the words to describe. Complications.

He recalled Castellanos's words in the terminal. "It always is with you guys." *That's my problem, isn't it? The complications.* What about Ferguson's...the...CIA's, plot that caused this damn mess in the first place? Should I just leave well enough alone and let it drop?

And what of Alek? He recalled her whispered words at the farmhouse in Chelyabinks, a lifetime ago: 'No, not this.' Her asset, al-Khultyer had betrayed her. Was she another victim? No, she was complicit. *Is she even still alive?* He had no idea. She'd probably been hauled off to Siberia never to be heard of again. But Grekov and Ferguson weren't the only loose ends in his life. He stared at his computer screen. *What do I about Marty and Emma?*

Chapter Sixty-One

603 23rd AVENUE SOUTHWEST
MIAMI, FLORIDA
FRIDAY 13 FEBRUARY

Nick pulled into Marty's driveway and turned off the ignition. He placed his hands back on the steering wheel, reluctant to leave the safety of his car. His left hand inched toward the handle and opened the door. *I have to do this.*

He rang the doorbell, uncertain of his own feelings, not sure what he was going to say. The door opened. "Hi, I'm not too late am I?"

"No, you're fine," Marty said, guiding him to the couch and handing him a glass of wine. "Emma's asleep. She had a good day, but it tired her."

"She's okay?"

"She doesn't really understand what happened."

"I'm sorry."

"Don't be. We'll get through this. All three of us will. Together."

Nick took a sip of his wine, avoiding eye contact. He didn't know where to begin.

"Will you be staying in Miami?" she asked, breaking through the awkward silence.

"I've got to go back tomorrow."

"You shouldn't be alone. Do you have someone to talk to?"

He thought a moment. *Mike Rohrbaugh? Michelle?* "I've got a couple friends."

"Will you call them?"

Nick fought the urge to retreat. "I almost lost you. I almost lost Emma."

Marty set her glass on the coffee table. "You saved our lives."

He looked down. "I don't know. I'm not sure about anything anymore. What I've done. What I've become..."

"You've got Emma. And you've got me, if you'll still have me."

He nodded and reached for her hand, his eyes glistening.

Emma's voice cut through the moment. "Daddy?"

"Go," Marty said. "She needs you. You're her valentine."

"Valentine?"

"You do know tomorrow is Valentine's Day?"

"Ah, no. I completely forgot."

He looked toward Emma's bedroom, hesitating.

She held up the spotted unicorn he'd bought.

"His name is Sprinkles."

"Thank you." He turned and went to his daughter.

She sat up and smiled, reaching her arms to him. "Hi, Daddy."

He sat down on the edge of her bed and handed her the unicorn. "Happy almost Valentine's Day."

Emma clutched the toy. "He's beautiful."

"So, Miss Emma. Tell me all about Mr. Sprinkles."

Sneak Preview of Arctic Menace (The Defenders Book 3)

THE CHUKCHI SEA
CAPE LISBURNE, ALASKA
MONDAY 30 OCTOBER

"*Zhè bù kěnéng!*" Li Tsang gasped in disbelief, the piercing sound amplified within the *Flying Fish's* cramped personnel sphere. His eyes must deceive him.

He clutched the mini-sub's joystick, peering through the vessel's six-inch viewport. "This can't be," he repeated.

Tsang switched his focus to the 3-D feed from the sub's external cameras and toggled the zoom for a better look. Clusters of black potato-shaped rocks blanketed the olive-gray mud flats of the Chukchi Sea's abyssal plane.

He knew what they were at a glance: polymetallic nodules. He'd seen them before, surrounding the hydrothermal vents spewing basaltic debris in the deep-sea trenches of the mid-Pacific and Indian Oceans. He'd read the reports, hearsay really, a fool's dream: nickel, platinum, gold, diamonds. A trillion dollars-worth of rare-earth minerals. Were the reports true? Geologically, his discovery made no sense. Would anyone even believe him?

He activated the video record and shot a glance at his co-pilot wedged into the seat beside him. At first, he mistook the quizzical expression on Chenglei's face for mutual disbelief at what they'd observed on the ocean floor. Then Chenglei turned to him, his eyes widened with alarm.

"Do you smell something?"

Tsang sniffed the scrubbed air and jerked back from the video display. His nostrils flared at the faint acrid odor of burning insulation. A paralyzing chill raced down his spine, dread replacing the euphoria of discovery. *There must be a short in one of their electrical systems—or something worse.*

He fought the suffocating fear that gripped his chest, forcing himself to scan the vessel's bank of computer monitors and service panels. An electrical fault, however minor, could burst into life-threatening fire. Did he detect a hint of smoke?

His eyes stopped, fixed on the readout of the electrical supply system. The amperage of their lithium-ion battery stacks indicated an unexpected drain. He'd already noted a loss of charge from the stacks earlier in their mission. He'd presumed the batteries were depleted supplying power to push the *Flying Fish* through the strong offshore currents of the Bering Strait. And he'd been wrong.

An ominous silence and the eerie red glow from the sub's interior lighting reinforced his unease. He held the back of his hand to one of the circulation vents. Nothing. *What would cause that? Are the ventilation fans down?* Without the fans, their scrubbers wouldn't function properly. The cabin's carbon dioxide levels ....

They had to return to their support ship or risk being trapped under the advancing ice pack, slowly poisoned by the cabin's foul air. But he couldn't return. Not yet.

He twisted toward Chenglei. His co-pilot's pupils were dilated in terror, the color drained from his face. "Check our operating voltage and discharge current."

Chenglei's head snapped toward the incandescent green

of a touchscreen mounted to his right. He tapped his index finger on the battery icon and studied the readouts: Temperature, discharge rate, operating voltage, remaining capacity. His eyes remained fixed on the monitors. "What's our position?"

Tsang looked at the real-time navigation display. He grunted before double-checking to confirm their track. A black dot marked their current position ten miles off the Alaskan coast west-northwest of a point named Cape Lisburne—well within American territorial waters. His pre-deployment brief included a side note that Cape Lisburne, the site of an old cold-war defense radar base, was being evaluated for re-activation.

He hissed a curse. *Wáng bā*! He'd been too distracted by his unexpected finding to notice the extent of the incursion.

He'd taken the submersible to the depths of the Mariana Trench, but faced an entirely different proposition navigating the shallow waters of the U.S. continental shelf. His orders directed him to collect bathometric data of the seafloor and document the peculiar convergence zones of the different currents, cascading isothermal layers, and salt gradients for the Navy's submarine force.

And now? Few, if any ships ventured this far north in late October. No one dared being trapped by an unexpected storm, their hull crushed by tons of ice. He read out the results. "68°52 North, 166°35 West."

Chenglei tapped *Flying Fish*'s touch-screen power control and life support icons. He cast a worried look at Tsang. "Our oxygen level is acceptable, but the cabin's carbon dioxide level is increasing."

"And if we—?"

Chenglei cut off his commander. "We must power down all unnecessary systems and return to the *Kexue* immediately."

Tsang exhaled through pursed lips, willing himself to remain calm. The expletive had un-nerved his companion.

"Yes ... Power down the systems. We must continue on this track a bit longer."

"But—"

"Patience."

Tsang eased the *Flying Fish* forward at three knots, adjusting their course to follow several dark-gray streaks from a recent mudflow. The bottom topography changed to a mix of light-gray and black pebbles swept from the limestone cliffs of Cape Lisburne. A ghost-white bottom fish drifted through the thin beam of light emanating from a string of LED lights set along the vessel's sampling arm. "There."

"Where?" Chenglei echoed. "What do you see?"

"A subduction zone. It's a fault line from an ancient seismic event." He sorted through the possibilities, seeking refuge from his stress with scientific exactitude. *The nodules may be metamorphic rocks from a pre-Cambrian Age uplift volcano, an extension of the Alaskan Brooks Range.* He voiced his conclusion. "That might explain it."

"Explain what?"

Tsang ignored the question and the fear in Chenglei's voice. There must be no room for error, no room for second-guessing. "We must collect samples for mineralogical and geochemical analysis."

"But, Li, our batteries and power control. We—"

"I understand that," he snapped. "I will notify our superiors on the *Kexue*."

They were nearly six hours into their mission at the edge of their effective communication range of twenty-five kilometers. He must try. He reached for the microphone, then dropped his hand. No, a text would be better. There would be no voice distortion from unexpected electromagnetic interference or from sending his signal through the thick surface ice. His fingers moved over the keyboard. *Unexpected finding.* He waited for the acknowledgement from their support ship. The cryptic response: *Unerstod. Ice rdiges orming.* He dismissed the operator's typos in the garbled message. They needed to return.

Tsang maneuvered the *Flying Fish* toward the nearest scattering of rocks relying on the vessel's auxiliary power unit. The submersible's forward beams cast their light for thirty meters through the clear water. He selected his first target. Turbulence buffeted the sub.

"What was that?"

Tsang glanced at Chenglei. Sweat dotted his forehead despite the chill permeating the sub's personnel sphere. Tsang turned back to the viewport. Microalgae and suspended particulate matter illuminated by the sub's lights undulated in the current. Beyond that, a black void. He sought to calm Chenglei. "Must be a pycnocline. Fresh water from the shoreline. Take a sample and note our position."

Tsang triggered the sub's thrusters to compensate for the turbulence and activated their vessel's hydraulic grabbling arm while maintaining position over a prospective target. "Here we go."

A dirty-gray cloud of billowing detritus and glacial silt obscured his vision. Tsang backed off, slowly lowered the sampling arm, and opened its jaws. He grasped the rock and dropped it in the sample basket. He added several more, one streaked with red iron oxide, another with a hint of yellow suggesting a high sulfur content. "Okay, let's go home."

Only nineteen meters separated him from the surface and the rapidly forming ice extending from the Alaskan coast. A polar low with gale force winds drove the flows and their ice keels that descended like daggers toward the *Kexue*. They were now barely making headway near the forward margin of the ice. Would his comrades be able to maintain station?

The eleven-centimeter thick titanium sphere of the *Flying Fish's* personnel compartment could survive a collision. The damage to the rest of his craft would cripple them. He chanced another look through the viewport dreading what he might see. Nobody had ever planned for or studied the implications of operating the submersible in the Arctic.

Questions flooded his mind. Would he be able to break through the surface ice or would they ram into an ice keel extending down from the bottom of the ice pack that would rip their craft open like a mere sardine can? Would there be a catastrophic failure of his electrical systems? And, even with perfect conditions, could he could still have to affect the rendezvous with the *Kexue* in complete darkness.

So, what if we are to perish? His wife and children would be provided for. *And me?* He resigned himself to his fate, pushing his concerns to the back of his mind. There were no other options. He sent another text to the *Kexue* informing them of his intent to return. That task completed, he entered a reciprocal course into the navigation system to the last known position of his support ship.

Time slowed, the basso thrumming of the *Flying Fish's* twin propellers dulling the turmoil raging in his mind. He tried to shut out the sound of tons of ice being crushed, driven into ridges, then torn apart by the winds of the approaching polar front. Deep rumbles like thunder, screeching, sharp cracks like those made by a splintering tree. Chirps and whistles echoed within the personnel sphere. The ice seemed alive, speaking to him, filling him with dread. He'd heard a name coined by the early Arctic explorers for the sounds: The Devil's Symphony.

He closed his eyes and fingered the jade amulet around his neck offering a silent prayer to Mazu, the Chinese goddess and patroness of the sea. There was nothing more to do. He pulled his woolen sweater tight across his shoulders. Only a few of the sub's critical systems were functioning and the sphere's temperature continued to fall. Despite shutting down all non-essential systems, they were now dependent on what little power remained in their emergency batteries.

He debated over-pressurizing the sphere to increase the cabin's temperature, but that would require releasing their reserves of pressurized oxygen. He discarded the idea focusing on the more immediate threat. If they didn't reach the *Kexue* soon, they'd be unable to maneuver—helpless, driven northeast by the offshore Alaskan current surging through the Bering Strait. Their power would be drained before their oxygen supply ran out, but by then ...?

The auspicious dates of his birth-chart as prescribed by The Four Pillars of Destiny had pre-determined his fate. *But didn't the precepts of Hòu Tiān also state that his fate could be affected by chance, risk, and trust and those aspects of life that he could control and achieve with effort?* Perhaps fate had reserved another path for him, intertwined with that of another person?

He keyed his microphone and sent a voice message to the *Kexue*, Nothing. He tried sending a text. His hands fumbled over the keyboard *earinm ladt knooow posijin. Rewuesr.* He stopped, concentrating, using his index finger to tap out the message. *Nearing last known position. Request instructions.*

His reply arrived within seconds: *Repeat your last.*

Tsang repeated his message.

The answer crackled over the overhead speaker. He leaned forward, straining to understand their directions. Were their communications being jammed?

Have you on sonar. Activate your homing beacon. Will guide you in.

Several more garbled messages followed, his mind benumbed, unable to decipher what the support ship had transmitted. What he did manage to understand was the support crew had managed to expand one of the polynyas, an open area in the ice near the ship. Clearance to surface would come soon. Convulsive shivers wracked his body. *So tired ... must wake Chenglei.*

"Shhehlei?" The engineer didn't respond to his slurred name. He reached over and shook his arm. "Shhehlei."

A shrill alarm pierced his ears. The capsule plunged into darkness. Several emergency lamps clicked on. They began to drift, widening their distance to the *Kexue*. He must surface or they would be lost. He managed to flip open the safety cover for the sub's emergency ballast system and pressed the red button enabling the relay switch. *Will it even work?*

The sub gave a small lurch as the vessel's electromagnets released their grip on the steel brackets holding the vessel's ballast. The 450-kilogram weights fell away and the *Flying Fish* began to ascend. Twenty meters, ten, five … He focused on the depth gauge.

Was that to the surface or to the bottom of the ice?

The answer came with a grinding crunch, the noise deafening within the confined sphere. He could only guess at the damage. Would the sample basket be dislodged? They had to retrieve it.

He felt movement. Were they in open water? Ice screeched against Flying Fish's hull. He dared not open the escape hatch. A text: *Nearing your position. Hold on.*

A thin veneer of ice covered his computer screens, moisture, condensed from his breath, frozen to his instruments. *Odd, I'm no longer shivering.* How long had they been waiting? It didn't matter. Nothing did. His mind numbed beyond caring.

A voice? No, a new sound. Metal clanging on metal.

He stared upward, trying to locate the sound. The dog lever on the hatch moved. Then stopped. The clanging intensified. The wheel gave way, spinning, and the hatch flung open. Several chunks of ice cascaded through the opening, pummeling his head and shoulders. He barely felt them.

"Tsang!"

He tried to answer. Silence. He tried again. A whisper escaped. "My specimens."

Hands reached down—grabbing his shoulders—pulling him up through the hatch onto the deck. A blast of freezing wind staggered him. He fell to his knees. Ghostly apparitions approached, their movements backlit by the eerie electric blue and green colors of the aurora borealis swirling above the horizon. Someone pulled a fleece ski hood over his head.

Another wrapped a thermal blanket around his shoulders, guiding him toward the *Kexue*'s Zodiac.

He lunged toward the bow of the *Flying Fish* intent on diving into the icy water to retrieve the specimen basket. A hand pulled him back to safety.

"He will retrieve them."

Tsang's eyes followed his rescuer's arm toward another clad in an orange full- emersion suit. "Chenglei?"

"We must return to the ship."

He stumbled around a hummock of ice. Two crewmen grasped his arms and dragged him forward. He would survive. *But Chenglei? What of him? Dead? And his Flying Fish?* She would be abandoned, a captive of the merciless Arctic ice…

Acknowledgments

I want to mention those incredible folks who, without their efforts, my draft of *Amber Dawn* would have remained, forlorn, as just another icon on my computer's desktop. First of these is Mr. Rick Ludwig, friend and fellow author, who provided the initial sanity check on my draft finding all manner of issues to address: Context, flow, viewpoint, and, yes, spelling. No novel, no matter how accomplished, will ever (or should never) go to print without the focused attention of the editors. They are essential to a clean manuscript where errors will stop a reader in their tracks. I own a huge debt of thanks to Ms. Alice Bernhardt for her editing and formatting skills. Ms. Savannah Thomas, even after dealing with all my foibles as a writer with my first novel, *Flash Point*, still took on the project as the primary editor for *Amber Dawn*. Beyound finding typos and grammatic errors, her suggestions as to tighten up and clarify any number of passages has made this a much better novel.

Next up in my Hall of Fame is Maria Novillo Sararia of BEAUTeBOOK. Maira took my initial concept of a cover design and took it took a different level. Her three elements for the cover captured Amber Dawn's theme: The American and

Chechen national ensigns, the smoke of an explosion, and the damaged sunflower all carry meaning. Indeed, you can tell a book by its cover. Writing a novel is one thing but getting it noticed is on an entire different level. In this, I own a special debt of gratitude to my publicist and fellow veteran, Ms. Sharon Jenkins, Sharon@mcwritingservices.com. Her untiring efforts to educate and guide this poor neophyte have truly been above and beyond. And finally, I must acknowledge my publisher at Babylon Books, New York Times best-selling author William Bernhardt. His friendship and patient mentoring have made my series possible. And now what? All of these folks have to buckle up. The final three novels of this series are on the way.

About the Author

Kenneth Andrus is a native of Columbus, Ohio. He obtained his undergraduate degree from Marietta College and his doctor of medicine from the Ohio State University College of Medicine. Following his internship, he joined the Navy and retired after twenty-four years of service with the rank of Captain.

His operational tours while on active duty included: Battalion Surgeon, Third Battalion Fourth Marines; Brigade Surgeon, Ninth Marine Amphibious Brigade, Operation Frequent Wind; Medical Officer, USS *Truxtun* CGN-35; Fleet Surgeon, Commander Seventh Fleet; Command Surgeon, U.S. Naval Forces Central Command, Desert Shield/Desert Storm; and Fleet Surgeon, U.S. Pacific Fleet.

His webpage can be found at: www.kennethandrus.com

About the Author

Also by Kenneth Andrus

The Defenders Series

Flash Point

Amber Dawn

Arctic Menace (Fall 2021)

Publisher's Note

Babylon Books is a division of Bernhardt Books, a family-owned publishing house founded in 1999 that specializes in showcasing emerging authors and compelling fiction.

Editor-in-Chief: Alice Bernhardt

Marketing Director: Ralph Bernhardt

Chief Financial Officer: Harrison Bernhardt

Lightning Source UK Ltd.
Milton Keynes UK
UKHW040735190321
380634UK00001B/24